SEATTLE SC

DEA

Rinker

RUTH STILLING

ISBN 978-1-0686000-2-9

Cover art by Andra Murarasu

Interior design and formatting by Summer Grove

Full editing and proofreading by Tina Otero

TRIGGER/CONTENT WARNINGS

You should be aware that while this book is a work of fiction and is, of course, a happily ever after, Dead Rinker does contain themes of the following:

Sexually explicit content, strong language, emotional and mental abuse by the parents of the female main character, mention of the death of a newborn child (off-page), and reference to an unfaithful former partner (not the main characters).

For those who feel like their purpose in life is to deliver on the expectations of others.

Fuck that.

PLAYLIST

You can find Jensen and Kate's playlist on Spotify.

Sabrina Carpenter — Bet u wanna
Ariana Grande — Love me harder
Arctic Monkeys — Do I wanna know?
Taylor Swift — Don't blame me
Hannah Wants — Cure my desire
The Weeknd — In your eyes
The Weeknd — Can't feel my face
Ed Sheeran — Shivers
Glass Animals — Heat waves
Bea Miller — Like that
Dermot Kennedy — Better days
John Legend — All of me

PROLOGUE

DECEMBER

KATE

Who knew dickheads could be so handsome?

Well, I do, and I'm looking at one right now.

I mean, really, who the fuck does he think he is?

First, he proposes we head back to his place for a night in bed, where he's *oh so convinced* he'll be the best I've *ever* had. And when I refuse to succumb to his apparent charm, he goes after someone else.

Just because I wore his jersey to the game tonight doesn't mean I'm going to instantly fall into bed with him.

Okay, there was a slim chance of that happening. But with the way he was so sure of himself *and me*, well, I wasn't handing anything over.

All this nonsense about jerseys and true love means nothing to me. Sure, he's hot, and I can't deny I've thought about what lies beneath those pads a time or two, but did he *really* think I was that easy? If I want to wear his jersey, then I'll wear it. There are thousands of jerseys in circulation, and not everyone who wears number eighty-eight automatically wants to get railed by the Scorpions goalie, despite what he might think.

And that's exactly what I said when I slid off his knee and told him to go fuck himself.

"Come on, babe. Why else would you be wearing my jersey? Let's get into it."

Ugh.

So I stormed to the bathroom and angrily fixed my blush before returning to the bar only to find Mr. Dickhead himself had moved on to another woman. A redhead with long, slender legs and a banging body, to be precise. She looks younger than me, too. At least five years, and with me being thirty-four, the fact that he's moving onto a younger model makes me feel even worse.

Is that all I was worth? A quick attempt to get me between the sheets? We're supposed to be part of the same friend group; all he wanted was to use me and then throw me away. I might enjoy casual sex from time to time, but I want him to at least *work* for it. One-night stands are not my thing.

So here I am, alone in a bar and sipping on a mojito of rejection.

"He's not even that hot," I grumble under my breath as I take another mouthful.

"Oh, I don't know. I don't think I'm bad looking," a deep voice says from behind me.

Slowly, I turn to locate the source.

Hmmm, not bad. Tall, dark, handsome, and probably younger than me.

I cautiously glance to my left and see Mr. Dickhead's hand has now found Red's lower back.

Yeah, well, two can play that game.

I take another sip of my cocktail and smile sweetly up at him. "No, I suppose you aren't."

He smiles and then leans down to whisper in my ear, and I instantly detect the strong smell of booze on his breath.

I'm mad at myself. Playing games to make Jensen Jones jealous has already backfired on me.

Ignoring completely what this guy has to say, I glance over at Mr. Dickhead once more. His back is to me as he stands at the high-top table with his arm now fully wrapped around Red's waist, and I can tell that look he has on his face because it's the look he was giving me not a half hour earlier.

But what really annoys me more than anything is the fact that I'm bothered. That I'm even the slightest bit affected by his attention being anywhere other than on me.

I might be loud and sometimes a bit brash, but I'm not an attention seeker, and I definitely do not want the attention of this guy standing next to me. So why do I want Jensen's?

"I'm Todd. What's your name, sweetheart?"

I fight back an eye roll and take another sip of my drink, swirling my straw around to mix the mint leaves. "Kate," I reply in a clipped tone.

He hums in appreciation and steps even closer. My back is against the bar, and he's standing in front of me. Another few inches and his body will be pressing into mine. "Are you here alone, Kate?" he asks in a lecherous voice.

Alone? I fucking hate that word. It frames my life.

I look up at him and narrow my eyes. "Why do you ask? Does it affect your next move?"

He chuckles quietly. "Well, if you're here with another guy, then yes."

"No guy with me. But I have no plans on leaving with someone tonight."

I look over at Jensen again. He still has his hand above Red's ass and his back firmly to me, like I don't even exist.

"Can I do anything to change your mind?"

I shake my head. "No. I don't leave with strangers."

"I wouldn't say I'm a stranger anymore."

Fuck me, Kate. You really got yourself into something here.

I pat him on the shoulder and go to turn my back, but just as I do, I catch a flash of red moving across the bar.

He's fucking taking her home.

Right in front of me.

Bastard.

I fight to close my gaping jaw at the audacity of this man just as he looks over his shoulder and throws me a wink and a goddamn grin.

His tousled dark hair falls over his tanned forehead, and his deep brown eyes sparkle with satisfaction. And when he throws me what I know is a faux sweet smile, the dimple in his right cheek pops. He's twenty feet away from me, but I know it's there. And it pisses me off.

He pisses me off.

Jensen Jones is officially at the top of my shit list.

But as I turn to face the bar fully and wave at the barman to bring me another drink, I wish I could hold onto my rage.

Through the mass of people rammed into Riley's Bar, I can still make out the way he helps the redhead into her jacket and then throws his arm over her shoulder. The streetlights outside make it unmissable.

That really fucking hurts.

He really fucking hurts.

Vulnerability shoots through me. We might be part of the same friend group, and my best friend might be dating his captain, but I'll never go near Jensen Jones again.

That man is dead to me.

CHAPTER ONE

MAY, EIGHTEEN MONTHS LATER

KATE

"Hmmm, I think I've decided what to go for. The lobster thermidor looks great. What about you, sweetheart?" Tom slides his hand across the table and places it on top of mine. I look down at the tender connection, but I feel no affection.

What I do feel is terrible.

Tom is one of the kindest men I've ever met, and he deserves far more than I can offer him. He wants a wife and family, and he definitely wants to move things along with us after nine months of on-and-off dating.

I keep putting the brakes on because I know that's not what I want. Never any of those things.

I look down at the menu again, none of the words on the page making any sense. "I can't decide," I reply quietly, shifting my hand from underneath his to turn the menu card over. I could've done it with my other, but this seemed like a good excuse to back away from him once again.

He clears his throat at the loss. I know he can feel it—that I'm not into this, that I'm pulling away.

Our relationship has run its course.

I'd tell him that he shouldn't take it personally if that wouldn't come off as insanely insensitive, but it's true—that's what I've always done. I'm not a serial dater, but typically, if I meet someone I like, I'll go on a few dates, enjoy some sex, and then be on my way before he catches feelings.

With Tom, I've gone further than I have with anyone in years. He's every bit my type, tall and handsome and an incredibly talented lawyer. We reconnected at a friend's wedding last year, having known each other since college, and to be honest, when he asked me out, I thought, why not? What harm can a bit of fun be?

But here I am, about to break his heart. And I feel shitty about it.

"Why don't you get the lamb, and then we can share? It was between that and the lobster for me," Tom interrupts my thoughts.

His handsome face is lit softly by the romantic setting and candlelight. This is a really lovely restaurant in downtown Seattle. He's brought me here a few times, and he never holds back from treating me, making me feel even worse.

"Yeah, sure," I say, passing the menu back to the waiter as he approaches our table and Tom confirms our order.

Once back alone, Tom pulls our wine from the ice bucket and refills my glass.

"You look stressed out." He raises an inquisitive brow at me. "Are Mark and David riding you hard?"

Mark and David Preston are brothers and joint owners of my law firm. They're hardheaded lawyers, but they never "ride me hard," given that I'm one of the top-performing litigation lawyers in Washington state. I should be, too. I'm a workaholic, and it's all I've ever known.

Our waiter returns with bread and olives and sets them on the table. I reach across and pop one in my mouth. They really are the superior snack—something my best friend, Felicity, and I bonded over.

I shrug. "It's intense but no different from normal."

Tom's brows pinch together. "So what's eating at you?"

Ugh, I really didn't want to do this now, right as we're about to eat, but honestly, when is the right time to break it off with someone?

I take a deep breath and look him in the eyes for what feels like the first time since he picked me up tonight. And after this, I'll likely be calling myself an Uber back home.

"I, I just—"

"It's me, isn't it? Well, I mean us." Tom sits back in his chair and tips his head to the ceiling. Closing his eyes, he shakes his head slowly.

"I'm so sorry, Tom. I just can't do this anymore. It's not..."

"Please don't tell me you were going to say 'it's not you; it's me' because that makes it even worse."

I flatten my lips and press them together. "I wasn't going to say that. I was going to tell you it's not what I want and that we both want different things. You want the two-point-four children and the picket fence, and I want..."

What *do I want* exactly?

"You want to be who you've always been," he finishes for me, twisting his water glass around in his hands as he leans forward and rests his elbows on the table. "You want to get to the top of your profession without any distractions."

My stomach knots at the way he says it. There's no bitterness to his tone, but he hits close to home with his words—that's exactly what I've always said I've wanted, and it's absolutely what I've gone after.

"Kate must conquer the world."

"Kate, you can't have the brains you do and let them go to waste."

"Kate, you were at the top of your class in Yale Law. Do not let this slide."

"You have our legacy to upkeep."

Lecture after lecture from my parents has drilled into me the only route I know in life.

I look up at Tom and nod, taking a sip of wine. "I'm really sorry."

He sits back again and folds his arms across his chest just as our dinner arrives. "Might as well eat this, and then I'll drop you back at your place."

THE REST OF MY "DATE" with Tom could be best described as awkward.

As always, he was polite and even offered to foot the bill, which ran into hundreds of dollars. But I couldn't allow him to do that, so I paid my share before he dropped me back at my apartment.

And that's where I am now, having changed into a pair of sweats and an old hoodie. I then watered all of my house plants and made myself a hot chocolate with whipped cream.

Folding my feet underneath me, I sit on my couch and reach for my sketch pad and calligraphy pen set. Pinks and purples today.

I started calligraphy last year when I took a random course with my super-gifted niece, Ava. In my day job as a lawyer, it's hard to get creative, and there's always that itch in my brain that wants to express itself.

Maybe it's a way to switch off since my mind is constantly on the go, searching for the next thing.

But no sooner have I started than I'm interrupted by my cell phone vibrating on the coffee table. I reach over and grab it. "Violet" lights up the screen. I can't remember the last time I referred to her as "Mom."

"Hi."

"Kate, how are you?"

You'd never think she was calling her daughter, more her assistant or colleague.

I set my sketch pad to the side and pick up my mug, holding the warmth in my hands while I prop the phone between my ear and shoulder.

Might as well get comfortable.

"Pleased it's the weekend. How are you both?"

"Why? Has work been intense?" she asks, entirely glossing over my question.

"No. Just ready to relax. I broke it off with Tom tonight, and that was intense."

"What do you mean?"

My brows knit together in confusion. "About Tom? Well, I—"

"No, no. I mean about work. It should *always* be intense."

I set my mug down and take hold of my phone. I'd happily throw it across the room if I didn't think it would break.

"It is intense, but I'm used to this kind of pressure. It doesn't mean I don't need downtime."

"Your father and I never had downtime; that leaves a chance for everyone else to catch up," she guffaws.

"Not everything is a competition, Violet," I say quietly, shifting on the couch and mindlessly playing with the tassels on the soft blue blanket draped over my knees.

"Huh, well, it is in the firm we run."

"Did you call for a reason?" I abruptly change course.

"Yes. Your brother is returning home for the weekend next week. It's an impromptu visit, and since he's been in Dubai for six months, we thought you'd want to see him. Only him, though; Ava is staying with her mom."

I'm surprised Easton hasn't told me he's coming since we're pretty close. Between us, we've shared the burden of pressure to succeed, handed down by our parents. My older brother has definitely succeeded, though, owning a multi-national private equity firm.

"I'll be there," I say, taking another sip of hot chocolate.

"Good. We're having a get-together with a few friends, so be sure to bring something nice with you."

I roll my eyes. "A get-together," in my parent's book, is basically a black-tie cocktail party.

"Okay."

"And nothing too short, Kate."

"Nothing too short," I repeat, already considering the tiniest dresses I have in my closet.

CHAPTER TWO

KATE

"The Blades are still high up on my shit list," I say, pointing to the game on the huge TV screen mounted on Zach and Luna's lounge wall.

"They should've made an example out of him," my friend, Luna Johnson, nods in agreement. Her now fiancé, Zach Evans, is the key defenseman and the Scorpions' assistant captain. Eighteen months ago, and thanks to his manipulative ex-girlfriend, Amie, he took a dirty hit on the ice courtesy of the former New York Blades' defenseman, Alex Schneider, and it left him hospitalized. Thankfully, Zach has been able to continue playing, but that hit could've killed him, and with the way Zach was unsteady coming into this season, he knew it, too.

"At least Schneider will never play again since no team wants to go within ten feet of a contract." Luna sits back on the couch and crosses her legs, sipping her tea. "I hope we absolutely trash them tonight."

"It would be poetic justice," Felicity adds from my other side as our close trio sits on the couch armed with all the snacks and drinks we could find in the store. Felicity is the Scorpions' captain, Jon Morgan's fiancée, but he already refers to her as his wife. She's also my best friend and colleague at Preston & Preston Law, although she's a human rights lawyer. We spend far too much of our time drinking coffee in the kitchenette and putting the world to rights.

My mind momentarily travels to my parents and how they would disapprove of me having any time to relax, especially at work.

"Fuck. Yes!" Felicity squeals, almost toppling the bowl of sweet and salty popcorn over as she leaps up and pumps the air.

The Scorpions go one-zero ahead thanks to a crashing slap-shot from forward Jessie Callaghan.

"Woah!" Luna gasps. "Look, this is a big game and all, but please, go easy on my popcorn."

I chuckle as she leans down, grabs the bowl from the coffee table, and rests it safely in her lap.

She has an addiction, that girl.

But she's right about the game, not the popcorn.

If the Scorpions win tonight, when they play the Blades at home, they are one step closer to the Stanley Cup for the third time in their history.

I've been a die-hard Scorpions fan my entire life since Easton has always been crazy about them. But my work schedule and constant studying have left me with no time to attend games. Only since I met Felicity several years ago and when she made a move out here with her then-husband, who we don't mention since he's the biggest dickhead there is, have I watched more games. Having two best friends dating and now engaged to the Scorpions captain and assistant captain definitely has its benefits.

Luna became part of our trio last year, and honestly, she completes us.

"Do you know what else will be poetic?" Felicity asks us both as she sits back in her seat, tucking her thick, wavy chocolate hair behind her ears. She glances at us both with her gorgeous emerald eyes.

"What's that, babe?" I say, leaning across to grab a cheesy nacho from her plate.

"The final act of Jon's career ending with him lifting the cup." Her sweet voice trembles slightly as she says out loud what we've all been avoiding since Jon officially announced his retirement will be at the end of this season.

"Zach won't talk about it. I think he's still in denial," Luna says, her eyes down and on the bowl of popcorn in front of her.

"It's time," I say on an exhale. "He finally found the girl, and now he's ready for his next chapter." I squeeze Felicity's thigh softly.

She turns to look at me, her eyes a little glassy.

Emotions. I'm not good at them.

I roll mine in response. "Don't get all sappy on me now, woman."

Leaning forward, I swipe my wine from the table and take a sip.

Swallowing down the fresh citrus taste, I change course. "Are we all set for June thirtieth?"

Tonight was not only a girls' sleepover since it was a Friday night but also a final check over the details for Jon and Felicity's wedding.

"I still can't get over that Jon pretty much organized the entire thing himself." Luna shakes her head in disbelief as she watches the game. "Zach thinks I'm expecting the same."

"Well, first, you need to set a date," Felicity replies, her mouth full of nachos.

Classy girl.

"Hmmm, yeah. Well, the wedding isn't our top priority."

Felicity squeals excitedly and reaches over to pat Luna's stomach. But in response, her brown eyes dull.

"Still nothing?" I ask cautiously.

She shakes her head. "Nope, but I guess it's still the early days, and we haven't been trying for more than a couple of months."

"It'll happen," Felicity soothes.

"I'd be gutted if it happened so quickly for me."

Wait, did I just say that out loud? Luna's unfiltered tendencies are rubbing off.

Both heads whip over to me. "What?" they say in unison.

I shrug it off. "Not that I'd have kids. I'm just saying that hypothetically, if I did, then I'd want the breeding sex to last for at least a while."

Felicity bangs Luna on the back to dislodge the piece of popcorn she's now choking on.

Catching her breath, she looks over at me. "Jesus, you really are something else, you know that."

I shrug. "Just because I'm single doesn't mean I can't have sexual thoughts."

They both nod. "Have you heard from Tom since you called it off?" Felicity asks.

I shake my head. "Nope. I think that's finally it. It's better this way, too. It wasn't fair for me to keep leading him on, hoping I'd get serious. Even though I told him from the start, I don't do serious."

Luna hums in agreement, and Felicity smiles at me with sympathy before she reaches over and plucks a strand of my blonde hair from my black Scorpions jersey.

As if sensing I want to move on, she resets her focus on the previous conversation.

"Jon has a breeding kink." Her eyes are now fixed on the game as the first period ends, and the Scorpions are still up by one.

"That doesn't surprise me at all," I reply. And it doesn't; that boy is all kinds of possessive when it comes to his girl.

"Zach is so desperate to get me knocked up. The night before he left for New York, he fucked me so hard, and when he came, he lifted my pelvis off the mattress convinced 'gravity would help.'"

"I think I fell pregnant just from hearing that." Felicity's jaw hangs open.

"In Jon's dreams," I say around the rim of my wine glass.

She waves a hand in the air as she rises from the couch and heads through the open plan space to the kitchen. "Meh, I don't think he's fussed. He's kind of adopted Jack these days."

"Things still bad with Elliott?" Luna shouts over to her.

She peers inside the freezer. "Yep, my ex-husband has finally shown his true colors to our son, and Jack is old enough to recognize that he's a manipulative jerk." She shuts the freezer door with her hip and pops the lid on a tub of chocolate fudge brownie. "And I have zero intention of doing anything about it. I can't hide who their father really is from my children anymore. Darcy will no doubt wake up to it sooner or later."

"Honestly, I don't know how you've kept your cool with that narcissist all these years. I'd have buried him under his English patio years ago," I bite out.

She strides back over to us in her sleep set and bunny slippers, frowning at the ice cream, still too hard to dig her spoon in. "Yeah, well, it's more powerful when they work it out for themselves. Plus, he can never claim I turned them against him."

"You're a better woman than me," I drawl.

"And me," Luna adds.

Felicity tucks her legs underneath her as she sits back on the couch between us. "Yeah, well, when you become moms, you'll get it."

"If," Luna whispers.

"When. You'll find a way, no matter what," Felicity corrects her.

The players re-take the ice for the start of the second period, and we all fall silent, knowing the game is reaching its business end. The next forty minutes will be key to clinching the Stanley Cup.

"He's been unbelievable tonight," Luna nods and then points at number eighty-eight as he takes to the ice.

"Sorry, who's that?"

She looks over at me, raising an unimpressed brow at my immaturity.

"You know who."

I definitely know who she's talking about. Despite my hatred of him, I haven't been able to tear my eyes from the way he stretches on the ice before games. The way he humps it in all his padded glory should be illegal and is *definitely* not suitable for family viewing.

I hate how I respond to him, even after eighteen months since the incident at Riley's Bar—he infuriates me. He makes me want to scream into the nearest pillow with rage at his crooked and cocky smile whenever I see it. But I especially hate how he makes my body flutter whenever I see him.

"He's been distinctly average, in my opinion. The Blades goalie has been far superior."

Luna balks at me. "How'd you work that one out? JJ is on for a shutout, and their goalie isn't."

JJ.

I catch sight of Felicity's head spinning to Luna, her eyes flaring at the use of that name.

"It's fine," I say, tipping my chin up. "Use that nickname all you want. It means nothing to me."

THE DRIVE to my parents is only ten minutes. They live on one of the most exclusive streets in Seattle in an ornate mansion that has been the Monroe family home for decades, inherited through several generations.

Being only a short drive, you'd think I'd be back home to

visit my family more often. The real truth is that I'm rarely here, and I have no intention of changing that any time soon.

It couldn't be further from a family home. It's cold and formal, which is everything my downtown apartment isn't.

When Easton left for college, I had to wait two years before I could move out and head for Connecticut.

Two of the longest years of my life.

Study, study, study.

As I pull through the black iron gates leading up to the property, I round the driveway and pull up behind my brother's black Porsche 911.

I haven't been "home" in months, and I'm only here because my brother is.

The gravel crunches under my feet as I step out of my car and look around the well-manicured gardens—all tended to by a team of gardeners. Violet and Henry, my dad, would never do something as manual as gardening.

I open the trunk of my car and pull out my cocktail dress and overnight bag just as the front door to the house swings open.

I can't help the whopping smile that breaks out across my face when I see him.

My brother's arms are folded across his chest, and he's leaning against one of the white pillars on the porch. His blond hair and tanned skin are blonder and darker thanks to the Arabic sun. And as I approach the bottom of the porch, I skip the final couple of steps before he wraps his arms around me in a tight bear hug.

The only hug I ever get from my family.

Other than my two girls, he is my safe space, and more than that, he gets what it's like to live under the ever-heavy expectations of our parents. Still, he has always been the favorite and the one they go easier on.

"Hey, Katherine," he whispers into my hair.

He's at least six inches taller than me, and I'm not petite at five-eight.

"You're the only one who can get away with using my full name. Do you know that, East?" I pull back and throw my arms around his neck, planting a kiss on his cheek.

"And you're the only one who calls me East. Just don't do it for the next twenty-four hours, yeah?" He winces and tips his head inside. "She's on one."

I press my lips together, anxiety rolling through me. "In what way?"

"The caterers messed up and didn't provide enough entrées, so she's had to place a last-minute order, and they have three hours to deliver them."

"Oh, dear," I mock. "It's almost as if her gluttonous rich friends will go hungry."

He quirks an amused brow. "It's a concern for sure."

"Kate!" I hear Violet's voice echo through the foyer. "Don't loiter on the porch. It looks bad."

Ugh.

My brother lifts my bag from my shoulder, and we turn to walk inside.

"I'm only here for you. You know that."

He smiles over his shoulder at me. "Likewise."

CHAPTER THREE

JENSEN

"There's got to be a reason."

My best man, Tim, smiles at me through his grimace. "Yeah, it's only a half hour. I'll call the driver again and see if they got caught in traffic."

I nod and fight back the knot forming in my stomach.

Everyone is here and waiting, looking at me, and now starting to whisper amongst themselves.

I know what they're thinking: she's not coming.

The difference is that I've been thinking about it for the past twenty-four hours since she stopped answering my calls. But deep down, I've known things haven't been right between us for a long time.

Fuck.

I ball my hand into a fist at my side and feel the edges of my nails dig into my palm, anything to break me from this nightmare.

I've felt her backing away from me, putting up her walls. We were supposed to be forever, goddammit.

No, Jensen, you're spiraling—she's probably held up on the freeway or something, just like Tim says. Although the church is a short five-minute drive from where she was staying, and there aren't any freeways, only country roads.

The priest looks at me again and then at his watch, clutching his Bible to his chest.

Yeah, say one for me, buddy.

He rocks forward on his toes and then back onto his heels, looking at me again. "You know we have that baptism later this afternoon. Normally, I wouldn't hold two ceremonies on the same day, but I know how much this date meant to your wi–girlfriend."

I nod and check my watch.

Nearly forty minutes late.

I glance over my shoulder, and fifty pairs of eyes shoot in my direction —no sign of her. The doors to the chapel remain closed, and an eerie silence descends on the room, almost as if the wedding guests have resigned themselves to my fate.

She's not coming. My childhood sweetheart, my everything.

I turn back to the priest and nod once at him, holding out my hand to shake his. I'm not staying here to be gawked at and then fawned over while people attempt to console me with their empty words.

He looks down at my hand and then back up to me, the corners of his eyes crinkling as he smiles warmly. "God has another plan for you, Jensen."

I BOLT up in bed as the sheets pool at my waist.

Cracking my neck from side to side, I swipe the back of my hand over my forehead and remove the sheen of sweat. It happens a lot, but each time it does, the dream breaks off at a different stage.

"Different plan my ass." I huff out a laugh to no one in particular. Every plan I've ever had has turned to shit. So I've given up planning to go with the flow and just accept whatever comes my way.

I turn the faucet on in my walk-in shower and step under the freezing water. I sleep naked since I seem to wake up in a cold sweat most mornings, and so I don't have to fuck about getting undressed. Ice-cold water works every time; it awakens my senses, especially before games. A couple minutes of this and then I'll slowly crank up the heat and ponder my day.

And today is big. Fucking seismic, in fact.

If we get the W tonight, we will clinch the cup for the second time in my career and during our captain's final game.

Pressure rolls up my spine; I need a shut-out against the Blades. It's nothing I haven't dealt with before, but it never gets any easier.

I turn the heat up on the shower, letting the rainfall cascade down my back as I lean my forearms against the tiles.

Feeling like it's my best option to ease some of the tension, I take my semi-hard cock into my left hand and move my fist up and down.

Damn, that feels good.

But just like during my morning routine and as if on cue, her face invades my mind.

And I'm not talking about my ex-fiancée, Lauren.

Kate Monroe. My fucking kryptonite.

The grip on my cock gets tighter as I pump it harder and with added frustration. She's like she always is in my fantasies: on her fucking knees with her silky blonde hair wrapped around my fist. Her piercing bright blue eyes stream, leaving mascara tracks down her rosy cheeks as she takes me further down her throat.

That's right, Princess. Take me. Take it all.

Let me fuck that sass and back talk right from that pretty mouth of yours.

I feel the pressure transfer from my spine to my balls as a powerful orgasm threatens to burst free.

I drop my forehead to the cold tile wall and squeeze my eyes shut as my hips begin to pump erratically. God, she's fucking good at sucking my dick in my imagination, and I know she'll be even better in reality. I'd fuck her through my mattress, given half a chance, even if she won't come within twenty feet of me.

Squeezing my dick harder, I come on a deep roar as streams of hot cum spray against the wall, and my jaw hangs open as I imagine her swallowing every single fucking drop.

Take it, Katherine.

A shudder wracks through my body as I come back down to earth, and frustration swells within me once more. For the past eighteen months, since that night in Riley's, all I can think about is her. And ever since she rejected me and then moved on to some random guy at the bar, she's triggered memories of that fateful day ten years ago when I was left standing at the altar.

But the kicker is that she's the one who thinks I moved on to some redheaded chick and took her home. Well, she's wrong. That redhead, Chloe, was actually my sister's best friend visiting her family for the holidays. We randomly bumped into each other, and the moment I saw she was drunk and planning to walk herself back to her parents' apartment in downtown Seattle, there was no way I was letting that happen.

So the immature little princess threw her toys out and concluded I'd moved on with someone else.

The hypocrisy.

I don't owe her shit, and like hell am I going to be the one to explain what happened. If she thinks I'm that kind of guy, then she clearly doesn't know me at all. She can live in her little world where she thinks she's always right.

Trouble is, she's ruined me.

From the moment I kissed her in Riley's, sparks flew. No one, not even Lauren, had anything on that hour we shared. Her in my jersey, sitting across my lap, my cock so fucking hard I could've fucked her through my dress pants. Yeah, I suggested we head back to my place, specifically my bed, and yeah, I wanted her. But not as a one-night stand. Fuck no. She owned me from the moment she turned up at the game wearing my name and number, and she's owned me ever since.

From the moment she slid off my lap and told me to go fuck myself, things have never been the same. I've never been the same. Every woman I've slept with has been Kate in my head. They could be brunette, but in my mind, they're blonde. As they take my dick into their mouths, all I can think about is Kate's lips wrapped around me.

And then, to add fucking insult to injury, she starts dating another man.

Fucking Tom Bennett.

Pretentious prick. I guess he suits her perfectly.

I yank the faucet off and step out of the shower, wrapping a towel around me as I head to the counter to brush my teeth.

I need to get over this woman, just like she clearly has with me.

We're part of the same friendship group, so I can't wipe her from my life, and honestly, I don't want to; I don't have it in me. Each time I see her, she looks more stunning than the last, and I want to tell her that every time. I want to tell her that I've given up sleeping with other women since it's pointless. She's the only one I want, the only one my dick wants. But I can't have her, and I can't even fuck her out of my system.

I'm fucking obsessed, jealous, angry, and even though she might not see it or care, I'm protective—I've kept my distance, but I swear to God, if anyone hurts her, I'll rip him limb from limb.

How am I supposed to go on like this? I'm fucked up and channeling every ounce of anger into my game. She'll be there tonight, ignoring me, taunting me, reminding me of all the ways she hates me.

But most of all, she scares the shit out of me with the way she makes me feel—out of control and powerless. Like a puppet being played with or better still, a toy once loved for a brief moment and then cast onto the heap while she moves on to something shinier.

I tell everyone I don't do commitment or relationships, and that's the absolute truth.

Because the one fucking woman I want hates me for something I didn't do, and like hell am I going to grovel.

Jensen Jones does not grovel.

I didn't grovel for Lauren to come back and marry me instead of running away with my then-best friend, and I'm sure as shit not groveling to Kate Monroe.

Especially when she's clearly over me and fucking another man.

CHAPTER FOUR

JENSEN

I push through the locker room doors, feeling just as nervous as I did this morning. You'd think my body and mind would be used to this kind of pressure after multiple seasons in the NHL, and a Stanley Cup win, but I'm not.

I embrace feeling this way. It's what makes me feel alive and reminds me that I still have a passion for the game I fell in love with when my dad first took me to our local rink in Alberta.

The key is not to let the nerves overpower the adrenaline.

"Yo!" Jessie Callaghan, my best friend and crazy fast winger fist bumps me as I take a seat at the bench with him.

With the win in New York a couple of days ago and our home-ice advantage from the regular season, we get to play tonight's pivotal game in front of a Scorpions home crowd, and that's a huge deal in our bid for the cup.

"Hey, buddy. How you doing?" I dump my kit bag down and take a deep breath, centering myself.

"I'm good. Body feels good, head's good, and the crowd is already buzzing. We're on for the cup. I can feel it."

"Fucking right we are!" Jon, our center and captain, shouts

from the opposite side of the locker room. He's sitting next to our assistant captain and defenseman, Zach Evans. Like true leaders, they're always the first to arrive and start prepping. Zach looks anxious, and I know it's a combination of factors, including the fact it's likely Jon's last game in his career, and after that, he will take the captaincy over. I'd love to be his assistant captain, but the NHL rules don't allow for goalies to have a captaincy role for practical purposes, so instead, the badge will go to Henderson, one of our experienced forwards.

One after the other, the boys begin to file into the dressing room, and an unusually heavy silence falls over the group. Normally, it's buzzing with life, but the entire team senses the occasion.

That's until Coach Burrows swings the door open. Game prep and clipboard in hand, he stands in the center and slowly casts his gaze at us all. "I don't need to stand here and say any more than what I've been saying all season and then again at morning skate. Tonight is historic."

He walks across to where our captain is sitting, his elbows resting on his knees and his hands clasped before him. Jon looks emotional, and when Coach speaks, I hear that emotion echoing in his voice. "You're not just a group of incredibly talented men, you're also my men. I've worked with some of you for a few short months and with others for years. But let me tell you this: I've never met a finer man or player than this guy right here." Coach leans forward and claps Jon on the shoulder. "I've seen this guy in his best and worst moments. But nothing will prepare me for tonight when the final buzzer goes, and we close out on one of the finest careers I've ever witnessed."

Our captain draws in a deep breath to center himself and comes to a stand. "We will clinch the W tonight because we owe it to ourselves. Months of prep and, in some cases, years of working and playing together all come down to this—three twenty-minute periods where we leave it all out there on the ice. Nothing is spared, no one is left behind, and everyone puts in their maximum shift. We don't accept anything other than the W tonight, and we give our fans exactly what they deserve—a night to remember."

"Fucking right!" Jessie jumps to his feet and fists the air.

Coach Burrows nods slowly and walks towards the door. "I think that's all that needs to be said. But I will say this, I'm proud of each and every one of you. And tonight, I want to celebrate with you in the bar. Now crush 'em!"

He leaves to a roar that reverberates off the walls.

And right here, the last of my nerves leaves my body to be replaced entirely by a thrumming need to secure my boys the shutout.

SWEAT DRIPS DOWN MY FOREHEAD, stinging my eyes.

This game is like no other. The Blades weren't going down without a fight, but neither were we. I'm not on for my shutout, having leaked two goals already, but as we reach the final few minutes in the third, we're a goal up, and the pressure crushes me as their center comes crashing down the ice.

There's no way Zach will catch up to him since he was left back at center ice.

Focus, Jensen.

It's effectively one-on-one, and if we concede now, we lose our slender three-two lead, opening the game right back up.

In reality, everything's happening so fast in front of me, but in my head, Robinson, the Blades' Center, is skating in slow motion. I've watched hours of game tape, examining his favored moves before he frequently sinks the puck.

He likes to go top left but tells you he's going right. I know his backhand might be his weaker side, but he likes to double-bluff goalies.

Not this time, though; he does exactly what I expected and

whips the puck to the top left corner in a Crosby-like move. I'm ready, glove outstretched, prepared to catch it and put this turnover to an end along with their Stanley Cup dreams.

The puck rockets into my glove with a thud as the crowd explodes.

There's all of thirty seconds left on the clock, barely enough time to restart play let alone draw level.

Jon skates over, clapping a hand on my shoulder. "Fucking yes!"

"Never in doubt," I reply, my voice as shaky as my knees. I was in total doubt. But they don't need to know that. No one needs to know what goes on in my head.

That's a one-way ticket to doing time for thought crimes.

Speaking of. I turn to face my goal and reset myself for the final play, but I can't help looking up at our family box. Mom, Dad, and my sister, Hollie, are here. But that's not who I'm looking for; Hollie and my mom have black hair, not blonde.

Next to them is a brunette and a redhead, Felicity and Luna. But they're not her.

Jon said she'd be here. But I've yet to catch a glimpse. And I've been looking every goddamn minute.

The biggest game of your life, Jensen, and you're still obsessing over the woman who hates your guts.

Pathetic.

The game restarts, but it's all over as the home crowd counts down the final ten seconds of play.

Cup winners, again.

In true Seattle fashion, rubber fish rain down onto the ice, making it nearly impossible to skate anywhere. I've never seen this many before, and I've never heard the crowd so loud my eardrums vibrate with the intensity.

But I need to get to him.

To Jon.

Through the sea of players making their way to him, I watch as he crouches down at center ice and pulls off his left glove.

Bringing his fingertips to his lips, he kisses them and then touches the freezing surface. A place where he's stood for so many puck drops, a place where he's heard his name chanted over and over again. A place he's called home for so many years. He's a living hockey legend who's called time on an insane career that's seen good, great, and some really tough times.

I stop skating and pull off my helmet, swiping a quick glove under my eye. But this time, it's not sweat impeding my vision.

My teammates give him this moment to connect with his home, with the ice, to say thank you but also farewell to the NHL. It's Zach who makes the first move over to him, which only seems right.

Pushing my feet forward once more, I'm second to arrive on the scene as we form a tight circle on the ice. More of our teammates arrive, but not one word is said. There's plenty of time to scream and get wrecked later.

Right now, in this moment, we pay homage to one of the greats. To our great.

Skating in a circle slowly, it's Jon who finally speaks. "I need to get wrecked, boys, or else I'm going to lose my shit right here and now."

Laughter buzzes around the circle.

"Now you're talking my language," I say, breaking from my position opposite Jon and skating over. There's no way I can lift all six-foot-four and two hundred and thirty pounds, but I'm an idiot, so I try anyway.

"Fuck me, put him down before you slip a disc, you dickhead," Zach scolds.

I've barely lifted him an inch before I set him back down. But Jon doesn't seem to have noticed at all since he's fixated over my shoulder.

And I know exactly what's captured his attention. Felicity, the woman who he has insisted since they got engaged, is already his wife. Soon to be in only four weeks.

But where there's Felicity, there's blonde and...

Wait.

Jessie Callaghan's fucking jersey?!

"You have *got* to be kidding me," I rumble darkly.

"Say what?" Zach nudges my shoulder with this. A smug grin on his face when he sets his eyes on Luna.

"Nothing," I bite out.

The circle breaks apart entirely, and the boys skate to their respective partners and family members. Mom and Dad haven't made it down yet, so I'm left standing here, simmering in my rage.

Usually, she barely makes eye contact with me, but tonight, she looks me straight in the eyes when Jon bends down and she hugs him, resting her chin on his padded shoulder.

She's barely twenty feet away, so I don't miss the smug twitch to her lips when she watches me scan her top half, taking in number forty-four stamped on the right sleeve of her black and white Scorpions jersey.

No, scratch that. Not her jersey—Jessie's.

I could rip it from her in one motion and revel in how the material tears apart.

Her lips curve into a full-blown smirk, and I know my expression screams rage. I keep my skates planted where they are. If I move any closer, I will likely go through with my thoughts.

Call the thought police.

My princess is full of surprises tonight as she pulls away from Jon and confidently steps across the ice in her white Converse and tight as fuck blue jeans. Did she spray those on? They'd be hard work to peel dow—

"Congratulations. Well played."

For the first time in weeks, even though we've spent time together as a group, she speaks directly to me. But her tone is as cold as the ice we're standing on, and her bright blue eyes are sharp as she folds her arms across her chest, looking up at me.

Her long blonde hair falls around her shoulders, and the tiny brown beauty spot sitting just below her left eye draws my attention, as it always does.

I wonder if it's make-up or natural. I wonder how much of Kate Monroe is real. She carries herself with confidence, but I've never been convinced she's as secure as she lets on.

There's an element of chaos beneath that perfectly put-together exterior.

"Thanks," I say, pulling off my gloves.

She scrunches her nose and looks me up and down with a tinge of disdain, her arms still crossed over her chest. "You smell terrible."

I lift an arm and smell my armpit before shrugging. "Healthy testosterone. No chick's ever complained before."

She scoffs. "They probably didn't get close enough to tell."

My six-three frame towers over her smaller stature, which is, at my best guess, five-eight. Add in my skates, and I have to really lean down to whisper, "Come a little closer and find out what all the fuss is about."

"Ha!" Uncrossing her arms, she reaches up and taps her palm on my right shoulder. Even through my jersey and pads, she brands me. It's the first time she's touched me since I can remember, maybe since that night in Riley's Bar. "Thanks, but I'm good."

I force a cocky smirk, my eyes still trained on hers. "First, you wear another man's jersey, and now you're flirting with me. Tom can't be happy."

Her eyebrows shoot to her hairline. "You can convince yourself of anything, can't you?"

I throw my head back and laugh. Fuck me, she's a handful.

"You didn't answer my question." I refocus, and surprisingly, she's still watching me when I return my eyes to hers.

"What exactly was your question?" she drawls.

"Tom. He can't be happy."

She pulls at the sleeve of her jersey and shrugs. "There's no flirting, and personally, I don't see what's wrong with wearing my favorite player's name."

Oh, you are something else.

"Lies."

"Unlikely, but don't sweat it for me, babe. I doubt he cares since we split."

I fight, with every ounce of goddamn will, to maintain an unaffected expression.

She's single.

I open my mouth to list off all the reasons why wearing a player's jersey speaks volumes and to ask her why the fuck *I'm* not her favorite Scorpion, but I'm interrupted by a gloved hand on my shoulder.

"So I've got a fan club after all." Jessie slides up next to me, jutting his chin at Kate. This guy is my best friend, but if he doesn't wipe that smug smile from his face in the next second, I'll remove it for him.

"All okay, Jensen?" Her sweet tone mocks me.

I won't let her have this.

Be a fucking swan, Jensen.

"Yeah," I retort. I'm thirty-two years old, but I'm not above acting thirteen. "Just thinking about tonight's celebrations since I was the designated party planner."

"I thought we were going to Riley's and then back to your place?" Jessie replies, sounding as confused as Kate looks.

I don't take my eyes off her when I reply, "Change of plans. Riley's and then onto Heat."

My dick might not respond to other women, but that doesn't mean I can't have a couple on my lap.

Game on, Princess.

CHAPTER FIVE

KATE

"Why the fuck are we here? I thought we were headed to your place!" Jon bites at Jensen.

We all roll out of the limo, and immediately the doormen usher us inside before security escorts our group to the VIP area on the second floor of Club Heat. Felicity shoots a wary glance at me as we walk down the lowly lit hallway. In front of us, Luna tightens her grip on Zach's arm. She hates these kinds of places.

I can't say I'm enamored. They're crawling with women *and men* looking to hook up with each other. If that's their bag, then fine. But it's not my scene.

I could answer Jon's question—he brought us here so he can hook up.

"I didn't want to spend my hangover day cleaning up my apartment," Jensen shouts over the beating music.

"You have a cleaner!" Jon shouts back. "You know I hate this place."

"Too many skeletons live here." Felicity leans into me as we walk hand in hand into the seating area complete with a private bar and plush black couches.

"Mmmm-hmmm," I respond. Jon's playboy days were largely spent here post-games; I doubt he wanted to be here tonight. "He's being a selfish wanker."

Felicity barks out a laugh as we take a tentative seat on one of the couches. "There's that British influence, again," she responds in her broad English accent.

"What was that?" Jensen comes to stand in front of me. Dressed in a crisp white shirt rolled up to his elbows, black dress pants that sit above his ankles, and loafers, I can't deny he looks delicious. His dress sense has always been impeccable. He never takes his eyes off me as he runs a hand through his glossy, almost black hair. He's every bit my type.

Every. Single. Bit.

Apart from the asshole factor.

I clear my throat and hold his gaze with determination. "I said, you're a selfish wanker." I cast a hand around the room at Jessie, Felicity, Jon, and Zach, who's got Luna protectively pinned to his side on the opposite couch. "No one wants to be here. Apart from you."

He shifts uncomfortably and looks across at his best friend, Jessie, for support. In response, he shoves his hands in his pockets and twists his lips to the side. "I mean, I don't mind. I'm up for a party."

Jensen steels his shoulders. "And I'm up for getting wrecked." He looks between his former and new captain. "For old times' sake."

"Fine," Jon replies. "But no girls."

SURPRISE, fucking surprise, there are girls.

And they're all over Jensen. Not that he's protesting; he invited the brunette onto his lap, and that's where she's been for the past ten minutes.

Which feels like ten hours.

She's young, pretty, and they've been talking nonstop. I think that's the worst part of having to witness this—the way they bounce off one another. But mainly, the way he hasn't looked at me once. If I wasn't sitting in public, I'd slap myself across the face to break me from my trance. I *never* get this way over a guy. I didn't get this way over a nice guy like Tom. But oh no, I go and get all antsy over a dickhead like Jensen Jones.

"Come down to the main bar with me." I've been so phased out that I don't notice Luna standing next to me while I sit, twisting the straps of my purse around in my hands.

"Huh?"

"Come down with me. Get away from him," she clarifies softly, holding out her hand.

"Away from who? I'm fine," I reply.

She cocks her head to the side and eyes me softly. "I don't believe you."

I scoff. "Babe, I love you, but you've got this all wrong. He..." I glance over at Jensen. "Does *not affect* me."

"So coming down for a drink with me shouldn't be an issue. Should it?"

I look across for my other best friend, but she's busy sitting on Jon's lap at the bar.

More laughter from the brunette has me looking their way once more, and I hate the way my stomach drops at the sight. Curling his hand around the nape of her neck, he pulls her head closer to whisper in her ear. My body betrays me again as goosebumps break out over my arms. The way she must feel right now.

Luna whips my bag from my grasp. "Come. Now."

Simply because I don't want to see anymore, I follow her lead as she takes my hand and guides us out of the VIP area.

"Be careful, Rocket. I'm right here if you need anything," Zach shouts up as we exit.

Smiling sweetly at him, she wastes no time pulling me down the stairs to the main club.

We take the only two stools left at the bar when Luna turns to me, a determined look on her face. "He's drunk."

"Is he?"

She rolls her eyes in frustration. "You know he is. You've been watching him sink tequila like it's going out of fashion."

I have. "Seems pretty with it to me. His new friend seems to be enjoying his company just fine." My response is laced with sarcasm, but I can't help it. I can't fight it back anymore, and I get the feeling Luna isn't going to drop this. She's been asking questions about us since last year.

"What happened, Kate?"

The VIP area can be seen from where we're sitting since it's a mezzanine, but I can't make out anyone sitting down, only Zach, who's standing up and keeping watch, although he's trying *and failing* to look like he's not.

I inwardly smirk at his obsession. Simp.

Sighing, I pull the mojito I ordered toward me. "There's not much more to tell than what I told you before. We were getting close one night at Riley's. He wanted a one-night thing, and I didn't. So when I said no, he got it elsewhere."

"With the redhead?"

I nod and take a sip.

"Felicity might've mentioned you were with another guy, too."

I nod again. I don't lie to people, let alone my best friends. "He approached me at the bar, and when I saw Jensen with another girl, I took advantage."

She smirks. "You two are like teenagers."

"He infuriates the shit out of me."

"Because you want him. He affects you. And I'm sorry to break it to you, but you aren't over that night."

I crash my straw down into the ice cubes, exhausted with the denial. "Tell me something I don't know."

"Well, that makes it even worse then. You've both been stewing over this for over a year but refuse to back down. You acknowledge each other only to make jibes."

I cast my eyes over the VIP area and immediately wish I hadn't. Hand in hand, Jensen and the brunette are walking over to the bar. I'm not surprised she's leading him since he looks even more unsteady than when we left. "He's over it. Take a look upstairs." I point Luna to where I'm looking.

Even from her side profile, I see the way her brows shoot to her hairline. "Yeah, he's drunk and being a dick." She turns back to me, clearing her throat. "I don't think wearing Jessie's jersey helped."

I shrug. "I wore his that night, and it meant nothing, so why would it mean anything to Jessie? He knows we're just friends."

"Jessie does, yeah."

Laughter erupts from across the club, and even over the loud music, we don't miss it.

Like history repeating itself, I watch as, with drinks in hand, Jensen stumbles behind the brunette as she leads him out of the VIP area and into the dark hallway.

I can't be here anymore. I don't need to watch this shit. If he is trying to make me jealous, then he's gone too far. But honestly, I don't think he could give two shits about me, my feelings, or anyone else's for that matter.

He's a selfish prick.

"I'm going home," I announce, pushing my stool back.

"Kate."

I shake my head, my hair falling around my face, hopefully shielding the shine to my eyes. "Whatever his game is, it's not about me. It's all about him because that's all he cares about."

"Kate, just talk to him."

I drop my head and then look back at Luna. "For what purpose? So he can tell me how good the redhead was? Because that's all he does—sleep around and have parties."

And get under my skin.

And live rent-free in my head.

And make me feel vulnerable.

"Let me and Zach take you home."

I shake my head and grab my purse from the side. "No. I just need to be alone. I've already said too much."

"But you can always talk to me. You know I would never say a thing to anyone."

I take a step back toward her and lean down, kissing her on the cheek. "I know, and I love you for that. But some people just can't be in the same room."

"It's not great for our group."

I draw in a deep breath. She's right. "I know. I need to work on that. With the wedding coming up and us being together for several days, we need to at least be civilized. Right now, though, I just need space to get my shit together."

She nods and throws me a soft Felicity-like smile. "It's okay to admit you have feelings for him."

Oh, I have feelings, alright. That I'd like to kick ass into next week.

I tuck my hair behind my ears and smile back at her. "I'm just disappointed in the way he behaved that night and then again tonight. He hauled us down here for his own needs and didn't consider anyone else's." My voice shakes as I fight to keep my tone even.

"Let us take you home."

"Stay. Zach is here to celebrate with the boys, and I'm a spare part anyway," I laugh.

Luna opens her mouth, no doubt to protest, but I get there first. "Stay. I'll grab an Uber."

Turning on my high heels, I blow her a kiss, a well-practiced faux grin, and high tail it out of there.

That's the final time Jensen fucking Jones humiliates me.

CHAPTER SIX

JENSEN

"I swear on all that is holy, if you puke one more time on my bathroom floor, I'll banish you from this apartment forever."

"Let me die, then," I reply, rolling over onto my side. I have no idea where I am, but I'm pretty sure that's Felicity's voice. You can't miss the British accent.

"Trust me. With the way you behaved last night, I'm tempted. But Jon likes you, so apparently, I have to keep you alive."

I groan in pain. "Where am I?"

"On my bathroom floor. Where you've been the entire night."

I try to sit up but crack my forehead on the underside of the toilet. "Fuck!"

"I'll reserve my sympathy if that's alright."

Prying an eye open, a very pissed off British woman slowly comes into view. In her sleepwear and bunny slippers, she stands there with her hands propped on her hips.

"What did I do wrong?" I manage, wincing at the pounding in my head as I come to sit up straight.

She scoffs and passes me a glass of water and two painkillers.

I down the water and tablets as slowly, but very fucking surely, the night starts to come back to me in hazy images. "We went to Riley's, right?"

"Yeah, keep going," Felicity drawls.

Scratching my bare chest, I hold out the empty glass. "I'm gonna need some more hydration for my brain to work."

Snatching the glass out of my hand, she turns the faucet and refills the glass, handing it back to me. "Would you like me to clarify last night for you, *JJ*?"

Damn, Jon must be scared shitless ninety percent of the time.

I've heard that nickname a handful of times and only ever from a blonde. But with the icy way Felicity says it, my skin prickles in response.

What the *fuck* did I do?

I nod once, forcing down the rising bile with water.

"Well, where do I start? Do you remember diverting us all to Club Heat after Riley's?"

I nod; yeah, I remember that since I made the decision while still sober.

"And do you remember announcing how trashed you planned to get?"

I nod again.

"The tequila?"

"How could I forget," I groan.

"And what about the busty brunette pinned to your side all night?"

My head whips up to look at her.

"Yes, Jensen. Although she was a part of your plan, right?"

There's no way I hooked up. I wouldn't. I don't anymore since it's fucking pointless. "I didn't hook up with her."

"I know you didn't." Her tone is slightly softer. "But is it true?"

"You'll have to clue me in. That's as much as I remember."

"Is it true you're crazy about her?"

"The brunette? I don't even remember her name."

"Not the brunette. Kate."

Embarrassment overtakes me. What *the fuck* did I tell her? I drag my hands down my face but pause when my right cheek stings.

Felicity chuckles. "That's where she slapped you."

Fuck! "Kate?"

"No, the brunette. She hauled you into a dark hallway. You were totally wrecked, so I chased after you to make sure you were alright. Next thing I knew, she was trying to climb you, but you said no and backed away. Then, in an incredibly slurry voice, you told her you were '*crazy about Princess Katherine, even if she can't stand me*.' And that's when she slapped you and stalked off."

Jesus. I called her Princess Katherine.

"So, is it true?"

Parting the fingers that still cover my eyes, I focus on Felicity. "This goes no further."

She drums her pink fingernails on the countertop in thought. "I don't keep secrets from Jon."

"Fine. No further than you and him."

"Deal."

"I'm...yeah...fucking obsessed with her."

Felicity's hands fly to her mouth as she audibly gasps. "I *knew it*."

I drop my hands and then my head between my shoulders. "I can't get her out of my mind. Not since that night at Riley's. I haven't hooked up with anyone in a while since I can't see anyone but her. Doesn't change anything, though; she hates me."

"Jensen. You had Kate on your lap one minute, and the next, you're copping off with some redhead!"

Shaking my head, I squeeze my eyes shut, my temples still pounding. "Sister's best friend."

"WHAT?!"

"Jesus, don't shout." I wince. "Not like that. She was drunk, so I walked her home. End of story. But *Katherine* always has to be right and decided I was hooking up immediately after she told me to go fuck myself."

Crossing her arms over her chest, she shakes her head in disbelief. "She's even more pissed at you after last night."

It just gets better. "What does she think I did?"

"The exact same thing. That you hooked up with another woman to make her jealous."

"Like she wore Jessie's jersey?"

"You two are insufferable, you know that?"

I lean back on the tiled wall with a thud and hold the glass out for another refill. "Yep."

"You need to talk to her. If this icy atmosphere is still around come our wedding day, I'll—"

"I know," I say on an exhale. "I know."

"What are you going to do?"

Gripping the back of my neck, I go over the options in my head. She's as stubborn as I am, so it'll take some work to bring her around after everything that's happened. "I'll call her and try to smooth things over."

She quirks a brow. "Well, that's a given. I meant, what are you going to do about telling her how you feel?"

I scoff. "Nothing. You think I'm going to lay it all on the line for the woman who invades my dreams at night but can barely look at me when I see her? You don't think feeling this way scares the shit out of me and that's why I've held back for so long?" I fight to keep my tone even, but my voice shakes at the end, and I hate that. I hate that I'm showing myself like this.

"Oh babe, I—"

I hold up a hand. "Don't go there, please."

"Okay, but I didn't realize you felt this way. Do you want me to talk to her?"

"No!" I bite out, way harsher than I want. "No, say nothing about any of this. I'll explain what happened both at Riley's and last night and the rest..." I grab my shirt from the bathroom floor. Fuck me, do I need my bed. "The rest is up to her."

JON

Felicity just told me. Want to talk about it?

ABOUT AS MUCH AS I want a hole in the head.

ME

No.

Okay, well, I'm here if you want. But you need to talk to her, buddy. Bottling this kind of shit up isn't healthy. You two have been toxic since I can remember, and now I find out you like her? Funny way of showing it.

Like? Nah. Try obsessed, try infatuated, try fucking insane with need. But how much of this is just lust, a craving to get her in my bed as many times as I can? Half the time, she pisses me off, and the other half, I'm doing the same. There's no denying my need to fuck her every way to Sunday. My need to fuck her out of my system. But I also can't deny the insane attraction runs deeper than my dick. Each time I've looked at her, I see past those faux smiles and cold blue eyes. There's pain there. I feel it in her. I feel it for her. And that shit makes me feel all kinds of confused.

I said I'll talk to her.

Okay.

Sitting at my kitchen counter, coffee in hand, I close out our message thread and scroll down to Kate's contact information. We haven't called or texted each other since I sent her a ton of wink emojis that night when she turned up to the game wearing my jersey.

The number of times I've scrolled back through those messages. When I changed my phone, I made sure they got transferred over, like a fucking simp.

ME

There's some cute blonde in the arena wearing my jersey. Happen to know who she is? **ten thousand wink faces**

KATE

Blushing faces Surprised you spotted me from the other side of the ice.

I'm not. You were the first and only thing I saw.

Fuck me. Where did all this go wrong?

I take a sip of coffee and then start typing out a vanilla message asking her to meet up or at least reply so I can explain, but who am I kidding? The only reply I'm likely to get is my second, *"Go fuck yourself."*

So instead, I tap on the top right, tentatively put my phone to my ear, and wait.

One ring.

Two rings.

Three rings.

Four.

She's not going to answer.

Voicemail.

I cut the call and begin typing out a message.

ME

Hey. I tried to call, but it went to your voicemail. Listen, can we talk? There are some things I need to say.

Like I dream about you nightly.

Sent.

I toss my phone to the side and groan. What a fucking mess. I don't expect us to be best friends, but if I'm going to bear the torture of being around her, then I need to at least get to a place where she doesn't want to rip my head off.

Rising from my stool, I head for an ice-cold shower but only get as far as the hallway when my cell buzzes.

I race back and snatch it up.

KATE

I don't think there's much to say, Jensen. I told Luna and Felicity I'd be civil with you, so that's what I'll be. But just know, I'm done with playing games.

"Argh!" I toss my phone at the kitchen wall. The crack is audible as it breaks into pieces, scattering across my light wood flooring. It probably came off better than my wall, though. There's a gouge in the crisp white paint exposing the plasterboard underneath.

I hate that I want her. I hate that she holds me in the palm of her hand, crushing me in her grip whenever she wants.

But mostly, in this moment right here, I hate the way she called me Jensen.

I'm JJ.

CHAPTER SEVEN

THREE WEEKS LATER

KATE

I haul my heavy suitcase out of the trunk of the Uber and settle up with the driver.

As the car pulls off, crunching along the gravel driveway, I look up at the picture-perfect English cottage. The entire drive here was like a scene out of *Bridgerton*. I've visited London before, but never Oxford and never this kind of countryside.

I can see why Jon was so determined to marry Felicity here, in her late parents' house. It's stunning. The purple wisteria wraps around the classic English white porch, the huge flower heads framing the entryway perfectly. The double-fronted stone cottage has flower baskets under each window, and I smile at the purple and green combination he's clearly gone for. I gotta hand it to him, he doesn't miss a detail. He never has when it comes to his soulmate.

I took a different flight than Luna and Felicity, who are already here. A case I thought I'd wrapped up took a last-minute left and I didn't trust anyone else to see it through. So, I backed out and caught a red-eye last night. I have to be here today since, in true Jon fashion, the celebrations last not just one day but two. Not that I'm complaining since I can't wait to spend every second with the happy couple. No one deserves a happily ever after more than these two.

I tap the big brass knocker twice, but my breath catches in my throat when the last person I expected to answer swings the door open.

"Kate. Um, hi."

There, standing in all his freakin' glory, is Jensen Jones. Argh. *Why does he have to wear backward caps?*

"Hi," I squeak out. Aside from a couple of pre-wedding meals we've both been at, we've barely spoken beyond handing each other the breadbasket and politely saying thank you.

"I thought you were the, um, the florist. They're coming to set up the archway today."

I nod as we hold awkward eye contact. "Nope. Just me."

He scratches at the thin white T-shirt he's wearing and then reaches out to grab my suitcase. I put my hand on the handle. "I got it, thanks."

I don't miss the way his eyes narrow at me, but I can't tell if it's frustration or that he simply likes me about as much as I do him. "Fine."

Stepping to one side, he holds the heavy white wooden door open, and I step into the hallway. "Where are the others?"

"In the garden. Jon's parents have just arrived with Adam, so they're spending some time showing him the garden and house. I came inside so there weren't too many of us around."

Adam, Jon's brother, is autistic and has some sensory processing needs. He can get overwhelmed with crowds of people, especially when he's in unfamiliar surroundings. But I'm betting he's doing just fine since he's with his number one person, Felicity. Those two are inseparable, with a bond like nothing else I've ever seen.

What does surprise me, though, is the way Jensen thought about someone else. He came inside to give Adam the space he needed.

I quickly shrug off the feeling. One moment doesn't undo the countless dickhead moves he's made. "Okay, do you know where my room is? I can go dump my suitcase."

I stand at the bottom of the wooden staircase. This place is seriously stunning. Jon's spent a fortune restoring its original features.

Jensen takes a step closer and holds out his hand to take my bag. "Your room is next to mine. I can take it up—it looks heavy."

I prop a frustrated hand on my hip. "You don't need to pretend, you know."

His eyebrows knit together in confusion. "Pretend what?"

"That you like me, that we like each other. We can just exist in the same space for the next two days and not fight and then go our separate ways for a detox."

Blowing out a humorless laugh, he shoves his hands into the front pockets of his low-riding black jeans. "I don't hate you."

"But you don't like me."

He drops his head between his shoulders and looks at the floor. "I thought you didn't want to talk."

"I don't want to talk."

"Then what are we doing here? Let me take your luggage upstairs. One, because it looks crazy heavy, and two," he pulls his head back up, looking at me with an intense expression that sends my knees weak, "because I'm a gentleman."

I scoff. "Ha! Okay."

He lurches forward, grabbing my suitcase by the strap.

"I wasn't saying okay to carrying my luggage. I was—"

"Whatever," he bites out as he stalks up the stairs, taking them two at a time.

Kicking off my sneakers, I chase after him. "Give me back my suitcase."

He stops mid-way to the top and whips around to me. "Remind me. When is it you turn thirty-six?"

"August."

"Start acting like it then."

He continues back up the stairs, and I chase him down the hallway until he stops outside a door I assume is to my bedroom.

"And what about you? When do you hit puberty?"

Placing his hand on the round brass doorknob, he twists it open and then turns to offer a smug smirk, which is way too sexy. "I already did. But you keep passing up the opportunity to find out."

There are so many ways I could dissect that statement. But I ignore all temptation to find out just how mature thirty-two-year-old Jensen Jones is.

Hard pass.

He disappears inside the room, and I follow. A king-sized bed with a brushed brass mental frame sits in the middle of the room. The decorations are soft pink and very girly; even the comforter is pink. I take in my surroundings for the next two days. "This should be Luna's room."

He chuckles and sets my case on the white wooden trunk at the foot of the bed. "They're all like this. Frilly and shit."

I fight back my laughter at his description—no need to encourage him.

"You can laugh, you know, even crack a smile at me."

I press my lips together. "I will when you say something funny."

He walks toward me, and the air crackles with charge. I know sleeping with him would be mind-blowingly amazing, and I hate how aware I am of it.

There's barely a foot between us when his earthy cologne hits me. I haven't been close enough to him to notice it lately, but with it comes a flashback of that night in Riley's when I was perched on his lap.

I squeeze my thighs together, remembering the way he made me feel, just like the reaction I'm having now.

"I'll make you smile at me if it's the last thing I do, Princess."

PRINCESS.

Oh, he thinks he's hilarious. The way he laced it with sarcasm, and I'm willing to bet he knew exactly how much it would piss me off too.

"More salad, Kate?" Jennie, Jon's mom, breaks me from my seething trance. Standing over me with a bowl, the others stare at me in silence as we sit around the huge, round outdoor table eating dinner.

How long have I been sitting like this?

"Hmm? Oh, no, no thanks," I finally respond.

Jennie smiles sweetly and turns on her heel, making for the kitchen.

"Okay, so let's go over the plans once more since a couple of things have changed," Jon begins. He leans down and fetches a folder from under his seat and starts flipping through the pages.

"Please tell me that isn't your wedding planner," I say, my eyes bugging out at the sheer volume of information. "I made fewer notes when studying for the bar."

A couple of snickers break out around the table, and I watch as Adam's shoulders shake with laughter. "Have you sprayed each page with Felicity's perfume?" he adds.

Jon points to him and then to me. "Don't you start. This is an intricate operation, and I want it to be perfect for my wife."

"It will be. So long as we say, 'I do,' then it will." Felicity places her hand over Jon's.

"She actually turned up, so that's a good sign," Jensen adds, but I don't look at him. I haven't since the moment I stormed out of that bedroom.

Jon rolls his eyes and continues. "So the changes are to the aisle order immediately after we're married. Originally, the lineup was me and Felicity, obviously, and then my best man and the maid of honor, then Jensen and Luna. But..." He clears his throat anxiously. "I've tweaked it so Luna and Zach walk together. It won't be long until they're walking down the aisle themselves."

"Sounds good," Jensen agrees.

No, this *does not* sound good.

I stab at the cherry tomato on my plate. *Keep calm, Kate. You need to remain civil. You're only linking arms with him; it'll be over in a flash.*

"And you, babe, is that okay with you?" Felicity asks from across the table.

I smile sweetly. "Of course. I'm happy to go along with whatever works best."

I can't help it. I glance over at Jensen, who's staring straight at me, a proud smirk across his face. I narrow my eyes at him and pick up my wine glass. In response, the asshole *fucking winks.*

Just a few seconds down the aisle, and you don't even have to look at him, Kate. I mentally calculate how long I can realistically hold my breath, that way I don't have to smell him, either.

"We should probably practice now since the flower arch and aisle are all set up. You know, like they do with rehearsals," Jensen suggests.

I would rather eat myself.

"I don't think that's necessary. How hard can it be?" I retort.

His lips tip up, clearly expecting that response. "It's more for pacing and timing, making sure we're in sync."

Jon turns to Jensen a couple of seats down from him. "For a guy who doesn't believe in marriage, you sure know a few things."

He does. I look back at the asshole, and it's clear a hint of redness stains his high cheekbones. He picks up his water glass and shrugs. "With the size of that folder, I'm surprised you don't. Hollie gets married in August, and she's been talking about rehearsals for ages."

Jon sits up straight. "Yeah, well, you've got a point, buddy." He drums his fingers on the table and then flicks through a few pages in the folder as Felicity's jaw hangs open at what she's reading. "The schedule is tight, but we'll make it fit."

Luna low chuckles in response.

"What?" Jon quirks a brow.

She giggles, but it's clearly to herself. "Romance girlie. Inside joke, don't worry."

Shaking his head, he goes back to his schedule. "Tomorrow morning at ten a.m. We'll all meet down in the garden after breakfast and go through the process."

Can't fucking wait.

CHAPTER EIGHT

JENSEN

The way her hand feels wrapped around my arm.

Through my T-shirt, her soft palm radiates heat into my body as we walk the few paces down the short aisle.

She hasn't looked at me once this morning, not even at breakfast, and by the way she loosely links her arm with mine, I can tell she'd rather be anywhere but here.

I expected nightmares of that fateful day in the chapel to come roaring back the moment I stepped under the flower archway. But Lauren hasn't entered my head once. All I can think about is the stunning blonde right next to me.

"See, it's not so bad," I quip as we follow behind Zach and Luna.

"Your chance to walk with a princess," she replies, deadpan.

I snicker. That nickname really got to her. I'm like a teenage boy constantly looking to get a rise out of her.

And I like it. I can't help myself. Anything to get her attention, even if it's for her icy heart to hate on me just a little bit more.

"Does that make me your prince?"

She scoffs. "It begins with a p, but *prince* is definitely not the word I'd use to describe you."

We reach the end of the walk, and she whips away from me at record speed.

"Perfect?" I muse. Her lips shake. "Is that a smile I see?"

"Prick. That would be more apt."

I bark out a laugh. "Such a filthy mouth for royalty."

The way her cheeks flush makes my cock twitch. That's it, Katherine, flirt back; you know you want to.

"And wouldn't you love to find out?" she pats me on the shoulder mockingly. "But unfortunately for you, that ship has sailed, long, loooong ago."

I fight to hide my disappointment. I don't know exactly what I want from this girl, but I do know it involves her being naked.

I've never wanted that more with any other woman in my life.

But with each second that passes, the realization gets stronger; just fucking her might not be enough.

"YOU GONNA EAT THAT?" Zach points to the untouched wing on my plate.

I hold it out to him as we sit on the swinging chair at the end of the long, manicured English garden. The rest of the group is a good fifty yards away, sitting around patio furniture, drinking wine and laughing.

He takes it and immediately starts chowing down.

"This is romantic," I say, "You, me, the birds tweeting, you piling food into your face."

Zach stops mid-bite and looks over at me, shrugging his shoulders. "What? I worked up an appetite, that's all."

"I don't want to know."

"Trying for a baby is hard work, man." He throws me a wink.

"I've had so much sex these past forty-eight hours, but when she's at that time of the month, you gotta take advantage."

"Nothing yet?"

He shrugs casually. "Nah. It'll happen, and meanwhile," he waggles his eyebrows at me, "I get to have a lot of fun. I've discovered positions I—"

"Yeah, great," I say, cutting him off. "Jon is the oversharer. Don't you start."

Loud laughter filters down the garden, and I watch as Kate throws her head back, laughing. She's got her back to me as her long blonde hair cascades down the back of her chair.

As if she can sense my eyes on her, she turns over her shoulder and pins me with her blue eyes.

I hold her gaze, refusing to be the one to look away first.

She narrows hers at me in challenge, so I throw her a wink and take another sip of my beer.

Finally, she breaks first, turning back to the group and then leaning across to pick up the bottle of wine they've been sharing and refills her glass. She's had way too much already, and she'll be feeling it for the ceremony tomorrow.

I wonder what she'd do if I marched down there, snatched the bottle from her hands, and told her she's had enough?

Probably slap me.

Shit, why do I like the thought of that?

"Well, this is an engaging conversation and all, but I'm gonna go take care of my—hopefully pregnant—fiancée." Zach stands from the swing chair, the loss of his weight sending it right back. He turns to look at me and smirks, "You look cute. Like a scene from *Mary Poppins* or some shit."

I shake my head. I'm always the butt of their jokes. "Go fuck your woman."

"See you tomorrow bright and early."

"Sure."

Zach turns to walk away. "Hey."

"Yeah?" He turns back.

I jut my chin at the group. "Ask Kate to come over, will ya?"

He knits his brows together. "What, like being summoned to the principal?"

Fucking hell, don't put ideas in my head.

"I'm just trying to build some bridges for tomorrow."

He nods his head in understanding, but he doesn't look confident about my chances. "Alright, see you tomorrow."

Taking another sip of my beer, I swing on the floral chair. This shit's relaxing, and I wonder if I could fit one on my balcony.

I watch as Zach approaches Kate, tapping her on the shoulder. She turns to me, a scornful look on her face. After a few more words to Zach, she grabs her wine glass and stands from her chair.

Cracking my neck side to side, I watch as she casually strolls into the garden, one foot on each stepping stone. Her long, black jersey dress scoops down at the front. It accentuates her taller frame, even in flat sandals. My dick stirs.

I've genuinely never seen a more beautiful sight.

Stopping a couple of yards in front of me, she props one hand on her hip and waits for me to speak.

I drop my other leg to the ground and spread my thighs apart, leaning back fully in the chair. "Come sit. It's relaxing. You look like you could use some unwind time."

She remains silent but lifts a brow.

"Sit." I point to the empty space beside me, my beer bottle still in my hand.

"Excuse me?"

I lean forward, my elbows on my knees. My eyes never leave hers. "I said, sit."

Her mouth hangs open as she runs her tongue lightly along her bottom lip. Looking to the side, her wine glass still in hand, she focuses her attention back on me. "I don't fraternize with the enemy."

"Neither do I, Princess. But for you, I'll make an exception." I tap my hand on the cushioned seat next to me. "Come."

Hesitantly, she takes a seat. She tries to look relaxed, but I notice the way her skin pebbles along her bare arms. "Feeling bossy tonight?" she drawls, trying to sound unaffected when I know she's anything but.

I reach over and take the wine glass from her hand. Her peach lip gloss stains the rim of the glass, and on instinct, I bring it to my lips, placing my mouth exactly over where hers just was. Downing the rest of the drink in one gulp, I set the glass down on the ground next to me and turn to look at her. "Pinot. Nice."

"What?!" she screeches.

I chuckle and rest my arm along the back of the seat behind her. "You're way past tipsy. I'm doing your head a favor."

She hesitates for a second as her blue eyes, slightly glazed with the effects of the alcohol, fall to my mouth. "You have gloss on your lips."

Leaning forward, I smirk but never break our eye contact as I swipe my tongue along my bottom lip. Her gloss tastes how it looks: sweet, fruity, and just like her.

For the briefest of moments, she pins her lips between her teeth but releases them quickly and looks to the ground. "Zach said you wanted to talk about something, and I'm really tired, so can we make this quick?"

Jesus, she's hard work.

"Sure, Princess."

Her head whips up. "Don't call me that."

"Why not?"

"Because you don't get to call me nicknames."

I lower my arm from the back of the seat until my hand rests just behind her ass. I'm not touching her, but I see the way she responds to my proximity. "I'd still let you call me JJ despite being a bitch half the time."

She scoffs. "I have no idea who JJ is. He died eighteen months ago."

"Well, that's just not true, is it? I can see evidence of him on your cheeks."

She flushes further, and I can't help the smug laugh that leaves me.

"I hate you. You know that, right?"

I pick my beer up and take another sip. "No, you don't."

"Don't tell me how I can and can't feel!" Her frustration, combined with the booze, has her voice raising several octaves higher, and I notice as Jon's head whips around from where he is making out with Felicity at the bottom of the garden like a pair of teenagers.

I set my bottle back down and run a hand through my hair. She's still sitting forward on the chair, her arms crossed protectively over her chest. "Here's the thing, Princess. If I don't take charge of this *situation* between us and leave it all to you, then I fear we'll never actually fuck. And I can't have that." I don't know if it's the beers and wine I've had tonight, but I take a huge gamble and shift my hand to her left hip, teasing her skin through the thick, black fabric of her dress.

Her lips part at the contact, but she fights to keep her arms folded across her chest. "Go find a redhead," she spits.

My grip tightens slightly. "You've got no idea what you're talking about."

"Mmm-hmm, I think I do."

"Tell me, is this incessant need to always be right with everyone or just when it comes to me?"

She pins me with a glare. "You."

I can't wipe the shit-eating grin off my face. "Good answer."

A long stretch of silence passes between us before I speak again. "You haven't asked me to move my hand."

"I hadn't noticed it was there."

I laugh and catch the slight lift of her lips, too.

"You were never a one-night stand to me, Katherine."

Her brows shoot to her hairline. "I hate that name even more."

"I don't."

She shakes her head and looks up into the now fully darkened sky, clearly not wanting to make eye contact. "You had your chance, and you blew it. Then you set it alight when you hooked up with that brunette three weeks ago."

"Here's my dilemma. Whatever I tell you happened, you won't believe. You'll choose your fictional version of events. Because you're a spoiled brat like that."

I probably shouldn't have added the last bit. Shit.

She sucks on her teeth and looks at me, anger blazing in her eyes.

Fuck me, she's hot like this.

"Then why in the world would you want to sleep with a spoiled brat?"

With my hand still on her hip, I pull her toward me. It's only a couple of inches, but our thighs are almost touching. Leaning down to whisper in the shell of her ear, I decide to give it to her straight. I'm done playing games. "Because you aren't a brat. Because you aren't always right, and you know you aren't. Because you know, deep down, I didn't sleep with the redhead that night, and I didn't hook up with the brunette either. Why? Because you invade my thoughts and drive me to the point of insanity. I have to have you, Princess. Trouble is, once I do, I'm not sure I'll be able to stop. There's not a chance in hell you'd be a one-night stand—I've been fucking you in my dreams since the day you pulled on my jersey and sat yourself across my lap."

CHAPTER NINE

KATE

I stumble into my bedroom and head straight for the en suite.

I need to wash my face or splash myself with cold water or something.

Jesus fucking *Christ,* what was that down there?

I squeeze my thighs together as I riffle through my cosmetic bag and find my makeup remover and a cloth.

Furiously, I scrub at my face. I feel woozy and lightheaded, but I can't tell if it's in response to the alcohol or the way Jensen Jones just looked at me.

I've been fucking you in my dreams since the day you pulled on my jersey and sat yourself across my lap.

My thighs squeeze harder of their own volition, and heat pools in response.

He's a fuckboy, and he's trying to get under your skin.

I set the cloth to the side and grab my moisturizer, knocking my toothbrush over in the process, and it rattles around the sink. Smearing some onto my face in a haphazard fashion, I grab my birth control and pop a pill. Drunk or not, I never forget.

I grab my toothbrush from the sink and squirt an unnecessary amount of toothpaste across it. "Fucking dickhead," I mumble to myself.

I'm aware I'm swaying as I reach my bed and pull back the covers.

Tomorrow is going to be top-notch. Avoiding Jensen and trying not to puke.

It's still dark outside when I wake and sit bolt upright in bed. Slamming my hand over my mouth, a wave of nausea hits me in the gut.

I'm going to puke.

Making it to the toilet just in time, I lift the lid and spill my guts.

Note to self: cocktails, shots, and wine will make you sick.

Hovering at the side of the toilet, I take a few deep breaths when the door to the bathroom opens.

I have nothing on apart from my black thong. In my drunken haze, I forgot I wasn't home and passed up nightwear. Plus, I never unpack my suitcase when I go away, and this trip is no different.

At the last minute, I slam my arm across my breasts, which does fuck all since I'm a DD cup, and bring my knees up in front of me. "Who is it?"

Please, *please* be Luna or Felicity.

The door opens further, and a bare foot appears. It's too big and male for it to be them.

"I'm naked...a-and sick!" I shout.

He steps into the room wearing only dark gray athletic shorts, number eighty-eight stamped above his right knee in white.

Holy hell, he's beautiful.

I look terrible. My messy bun is out of control.

"Get out!"

He stands there wearing a smug smirk, looking me straight in the eyes, not once gazing down my body.

"I'm naked!"

"I can see that, Princess."

"Stop calling me Princess!" I exclaim and then wince at the pain throbbing through my head.

Reaching over, he pulls the overhead chain to the old-fashioned toilet and shuts the lid before turning to walk out of the bathroom.

"Where are you going?" I ask, my boobs still covered by my arm.

Returning a few moments later, he hands me a glass of water and then a T-shirt. I set the water down to free up my only hand and snatch the shirt.

Wait, this isn't mine.

Holding it by the collar, I twist it around in my hand. It's crumpled, but when I see "J," I throw it back at him.

"I'd rather show you my tits than wear your name again."

"All in good time." He chuckles and walks out of the doorway. "I've left some Tylenol on the nightstand. I suggest you take them."

The door to my bedroom shuts with a soft click, and I drop my arm and slowly rise to my feet.

I look like hell as I brush my teeth for the second time tonight and then pad into the bedroom and crawl into bed, swallowing the two pills and cursing the shirt on the floor.

LIGHT STREAMS in through the pink curtains, and I stir, my head pounding but no doubt less, thanks to the Tylenol.

At least he has one kind bone in his body.

Voices filter from downstairs when I reach over and check my phone.

Shit, shit, SHIT. It's past ten fucking a.m.!

But wait, where the fuck is my suitcase? It was on the trunk at the foot of my bed last night...

He didn't.

Racing over to the dresser I know I didn't fill, I pull each drawer open to find nothing in there. Same with the closet.

The only item of clothing left in this room, other than the thong I'm wearing, is Jensen's training shirt.

"That absolute *bastard!*" I curse under my breath.

But in truth, there's a part of me that wants to laugh. And that pisses me off even more.

I'd rather show you my tits than wear your name again.

That's right, Jensen. I really fucking would.

Yanking the bedroom door open, I take a huge risk of being spotted and march a few paces to his bedroom. Not bothering to knock, I burst through the door, my breasts on full display as he stands in the middle of the room wrapped in a fluffy white towel. He looks bewildered, rubbing the hair on the back of his head.

"Excuse me, please," I say as his eyes bug out of his head, and I look down at myself. "What's up, babe? Never seen a pair of tits before?"

I snatch up my suitcase and throw his shirt as he catches it against his chest and then brings it to his nose. "You didn't wear it."

"No. I'd rather show you my tits, remember."

He walks a couple of paces toward me and hooks his fingers underneath his towel, letting it fall to the floor at our feet.

Our chests are only a few inches apart when, finally, his eyes drop to my body. He pins his lip between his teeth and shakes his head with a look of awe.

My entire body ignites, but I fully burst into flames when I, too, drop my gaze.

He's hard as a rock, and the girth and length of this man is mind-blowing.

Holy. HELL. He would break me in two.

Reaching out, he takes the suitcase from my hand and drops it on the floor before twining our fingers together. With his other, he hooks a finger under my chin to bring my eyes back to his.

The next thing I feel is my hand resting on the top of his dick, and on instinct, I wrap my fingers around his shaft.

He closes his eyes as a rumble leaves his chest.

"I'm still pissed that you left me for other women," I say, squeezing him tight in my grasp.

His head falls forward between his shoulders. "Good." He looks at me once more, his brown eyes burning, his pupils blown. "You'll ride my dick harder when I ultimately get you in my bed tonight."

I pump him again and he groans. "I won't be wasting any of my energy on you. You can do all of the work making it up to me."

He still hasn't touched me, but my body cries out for him to take his hand and swipe his fingers through my throbbing pussy.

Wrapping an arm around my waist, he presses me into him, my hand around his dick pinned between us. At first, I think he's going to kiss me, but he doesn't. He just wears that shit-eating trademark grin. "We need to start you off steady. If you let me do what I want tonight, then I'll be carrying you out of this place in the morning."

"You know nothing about me and my limitations."

He smirks. "Okay, since your hand is wrapped around my cock, and I'm desperate to bite down on those nipple piercings you have, let's say this. One night."

I glare at him, but he holds up his other hand. "Wait. Give me one night to show you what it's like to be with me. To show you what you keep walking away from. I guarantee you'll want more, and when you do, I'll be waiting."

Pre-cum leaks out the tip of his cock, and I swipe my thumb across the top. He winces with torturous pleasure.

"Tom was a nice guy, but unfortunately, that translated to the bedroom as well. And that's not my scene. I don't do emotional sex." I put my thumb to my lips and taste him. His eyes hood at the sight. "Are you good with that?"

He brings his lips to my ear, twisting a lock of my hair around his forefinger. "No." I go to pull away, but he pulls hard on a lock, keeping me in place. "I'm fucking great with it, Princess."

Reaching down, he removes my hand from his dick and then rips the side of my thong apart with both hands, and it falls to the floor in pieces.

"You ruined my favorite thong. Asshole."

"No underwear today, and no touching yourself when you get back to your room. I'll know if you have."

"Jensen, I'll leak through my dress. I—"

"Better get a handle on yourself. If you manage all the above, then I'll put my hands on you tonight."

"Wha—"

"I don't want to make you beg for me, Katherine. Just be a good girl, and I'll give you what Tom could only watch on his phone."

CHAPTER TEN

JENSEN

The number of times I've wanted to trace my hand over her dress and check if she's wearing underwear. It's only been a couple of hours since I had her naked in my bedroom.

It's unhealthy.

Zach, James, Adam, Jack, and I stand next to Jon as we watch Felicity take the few steps up the short aisle, Khalid's "Better" their chosen soundtrack.

Jon wobbles as his fiancée, dressed in a sleek and silky ivory gown, her hair down and around her shoulders, comes to stand by his side.

But I can't keep my eyes off the blonde woman in emerald as she takes Felicity's small white peony bouquet and holds it with hers. Her hair is partly pinned, the rest cascading around her shoulders, stopping in the center of her back.

Today there's a look of innocence about her that grounds me as I stand in a similar place to where I was once left humiliated and rejected. For the first time, I catch myself thinking about what it would be like to take it slow with Kate Monroe, to savor the way she would melt and yield beneath my touch. I don't do tender, and I don't open my heart up to anyone, ever. But the way I want to share truths about myself with her, not even my own sister knows...that's some scary shit.

Once again, she's barely made eye contact with me, yet that still hasn't stopped me staring every chance I get.

Jon and Felicity opted to keep the ceremony short and simple with a relaxed afterparty, and as the bride and groom take their first kiss as newlyweds and make for the aisle, my body hums with anticipation for the next twenty seconds I'll get to spend with Kate by my side.

Unlike yesterday, she doesn't roll her eyes when I hold out my arm for her to take. Instead, her palm grips my bicep firmly.

Seizing what might be one of my only opportunities, I lean toward her. "Did anyone ever tell you that it's not cool to upstage the bride? Especially when you're the maid of honor."

She side-eyes me cautiously. "I'm wearing the same as Luna and the other bridesmaids."

"Are you?" I reply. "I hadn't noticed anyone else."

Coming to a stop at the end of the aisle, we wait as Jon and Felicity pose for a couple of pictures.

Inconspicuously, I run my hand down her side and over her hip, and she shivers in response. "No underwear. Good girl," I croon before I break away and I head over to shake Jon's hand.

KATE

"Mrs. Felicity Morgan. It suits you perfectly."

My best friend chuckles. "Never did I think I'd get married again. Just goes to show, you find the right man, and anything is possible."

"Totally true," Luna agrees, glancing over at Zach, who's sitting with Jon and Jensen. We all changed out of our formal wear after the ceremony and into more relaxed evening clothes. Jensen looks delicious in a white shirt, sleeves rolled up to his elbows, and pale gray chinos. His pants stop just above his ankle, and he wears tan loafers.

Good Lord, he's hot.

My body vibrates with anticipation for tonight. Am I really going to go through with this and sleep with him?

Hate sex. That's what this is.

"Kate?"

"Huh?"

"More wine?" Felicity hovers the bottle over my glass, but I place my palm over the top. "I think I might switch to water."

Luna fakes falling off her chair in shock.

"Ha-ha," I mock. "Hilarious. But I'm still feeling hungover from last night, and I'm jetlagged to hell. I've already had three glasses, and it's only six p.m."

"Never stopped you before." A deep voice filters from behind, and then Jensen comes to sit next to me in the empty seat. A slight breeze casts across the garden and his cologne hits me square in the face, sending tingles throughout my body.

I reset myself and shrug my shoulders. "I refuse to spend tonight with my head in a toilet."

He drops his head so Felicity and Luna, who are busy talking, can't hear. "No, you're right. I'm gonna need your mouth elsewhere."

Heat pools between my thighs, and he chuckles in delight.

Bastard.

"Still bare for me?"

"No," I say, turning to him. "I put underwear on when I got changed."

A hand lands on the inside of my thigh underneath the table, and I shudder at the way his fingertips dance up the inside, traveling toward my apex. I turn to look at him just as his fingers trace over my lace thong. "I don't like being told what to do."

He quirks a brow at me. "Oh, Princess, I can't wait to have you on your knees for me."

Snatching his hand away, he pushes back his chair and stands, disappearing into the house.

Clearing my throat, I cross my legs and squeeze my thighs, fighting back my needy desperation.

"When do you head out for the airport?" I turn to Felicity.

She checks her watch. "In a couple of hours." Throwing her head back, she groans in pleasure. "Two weeks on a Caribbean beach, come to Mama."

I snort. "Don't worry, I'll hold the fort down at work."

"Where's Darcy?" Luna looks around, searching for Felicity's daughter.

She rolls her eyes. "On the phone with Liam asking where he is. He was supposed to be here an hour ago."

"Oh," I say, taking a sip of water. "What's the issue there?"

Puffing out a breath, she runs her finger around the rim of her glass. "They're just fighting more. Which doesn't bode well given they're both attending the same college this year."

I wince. "It's really young to be so serious."

She nods. "Yeah, but they've always been kindreds."

"He's acting like a dick," Jack pipes up from where he's sitting across the table. Felicity eyes him, but he sits back in his chair and crosses his arms. "He is! Every time I see my sister, she's crying over him."

"Well," I announce. "That's the trouble with men. They're all dickheads, some are just more self-aware and rein it in better."

Luna snorts. "Tell me that again when you find the one."

"Not happening. I'm young, free, single, and actually, I'm having another glass of wine."

Luna snorts another laugh, but loudly this time, and she slams her hand over her mouth. "God, I'm so embarrassing!"

"Angel, I've got Jessie on the line." Jon appears, handing Felicity his phone, and she stands from the table to take the call.

"Why couldn't he come?" Luna asks. "He said something about family commitments?"

I pinch my lips together. I know very little about Jessie

Callaghan, but from what's circulated in the media, he doesn't have a great family. "I think he had to stay and look after his mom or something."

"Oh," Luna replies, clearly wanting to ask more. "That's a shame. He seems nice."

I nod. I know Jensen is close to him, but that doesn't surprise me. They're both closed books, sharing little about themselves. In the time we've all been hanging out, Jessie has never said much about his personal life or past.

"This will be you next," I say, looking around the garden set up for a wedding.

Luna smiles. "I hope so. Although, it's never really been the day that interests me, more the night," she giggles.

I waggle my brows. "Is that so, Luna Johnson?"

Jack clears his throat and stands. "Gross."

Luna smirks at me. "Oh yes. Allllll the hot sex."

I open my mouth to tell her I'm hoping for some of that tonight, but I check myself right at the last second. Whatever Jensen and I have going on needs to be kept under the vest. It's just sex.

Hot sex.

DICKHEAD

Come upstairs.

I LOOK DOWN at the text as I hold my phone with shaky hands. It's past eleven, and Jon and Felicity left for their honeymoon hours ago. Most day guests have left, leaving only a few behind, and they're pretty much all couples.

Alone, I sit rocking on the swinging chair at the back of the garden and consider my options.

ME

Come get me if you want me.

Stop playing games, Katherine. You want to fuck me, and I'm desperate to fuck you. For once in your life, just do what I ask.

I down the rest of my wine and make my way out of the garden. He can have this round. I feel rude about ignoring everyone, but equally, I don't want to attract attention to myself and where I'm about to go.

At the bottom of the wooden staircase, I inhale a deep breath and take each step, holding my long summer dress up so I don't trip.

When I push open his bedroom door, my breath catches in my throat. Standing in the middle of the bedroom, he wears the same outfit and hot as fuck white shirt, his hands in the pockets of his pants. Like he's waiting for me, his deep brown eyes are even darker with feral need, and his sleek dark hair falls over his forehead and eyes.

Excitement races through me.

I'm going to get absolutely railed, and I'm fucking here for it.

We stand about three feet apart; his chest is heaving, and I can feel my pulse beating in my ears.

"Your move, Jones," I say, throwing my purse and phone down on the cushioned seat in the corner.

He doesn't move for several moments but then cocks his head toward the bed. "Take off that dress so I can see you in the thong you were bratty enough to wear. Then get on the bed and on your knees."

For the first time in my life, I don't want to argue with him. Unhooking the thin straps from over my shoulders, the dress falls to the floor with ease.

His eyes widen at the sight of me standing before him in only my underwear.

Unclipping the clasp, I take off my bra and then hook my

thumb under the waistband of my thong, and all the while, he watches, his bottom lip caught between his teeth. "You should know that I only do things on my terms, Jensen."

Confidently, I climb onto the bed, but I don't kneel for him. Instead, I climb under the covers. His cologne envelops me, sending heat straight to my core.

"Take your clothes off." I wave a hand in front of me.

With a shit-eating grin, he slowly unbuttons his shirt and pulls down his sleeves, removing it fully to reveal his gorgeous torso and eight pack. My mouth waters at the sight. Next is his pants as he unzips them, his eyes pinning me in place. They pool at his feet, and my gaze drops to his cock, which fights to break free from the black boxer briefs that hug his thick goalie thighs. Everything he wears fits him perfectly.

"Are your boxers tailored?"

He takes off his gold watch and sets it on the side, then unclasps the gold chain he wears every time I see him. "Everything about me is tailored, Princess." He pushes his briefs to the floor and then takes his cock in his hand and pumps it as he walks to the edge of the bed. "Crawl to me."

"Fuck off."

He laughs, but I do want to taste him, so I concede.

Finally, he has me where he wants me as I sit on the edge of the bed and wait for him to give me his dick.

He pulls on my hair, gathering it up and away from my face. "You have no idea how many times I've wanted to wrap this hair around my fist. Now, swallow me."

I take his long, hard cock into my mouth, and he doesn't hold back as he pushes himself to the back of my throat and groans loudly. "Suck my dick. That's right. Suck it."

He tastes insanely good as pre-cum spills from him and onto my tongue. I pull off him with a pop. "You'll come and—"

Throwing his head back, he laughs. "You think if I come, I'm done?" He tips my chin up with his forefinger, and I look him in the eyes. "You don't know me at all, do you?"

"The same could be said about you."

"I see you, Kate. More than you want me to, and one day, I'll see it all."

In a flash, he drops his hand and then lifts me from the bed. His fingertips dig into my ass, and I wrap my legs around his waist as we come face to face. I'm not petite, but he holds me like I weigh nothing.

Uncertainty washes over me as his fierce eyes soften and, surprising me further, he holds me with one arm and caresses my right cheek with his free hand. "I promised myself I wouldn't kiss you. But promises are made to be broken."

I did, too. But that doesn't stop me from opening for him when he swipes his tongue across my lower lip. He pushes his hand through my hair, and I whimper as he kisses me until my lips feel sore. The scruff of his jaw is rough and sharp against my chin, but it's a delicious sensation.

Setting me back down on the bed, he parts my legs and holds them open with his hands. "You didn't play with yourself. At least you got that right."

"How can you tell?"

"Because, Princess, this pussy is begging to be touched, and only my fingers will do."

He swipes a finger through me, and I fall back onto my elbows. "More."

"No."

I want to scream in frustration.

"I'll fuck you first, play with you later."

CHAPTER ELEVEN

JENSEN

Crawling over her body, I can tell she's feeling less sure of herself than she lets on.

She's nervous to be with me, even though her stern façade tries to say differently.

Reaching down between us, I pull one of her legs around my waist. "You look nervous."

She balks, but it's fake. "I'm not. Just fuck me."

My thumb finds her clit as I begin kissing my way down her throat. "How hard, Princess?"

"Hard. And stop calling me Princess." She gasps.

Scissoring into her with two fingers, her mouth falls open in surprise.

"You've got a tight pussy."

"Yes, I...yes, that's so fucking good."

"Finally, I've got you right where I want you." My tongue falls to her breasts, and I run hot circles over her pierced nipples. I've been with a lot of women, more than I can count, but never anyone pierced.

She squirms beneath me. "I want your dick."

In an instant, I'm on my haunches as I lift her onto her hands and knees. Burying my face between her cheeks, I spread her wide and eat her pussy like it's my last meal. It might as well be; nothing will ever taste this fucking good.

She cries out.

"The whole wedding party is going to know we're fucking. Is that what you want, Princess? Do you want them to know I've got my tongue buried deep in your cunt?"

She doesn't answer. But I hand her this reprieve.

Feral need washes over me, the sight of her on her knees, her glistening pussy ready for me to take. "Birth control?" I bite out.

"Yes."

On my knees behind her, I sink all the way inside Katherine fucking Monroe. "Fuuuck," I groan as I move further inside until I'm fully seated. "You know what else is tailored to me? This cunt."

I smack her ass once. "That's for making it so hard to finally fuck you."

Twice. "That's for your bratty mouth."

She cries out with pleasure.

Three times, my handprint raised on her left cheek. "And that's for not going bare when I said how I wanted you."

My hips piston into her as I run my fingertips over the raised red skin on her ass. "I don't think you'll be able to sit on the plane tomorrow, but let's test that out now."

Sitting back on my heels, I pull her down with me. With her riding my cock, I reach up and wrap my hand around her throat. I can't see her face, but by the way she whimpers with need, I know she likes it. "My Princess does like it rough, huh?"

"Make me come."

"Beg for it."

Rising up, she slams back down on my rock-hard dick. "I don't beg. I take what I want."

Teasing the bar through her nipple between my thumb and forefinger, I lean forward and whisper in her ear. "If I give you what you want, you have to promise me that tonight won't be the only night I'm inside you."

Finishing with a kiss to the shell of her ear, her head falls forward as I thrust up and into her. My hand is still wrapped around her throat, her hair twisted around my other. "I'm going to unload any second."

"I'm coming! Oh fuck, Jensen, I'm coming."

I'm done. Fucking gone. Coming inside her with a roar. "All. Fucking. Mine."

KATE

Best. Night's. Sleep. Ever.

I stretch out but only get so far before I'm met with resistance.

Male resistance.

No. Way.

Yes. Way.

"Jensen!" I whisper-shout.

Peeling his arm that's draped across my breasts, he groans into his pillow.

"Get your big body off me. I slept in your room overnight!"

I don't know why I'm acting surprised since we didn't stop going at it until the early hours of this morning. And that was because I finally broke and told him I was too sensitive to continue. Honestly, I think he could've gone through to sunrise.

This fucking kills me to say, but he's a machine. A sex god, and he knows it.

"I literally couldn't care less," he mumbles.

"Yeah? Well, I do."

From over my shoulder, he turns his sleepy face to look at me and smiles. "Turn around and face me."

"No."

The arm he's refused to move grips my hip and slowly rolls me onto my back. I yield and look at him. "What?"

"Are you ashamed of me?"

I balk. "No. I—"

"She was my sister's best friend; she was drunk, and she needed someone to make sure she got home safely."

I pull back and look at him. "You're not bullshitting me, are you?"

He shakes his head. "No, Princess. I'm not."

"And the brunette on your lap?"

He sighs. "I didn't do anything with her, either."

"I find that hard to believe."

Rolling onto his back, he runs a palm across his face. "I wanted to make you jealous."

"Prick."

He barks out a laugh. "You're joking, right? You came to the Stanley Cup finals wearing my best friend's jersey and a smug look on your face and didn't expect me to react?"

"I can wear whoever's jersey I want!"

Rolling his tongue to the roof of his mouth, the fierce look his eyes wore last night returns. He stares up at the ceiling and cracks his neck to the side. "No. You can't."

I sit up, and the sheets fall from my naked body. Noticing the way his eyes float across my skin, I inwardly curse myself for the way it makes me feel. Needy for him to put his huge hands on me again. "Um, I think you'll find I can."

Sitting up, too, his hand shoots up and grips the tip of my chin between his thumb and forefinger. Turning my head to his, he runs his tongue along his bottom lip. "So you're telling me when you wore my jersey that day, you didn't want my cock buried inside you like it was last night? You didn't want to hand yourself over for me to play with? And your pussy wasn't throbbing with anticipation of how I would react when I saw my name stamped across your back?"

"No."

"You're a fucking liar. And stubborn as hell. You want me; you want this. I'm the first person in your life who's got the full measure of you, and you can't deal with it. So what do you do? You get pissy with me."

Who the *fuck* does he think he is?!

Anger climbs up my spine as I desperately try to search for a response. A comeback to prove him wrong. He doesn't know me, and he doesn't get to pass out judgments either.

This whole thing was the biggest mistake of my life.

I shoot out of bed and grab my dress from the floor. Snatching up my phone and purse, I turn to look at him, still naked. He wears an appreciative grin at the sight. "I'll tell you what I did lie about."

"What's that, Princess?"

"One-night stands. Apparently, I do have them." I wrap my dress around me and make for the door. "Starting from last night."

"Kate!"

"Fuck off."

Slamming his door, I storm down the hall into my bedroom and throw on some clothes. *Now* I know why I don't unpack my suitcase. Brushing my teeth, I throw the final toiletries into my bag and zip it shut when the toothbrush joins.

"Kate."

"No."

"Where are you going?"

"Home." I whip around to face him. His hands grip the door frame above his head, and I refuse to look at his abs or the deep protruding v leading from the athletic shorts he's wearing. "Move out of my way." My voice cracks on the final word.

"Just slow down."

Panic rises in me. "Last night was a mistake."

For the first time ever, I watch as Jensen's face twists with hurt. "No. It wasn't."

"It was. We agreed to be civil, and that was it."

His grin returns. "Oh, last night was far more than civil."

Dragging my hands down my face, I regret everything we did. "Please just let me leave."

"Kate?" Luna comes to stand next to Jensen in the doorway. "Is everything okay?" She looks between us both, concern etched across her pixie features.

"Yeah, it's fine, babe." I pick up my phone and scroll to the Uber app, booking a car to come pick me up ASAP. "I just overslept and realized my flight leaves earlier than I thought."

"Oh." She side-eyes Jensen, who's dressed in very little. "Okay. I thought you had the same flight as us?"

Not anymore, I don't.

"No. I changed it last minute so I can get back early to work on this case. It, um, it needs my full attention."

Picking up my suitcase, I point to the doorway they're both blocking. I just want to go home and work on forgetting this ever happened. Also, scour the internet for one of those red-light flashy thingies that wipe your memory, like in *Men In Black*. "I have to go."

Luna steps to one side, but Jensen stays exactly where he is. He thinks *I'm* stubborn. "I can get you a seat on my flight in first class."

I scoff but then straighten up, remembering we have an audience. "That will be too late, and besides..." I pull up the handle on my case for effect. "I already have a seat in first."

With Luna halfway down the stairs and out of sight, I go to push past him, but he shoots his arm out across my body and braces it on the opposite frame. "Stay."

"We all leave today anyway."

"Don't leave like this. Not after what we shared last night."

"It was just a hate fuck, and it's a shame you had to go and ruin it this morning. You don't own me."

His jaw ticks, but he drops his hand from the frame. "You're right. I don't." I go to leave, but he grabs me by the arm. "But one day, I'll make you mine."

CHAPTER TWELVE

KATE

"Hey, Margo. Any messages for me?"

"Only that your eleven o'clock has pushed back to twelve, but your calendar was clear, so I went ahead and confirmed. How were your morning meetings?"

"Yeah, okay," I say with a yawn, standing at the reception desk of Preston & Preston, the law firm I've worked at for the past six years.

"You did, um...get one more, but I don't think it's work-related."

I stop scrolling through the emails on my phone. "Oh yeah?"

"From Tom Bennett. He said he'd tried to reach you over the weekend but was sent to voicemail. He was concerned and asked that you call him." Margo wears an unsure smile as she delivers the message from my ex-boyfriend.

"Thank you for letting me know. I can take it all from here." Signing the half dozen letters set out to go in the mail for various clients, I turn on my heel and move toward my desk. Felicity's remains empty and has been for the past ten days. I've found myself counting down the time until she returns from her honeymoon. The pictures she's sent from Barbados look insane, but I can't wait to have my best friend back.

Setting my bag and jacket down, I begin replying to various emails that have come in over the weekend.

I'm halfway through an email when my phone vibrates, and a text appears at the top of the screen.

TOM

I miss you. Talk to me, and we can take things at your own pace.

It's been like this for the past ten days since I got back from Oxford. I've sent him a few short replies, but really, how many ways can you kindly tell someone it's over?

I'm sure he'd feel differently if he knew I'd slept with someone else.

And there's the issue—Tom keeps blowing up my phone, but the guy I can't get off my mind has sent two measly texts.

Two.

DICKHEAD

Landed ten minutes late. I hope you didn't miss your important work commitments.

ME

You tracked my plane?

Flight BA1749.

That's the extent of it. I slept with him, he pissed me off the next morning, and other than track my flight, he hasn't been in touch.

Argh, why does that bother me?!

This is where I need a morning coffee in the kitchenette with Felicity. Except I can't tell her about what happened. Not because I'm ashamed, but because she'd ask questions about us that I'm not prepared to answer.

I hate that I like him.

I hate that I should be replying to nice guy Tom and not sitting and waiting for Mr. Dickhead himself to show just a little bit of interest in me.

He only tracked my flight so he could message me and call me out for my bullshit work excuse. And he'd be right.

And he knows it.

He also knows what he's doing in bed.

For the hundredth time, I squeeze my thighs together at the memories. The way he sunk inside me from behind and wrapped his hand around my throat. Fuck, he was good. Just like he promised. And just like he predicted, I want more. Correction, my body wants more, but my brain reminds me of all the ways I was stupid for climbing into his bed in the first place.

"Kate."

"Hmmm?"

"Your client is here. The eleven o' clock. Mr. Jones."

"Huh?"

"The one who had to push back an hour due to another meeting he had." Margo points to the meeting room around the corner. "He's ready and waiting."

"Oh. Sure." I stand from my desk and pick up the file. Not that it's any use since there was barely any information included.

I'll just wing it.

Pushing the door open to the room, I glance down at my watch. "Apologies, Mr. Jones. I was held up on another call."

"Don't tell lies, Princess."

Oh, holy hell.

"What are you doing here?"

Jensen smirks at me. Leaning back in his chair, with his bent leg resting across the opposite knee, he takes a sip of water. "Here to take you out to lunch."

My body buzzes with excitement, not that he needs to know that. Propping a hand on my hip, I lie, "I don't have time, I've another client in a half hour."

He stands and shoves his hands into his pockets, rounding

the table slowly. We're only two feet apart when he finally comes to a stop. "Margo said your calendar is free this afternoon."

Damn it, Margo.

"Why do you want lunch with me?"

"To talk. I'm not a fan of texting. I prefer the old-fashioned way."

"Jensen. I'm not sure—"

"Stop fighting it, Princess. I've got a table booked at an Italian restaurant in five minutes."

"I still don't know what you want to talk about. I've got nothing to say to you."

He takes a small step toward me. "Since you're full of bullshit today, why don't you go ahead and lie some more. Lie and say you haven't thought about what I did to you that night, how I made you feel?"

All the time.

"I haven't. It wasn't especially memorable."

He puffs out a disbelieving breath and shakes his head slowly. "Wrong answer, Princess."

"I'm not going to lunch with you. My calendar is clear because I have a ton of work to get through."

Just as I finish my latest lie, a sharp stabbing pain hits me in the lower right-hand side. "Ouch."

"Kate?" Jensen's tone changes dramatically.

"Ow!"

I meet his eyes, which hold the same level of concern. "What's wrong?"

Shaking my head, I drop my hand from the area it was covering. "Nothing."

His hand darts out to replace mine, and my body fizzes with another dose of excitement. "Sure didn't look like nothing."

Taking a deep breath, I center myself and then take a step back, far enough so I'm now out of reach. "I'm fine, but I am really busy."

"I want to fuck you again."

My eyebrows shoot to my hairline in surprise. I thought I was the queen of come out and say it. "I'm sorry?"

He closes the space between us again, and I step back once more. But this time, my back is met with the wall. He places his palm above my head and leans into me, his breath dancing across my collarbone. "No one finishes a meal after only the appetizer. Especially when it was that good. I want more. The entire menu."

Heat pools at my core.

"It wasn't that good."

Throwing his head back, he laughs, and I'm one hundred percent sure the office can hear.

"Shh! What the fuck are you doing?"

"Jesus, Kate. You're so full of bullshit." He sounds incredulous.

"Aww, does it hurt your manhood that a woman finally turned you down?"

"No one's turning anyone down. All I see is a silly little girl playing silly little games."

Placing a palm on his chest, I wear a mocking smile. "And all I see is a deluded man. It's not happening again. End of story." Whipping from under his arm, I take a couple of paces and pull open the door. "I hope the restaurant accepts tables for one."

ALL DAY I've swung back and forth, cursing and congratulating myself for turning Jensen down for lunch. He said he wanted to talk, but it's obvious what he's really after—proving to me that I can't resist him.

Well, Kate Monroe has more willpower than that.

My meal for one pings in the microwave, and I throw a tossed salad onto my plate to accompany the lasagna. Appetizing. But when you work until almost eight in the evening each night, getting home and cooking a gourmet meal is far less appealing.

Especially when it's just for yourself.

I've been avoiding Tom all day, but I can't put it off any longer, so as I take a seat on my couch, my plate balancing on my knee, I tap out a reply.

ME

Hey, I'm fine. I just don't have a lot to say. I hope you're doing okay.

Very vanilla.

A response comes through in seconds.

TOM

I'm sorry if I pushed you too hard. I don't want things to end between us.

I wish I didn't have to hurt him.

I don't want to hurt you, but you need to know I don't want to try again.

I set my phone down and begin flicking through channels.

Are you still coming to Marissa and Brad's engagement party in September?

I pinch my brows together. Why is he asking that?

Yes, why?

I want to give you some space to think everything through, but I'd really like you to be my date.

He's pushing really hard on this. He needs to know the truth.

Tom, I slept with someone else. There's no kind way of telling you that, but I've moved on, and I don't want you to hold out for me. I'm so sorry.

I push my plate off my lap and onto the coffee table in front of me. My appetite has deserted me and been replaced with a nauseating feeling. I might be as direct as they come, but that doesn't mean I don't have empathy. I hate hurting people, but stringing Tom along is arguably even worse.

My phone vibrates again, but this time, the text makes me smile.

LUNA

Lunch on Saturday? I think we need to catch up. It'll be two weeks since I saw my girls, and that is way too long. Felicity, you aren't allowed to go on anymore honeymoons, and Kate, you aren't allowed to disappear into your working cave.

My girls, just when I need them.

FELICITY

The sun is shining so bright on my screen that I can barely make out what I'm typing, but trust me, I do not plan on any more marriages, but maybe extended honeymoons...

ME

Rub it in with the sun. It's pouring here. Yeah, Saturday is good with me.

LUNA

Great. I'll book the table at Luigi's for one p.m. I can't wait to see you!

CHAPTER THIRTEEN

KATE

Work is officially kicking my ass, and I'm moody. No matter how hard I try, the funk I've been in for these past three days won't shift.

"I need your notes on the Taylor file ASAP, Kate."

Facing my computer screen, I roll my eyes. "I'll get them to you as quickly as I can, Derek."

He huffs out a breath and comes to stand next to me, eyeing my screen. "So they aren't ready yet?"

Closing down the window so he can't spy on private client information, I turn to look at him. "No. If they were, then they would be on your desk, so you aren't standing at mine interrupting me."

Borderline rude, I'll admit. But Derek has been hounding me for days over a non-urgent case.

He looks taken aback. "Easy now, Kate. That time of the month?"

I'm incandescent with rage and ready to crop him at the kneecaps when I stop dead in my tracks...

Everything, even annoying Derek, fades into the background. Today is July fourteenth. I took my last pill three days ago.

Where is it?

I shoot up from my desk, my chair spinning back. "Excuse me, Derek." I rush out.

Grabbing my bag and jacket from the back of the chair, I move toward the exit but stop at reception. "Margo, I need to head out for a couple of hours. Is there any chance you can push the Parker meeting to Monday?"

She winces. "Your calendar is stacked on Monday."

It's Thursday, and I already know tomorrow is packed. "I'll offer them a late-night appointment on Monday."

She folds her hands together on her desk and eyes me cautiously. "Kate, I've worked with you for six years, and in that time, I think we've grown close."

My brows knit together. "Go on."

"You're going to make yourself sick, honey. You never stop. You're the first one to arrive, the last one to leave, and now you're asking me to schedule in an appointment, which will likely take at least two hours after six in the evening."

I don't need this. I know she's trying to be kind, but right now, I'm on the verge of a breakdown for very different reasons. "I'm honestly fine. Book them in and shoot me an email to confirm." I turn to leave but stop. "Margo?"

"Yes?"

"Thank you for checking on me." My voice trembles on the last words, but I have no idea if she notices as I race for the elevator.

The descent to the lobby happens in slow motion as I lean against the back railing and mentally calculate the timeline. My period always starts on the twelfth of each month, never a day early or late. Pulling out my phone, I begin scrolling through my period tracking app. Month after month, year after year, and never a delay. Sure, I could forgive a day, but not this long. Why am I even going to the drugstore? I can't be. I take my pill every day without fail. I know I was twelve hours late that morning after Jensen and I—

"Hey, whoa, watch what you're doing!" A man crashes into me from behind as I come to a sudden halt on the bustling sidewalk.

My trembling hands fly to cover my face.

Fuck, fuck, fuck, fuck, FUCK!

I threw my pill up. And then took the next one half a day late. In between that time, Jensen and I had sex, without a condom, more times than I can count. He barely let me sleep.

I am, aren't I?

Standing in the middle of downtown Seattle, traffic and people rush past me, but I'm rooted to the spot—screw drugstore tests. Scrolling through my contacts, I hit call on the number for my OBGYN.

"KATE, TAKE A SEAT." Doctor Radwanska waves a hand to the black leather couch situated along the back wall of her consultation room.

Offering me a sweet smile, she waits for me to explain the reason for my panicked call requesting an urgent appointment.

Taking a deep breath, I cut to the chase. "I need you to run a test. I think I might..." I trail off and bite down on my bottom lip, "...be pregnant."

Her eyes flare in surprise, but she quickly resets her professional exterior. Clearing her throat, she flicks through a couple of screens on her computer and then turns back to me, her comforting smile returning. "Okay, we can definitely do that. Do you have any idea of the timeline?"

"Well, my last period was June twelfth."

She nods and makes a note. "When did you last have unprotected sex?"

"Birth control?"

Jensen's clipped question just before he entered me races through my memory as I squeeze my eyes shut. "It was one night on June thirtieth. I'd been sick the night before, and there's a possibility my birth control didn't get a chance to work. Plus, the following morning, I took my next one twelve hours late. I was right in the middle of my cycle. I'm certain that's the only time I could've conceived."

Doctor Radwanska presses her lips together in a thin line. "So this potential pregnancy isn't planned?"

I shake my head and bite down hard, but on the inside of my cheek this time. "No."

She sets her pen down and reaches across into a drawer. Pulling out a urine collection container in a clear sealable bag, she hands it to me. "Okay, let's get the facts before we go any further. If you're able to provide me a sample, I can run the test for you immediately, and then we can go from there."

The tremble in my hands returns tenfold as I take the bag from her and stand.

"It's all going to be okay, Kate."

I wear my most relaxed smile. "Sure."

SILENCE DESCENDS over the room as we wait for the test to run and the results to come through.

"I'm not with the potential father," I blurt out. I've been seeing Doctor Radwanska for years, so she knows all my medical history and that I never planned to have children.

"Whatever the results, Kate, there are many people who co-parent and do it very successfully."

But do they fight like cats and dogs?

The timer goes off, and I hold my breath in anticipation. The doctor takes a look at the results and then makes a quick note before turning to me, crossing her legs over, and folding her hands in her lap. "It's positive, and the timeline matches your prediction, giving you an estimated due date of March twenty-third. Your first-trimester ultrasound will be around the eight-week mark, and it will provide a more accurate date, but I'll schedule that and be in touch."

I've stopped breathing.

"Kate?"

Words die on my tongue as I open my mouth, but nothing materializes.

"Kate? Do you want a glass of water?" Doctor Radwanska comes to sit on the chair beside me, placing her hand on my knee.

Overwhelmed. That's the best way to describe this moment. Panic—that's also apt right now. I've spent my entire adulthood meticulously planning my life to the last detail, and here we are, at thirty-five years old, and an atomic bomb drops right in the center of everything.

"He's going to run," I say. My head is spinning out. I reach to steady myself on the arm of the chair.

"Okay, you're okay." The doctor gently presses her hand against my chest, asking me to sit back in my seat. "Take a few deep breaths for me, Kate."

"My parents will disown me." Panic gnaws away at my insides. "I'll need to move to a new apartment. Mine's not big enough for me and the baby." My breathing turns erratic.

"In through the nose, out through your mouth."

"Slap me."

"I'm sorry, what?"

I turn to my doctor. "Slap me and wake me up from this."

She chuckles softly. "We can put together a plan for all your prenatal appointments. Right now, though, I just want you to go home and relax, talk to and tell whoever you need. It's still very early days, but you will need support. How are you feeling physically?"

"Fine," I say blankly, staring out into space. I think back to the moment in the office with Jensen. "I've had a couple of sharp pains but no bleeding."

"When was that?"

"A few days ago," I confirm.

"Okay. Sounds to me like implantation. Sometimes women feel it but don't always know what it is."

I was implanting while telling him to shove his Italian lunch up his ass.

Ideal Kate, ideal.

"Okay, I'm going to put together a prescription for the recommended prenatal vitamins and get the nurse to grab you a glass of water. Can I get you anything else?"

Breaking my gaze from the cream-colored wall, I look at the doctor. "A glass of wine?"

She wears an amused look. "In nine months, no problem."

STILL IN DEEP SHOCK, I walk back into my apartment, having totally forgotten to return to work, collect my car, or tell anyone I wouldn't be back until tomorrow.

I need a minute to process. But I need to do it alone.

I'm going to be a mom. To Jensen Jones' baby.

There's absolutely no way it can be Tom's since the timelines don't align, and we hadn't slept together in a while.

He's going to freak the fuck out when I tell him.

I head into the kitchen and search through my cupboards. I'm sure Felicity left some chamomile tea here once. She tells me it's calming.

Lifting the lid on the box, I open two paper pouches, stick them in my cup, and fill it with boiling water. It looks like actual piss. "What is wrong with her?"

Taking a sip, I hold the dreadful taste in my mouth before spitting it into the sink. "Blah!"

Wait, can I even have that shit when pregnant? Snatching up my phone, I begin frantically scouring the internet. "Shit." Chamomile is not recommended. Once again, I begin to panic, tears pricking in my eyes. I have no idea what I'm doing here.

I hit dial on my doctor's office number.

"Good afternoon," the receptionist greets me in a breezy tone.

"Hi, um, it's Kate Monroe here. I came in to see Dr. Radwanska earlier."

"Yes, I remember. Is everything okay?"

"Yes, no, well, I don't know." I panic. "I need to ask her a question, and I'm wondering if she's available?"

"She's very busy today, but let me pass on a message to her. Is it urgent?"

"I don't know," I squeak out. "Maybe."

"Okay, Ms. Monroe. I'll get right on it and pass the message along."

Ending the call, I pace my kitchen and then living space, all the while tapping my phone against my hip.

It must be ten minutes when my phone buzzes in my hand, the call from an unknown number.

"Hello?"

"Hello Kate, it's Doctor Radwanska. I'm returning your call."

Relief floods me. "Thank you for getting back to me, and I'm sorry to bother you."

"It's fine, Kate. Don't worry. Is anything wrong?"

I run a worried palm across my forehead. "I drank some chamomile tea. Well, more spat it out. Then I checked online, and it says it could be dangerous for the baby, and I don't know what to do."

I've *always* known what to do. Always had a plan for everything. Not this time, and my stomach knots with anxiety.

"Well it sounds like you didn't drink any, but please do not be concerned. Everything is fine. I was just in the middle of emailing you over some information and recommended reading to help you through your pregnancy."

Pregnancy. I'm pregnant.

"Okay, t-that's great, thanks."

Hold it together, Kate. Always. Hold. It. Together.

No one wants to deal with unhappy, crying people. Just like my parents have always told me.

"I promise you it's all going to be okay," Doctor Radwanska reassures me a final time.

"Yeah, I've got this." But reality couldn't be any further from that.

CHAPTER FOURTEEN

KATE

On Saturday afternoon, I push through the door to Luigi's Italian. It's our group's favorite place to eat, and as I locate a very smiley Luna and a very tanned Felicity, I can't help wondering if this was the place Jensen booked.

"I'm sorry I'm late," I say to my two besties. "I overslept."

Felicity throws me a look like I'm from another planet. "First, you're running late, and then you tell me you've overslept. Okay, who are you, and what have you done with my friend?"

I snort a laugh. "I couldn't sleep for some reason."

That reason being the unborn child I'm carrying from the man I can't stand, and somehow, I need to tell you both about it, probably in the next half hour.

"I thought British people didn't tan?" I ask, deflecting my own thoughts.

On instinct, I take the wine list when Luna hands it to me. There's quite literally nothing I can have on here. I'm going to murder Jensen Jones.

Felicity spins her forearm around in front of her, admiring

her olive glow. "Trust me, this baby took work. Jon sits there for an hour and looks like he's been away for three weeks."

"I'm sorry, but are you really complaining about struggling to tan." Luna flicks the page in the menu. "I have never tanned in my life, only burned. And I'm from Florida!"

"Babe, no one needs to tan with a complexion like yours," Felicity croons. "It's flawless."

"Are you ready to order?" The waitress approaches our table. "I can take drinks first."

"I'll have a glass of your Italian Pinot, please." Felicity glances around our table and tips her chin. "Make that three glasses, nine ounces, thank you."

"No!" Both Luna and I shout in unison.

Felicity's head whips to me, and then Luna in surprise, along with a couple more in the restaurant. Luna eyes me carefully, and I can tell Felicity is waiting for my explanation. I clear my throat. "I've been feeling a little off lately." I close the wine list and hand it back to the waitress. "I'll take an orange juice, please."

"Kate."

"Yes, Felicity?" I reply.

"Are you okay?"

I don't answer, but look to Luna. "We both said no. Sometimes we just don't feel like it, right babe?"

Luna's face flashes with excitement. "Well, actually," she giggles. "I'm off alcohol completely."

"Wait, what?!" Felicity announces, turning more heads our way.

"I can't hold it in any longer. I'm pregnant!" Luna squeaks. "Zach and I are pregnant!" She wipes under her eye. "Happy tears."

Standing from her chair, Felicity gathers Luna in her arms. "Oh my goodness! I know how much you have both wanted this, how hard Zach's tried." She laughs. "You are going to make the best mummy in the world."

My heart implodes, curling in on itself as tears begin to tumble down my cheeks. In desperation to hide my reaction to such incredible news for my friends, I snatch at the napkin underneath my knife and fork, sending them crashing to the floor with a clatter. "Oh, shit."

Luna leaps from her seat. "Kate, what's wrong?!"

"I'm good. I'm great." Quickly, I swipe everything from the floor and set my knife and fork back down on the table. "Everything is just...great."

"Talk to us." Felicity sits back down and pins me with a serious, no shit taken glare.

"Can we just concentrate on Luna's news for a moment?" I say, holding my hand out for her to take. "I'm truly so happy for you, friend. I know how much you've both wanted to start a family. You will make the best mommy." Tears continue to stream from my eyes.

She smiles but holds concern for me in her gaze. "What is it, Kate?"

"When are you due?" I ask.

"March twentieth," she confirms.

Almost the same date as me.

Silence descends on our table, and I look from Luna to Felicity and back to Luna, both of them waiting for me to share what's going on.

Relaxing my shoulders, I take in a deep gulp of air. "I'm due March twenty-third."

Audible gasps ring from both of my best friends.

"Kate, are you being serious?" Felicity eventually speaks first.

I nod, looking down, trying to hide my damp eyes. "Yep."

"Have you been in touch with Tom?" Luna asks.

I shake my head. "No, and I don't intend to, either."

"Babe, I know this is a shock and will take time to process, but he really needs to know as soon as possible," Felicity says.

Finally, I look at them both. I squeeze my eyes shut for a second, readying to drop the next bombshell. "He's not the dad."

"Okay, I have two juices and a large wine." Our server stands next to us with an expectant look on her face.

Felicity doesn't take her eyes off me when she replies, "Just leave them on the table, and we'll sort, thanks."

"Sure! Are you ready to order?"

"Nowhere near," Luna says, equally dazed.

"Oh, okay. I'll give you guys another few minutes."

"It's Jensen's."

Luna's jaw hits the floor as her dainty hand flies up to cover her mouth. "As in Jones? Jensen Jones, the goalie, our goalie... ohmygod, Jensen?!"

Offering a pathetic smile, I nod slowly.

"How much for the entire bottle?" Felicity begins searching through her wine list once more.

Despite everything, I snort a laugh. "Well, you might as well have one for me since I can't drink."

"Yeah, me too," Luna adds.

Felicity takes a deep breath, matched by her long sip of wine. "So if you're due at the same time as Luna, that must mean..." she pauses, mentally calculating a possible timeline. "Around the time of our wedding?"

"Yeah," I confirm.

"How long have you known?" Felicity asks.

I look at both my friends. "Couple of days. But you're both the first people I've told. No one knows but my doctor. I needed a minute to try and process everything and calm down."

Not that its worked.

"Not even your parents?"

I look at Luna and smirk. "They're the last people I plan on telling."

Felicity nods in understanding. "Violet is quite possibly the biggest hypocrite I've ever met—the woman who expects her daughter to have zero personal life and focus entirely on work yet has two children herself."

"I wondered why you never mentioned her. She sounds

delightful. Perhaps we can compare notes on supportive moms one day." Luna takes a sip of juice and sets the glass back down. "Was it just one time with him?"

Flutters float through my body as that same memory of him behind comes racing back. "It was the night of the wedding." I flick my hair over my shoulder. "It's like I hate him and the way he seems able to crawl under my skin and call me out. The sexual tension has been building for ages—"

"Mmm-hmm," Felicity says around her glass.

I drop my shoulders and raise a brow at her. "As I was saying, it's been building for a while, and, well, on the day of the wedding, he asked me to spend a night with him. He said I would be back for more."

"And obviously, you took him up on his offer."

I look at Luna and trace a circle over my stomach. "Obviously."

"I'm sorry, but I have to ask. Was it good, and therefore, will you be 'back for more?'"

I throw her an incredulous look. "What do you think, Felicity?"

"I think you went all night long with him, and despite the current conditions, you will, in fact, be 'back for more.' But you hate the fact you want to." She sets down her wine glass. "Let's be real for a second, though; more sex with Jensen Jones is low on the list of priorities."

"No kidding," I agree sarcastically.

"You need to tell him, like yesterday."

"Seconded," Luna declares.

I sit back in my chair and cross my legs over at the knee. "Are we forgetting he's a dickhead who doesn't do commitment? The moment I tell him I'm carrying his child, he's going to run so fast in the opposite direction that the Scorpions will be looking for a new goalie."

"I wouldn't be so sure about that. Also, can I just point out that you are more alike than you care to admit? And I think that's why you clash. You don't do commitment, but I don't see you running away from your responsibilities, ever." Felicity points out.

"He is your doppelganger," Luna nods.

"What?"

"Deny it all you want, babe, but that's why he's under your skin so much and likely you under his. You both infuriate each other, but you're also like magnets, physically attracted to one another." Felicity makes yet another accurate statement.

I drop my head between my shoulders, my hair falling in front of my face as I let out a low groan. "I'm not built to be a mom, and I can't see him relishing being a dad, especially to the baby of a 'spoiled princess.'" I hold up my fingers and air quote the last two words.

"He said that?" Luna exclaims.

"He doesn't mean it," Felicity quickly counters.

My head whips up. "Why are you defending him?"

She leans forward, clasping her hands together on the table. "Like it or not, babe, you're now having a baby with him. I'm not saying fall madly in love with the guy, but I am saying you need to get along, for both of your sakes. I'm also saying you need to give him a chance because I think he might just surprise you."

I purse my lips together and nod. "I agree with you, apart from the last bit. I just don't see him stepping up."

"Also, you're going to be a great mom, and you know why? Because everything you set your mind to, you do with determination and heart. Yes, this isn't where you expected to be, but you will nail it, and you have us to support you." Felicity gestures between herself and Luna.

"We can share our pregnancy journeys!" Luna squeaks with excitement.

I smile sweetly at her. "Other than our gestation period and due dates, I don't think our journeys will look very similar."

Reaching across, Luna places her hand over mine. "Talk to him. Let him support you. I think Felicity's right."

"I will," I say, looking at the menu to finally decide what I want. "As soon as possible."

"Today," Felicity insists. "Right after this lunch. He's at home packing and relaxing before he heads to Alberta."

A wave of disappointment hits me, and I hate it. "He's heading out of town?"

I swear she notices and smirks at the way I try to hide my reaction. "Yes. He leaves in a day or two—I can't remember exactly when Jon said—but he's at home. He's been more withdrawn lately. Not the same Jensen."

"He has?"

"Especially since you stormed out of his room and flew back to Seattle." Luna winces. "I'm guessing I walked in on the morning after?"

"Yep." I pop my p.

"Today, babe," Felicity repeats.

I roll my eyes, knowing she's right.

"Okay, are we all set?"

Felicity closes her menu and smiles at the waitress. "Yes. Never been clearer."

CHAPTER FIFTEEN

JENSEN

Setting my weight on the rack, I sit up on the bench and grab my towel, running it across the back of my neck.

A few days back home in Alberta to see my parents and going for final suit fittings will leave me next to no time to work out. Hollie's schedule makes Jon's look like a free skate.

Rising from the bench, I make my way over to the leg press when I hear a thud above the eighties rock music playing from my speakers.

I grab my phone and open the smart camera app.

Kate.

What's she doing here? And should I throw on a shirt?

Nah, fuck it. Might as well make her Saturday night, remind her of what she's missing.

Another knock sounds as I step out of the gym and move for the front door. "Patience, Princess!" I shout loud enough so I know she can hear it and no doubt offer me her trademark snarl when I open the door.

Pissed off Kate is the hottest kind of Kate.

But she doesn't wear a snarl as I open the door to my apartment. Her expression is completely unreadable. For the first time in forever, I can't read her.

"Hey," I say, holding the door open in one hand and a bottle of water in the other.

"Hey." Stepping into my apartment, a place she's been to many times before as part of a group but never alone, she doesn't pause for one second to admire my bare chest.

Shutting the door behind us with a soft click, I turn and rest my back against it, crossing my ankles.

She looks beautiful today, almost radiant. Her usually thick and luscious blonde hair somehow looks even thicker. Her cheeks glow, and her eyes sparkle.

Twitching her nose, she looks around in disgust. "What's that smell?"

Because I can't help myself, I lift an arm and sniff. "One hundred percent man, Princess."

"Stop calling me that! And I'm not talking about you. What did you have for dinner?"

I run a palm over my mouth to hide my satisfied smile. She didn't deny that I'm all man. "I wasn't that hungry, so I made myself a bacon sandwich."

She slams a hand over her mouth like she's about to puke. "That is gross!"

"Bacon?"

"Yes!" Her voice muffled by her hand. "Bacon, meat." She heaves again. "Meat is gross."

No cock jokes, Jones. Hold it in.

"I didn't know you didn't like meat," I say, pushing off the door and making my way into the living room.

She follows behind me, her clutch between her hands. She's clearly been out somewhere; the fitted cream pants and black blouse she wears are hot as fuck and definitely not everyday clothes.

Looking as surprised as me, she sets her clutch down as we both take a seat on the black leather couches opposite each other. "Apparently, it's a new thing."

I narrow my eyes at her. "I gotta admit, I wasn't expecting it to be you interrupting my workout."

"Yeah, well, I wasn't expecting to be here today either."

She's being weird. "Can I get you a drink or something?"

"Um, a glass of water would be great. Thanks."

I fight the urge to hand her the bottle I'm drinking from just to test her reaction. Instead, I stand and walk to the kitchen.

Again, she follows me and stands at the island, looking around the vast space. "You have a nice place."

I look over my shoulder from where I'm standing with the fridge door half open. "Thanks." I sound unsure. She's never complimented anything about me, not since that night in Riley's.

Handing her a water, she twists the cap and takes several large gulps. "It's hot out there today. I'm really hot."

"Damn right, you are." I throw her a wink.

Rolling her eyes, she sits at my island and places her clutch next to her.

"Can I be honest?"

"Yeah, I guess," she replies, still taking in my place like it's the first time she's seen it.

"You look different; you're acting it too."

She flushes. "Different, how?"

I come to stand on the opposite end of the island and lean forward, resting my forearms on the white marble. Pinning her with my eyes, I smile a genuine smile this time. "Well, for one, you're not being a straight-up bitch to me. And two—" I round the island and stop, swiveling her stool towards me but not touching her *yet*. "You look more stunning than ever."

She takes a sharp breath. "Has anyone ever told you that you're really forward?"

I shake my head and smile again. "Nah, they normally do all the work. You're the exception, Princess."

God, I love the way I can make her flush with such ease.

That night in Oxford lives rent-free in her head. She *definitely* wants more.

Looking down at her gold sandals resting on the stool, she twists her hands together. But the next surprise she has for me tears my heart clean apart. Her lips start to shake.

Is she *crying?*

Katherine Violet Monroe...crying?

"Hey, hey." I tip her face back up to mine with my index finger.

She looks up at me, and she's definitely fighting back tears. "I'm really sorry. I shouldn't have come. I'm not ready to tell y—"

"Tell me what, Kate?" My damaged heart stops beating altogether. "Tell me *what?*"

"I'm really sorry. In fact, no, I'm not that sorry. It's both of our responsibility. But for the love of all that is holy, please don't freak out on me." She twists her hands together again.

"Kate, I'm gonna be really honest right now. You're scaring the shit out of me. What's going on?"

Twisting hands fly in front of her face, but I reach up and pull them apart. "Don't hold out on me, Princess. You turned up at my apartment, drank my water, and now you've started crying on me. What's wrong?" A growl rumbles from my chest. "Is it Tom? Has he hurt you? I'll fucking *murder* him."

"You're kind of scary and a bit over the top, you know that?" Her blue eyes look deep into mine.

Thump, thump, thump. My heart races faster.

"Has he hurt you?" I repeat.

"No," she whispers. Our eyes are still locked, and my hands are still over hers, framing each side of her face. "I'm pregnant, Jensen."

What? She's having his baby. *I'm* going to puke now.

"With Tom's baby? Did you know before we—"

"No." Another whisper. "It's yours. My doctor confirmed it."

Sh-she's having my...baby?

The girl of my fucking dreams, literally my dreams, the girl I can't stop obsessing over. The girl I've shared the best night of my life with is...having my baby.

Silence.

I pin my bottom lip between my teeth, trying to hide my smile—Jensen Jones, Mr. Non-Commitment, surprised by his own reaction to being a daddy.

For her, I'll be anyone.

"Why would I freak out, Kate?"

She rolls her eyes. "Duh, you don't do relationships, let alone with a 'spoiled princess.' And now you find out I'm pregnant with your baby."

"Say that again."

"Spoiled princess."

"No. The last part. Say it again."

"I'm pregnant with your baby." Her voice is breathy as she repeats the words that cast over me like velvet.

Hands still on either side of her face, I lean forward and brush my mouth across hers, smiling against her lips. "I got you pregnant."

"Well, yes."

Kissing her gently, I close my eyes. Fuck me, she tastes like heaven. "Don't you go freaking out on *me* now. But all I can think about is doing it again, just to be sure."

She pulls back, wiping her deep blue manicured nails across her bottom lip. "What?"

I don't even hesitate as I pull her back into my bare chest. Kate sitting on a high stool is perfect kissing height. "You think you know everything about me. That you have me all figured out. The truth is, Princess, you know nothing about me at all. But I know every single part of you. What makes you tick, what makes your thighs clench, what makes you seethe with rage. I know your favorite dishes and your favorite restaurants. I know what cases you've recently won at work and that the nail polish you're wearing right now is your favorite since you wear it six months out of the year. You hate me because I keep you guessing. I challenge you. And for once in your fucking life, I make you *want* someone for something more than just a few dates and a fuck. And that scares the shit out of you. I know it does because it scares the shit out of me too."

Her breath catches in her throat, and I go to kiss her, but more deeply this time.

"No."

"No, what?"

"No, don't kiss me again."

I close my eyes and brace my hands on the arms of her stool, squeezing the bars in my palms. "Don't freak out on me, Katherine."

"I've just told you, the person you apparently can't stand, that I'm having your baby. And then you come with all of this? How am I not going to freak out? I was already freaking out at the baby part. You, on the other hand, want to put *another* baby in me."

Scratching at my chest, I smile at her. "I didn't mean another, but since you suggested it..." I turn serious at the look of horror on her face. "I'm obsessed with you. I've been obsessed with you since the moment you wore my jersey and sat on my lap. Since the moment you placed your lips against mine. Sure, I didn't plan on having a baby. And it's true I'm not into commitment. I've got my reasons for that." I sigh. Taking one of her hands in mine. "But with you, and only you, I'm not scared to have a baby. Just like I'm not scared to be with you. I've been fantasizing about it for too long."

"Together?! Oh, you're way too much!" She pushes off the stool and grabs her clutch, racing over to the front door. Just as she makes it, she trips on the mat and stumbles forward, crashing hard onto the wood.

"Fuck!" I bolt across and gather her in my arms. "Are you okay?" Pressing my palm across her lower stomach. "For fuck's sake, Kate, be careful."

"I-I need to leave."

A red bump starts to appear on her forehead. "No way are you leaving. My pregnant girl just crashed into a door. There's no way I'm letting you out of my sight."

She scoffs. "Let me make a couple of things really clear for you, Jensen. I'm *not* your girl. I'm Kate Monroe. I might be carrying your child, but we are not together. Also, I am leaving, thank you very much. I'm fine."

Kate rests her hand on the handle behind her, but I shoot an arm out and press my hand firmly against the door to prevent it from opening. Her back is to me as I squeeze my eyes shut, her citrus scent swirling around me. "Don't go. I'm sorry I came on strong. But eighteen months of you driving me wild, and then this news lit the simmering fire I've been burning for you. I'll give you time to think about us, to come to terms with how we're meant for each other. But while you do that, just know I'm going to be at your every beck and call. I'm going to spoil the shit out of you and *my* baby. You're my princess, Katherine."

She doesn't say another word as she pulls on the handle, and this time, I release my arm, letting her leave.

Pulling the door shut behind her, she leaves me standing in my empty apartment, processing everything that's just happened and all that I've admitted out loud. Just like popping the cork on a champagne bottle, I exploded, unable to reel in my feelings anymore. But how the fuck was I supposed to hold everything back when she turned up at my place and brought me the greatest news of my life on what has always been the hardest day? July sixteenth—the day Lauren walked out of my life and left me standing at the altar but now, the day Kate Monroe offered me the best gift I've ever received.

CHAPTER SIXTEEN

JENSEN

ME

Are you at home?

PRINCESS

Yes.

Then why won't you answer your door?

Technically, I'm not in my apartment, but I am in my building.

Doing what?

Having a coffee with a friend. I'll be a half hour.

I stand in front of her door, typing out a response. I didn't know Kate had friends outside of our group, and definitely not one living in the same building as her.

I have to be at the airport in an hour, so I was stopping by to drop off a few things. But give me this friend's apartment number and I can stop by and say hi.

AUDREY is eighty years old and is nervous about strange men. What "things" are you dropping off?

Come down, and you'll find out. It would make sense for me to have a key to your place, just in case you need me.

Yeah, not happening. I've gotten by fine these past thirty-five years.

That was before you were carrying my baby.

I'll be down in a minute.

It has to be ten minutes before Kate rounds the corner, walking toward me down her corridor.

Dressed in a long black flowing skirt and a white cropped T-shirt. Her hair is up in a high-top ponytail with a few pieces framing her face.

What is it going to take to get this girl on my side?

Sliding her key into the lock, she opens the door and waves her arm inside for me to enter.

"What have you got there?" She eyes the bags I'm holding as we both walk across to her kitchen counter.

I've only been here a handful of times with the boys, but her apartment was the first real insight into the true Kate. When she doesn't think the rest of the world is watching, she likes to do calligraphy in bright colors. She has favorite plates and mugs that are chipped and worn, but they sit at the front of her cupboards, the ones she uses all the time.

"How do you keep on top of all these houseplants?" I say, looking around. She must have at least ten in her teal living room alone. There are two more floor plants in the entryway.

She shrugs. "It's nice. They oxygenate my apartment, and I enjoy looking after them. That's Herbert." She nods at a spider plant. It hangs from the corner of the ceiling above her TV.

I smile and set the bags down on the countertop. She's so fucking cute, and she doesn't even know it.

Her eyes flare as I start unloading the bags. "What's all this?" Coming to stand next to me, she peers into one of the bags. "Jensen, what is all this?!"

"My flight to Alberta leaves in three hours. I've gotta check in and head through security. But I wanted to make sure you're all set while I'm away. I was going for a week but shortened it to four nights, so I'll be back sooner."

"These must've cost a fortune!" She picks up half a dozen parent and baby books. "Did you buy the entire store?!"

I point at one with a pink cover. "That one's great."

She looks up at me in surprise. "How do you know?"

I continue to unload the bags. "I read seventy percent last night."

And fell asleep with it on my chest. Then I read the rest this morning.

Kate's a decent cook. I know this from when I've been around, and she's made dinner for us all. But like hell am I having her work the crazy hours she does and then come home and prepare her own food.

So, I batch-cooked a bunch of vegetarian options. There's enough to get through the next four days, and I have Jon on standby. He's an okay chef, but he's not me. Taking out the freezable containers, I stride over to her freezer and begin loading them in. "No meat in any of them."

"Jon made these?"

I roll my eyes and shut the freezer door. "Nah, I did."

Kate fights to hide her surprise.

You think you've got me all figured out, don't you, Princess?

"Um, well, thank you. It really wasn't necess—"

"It was. You get home from work at, like, what, eight in the evening? Let me guess... then this goes on." I open the door on the microwave, and the food splatters inside tell the story.

Rushing over, she slams it shut and stands in front, her face flushing red. "Microwave meals have come a long way."

Reaching out, I lightly run the back of my knuckles across her stomach. "Do I need to repeat what I said yesterday?"

"No."

"I'm going to anyway. I'm going to treat you like a princess, Princess."

ME

I'm boarding my flight. Jon, can you check on meal levels? Zach, I've booked Kate in for her first prenatal class and another space if Luna wants to go. Let me know. Jessie, just keep a watch out for me.

JESSIE

Watch out, as in like a stalker?

JON

Oh how the tables have turned. I'm here with popcorn.

ZACH

When is the class?

ME

This Saturday. I'll be back early Friday, so I'm going too. If you need to stalk, then stalk, and Jon, fuck off.

ZACH

I'm surprised she agreed to it.

ME

She hasn't, but she will on Saturday.

ZACH

Are you trying to get a slap?

I CLOSE out the message thread and hand over my boarding pass to be scanned.

My phone buzzes in my pocket.

"Sir, all phones beyond this point should be switched into airplane mode."

"Sure, give me one second."

I step to the side and answer. "Yo, what's up?"

"You want me to stalk a lawyer?"

I turn my back on the other passengers boarding the plane. "Just make sure she's doing okay."

"She's thirty-five years old. I'm sure she can take care of herself," Jessie replies.

Not in the way I can.

"Just stop by one night this week to check if the stock of meals is going down."

Jessie huffs out a breath. "Let's get real for a second. I get that she's pregnant, and you want to take care of her, but you sound obsessed. Not just with the baby, but with her too."

You have no idea.

"I'm just trying to step up."

"I know, I know. You'd tell me if there was more, right?"

I should tell him more; I owe my best friend that since I'm the only one he's confided in about what happened in Texas and the whole reason he was traded to the Scorpions against his will. Even worse, Jon knows how I feel about Kate since Felicity saw what she saw. I feel like a shit friend for keeping secrets like this when he's been so candid with me and only me.

But now isn't the time.

"I'm about to board my flight."

"So there is something?"

"When I get back, I'll come over; we'll have a few beers and shoot the shit."

"Right, well, I'm heading back to Dallas next week, so make it soon. Damn man, I thought you told me everything."

"Up until yesterday, there wasn't much to tell."

For a few beats, he goes silent on the other end of the line. "Alright."

"Heading back to see your mom?" I ask.

"Yeah. She needs me. Dad turned up again last night."

"Is she okay?"

"She will be."

I nod and then look up to see a very angry member of the cabin crew. "Look, I gotta go. I'll be in touch."

"Alright."

Finding my seat in first, I sit back for the short one hour forty-minute plane ride I've taken more times than I can count. Usually, I love heading home since I have a close family, but right now, I want and need to be in Seattle.

But I can't let my sister down.

Connecting my phone to the plane's WIFI, I realize there's a question I forgot to ask her.

ME

Are you okay?

PRINCESS

Since you last asked? Yes. Nothing has changed in the past three hours.

I want to tell my parents. I'll be home with family, and you know we're close. Doesn't seem right keeping it from them. Unless you don't want me to?

You can tell them, but it will probably leak to the media.

The media know nothing about me and my personal life. My family is as loyal as they come.

I won't be telling mine. Maybe Easton at some point, but not my parents.

She is; she's ashamed of me. I know Kate is from a family

with serious money and social status. Her family owns one of the largest law firms with offices across the country. They probably wouldn't approve of rough-and-ready Jensen Jones from Alberta. I've got money, but I'm a working-class boy.

Why not?

She begins typing a message and then stops. It is me. My heart sinks. It's not just that I drive her to the point of insanity but because of who I am and who they would *or wouldn't* approve. And that pisses me off.

Why not, Kate?

Finally, she begins typing again. I'm so focused on my screen that I don't notice we're about to take off until the same airline attendant asks me to buckle my seat belt.

Let's just say it won't sit well with my parents...

"Fuck."

My new best friend and biggest fan spins around in the aisle and pins me with a glare.

"Sorry."

Wincing, I get back to my phone.

You have a real way of making me feel good, Kate.

It wouldn't matter if I was having a baby with Jesus Christ himself—it still wouldn't be good enough.

I'm going to tell my parents about the baby on this trip home, and when I get back, I'm going to go with you to tell yours. They can tell me I'm not good enough for you to my face.

It's not about whether YOU'RE good enough for me. It's the fact that I'm having a baby, period.

They don't want you to have a family?!

Can we talk about this another time? Maybe not over text?

Who the fuck are these people? The Monroes just went straight to the top of my shit list.

Damn right we are. What the fuck, Kate? You're thirty-six!

Thirty-five.

You drive me crazy; you know that?

Hard same.

I catch myself smiling. Somehow, in the space of ten seconds, it's morphed from a full-blown scowl.

It turns me on. I've got a boner at thirty thousand feet.

Insufferable.

CHAPTER SEVENTEEN

KATE

The following day, I sit up in bed feeling like total shit.

One minute, I'm fine; the next, it feels like I could fall through the floor. Dizziness and nausea have really taken hold.

Grabbing one of Jensen's books from my bedroom floor, I quickly scan the pages until I find the section on morning sickness. Self-help it is. No need to call the doctor.

The key symptoms are everything I'm feeling, including loss of appetite.

Padding through to my kitchen, I flick the coffee maker on but quickly stop it. Blah, even that makes me gag. How in the hell am I supposed to make it through the day and then to the rescheduled meeting at six p.m. with the Parkers when I feel like this? I guess they call it morning sickness for a reason, and hopefully, by the afternoon, I'll be feeling better.

I need to feel better.

A half-hour later, I've dragged my sorry ass around my apartment and made the best effort I could to get ready. I genuinely cannot bear the thought of food, so I forego my breakfast and take a few sips of water. At least Felicity will be back at work today.

Snatching up my keys, I make my way down to the parking lot and get in my car.

God, this isn't getting any better, if anything worse.

"No excuses." Violet's mantra rings over in my head.

Cranking the engine, I back out of my space and head for work, stopping at a stoplight a couple of blocks away from my office when my phone buzzes.

Then buzzes again.

Connecting it to the Bluetooth, I pick up but don't bother to check who's calling. "Hello?"

"Kate, it's Margo. Sorry about this, but the Parkers are here and waiting for their appointment. There's been a mix-up with timings." She pauses, and I hear a few clicks of a computer mouse. "You have an opening for an hour right now if you can see them?"

"I thought it would take at least two hours, given the paperwork they wanted help with."

"They're confident they can squeeze it into an hour."

The lights turn green, and I pull away, taking a left onto the street where our office is located. "Okay, I'll be there in five minutes. Get them a drink, and I can take it from there."

Margo hesitates for a second before answering. "Okay...no problem. Just take your time on the road."

"NO PROBLEM, Mr. and Mrs. Parker; I can draft the pleadings as soon as possible and have everything moving forward."

My stomach rolls again.

"Thank you, Kate. We're so glad we held out to see you. I know you have a busy schedule, but you have one of the best reputations in Seattle." Mrs. Parker smiles sweetly at me.

"Thank you, I really appreciate th—"

I throw a hand over my mouth, unable to contain the nausea any longer.

Resetting myself, I take a deep breath and go to open the door.

Another wave.

"I'm so sorry," I rush out. "I'll have Margo show you out."

Racing to the bathroom in high heels, I swing the door open but don't make it far enough when I puke straight into one of the sinks.

Then I puke again.

And again, until I'm a crumpled mess on the floor, my suit dress gathering muck. Kicking off my heels, I curl in on myself and close my eyes. The room won't stop spinning, and I know it's because I haven't eaten anything since yesterday at lunchtime when the nausea bouts began.

"Kate?!" Felicity barges through the door, dropping to her knees beside me. "Are you okay?"

"Never better," I slur.

"Come on, we need to get you up and home."

"I'm good. My day is packed. I can't miss any more appointments."

My best friend glares at me in a way that sears straight through my bones; she isn't messing around. "You're probably the most beautiful woman I've ever seen, and I thought that from the moment I saw you. But right now, you look like absolute hell. I won't accept anything other than you going home and getting into bed. You're in your first trimester and have bad sickness." She wraps an arm around my waist to support me. "Trust me, I had it with Jack, and it was the worst."

"I'm good," I repeat, trying to smile and failing.

She holds out her phone to me. "Call Jensen, please."

I throw her a puzzled look. "Why?"

"Because he tried to text you, and you haven't answered in all of ten minutes, so now he's blowing up mine."

"Really?"

"Yep. He makes Jon look like a slacker."

"He's just got the first-trimester jitters."

Felicity blows out a breath and looks at me. "You really believe that? That this is just about the baby and nothing else?"

"I don't know what to believe anymore, babe."

"He's obsessed with you. He has been for a long time."

"I know. But I don't want that. I just want to co-parent and keep some independence."

"Who said being in a relationship means giving up your independence?"

I throw a hand over my mouth and hold up a finger, burping slightly.

"Lovely." She scrunches up her nose.

"Acid." I wince and then start to puke all over the floor in front of me.

My best friend rubs my back. "Yeah, it's home time now, babe."

FELICITY SETS a glass of water on my nightstand and then helps me into bed, pulling the duvet over me. "Thanks, Mom."

"How are you feeling now?"

"About as well as when you pulled over for me to puke on the sidewalk."

"Yeah, that wasn't a good look." She hands me the glass of water. "Try and take a few sips."

Holding the glass to my lips, I roll my eyes. "Only Jensen's baby could be this troublesome."

Giggling, she searches through her large black tote. "Here, try nibbling on some of these tonight. I know you don't feel like eating, but the most important thing is fluids, and these biscuits may help. Ginger can also help settle the stomach." She hands me the packet.

"Where the hell did you get those?"

She shrugs. "They're one of my favorite snacks. I always keep a packet on hand."

"You are Mary Poppins; you know that right?"

"Have you called Jensen back?"

"Nope. I texted him."

"And told him what exactly."

Tentatively, I nibble on the edge of the biscuit. "This isn't as bad as that chamomile crap you consume. That looks like piss, but it's actually worse."

She ignores my mindless jabbering. "Told him what?"

"I told him I was at work and busy in meetings and not to worry."

"So you didn't mention that you were texting him from a bathroom floor, covered in your own puke?"

"It's just the usual morning sickness, babe. I'll be fine tomorrow."

My stomach rolls again, and I sit back in my pillows and groan. "I hope."

"Please do not come into work tomorrow if you aren't up to it. I get that you don't want to say anything until twelve weeks, but if this carries on, then you might need to."

"I'll tell Easton after the twelve-week mark, but I'm not telling my parents. Ever."

"Hmm." My best friend comes to sit on the bed next to me. "I say rip the band-aid off and tell them ASAP."

"You've met them a couple of times, and they're only nice to you because you work with me, and you aren't direct 'competition.' It would be pointless telling them, more trouble than it's worth." I scoff and then burp again. "It's not like they would step up and support me. And don't get me started on the way they'd treat Jensen."

Felicity knits her brows together. "Why? Yeah, he's a bit over the top, but he's a good man and will more than step up."

"A *bit* over the top?! Girl, you're way too conditioned by Jon."

"Okay, he's a bit more than over the top. But he's, you know, he's got..." She trails off and purses her lips together.

"He's got what?" I throw her my look reserved for do not fuck with me moments.

"Ugh, I promised him I wouldn't say anything. Only Jon knows."

"Jon knows *what*?"

"You know how he was hammered at the club the night of the Stanley Cup win?"

I think back to sitting at the bar with Luna, watching him stroll off with the brunette. "The night he allegedly used a brunette to make me jealous."

She clears her throat. "Yeah, well. I followed them into the hallway when she dragged him off. He obviously went willingly, and I kind of felt like I was sticking my nose where it didn't belong, but the next thing I see is her trying to climb Jensen and him saying no."

Nausea hits me again. "He told me the morning after we slept together that he didn't touch the redhead either. It was his sister's drunk best friend or something."

She nods. "Yeah...I think you should know that when that brunette was coming onto him, he said he wasn't hooking up with anyone else because he was..." She smirks with amusement. "'Crazy about Princess Katherine, even if she can't stand me.'"

I pick at the white lace on my duvet but don't say anything.

"I don't think he's been with anyone else in a long time, babe. I think you were his first time in a while."

"He basically said he wanted to be together when I broke the news to him about the pregnancy. He didn't freak out at all. In fact, he was totally over the top about it."

"Oh, he's over something alright. Head over heels for you.

And now that you're having his baby, he's like a caveman on steroids."

I laugh. "I don't want a serious relationship. Not with anyone. I want to try co-parenting. I don't want to give every last piece of me away. A week ago, I was Kate Monroe. Today, I'm mommy-to-be and Jensen Jones' girl, if he has his way."

Felicity nods. "I can definitely relate to that from when I had my children, but babe, Jensen is *nothing* like Elliott. At least keep your mind open to the possibility."

I shake my head. "I'm attracted to him, but I just don't think I feel that way. We clash too much."

She rises from my bed and picks up my water glass. "Drink some more and get some rest."

I take the glass and take a few sips.

"Try not to make any finite decisions one way or another. Your entire world has just been flipped on its head."

Another wave of acid. "Yeah."

"I will say this though."

"What's that?"

Smiling knowingly, she looks down at the rings on her left hand. "There's nothing wrong with a boy obsessed."

CHAPTER EIGHTEEN

KATE

Thump, thump, thump.

"Ugh, go away!" I groan from my bed, although it's pointless, given that the person hammering on the other side of my apartment door can definitely not hear me.

Thump, thump, thump.

"I'm sick, so please go away," I croak from under my comforter.

Thump, thump, thump.

Pushing back the cover, I climb out of bed.

This had better not be another delivery to the wrong apartment.

Thump, thump...

"Yes, okay!" I shout, but this time, I'm close enough so they can hear. I have no idea who's on the other side of that door, but whoever it is deserves to witness whatever state I'm in just for dragging me out of my bed. It might be two in the afternoon, but I haven't eaten anything other than ginger biscuits in days, and I'm just about keeping fluid down.

"Jessie?" Peering through the spy hole, I see him on the other side. His hands are in the pockets of his jeans, and he's looking from side to side down the hallway.

"Hey," I say, pulling the door open.

At the sight of me, his eyes go wide. "Kate, um." He scans my body, but not in an appreciative way, more taking in my mess. "Are you okay?"

"I've been better. Come in."

Once inside, he looks around my apartment, which he's never been to. "I hope you don't mind me saying this, but you don't look great, and your apartment isn't much better."

"Tell me something I don't know." I burp the final word. "I'm assuming Jensen's told you."

He nods. "That's why I'm here, actually. To check on you. He wanted me to make sure you were doing alright, but..." He casts his gaze around my apartment once more and then again on me. "Have you been eating the meals he prepared?"

"What is this?" I say, propping a hand on my hip.

Jessie winces. "He's just worried about you."

"I'm fine." Even I don't believe that anymore.

He makes his way over and into my kitchen. Heading for my freezer, he pulls the door open and then starts counting the meals Jensen left in there. "You haven't had any."

"This is crazy."

"You look dehydrated, Kate, and gray, and your hair is..." He circles his finger in my direction. "You just look like—"

"Shit?" I finish for him. "Yes, I know, because that's exactly how I feel." Tears well in my eyes. I'm so fucking emotional all the time.

Jessie reaches into his back pocket, pulls out his phone, and begins scrolling.

"What are you doing?"

"I was under strict instruction to let him know how you are, so I'm doing that."

"Jessie..." I drawl.

"I can't lie to him, Kate, and seeing you like this is worrying me too. I think you need medication or something."

Right as he says it, the burning sensation in my chest sends up another wave of acid and I heave, running to my bathroom.

As I sit on the end of the bath, my hand rests on the side of the open toilet, and I feel the tears start to roll down my cheeks. I hear a murmur of a conversation, no doubt between Jessie and Jensen.

After a few minutes, Jessie appears in my doorway. "He's on his way. Who's your doctor?"

"I wish you hadn't called him. I've got this."

"No, Kate, you don't. You need someone to help. You could barely answer the door. How long has it been like this?"

"A couple of days."

He presses his lips together. "My mom was like this with me and my brother."

"You have a brother?"

He doesn't answer but instead grabs the empty water glass off the side and heads into the kitchen to refill it. "Take sips of this and get back into bed. Have you got anything ginger?"

I snort a laugh. "I ran out of the biscuits Felicity gave me. I was going to ask her to bring some more when she's finished at work. They're the only thing I can keep down and seem to help."

He smiles. "Leave it with me."

JENSEN

It took me four hours to get from my mom's living room to where I am now, standing outside Kate's door.

I'm pissed she lied to me, texting me to say she's fine when based on what Jessie told me, she's less than great.

Knocking a couple of times, I wait for her to answer the door. "Hang on," a familiar male voice echoes.

Jessie pulls the door open, and immediately, I'm inside, looking around for her. "Where is she?"

He points through to her bedroom. "In bed, sleeping. I went to the store to grab her some more ginger biscuits. It's the only thing she'll eat. The only thing she can keep down."

"The *fuck*?!"

"She's stopped puking now, though, and had some water."

I drag my hands down my face. "I shouldn't have left her."

"You think she's going to let you fawn over her? That girl is shit scary."

Pulling open the freezer door, I count the meals left. "You weren't kidding. She hasn't eaten anything?"

Jessie shakes his head and looks around her apartment. "Never expected this."

"What?"

"I dunno, life? Plants?"

I snort a laugh. "Trust me, my girl's got layers."

"Oh, so you *are* dating?" He walks over to grab his bag from the couch.

Christ, I wish I could answer that question differently. "Nah. Not yet."

"Not yet?"

Twisting the cap on a bottle of water, I wipe the back of my hand across my mouth. "When she comes to her senses, she'll realize I'm the only guy for her. It's a matter of time."

He eyes me closely. "You sound unhinged. I mean, I thought you liked her, but, wow, you're in deep."

I shrug and take another sip of water. "Some people are made for each other. Our baby confirms it."

"She's it for you?"

"Yep." I throw the empty water bottle in the recycling can.

He scratches the back of his neck. "This can't be new. Why didn't you tell me?"

"What's the point when she's dating another guy and can't stand the sight of me?"

He laughs. "Other than the other guy, I don't think much has changed."

"It has."

"What. Because you slept with her?"

"Nah, because she wants me too. I can feel it."

Shoulders shaking with silent humor, he walks toward the door to leave. "I gotta head out. I've been here way longer than I intended. I'll be back in a couple of weeks."

I pause on obsessing and take a long look at my best friend. "Why do I feel like you're holding out on me now?"

"Like you, there's not much to say. Mom's still struggling, and Dad's never around. It's down to me to care for her."

"Where is he this time?" God, he's a prick, and fuck knows how a man like Jessie Callaghan came from his DNA.

"Probably shacked up with another chick."

"Why doesn't she just leave him? You could set her up with everything she needs."

Jessie blows out a disbelieving breath. "You're kidding, right? They've been married for twenty-five years. She doesn't think she'd be able to cope on her own."

I nod. Families can be a fucking nightmare. I'm so grateful for the one I was blessed with. "Have you spoken to your dad?"

"Ha! I'm more likely to break his jaw than speak to him."

"Yeah, don't do that." Although I totally get why he would.

"I'm gonna head out and finish up packing for Dallas." He nods down the hallway to Kate's room. "Good luck with getting the girl."

I walk over and fist-bump him. "If all else fails, there's always handcuffs. Thanks for checking on her, bro. I owe you."

He pauses halfway out the door. "You're joking, aren't you?"

"Of course I am. It won't come to that. Another few weeks, and she'll be mine."

He shakes his head and walks down the hallway toward the elevators. "Later."

No sooner is the door closed than I'm striding into Kate's bedroom. Lying on her side, she faces me, her hair fluttering from the ceiling fan. How is it even possible to be that goddamn beautiful? I've only been away a couple of nights, but there's no doubt she's more gorgeous than when I left.

I know I shouldn't. I shouldn't climb under the comforter and lie beside her, but fuck it, I'm doing it anyway. How in the hell I manage to get my six-three frame in without waking her, I'll never know. She's fucking exhausted, I know that. Resting my head on her soft white pillow, the raw need to pull her into my chest and never let her or our baby go claws at me, testing every inch of willpower I have. I need to touch her again, need to taste the way she feels on my lips, on my tongue, the way she molds to me.

Conveniently, a piece of hair swirls and sticks to her upper lip, which protrudes just slightly above her lower. It always does, whether she's smiling, laughing, crying, or scowling, the latter being the version I get most often—for now.

Reaching up carefully, I pull the strand of hair away and tuck it behind her right ear. Her eyelids flutter slightly, but she stays perfectly asleep. Everything about her is perfect—even her snarky mouth.

"What is it going to take for you to fall for me?" I whisper the words so quietly I can barely hear them myself, though I've repeated them in my head more times than I can count. "Let me love you both like I know I can."

"I'M gonna need you to eat some of it for me, Princess."

I'm sitting next to Kate, who finally woke up around nine

p.m. I watch her push the vegetable stir fry around her plate. "I just don't think I can stomach it."

"What else can I get you? If it continues like this, then we're going to the doctor." Walking the plate through to her kitchen, I pull out my phone and text the boys.

ME

Can someone with a key to my place head over and pack me a bag for at least a week? There's no way I'm leaving her like this.

Like the fine friends they all are, every single member of the group begins typing immediately.

JON

How is she? Yeah, I can sort it.

ZACH

What else do you need? Luna and I are headed to the store in a sec, so we can grab you anything you need.

JESSIE

Say the word and it's yours. I don't fly until tomorrow.

ME

Jon, you're probably closest, so makes sense. Zach, I'm good. I just ordered in for me, and Kate has a lifetime supply of those god-awful ginger biscuits, thanks to Jessie.

JON

I'll be there in an hour.

"Yeah. I think my schedule is free then." Kate's voice filters through to the kitchen.

"Who are you talking to?" As soon as I appear in the doorway, a guilty look crosses her face as she hits end on her work cell. And she thinks *I'm* insufferable? "Who was that?"

She shrugs. "Margo."

"At..." I check my watch. "Half past nine in the evening you're making work calls?"

She winces. "I didn't realize the time, but I always call her after hours if there's an important meeting coming up. I needed to deal with it now."

"Why not tomorrow, or better yet, when you're better?" I try not to sound like I'm barking orders, but I'm worried she's not putting herself first.

She takes a sip of water. Good. "That would be too late. The meeting's tomorrow."

Not good.

"You really think I'm going to allow you to work tomorrow when you've been this sick?"

She scoffs. "What are you going to do about it? Tie me up?" Her eyes flare at her own suggestion. "Wait, don't answer that. But seriously, you live on the other side of the city. You can't constantly keep me under watch."

Walking around to her side of the bed, I tip my finger under her chin and look her straight in the eyes. "Wanna bet? I'm moving in."

CHAPTER NINETEEN

JENSEN

Night after night on this couch is killing my back. It's in pieces.

Trying to stretch out in the tiny space, I hit accept on my usual early morning call from Mom. I didn't get a chance to break the news of me being an expectant dad before I raced back to Seattle, so they're still in the dark. My plan is to tell them face to face and after the wedding. Hollie and Ed, her fiancé, really don't need their day overshadowed by my bombshell.

"Bright and early as per," I say, keeping my voice low so I don't wake Kate. Yesterday was the first day without any sickness. Thank fuck. But she's lost visible weight.

"T-minus two weeks until the big day!"

"That's what you called to tell me at six in the morning?"

"No, I called you to tell you your dad and I are coming to town this weekend. We're staying with Chloe's parents and going to watch a show. Will you be around?"

"What day do you want to meet?"

"We were thinking on Friday, lunchtime."

It might be a good time to tell them about my news... "Yeah, it should be fine." The temptation to invite Kate to meet them opens my mouth, but I quickly clamp it shut. Mom, especially, is going to have so many questions about us, mainly if we're together.

Yeah, me too, Mom.

"Great. Make a reservation at that cute Italian place for us, will you?"

"Yeah, sure." I wince, my back cracking when I stretch again. This fucking couch.

"Everything okay?" she enquires, not missing a beat.

"Yeah. Just not sleeping well."

"Hmm. You sound preoccupied."

"I'm fine. Just got a lot on my mind, that's all."

"In the offseason?"

"Yeah."

"Jensen. Don't bullshit a bullshitter."

I bark out a laugh. "Mom!" Leaning back, I look down the hallway and wince. She's already about to kill me for moving in, never mind waking her, too.

"Are you seeing someone?"

"How in the hell did you guess that?"

"So you are?"

"No." *Un-fucking-fortunately.* "What have I said or done in the last sixty seconds that's brought you to that conclusion?"

"You're tired. You don't sound like you're at home since your voice is echoing, and your bedroom doesn't echo. And you're clearly trying not to wake someone."

Fuck me, she's good.

"I'm staying at a friend's place."

"Friend being a girl?" Her voice raises with undeniable excitement.

"It's a girl, yeah, but she isn't my girlfriend."

"Do you want her to be?"

"Why are you talking to me like I'm sixteen?"

"Because you're hiding things like a teenager."

I groan. "I'll fill you in on Friday."

"Why not now?"

"Because she's down the other end of the hallway!"

"Ah-hah! Wait, you aren't in bed together?"

"Yeah, this is my cue to end the call. Bye, Mom, see you on Friday!"

"Hang on a min—"

I throw my phone down on the comforter in front of me.

"I would pay good money to hear that all again."

Kate stands at the entryway to her bedroom, dressed in a fitted black suit. Her hair is up in a bun this morning.

Striding into the kitchen, she hunts through the fridge and pulls out the morning smoothie I've started preparing for her, packed with all the vitamins she needs. "You're making my place messy. It looks like shit."

"My back feels like shit." Rising from the couch, I straighten out and feel another crack. "I'm going to order an airbed."

She goes to speak, but I hold up a hand. "Before you say no, I'll take it down every day."

"That wasn't what I was going to say." Her gaze lingers just long enough on my bare chest before she snaps her head away and turns to the cupboard, pulling out some cereal.

"What were you going to say? And are you feeling well enough to go to work?"

She turns back to the counter and sets the cereal box down.

Lucky Charms? *Just pour yourself a bowl of gestational diabetes, Katherine.*

"Yes, I'm taking the chance while I don't want to puke my guts up. The longer I can put off telling work, the better. Also..." She pauses while pouring the cereal into her bowl. "If you want, we can share a bed. Mine is huge, and we can form some sort of pillow barrier."

She looks up nervously at me, and my dick twitches in the athletic shorts I'm wearing.

Walking towards the kitchen, I come to stand right next to her, and instantly, I'm hit with her familiar fruity scent. "I'm not getting in your bed, Kate."

I begin inspecting the nutritional facts on the back of the box. I have no intention of stopping her from eating what she wants, but I know it'll rile her up.

"Why not?" She grabs the box from me and sets it back down on the other side of her.

As I lean, I see the way her skin reacts to my proximity. "Because I want you and not your pity."

Her breath snags in her throat, and I see the way her chest moves up and down more rapidly. "You know that's not happening."

"Your body tells me differently." Moving behind her, I stand with my bare chest to her back, and I swear she moves back to press into my fully aroused cock. Picking up the milk, my hands work either side of her as I unscrew the carton and begin pouring it into her cereal. "Silly, traitorous body telling me everything you don't with your words."

Once I'm finished pouring, my hand moves lower, and I spread my left palm across her stomach. "When is your first scan?"

She's breathless when she whispers. "This Friday at three. I was going to tell you today; I got the email confirmation late last night."

Quick lunch with Mom and Dad, then.

"Do you want to find out what we're having?" I whisper into the shell of her ear.

"I guess it makes it easier to plan everything, but I haven't decided yet. Do you?"

Yes. "I do. But this is your call, Mommy."

She doesn't fight to move away from me, and warmth floods my chest.

Only a matter of time, Katherine.

"When you want me in your bed again, and not just because

of my back, just say the word. But until then, it's the air mattress."

Her chest continues to rise and fall rapidly. "I need to eat this and get to work."

"I'll take you."

KATE

The level of tired I am as I walk through the front door and mindlessly pull off my heels is staggering.

Is this normal? If so, snaps to any woman who goes through pregnancy more than once because I'm approaching only seven weeks and already a mess.

"Hey." Jensen walks out of the bathroom and strides toward me. He's still in the gym wear he dropped me off in earlier and has spent most of today at his place working out. "I was going to pick you up, remember?" He takes my laptop bag from my shoulder and sets it down by the front door.

"Final meeting got canceled, so I took an Uber."

"You could've called me." He narrows his brows, "No, you should've called me. But since you're back now, can I talk to you for a second?"

"Yeah, sure." I stand there waiting for him to begin.

Reaching out, he takes my left hand in his. The feel of his palm against mine sparks tingles throughout my body. He guides me toward the couch, his blanket neatly folded over the arm and pillow to one side.

I look around. "Did you get an air bed?"

"Yeah, but I told you, I'll set up right before bed and take it down each morning."

"Jensen, just come and sleep in my bed. Or I can clear out the mess in the spare room and set you up a bed if you insist on staying here. Which you don't need to, by the way. I'm feeling better."

"Are you Kate? Or are you just pretending like you aren't exhausted and constantly nauseous?"

God, I hate it when he's right. Which is all the fucking time.

"What did you want to talk to me about?"

Looking down at his sneakers, he scuffs the floor lightly. "My sister, Hollie, is getting married in a couple of weeks. I want you to come with me. It'll be a chance to meet my family."

"I don't think I can. I have a crazy month in August. With all the time I've taken off with sickness, I'm so far behind with my clients."

"You can't fly out on the Friday and then home on the Sunday?"

I shake my head. "I can't take *any* time off."

I watch the way his jaw ticks, and I can tell what he's thinking—I'm avoiding meeting his family, and I'm keeping him and his loved ones at arm's length. "Is this really about work, because in around seven months, you're going to be off for a year."

A year? Unlikely. "All the more reason for me to push on with work now."

"You're going to run yourself into the ground."

"I can handle it," I reply.

"At least let me take you out for your birthday. It's a couple of days before I have to leave town for the wedding. When I get back, I'll be straight into preseason conditioning."

I pull back. "Like as part of the group or just us?"

He turns to me on the couch, and he's so freakin' handsome. "Just us."

"Not a date, though, right?"

He blows out a breath, sounding frustrated. "No, Princess, not a date. I couldn't possibly subject you to one of those with me. But maybe as your friend? If you'll consider me as that now."

I think back to all Felicity said a few days ago and how he's told me he wants us to be more. I've just come out of one relationship with a guy who wanted more, and now I find myself pregnant with the baby of another. It's too much, too soon. But equally, the more I get to know the man sitting next to me, the more he surprises me with his loyalty. He didn't run. He's standing by me, and that earns a lot of respect in my book.

"Yeah." I smile at him and take his hand back in mine. "Sure, as friends, why not. Just...nowhere that serves meat."

CHAPTER TWENTY

JENSEN

"So, who is she?" my mother asks.

"Who's who?" I say, playing stupid.

"Don't leave your mother in suspense any longer, son," Dad says, perusing the menu. "Other than the wedding, speculating on who your new lady is has taken over every single conversation."

Checking the time once more, I sit back in my seat and fold my arms across my chest. "I'll be honest with you. I don't have a girlfriend at this point."

"At this point? What's that supposed to mean?" Mom responds.

Scrubbing a hand over my face, I consider my next words carefully. No matter how I put this next thirty seconds, the glass of beer currently in my dad's hand is likely to end up in his lap. "I'm going to be a dad, and the woman carrying my baby isn't my biggest fan. We're stepping into the friendship zone, but she doesn't want a romantic relationship with me."

There, that should do it.

"Jesus," Dad slurs, quickly setting his glass back on the table.

Mom's mouth continues to hang open.

"My intention was to tell you when I came back home for the suit fittings, but you remember how I had to rush back to Seattle, right?"

Mom's head nods slowly, but still, no words materialize.

"She's been struggling with morning sickness, which turns out to be more like all-day sickness." I pick up my drink and take a sip, checking my watch again. "Anyway, I needed to get back and help her."

"Do we know this girl?" my mom asks.

They've met Kate a few times at games, but other than that, I've only mentioned her to my parents in passing and normally as part of a conversation about our wider group. "Kind of. Her name's Kate."

Or Princess.

"Why isn't she here today?" Mom still looks phased out. The news is clearly not sinking in.

"She's at work. She's a lawyer."

"Oh, Kate! Felicity's friend, right?" Dad snaps his fingers.

"When is she due?" Mom asks.

"Actually, we're heading for her first scan this afternoon. We should get a better idea of the date, but it's estimated to be March twenty-third."

"Wow. Jensen, I'm literally speechless." Mom continues to stare at me. "Was it something that just happened? I mean, I know the baby isn't planned, but you seem really thrilled." She smiles at me sweetly.

The smile I've worn this entire time grows wider. "No, it wasn't planned, but it was meant to be."

Mom cocks her head to the side. "What do you mean?"

I think back to the day she told me and specifically the date, July sixteenth. "Do you believe in fate?"

"Absolutely," Dad chimes in.

"Well, this is it for me. She's it for me."

"But you're just friends?" Mom questions.

"For now, yeah. But I'm working on it. She doesn't do commitment."

"Neither have you since..." Dad hesitates before saying her name. "Well, since Lauren."

"She's what I want," I reply. "No girl has come close to her."

Dad nods in understanding. "Then go get her."

"And bring her to the wedding," Mom adds. "I need to meet her."

I wince. "She's working and can't get the time off." I sigh. "She's a workaholic, and this whole baby thing has left her reeling."

Mom smiles empathetically. "You've got your work cut out for you if you want to start dating her and upgrade from a co-parent."

Shaking my head, I raise a hand to attract a server's attention. "Dating is just a steppingstone to being my wife."

KATE

"Katherine Monroe," the sonographer calls out across the empty waiting room.

Jensen leaps out of his seat and smiles down at me, holding out his hand for me to take. "I can walk by myself. You do know that, right?"

"Sure, Princess, but this is the best part. The first time we get to hear our baby's heartbeat. So," he waggles his fingers to invite me once again, "take my hand."

Sliding mine into his, I can't deny that the nerves I've been feeling since the moment this appointment was confirmed die down almost completely.

I look up at him. "You do know you can start using my real name whenever you're ready."

We begin walking toward the scan room when Jensen leans into me. "I'll make you a deal. I'll stop calling you Princess when you start calling me JJ."

I scoff. "Why is that so important to you?"

He goes to answer but doesn't get time to reply before the sonographer speaks. "So nice to meet you both. I'm Jayne, and I'll be conducting your prenatal ultrasound." She looks over at me and smiles. "If you can hop onto the bed here, we need to get everything ready so you can meet your baby for the first time." She then looks at Jensen, but I'm certain she doesn't recognize who he is, clearly not a hockey fan. "Is this dad?"

"Yes indeed," he replies without hesitation.

I kick off my heels and lie on the bed, getting myself comfortable. As I stare up at the poster of the stages of pregnancy, the nerves that Jensen seemed to calm come racing back to me. I can't be a mom. I wasn't built to be a mom. Moms think about their babies years before they're born, and here's me, lying here with no plan or fucking clue what I'm doing.

"Hey." Jensen pulls his chair closer to my bed and reaches out, taking hold of my hand. "All okay?"

"Yep," I reply, still staring straight up at the poster, totally overwhelmed.

"Okay." Jayne tucks a sheet into the top of my work pants and rolls my white blouse up to just below my bra. Holding a bottle of jelly substance, she squeezes some onto the probe. "Let's meet your bundle of joy. This might feel a little cold at first."

She isn't wrong. As soon as the jelly and probe hit my warm skin, I shudder. Jensen squeezes my hand tighter.

"Okay. Let's find that heartbeat."

Moving the probe around, silence falls across the room. Jensen continues squeezing my hand while we both stare expectantly at the screen.

"Where are you, little one?" I ask.

"Oh, don't worry, it can take a moment to find them, especially at this early stage."

I look to Jensen. "Yeah, it'll be fine."

He looks back at me. "I know. Jayne was responding to you, Princess."

Wait, did I say that?

"Oh right, okay," Jayne says in a surprised way.

Jensen's eyes flash to the screen, as do mine.

"What is it?" he asks, his tone less relaxed than before.

"Well, we don't have a 'little one.'" She smiles at us both warmly. "Rather a little two!"

"Ohmygod!" I gasp as Jayne makes some adjustments to the image, and two tiny heartbeats come through the speaker into clear focus on the monitor.

"I, I..." I turn back to Jensen, whose head is dropped between his shoulders.

When I squeeze his hand, he raises his head, and I see the tears shining in his eyes. "Two?" he croaks out and then clears his throat. "We have two babies?"

"Yes, both with healthy, strong heartbeats."

"Wow." I watch the screen in awe—in awe of nature, of my body, and the magic unfolding before me. The whole experience feels surreal.

"Congratulations to you both. You have an instant family." Jayne begins cleaning me up. "As you're eight weeks, you do now have the option of a blood test to determine the sex of the babies. Is this something you would like? It's a very personal choice, of course."

I look over at Jensen, who gives me a nod, indicating it's my call. "Can we make that decision afterward? It's just with this news and all the information..." Plus, I kind of had my heart set on finding out the sex via a scan. Something about that feels more special.

Jayne smiles. "Of course. Your next scan will be scheduled for eighteen weeks, and there is an opportunity to find out then, when you've had more time to talk."

Jensen squeezes my hand in reassurance and then rises from his chair and stands over me, placing a chaste kiss on my forehead before whispering, "I'm so fucking proud of you."

THE DRIVE back to my apartment is drenched in silence, John Legend playing softly in the background.

Jensen eventually speaks first. "The season will be in full swing in March."

Jayne mentioned that with twins, I'm unlikely to go the full term, but even if they do deliver the babies early, it will still be right in the middle of the NHL season.

Babies, as in more than one. I will not hyperventilate. I. Will. Not.

I swear to God, if someone had told me back in June that I'd be expecting twins in March with Jensen Jones, I'd have checked on their drug of choice.

"I'll have plenty of people around if anything happens and you're not with me."

"Hmmm." He signals to take a left onto my street. "I'm going to buy us an SUV. Your Mercedes is too small, and I want something safer."

He's probably right about my A-Class. "This is fine," I say, looking around his Tesla.

"I'll keep it because it's a great car. But I want something bigger for family days."

"What did you have in mind?"

He looks over at me, his sunglasses hiding his eyes but not his smirk. "For the car or family days?"

I can't help myself; I want to know. "Family days."

"Well, first, we'll need a bigger trunk for a double stroller.

Then, we'll need to buy a bigger diaper bag for double the stuff. Then you've got all the toys and equipment."

"Yeah, I guess so."

"And my girl. She doesn't travel light."

"You never stop, do you? Any excuse to goad me."

He pulls into the allocated visitor space next to my car and takes off his glasses. "I'm not goading you, Princess. I just want you to stop fooling yourself."

He climbs out of the car and rounds it, pulling my passenger door open. Holding out his hand, I slip mine into his for the second time today. "I'll give you one thing."

He waggles his brows at me in jest. "Oh yeah, what's that?"

"You're more of a gentleman than I gave you credit."

We walk across to the stairwell and begin climbing the couple of flights to my apartment. "You are going to make some lucky girl very happy one day."

Jensen stops, coming to a complete halt.

I turn around and look at him. "I mean it. You really will."

I'm three steps higher than him, and even though he has several inches on me at six-three, I look down at his constricted pupils.

He counters the difference and steps up so we're face to face and only inches apart. "Kate. Have you not been listening to a thing I've been saying these past few weeks?" His breath heats my entire body.

"I could say the same thing. You know what this is, Jensen. A friendship."

Shaking his head, he looks off to the side and then back at me. "I could make you so damn happy every single day. And when you finally drop your walls and let me in, you'll wonder what your life looked like before you had me holding you, kissing you, and warming your body each night." He reaches out and runs a hand through my hair, his palm coming to rest at the back of my head. "There are two hearts on the line here."

"I don't think that's true. People co-parent all the time and provide loving surroundings for their children."

"No. That's not what I mean." He closes his eyes, almost like he's in pain. "I'm not talking about our babies; I'm talking about *us*. You won't be only denying your heart a chance at happiness. You'll crush mine, too. There's only one place it wants to be, and that's in your hands. You're holding it in your hands. Just be careful with it, okay, Princess?"

My knees go weak. *Holy fuck.*

"That's what I'm trying to do, Jensen. I'm trying to keep the lines between us clear. I don't want to hurt anyone in all this. I think you're going to be the best daddy ever, and I don't want to fuck anything up between us. We're building a great friendship."

"Stop using the F word."

"Fuck? I use it all the time."

He smirks. "I know you do, potty mouth. The other F word. Friendship. It offends me when it leaves your lips."

"But that's what this is. A friendship, and we're a team."

"You know when you fall in love with me, I'm never going to let you live this down. Every time I slide inside you, I'm going to remind you that friends don't do this." He looks down at my pinched, traitorous thighs and then back up at me, his brown eyes more of an amber from the flames. "Just like your body is reminding you of that night. The night I put not one, but two babies inside you."

CHAPTER TWENTY-ONE

KATE

"Don't tell me you're pregnant now, too?"

Felicity and Luna walk towards me down the hallway outside the room where my and Luna's prenatal class is about to begin.

"No, thank the Lord. Jon and I barely have enough time to see each other, let alone throw a baby into the mix!"

"Aww, but just imagine a cute baby Morgan toddling around the place," Luna croons.

Felicity props a hand on her hip. "Hmm, I have enough on with the thirty-five-year-old baby I have at home. Since he's been working full-time with Jack's college team, I swear he's regressing in maturity."

I snort a laugh. "What are you doing here, anyway?"

"Dropping Luna off."

"Zach's meeting with his agent clashed with this," Luna clarifies.

"And I was heading this way, so I forced her to take a ride with me. Plus, I need to give you this." Felicity hands me a pink envelope and plants a kiss on my cheek. "Happy birthday, sweetie."

"Thank you." I pull open the envelope and look at the card. A group of three girls walking down the street, arm in arm, with "Happy Birthday Boss Bitch" stamped across the top.

"You got the bouquet, right?" Luna asks.

"I did. Thank you so much. They're beautiful."

"We thought you had enough houseplants, so we decided to go in on a ridiculous number of flowers," Felicity laughs. "You can never have too many blooms."

"You're the best, you know that?"

Luna smiles and gives me a hug. "We know, but we miss you. Feels like we only meet every couple of weeks or so for these classes."

"I know," I drawl. "Work is kicking my ass, and so are these babies."

"I can't believe you're having twins!" Felicity rests her flat palm over my stomach. "Have they said anything about whether they'll take you to full term?"

"My doctor says we'll see how things progress." I look down at where her hand is over my still-flat stomach and groan. "I'm going to be massive, aren't I?"

Felicity nods. "I won't lie. Yes."

"I won't be able to see my vagina, will I?"

"I said this to Zach the other day. He said—"

Quickly, I hold up a hand. "I'm gonna stop you right there. I'm down for anyone having a good sex life, but since mine is non-existent, I need to wallow in my self-pity."

"So Jensen really is sleeping on the couch then?" Luna sounds surprised.

"He's got an air mattress. We're going to organize my spare bedroom so he can move in there."

"Why doesn't he just go back to his?"

Felicity asks a fair question, and one I really don't have an answer to. The truth is he could easily head back to his place now that I'm not sick, and I could insist he does. But I like having him around. I think I'd miss him if he wasn't there. Even his attempts to get under my skin are kind of endearing.

I look down at my feet. "I guess I won't be able to see these either?"

"Don't deflect," Felicity scolds.

"What can I say?" I look back up at her and Luna. "We're working on a friendship, and when preseason kicks in, he'll be out most of the time anyway."

"Hmmm..."

"Hmmm..." Luna echoes Felicity.

"I'm not sleeping with him."

"It wouldn't matter if you are," Luna says.

"He's just a friend, and anyway, can you imagine if we got together?" I scoff. "It would be like taming wildfire."

"That I can agree with." Felicity reaches into her tote and pulls out the keys to her Mini. "You are both as bad as each other."

"I'm impressed with how well you're working together though. He's so attentive!" Luna says, sounding more than impressed.

I nod. "Oh, I know. It took me most of this week to convince him he didn't need to attend today's session on relaxation techniques during pregnancy."

"I genuinely think he'd eat, sleep, go to the bathroom, and poop for you if he could."

I look at Luna. "You really just say it, don't you."

"The filter is entirely lifted these days, babe." She hooks her arm through mine as Felicity turns to walk away.

"See you two preggos later. I'm off for a nice glass of crisp wine."

"Fuck off," I mouth back.

"JENSEN, this place is booked out months in advance," I say as we pull up outside the grand entrance of *Auberge,* one of the finest French restaurants in Washington state.

"And?" He turns to me in the driver's seat. Dressed in all black, his shirt is open at the top, revealing a tantalizing glimpse of his sculpted chest along with his gold chain.

"I know you're famous, but how did you get a table so last minute?"

He shakes his head. "You just don't get it, do you, Princess? But since it's your birthday, I'll let you off."

The valet opens our car doors, and I climb out. Tonight, I'm wearing my favorite dress with a corset bodice. The red lace skirt fans out from the waist, stopping just above my knee. I'll be the first to admit I struggled to zip it up. Either I'm putting on weight, or my belly is growing, and at almost nine weeks pregnant with twins, I guess it's no wonder.

"Don't get what?" I say, taking the hand he's offering me and walking inside.

"I didn't book this last minute."

My heart trips out as the host guides us to our table, set up with a small lamp in the center. "You've been planning this?"

How many more times is this man going to surprise me? But more than that, how many times am I going to surprise myself? A man booking a table well in advance of my acceptance, assuming I'd say yes or even want to go with him, would be the biggest red flag for me.

And here's the real kicker in all this—even though I insisted we'd be going as friends, a growing part of me wishes tonight was more than that. The last time I was at a restaurant with a man, I was searching for an opportunity to let him down gently. Yet tonight, I'm cussing myself for putting the brakes on and backing away.

Jensen declines the host's invitation and instead pulls out my chair. "Take a seat, Princess."

I narrow my eyes at him. "I have a confession."

Now seated, he pauses with a glass of water to his mouth. "What's that?"

"You once asked me if I thought I was always right when it came to you. And I said yes."

"You did. I think it was right before we fucked."

I pinch my thighs together for the hundredth time tonight and steady myself. *This man.* "Well, actually, I don't think I know much about you at all."

He smiles a triumphant grin. "You're forgiven. Not many people do."

"Oh, it wasn't an apology. It was a statement." I return his smug smile and tear a piece of warm bread from the baskets provided, dipping it in the selection of oils. "Not even Jessie?"

He shrugs. "Kind of. He knows more than most. Just like I do about him."

Jensen successfully gets under my skin, but the way I want to tear away at the wrapping and reveal the real man beneath is profound. "I get that. I'm a pretty closed book myself."

Picking up the oil I keep dipping into, he slides it across to me so I have it all to myself. "You don't say. I don't think even Luna and Felicity know the full Katherine Monroe."

I quirk a challenging brow. "And you think you've got me all figured out."

He nods, chewing around some bread himself. "Only one part I'm struggling with."

"What's that?"

"Your family. Specifically your parents."

My stomach drops. I'm reluctant to talk about myself, but I'm dead set against discussing my parents. The restaurant is hot and clammy all of a sudden, and my dress feels even tighter than when I fought to do up the zip.

My heart races for all the wrong reasons when I finally look back at Jensen. "Don't even go there. They just are the way they are, and they'll never change."

His jaw visibly tightens, and I watch the way he swallows his mouthful, like a dog ready to pounce for threatening something he's desperate to protect.

He sits back in his chair and scratches at his temple, and I know he's slowly working out the reasons why I keep myself so locked away.

Eventually, he sits forward, his thick forearms resting on the table, his hands clasped together, as he pins me in place with his brown eyes.

I'm powerless to move as I wait for the question I know is coming.

"Are they mean to you, Princess?"

And there it is.

My head screams at me to slam the door shut in his face, to deflect this conversation.

Where is the waiter? Aren't they ready to serve us our next course or something? I look around the room.

"Kate." Jensen reins me in softly with his voice.

"What?" I whisper.

"I'm going to need you to tell me baby. Are they mean to you?"

I need out of this hot as fuck restaurant.

Reaching across the table, he takes my hand in his and interlaces our fingers. Stroking his calloused thumb softly against my skin, the calming sensation is grounding.

I take a deep breath and blow it out slowly, my heart rate returning to something like normal. "Not in the classic sense."

I swear to God, I hear him growl above the ambient music playing in the background. "Classic sense?"

"Do we have to talk about them?" I try once more to deflect.

He nods slowly. "They're grandparents to my babies and mean to my girl. So yeah, I say we do." I can hear the way he fights back the anger and works to keep his tone soft. Jensen Jones is all kinds of caveman.

To think I once thought he didn't give a shit about anyone

but himself. If this conversation wasn't anything but funny, I'd laugh at my comical misjudgments.

With a deep sigh, I try and keep this as succinct as possible. "My brother, Easton, is the only real blood family I have. My parents, Violet and Henry, are cold. They see East and I more as projects and trophy cabinets. They spend more time boasting about who we are and what we do than paying attention to us as people. Easton is the favorite since he's an incredibly successful entrepreneur and the CEO of a multi-national private equity firm based in Dubai. He's out there most of the time with his wife and my niece, Ava. They are my only real family, but I can't exactly drop by for a coffee on the weekend." I offer my best fake smile.

Where is the server?

Jensen stares down at the pristine white tablecloth, grinding his molars. "So Easton is married with a family, but you told me in the text that your parents wouldn't do well knowing your news."

I press my lips together to stop them from shaking. "Easton is the eldest and the favorite. He's also a man who doesn't need to stay home and take care of the baby or take maternity leave."

Snatching up the elderflower spritz I ordered, I take a large mouthful to try and quench my dry mouth. It's gross, and I forcefully swallow it and then rinse my mouth with water.

Turning back to Jensen, he remains fixed in place, clearly digesting what I've told him. There's a murderous look to him that I'm not sure many have seen before. But it doesn't scare me. I know he's hurting on my behalf. I guess to someone like him with supportive parents, this must be hard to believe and nearly impossible to wrap your head around.

"That's what they expect? For you to prioritize your career above everything else? Fuck what you really want?" he bites.

I nod cautiously. "They paid for a lot of my education, for the best schools, and with their connections in the legal world, they secured the best placements when I was younger. They got me my current job with Mark Preston."

He balks. "You're kidding, right? Surely you don't believe that kind of bullshit, Kate." Taking a steadying breath and with the free hand that's not in mine, he drums his pointer finger on the table in sync with his words. "*You* got that job yourself. Your talent, your drive, the fact that you work yourself into the ground day and night. I've never seen anyone with more commitment."

I flush at the onslaught of compliments. "Thank you."

"Why do you put up with it, Kate? They're treating you like an extension of themselves. Everything you do is for them."

"It's not. My career is what I want." I repeat the same words I've regurgitated more times than I can count.

His thumb begins tracing patterns over the top of my hand again, and shivers trickle throughout my body. "When was the last time they hugged you?"

I want to cry, but I'm determined not to. I hate this conversation, but I also love it at the same time. I appreciate that he's pushing me to say all this out loud, but I hate the way it makes me feel to admit it—like their treatment of me truly is abhorrent.

"I can't remember," I whisper.

He bites the inside of his cheek this time. "When was the last time they told you they loved you?"

Too much. Too far.

"Why do you care?" I scold, not meaning it at all, but this is way too close for comfort now.

"Don't push me away. Don't shut me out. You know I care." He squeezes our hands tighter.

I say nothing but drop my head, my long hair coming to my rescue again.

"When, Kate?" he repeats softly.

"I don't know, okay? I can't remember."

Desperate to get away and hide emotions I'm still not ready

to share, I push back my chair and pull my hand away, grabbing my purse from the table. "I need to use the bathroom. Order me whatever you're having. Just not—"

"Meat, vegetable stir fry, or another elderflower spritz," he finishes for me. I can tell he's disappointed I won't open up further, but I also see the understanding look in his eyes. He knows he's taken me as far as I can go for now.

"Yeah," I smile. "Just not those."

"I HAD AN AMAZING NIGHT. THANK YOU," I say, walking back to the valet to collect Jensen's car. I truly did. When I returned to the table, having fixed my blush and taken a few deep breaths, it was like he knew we needed to switch gears. So, instead of talking about my parents, he told me all about his route to the NHL. Turns out, while I was studying hard for Yale, he was spending every waking hour on the ice which, for once, doesn't leave me surprised but does turn me on. This man's commitment and loyalty to what he loves is...yeah, wow.

Making our way outside, he grabs my hand and pulls me into him, his familiar cologne overtaking my senses. In my heels, I'm closer to his height, but he tips my chin up so I look straight into his eyes. "I've heard that on their birthdays, Princesses should be kissed."

I roll my eyes; butterflies are *absolutely* not present right now. "Insufferable. But okay, if it's on the cheek."

He nods lightly and smiles. "That's open to interpretation."

And now I'm thinking about him touching my ass. "You know what I mean."

He brings his hand to my stomach and smooths his palm over the red fabric. "I'll never stop asking, you know that, right?" Leaning down, he kisses me lightly on the cheek, memories of the night at Riley's and then in Oxford flashing through my mind like a slideshow.

Another flash, but this time not in my mind.

Flash again.

"Hey!" Jensen shouts, striding over to the guy who just took our picture. "What are you doing?"

"Jensen Jones, right?" The man holds out his hand for Jensen to shake, but he doesn't.

"Why are you taking a picture of me and my...my friend."

"Dude, she is *not* your friend," the man taking photos counters.

"Why are you taking a picture?" Jensen grits out once more.

He shrugs an entitled shrug. "You know how it is. You see someone famous; you take a picture and post it."

"No. I don't, actually. It's an invasion of our privacy. Delete it, please." Jensen tags on the please, trying to remain professional, but I can tell he's seething.

"You're mauling your girl in the middle of a restaurant parking lot. I'd say that's not private."

"Please just delete it."

"Jesus, fine. Chill out." The guy takes his phone out of his pocket and taps the screen a couple of times, showing the evidence. "Done."

Jensen nods. "Got a pen?"

"Huh?" the man responds.

I reach into my bag and fetch one out. I go nowhere without a pen. "Here you go."

Jensen pops the cap on the Sharpie and points to the white Scorpions baseball cap the guy's wearing. "I'll sign it for you."

His eyes light up as he pulls it off and hands it over. "Amazing, thanks."

Jensen moves across to his car, which is now parked by the valet, leans against it, and begins writing across the brim.

"Here you go, buddy. Have a good night." He sets it back on

the guy's head and then retakes my hand, leading me to the passenger door.

"Hey!" The guy shouts just as Jensen gets in the driver's side and takes off.

I watch over my shoulder as the man starts waving his arms around. "What's the matter with him? He got a signature, didn't he?" I turn back to Jensen.

He pulls out of the restaurant driveway and heads for the freeway. "Must be what I wrote."

"Which was?"

"Well, obviously, my signature. Followed by a friendly reminder not to be a prick."

I snort a laugh. "Takes one to know one, I guess."

Reaching over the center console, he smooths his hand over my stomach. "I had my hand on your stomach and my lips to your cheek. It was questionable at best. The media won't find out until we say it's time."

CHAPTER TWENTY-TWO

JENSEN

Last night was perfect. The only thing that would've made it better was taking my girl to bed and showing her just how perfect she is.

But I got the next best thing—she opened up to me for the first time since I laid eyes on her. Kate Monroe does not open up to people unless they're part of her inner circle, that much is obvious, and last night, she told me about her parents. Something I don't think she's ever spoken about before.

No, she told me about Violet and Henry. They aren't parents; no parents measure their child by her success and then set the bar so high she'll never be good enough.

They never hugged her or kissed her. I'm not even sure if they've ever told her they love her. She shut down on me at that point, and it broke my fucking heart to witness the pain she's still in even years after she left home.

I want to *annihilate* them.

Last night, when she went to bed, I spent hours researching their law practice and then looking up her brother. I think I got only a small glimpse into her family and her childhood, but

Easton knows it all. He has to. It took everything in me last night not to contact him. The only thing that stopped me was knowing that if I had, Kate would never forgive me. I'm already treading on volatile ground, and it takes only one false move for the land mine to go off in my face.

And that's the issue right there—it takes a lot to open the door to her trust, but only a tiny infraction for it to slam shut, the bolt to slide across, and the drawbridge to rise.

To everyone else, she's an enigma. But not to me. I don't even need a map. I just need her to see that I've got her, and she doesn't have to be anyone else with me.

"Morning." Kate yawns her way into her kitchen, pulling open the cupboards to find her favorite mug. "Hey, have you seen the...uh...Sleeping Beauty mug? It was in here yesterday." She moves a few mugs around to search the back.

"It's normally at the front, right?" I rise from the air bed and stroll over to her. Her black silky sleep shorts rise just above the curve of her ass as she reaches up to the top cupboard.

Fucking hell, she's got everything.

"Yeah. I normally have my one cup of caffeine in it every morning."

I know, Princess.

I also know exactly where the mug is.

Coming up behind her, she stills when I press my chest to her back and slowly reach around her, my palm splayed out across her stomach as I maneuver her to face me.

She looks up at me, her blonde hair still disheveled from sleep, although not nearly messy enough for my liking.

Placing both hands on either side of the counter, I lean down until we're nose to nose. "It's on the coffee machine, ready to brew."

"It is?"

I nod and lean into the side of her neck, my lips not touching the sensitive flesh but my breath firing off every reaction across her body. "It is."

"How did you kn—"

"You aren't seriously going to ask me how I know that's your favorite mug, are you? Time and time again, you do me a disservice, baby."

"Jensen, you can't keep doing this."

"Because you want me to kiss you, yeah?"

"No."

"Your body doesn't lie to me, even if your mouth does."

She places a hand on my chest and slowly pushes me back. "What plans do you have today?"

Sensing this is as far as she'll let me go, I walk back over to my air mattress and begin letting it down. "I needed to talk to you about that."

Mug between her hands, she walks over and sits on the couch, eyeing me. "Shoot."

"I think I'm gonna move back into my place."

Silence for a few beats before she clears her throat. I keep my back to her while I start folding the air bed away.

"Preseason will start as soon as I'm back from Alberta. I don't want to get in your way when I'm back and forth with traveling."

"Yeah...okay, I guess the sickness has stopped, and if you want, I can give you a key to here just in case."

Shoving the mattress back in its bag, I turn to the blonde-haired beauty sitting on her couch, her favorite Disney Princess in hand. "Just in case of what?"

"Well, um, just in case you forgot something or want to stop by for any reason."

I smirk and make my way through to the bathroom. "Okay, Princess."

"So I guess I'll see you when you get back from the wedding? Tell your sister I said congratulations."

Kate stands in the entryway as I check over the apartment for anything I've left behind. I don't want to leave, but two things are forcing me. The air mattress and the fact I don't want her to set up a spare room for me when she'll need all the storage space she can get for the million baby products I plan on buying, especially since it's now double of everything. But I also need to change up my game. It's risky, but I need to remove myself from her space and hope she'll feel my absence in the same way I'm going to miss the shit out of her.

Bags finally on my back, I stop next to her at the door, taking her chin between my thumb and forefinger. "What are you doing when I get back from Alberta?"

"Working."

"No shit, you're always working. After work, what are you doing?"

"Nothing, I guess."

"Keep it that way. I'll pick you up from work on Monday, and we'll go baby shopping."

I don't miss the flash of excitement across her face. "Aren't we supposed to wait until I'm twelve weeks before we start buying? You know, when we're out of the danger zone?"

"The sonographer and doctors were all happy at the initial visits. Plus, we need to talk about setting up two nurseries—one here and one at mine."

She pinches her brows together in surprise at my statement. Or is it disappointment? I fucking hope so. "Yeah, I guess they will have two homes."

They won't have two homes. They'll have one, and so will my girl—my apartment.

But I decide to play along for now. "Twice the love."

Kissing her on the cheek, I open the door and close it quietly behind me, walking down the hallway and away from the girl I desperately don't want to leave.

"Jensen!"

Whipping around from where I'm waiting at the elevator, Kate comes flying toward me. At first, I fight to remove the shit-eating grin from my face because that didn't take long. But the closer she gets, the more panic-stricken she is.

Waving her cell in her hand, the screen is lit up. "They know!" she blurts out.

Holding both arms out, she crashes into me, and I wrap myself around her in a bear hug. "Who knows?"

"My parents, Violet and Henry. Either that guy at the restaurant didn't delete the images like he said he did, or someone else took shots, too."

She hands me her phone and I begin scrolling through the last few texts from Violet.

VIOLET

Care to explain what the hell is going on here?

Image at the restaurant.

I don't watch ice hockey, but this is the Scorpions' goalkeeper, right? The one who is pictured with a different female each night. The one who has no respect for women and seems proud of it.

And my daughter has become his latest victim. Or is it that she willingly lowered herself to him?

You look cheap. Consider your career over.

They are finished.

"Where do they live?" I growl.

She takes the phone back from me, her eyes shining with tears. The strong, powerful, confident, and sassy Kate is totally gone, and in her place is a shy, defenseless girl. Her transformation needs no explanation now that I've read the utter bullshit in those messages coupled with her revelations last night.

"Across town. But they're probably at church. They go most mornings."

These people are "religious?"

"Doesn't matter. I'll wait for them to get home from their morning sermon and then offer them one they'll never forget."

Her eyes widen with fear. "You're going over there?"

The elevator doors open. "We both are. You think I'm just going to sit back and watch you get treated like this?"

"It's not your battle to fight, Jensen."

The elevator doors close behind me, and I frame her face with my palms. "People go to war to protect their country and freedoms. I go to war for my world."

She bites down on her bottom lip, and I don't know if it's to hide her smile or anxiety, but she's aware that she won't change my mind on this. "I need to change and grab my purse; I'll meet you downstairs."

"HOW LONG DOES the service usually take?" I glance down at my watch. We've been sitting in my car and waiting in their driveway for at least forty minutes. Ideally, I'd have gone in and made myself comfortable, eaten some of their luxurious food, and kicked back, but Kate doesn't have a key.

To her childhood home.

"They should be back any minute."

Her left knee bounces up and down as she sits in the passenger seat, her large sunglasses covering her pretty eyes. It's not even sunny out.

I place my hand on her knee to stop the bouncing and lean across to pull off her shades. "Look at me."

Biting her bottom lip again, she continues to stare straight ahead at the enormous mansion in front of us. "Look at me, Princess."

"Do you know what my parents will do if they hear you calling me that?"

Like I give a fuck.

"Kate. Look. At. Me."

Finally, she turns to look at me, her eyes puffy from the tears I know she's cried and fought to hide all the way here. "What?"

"You don't need these people and don't owe them a thing. You hear me?" I know she doesn't hear me. She thinks this whole thing is a terrible idea, and I can see it just by feeling the way she trembles beneath my touch.

"You don't know them like I do. All my life, it's been 'toe the line we set or pick up the pieces of the mess we'll make of your life.'"

"Life? By that, I assume you mean your career?"

"Yes, Jensen. My career, my job, aka my life."

"Your success doesn't define you, and neither do they."

Kate opens her mouth but then closes it quickly, casting her eyes from where my hand is resting in her lap up to the rearview mirror. "They're here."

CHAPTER TWENTY-THREE

KATE

"Ready?"

I watch as Henry gets out of their Land Rover and stalks toward the back of Jensen's car, his face twisted with anger.

My trembles intensify. "No."

"I'll do the talking."

Jensen opens his door and begins to climb out, but I grab his arm at the last minute. "Promise me." I look straight into his brown eyes, praying I can trust him. "Promise it's going to be okay."

Lifting my hand, he gently traces his lips across my knuckles. "One day, you won't need me to promise you anything. You'll just know."

A harsh throat clears from behind us, and when Jensen gets out of the car and closes the door behind him, I'm left in the passenger seat staring out of the driver's window at the way Henry scowls at him. His hands are on his hips, his glasses halfway down his nose, and a look of superiority written right across his face.

That look has never changed since the day I was born.

Oh, hell no, he isn't doing this to Jensen as well. I reach for the car door handle.

"Kate, nice of you to join us." Violet stands a couple of feet away from the men, clearly waiting for me to get out of the car.

"I don't have a key to the house, so we waited for you to get home."

"You don't have a key because it's not your home."

Jensen stops whatever he's saying and whips his head over. "What do you mean 'not your home?' She's your blood."

In response, she holds up a condescending hand. "Technically, you're trespassing here, but since you made the effort to wait around for us, let's go inside. I don't do discussions on my driveway."

Violet and Henry walk side by side up to the porch and then into the house as we follow. I can practically feel the anger flowing from Jensen as we step into the grand entrance, and he takes a look around.

There are no family pictures, only ones of us accepting degrees and achievements. The remaining images are of my parents meeting and socializing with big names and people in high places.

"Fuck me. This place is a shrine to them," Jensen says under his breath.

"Sure is." Touching his arm, I lead him to the study, where they hold all their meetings. "They won't offer you a drink."

Chuckling, he causally walks across the marble flooring, his hands in the pockets of his pants. "With the way your mom just looked at me, I'm happy to pass it up."

"Violet. I call her Violet. Don't refer to her as mom."

"She doesn't let you call her mom?"

I push on the large mahogany door that leads to the study. "I just prefer it that way."

"Jensen Jones?" Violet sits on one of the cold, black leather couches. "That's your name, correct?"

Without being invited, Jensen takes my hand in his and sits me right down next to him on a matching couch opposite my parents. "Not hockey fans, then?"

"No. We don't appreciate sports, especially..." Violet points at him. "Ones that aren't particularly refined."

Pulling his cap off his head, I think he's about to remove it since he's sitting in front of my parents, but instead, he turns it around and replaces it backward. "Oh well, nah, you won't like hockey then. You probably won't like me much thinking about it."

I smirk and Henry notices, raising an unimpressed brow. "I assume you're here to explain the pictures."

"We're here to respond to your texts. As I've always said to Kate, I prefer the old-fashioned way of communication," Jensen counters.

"I'm sorry, but the last time I checked, my daughter had the ability to speak."

Jensen eyes Violet. Crossing his leg over at the knee and making himself super comfortable, he replies, "Oh, so you are aware she's your daughter?"

"What the hell is that supposed to mean," Henry bites out.

"Would you like me to refer you to the texts you sent this morning, the things your *daughter* has told me, or the shameful way you look at her? Your call."

Removing his glasses, Henry looks Jensen straight in the eyes. He must be intimidated by his surroundings, but he doesn't show it, not one bit. "Son. Do you know who you're talking to?"

"Not really. I haven't given it much thought, to be honest. It's a bit like when I'm in a game—I assess the ice for threats and focus on those that pose the greatest risk. I don't see anything here."

I choke on my own saliva and sputter out a cough. *He really isn't intimidated.*

"Katherine. Can I have a word, please?" Violet stands and indicates she wants me to leave with her.

"What can't be said in this room?"

She looks to Jensen. "You aren't a part of this family, and whether you are having relations with our daughter or not doesn't make a difference. You aren't welcome here. You don't belong."

"He does," I blurt out. "He does belong, and soon enough, he will be a part of my family."

Jensen's hand finds my knee as Violet's face turns from enraged to horrified. Slowly, she sits back on the couch, analyzing my stomach. "We weren't imagining it, Henry. She is. The silly little girl has gone and got herself pregnant with some low-life's child."

Shame washes over me. Deep down, my subconscious battles with my deeply ingrained paranoia—I know I have nothing to be ashamed of, but the way my parents look at me makes me feel like nothing. Like I've thrown my entire life away.

Shame is quickly replaced with anger—*low-life?!* She knows nothing about him.

"Children."

"Pardon?" Violet's voice quakes.

"Plural, Violet. Children. Kate and I are having twins."

At over seventy years old, both my parents look like they're about to head into cardiac arrest. "Twins?" they whisper in unison.

"Yeah. We're due in March," Jensen clarifies, not a wavering in his voice.

"You stupid girl," Violet spits. "You aren't even married! Give it two months, and he'll be off finding another woman to knock up!"

"He won't," I argue. "Plus, we aren't together. We're going to co-parent."

Bedside me, I feel Jensen tense up. It's the first time he's shown a modicum of unease.

"Oh, this just gets better and better and better, Violet."

Henry scrubs a hand over his face. "Get out of my house, the pair of you."

"What?" Panic races through me.

"Get out of my house! You come here, insult us, and then drag our family name through the mud with this scandal."

"Scandal?!" Jensen inches forward on the couch, resting his elbows on his knees. "You're telling me you view your daughter's pregnancy and the fact that I am standing by her, wanting these babies with all my heart, as a fucking scandal? You're telling me you view your unborn grandchildren as a scandal?"

"Get out!" Violet spits.

Jensen doesn't move, and I stay rooted to the spot when he looks Violet dead in the eyes. "Did you view Ava as a *scandal,* too?"

"How dare you!"

"Or is that cool just because it's Easton and he's a guy?"

Violet ignores Jensen and looks at me. "Your career is over, Katherine. Congratulations. I shouldn't be surprised, though; I always knew you would fuck up."

"You're a hypocrite. You had me." Felicity's words play back in my memory.

"I had you with your father in a supportive home, and once we owned our own business, built it up from the ground and could call the shots. No one was waiting in the wings to replace me when I went off to have children."

"I've never heard such crap in my life," Jensen laughs. "This shit's hilarious."

Violet looks at Jensen and then at me, poison pouring from her. "But I should've stopped at one."

Jensen stops laughing. "I'm sorry, what was that?"

"I said—" Violet stands from the couch again, and Henry joins her, clearly in support. "We should've stopped at Easton."

The roar I hear from Jensen is enough to shake the entire house at its foundations. He lurches forward, but I can tell he won't touch my parents, even if the look on his face suggests exactly that. "You make me fucking sick," he snarls, his lips curling with rage. "Take a good long look at your stunning daughter and marvel at how you birthed her. I know I am. In fact, I'm starting to question if creatures like you are even capable of creating such perfection."

I place my hand on his arm to try to calm him. My walls are up, and I am in freeze mode, firmly holding in my feelings so the pain of Violet's words doesn't penetrate my heart. "Let's just get out of here, please."

JENSEN

I've done next to zero packing for the flight I absolutely have to take back to Alberta tomorrow morning.

But I can't leave her tonight.

I won't leave her.

I don't *want* to leave her.

What I want to do is haul her into me, have her arms wrapped around me for solace instead of her comforter. I've wanted to hold her all day, but she's refused to let me in, retreating further into her shell.

Who the fuck says that to their kids? Who the fuck treats anyone like that, let alone their own offspring.

The boiling blood pumping through my veins surges faster. I need to go to her. But she wouldn't let me hold her, comfort her in all ways I know she needs and craves.

"Fuck!" Sitting up on the air mattress I blew up ten minutes earlier, I pull out my phone.

"You know what time it is?" Jessie groans.

"She's not letting me in."

"But she gave you a key, right?"

I roll my eyes in the dark. "Not literally. Metaphorically, she's not letting me in. I'm getting nowhere."

"No fucking idea why you're coming to me with this. You know my track record with women," he says on a yawn. "Just tell her you love her or something."

"Yeah, that's not going to work here. She doesn't want me to love her."

"How do you work that one out?"

"Because her parents don't, so she thinks, why would anyone else."

"And you know this for a fact."

"Yeah. It was pretty clear from the delightful encounter I had with them in their study today."

"Shit."

"They're a piece of work, bro, both of them."

Jessie blows a breath down the phone. I know this is close to home for him. I can practically hear his memory whirling, recalling what happened in Dallas. "Well, you know how it ended up for me when I tried to take the parents on. I'm not the best guy to come to for positive affirmations or advice." He pauses. "I can give you a step-by-step guide on what *not* to do."

"Yeah, I think I've got that part nailed down, man."

"Look, just keep supporting her. That's all you can do. It might be that she genuinely doesn't want anything more than a good friendship with you."

I flinch. "I won't consider that as a possibility."

"I think you have to. She freely admits she doesn't do relationships. I'm going to be real honest with you here." Jessie pauses. "But first, I need you to promise you won't go off at me for saying it."

I might. "I won't. Shoot."

"How much of this is how you feel about her versus your need to prove Lauren was an idiot for leaving you...which she was, by the way."

Fuck, apparently this conversation is about to hit close to

home for us both. "I have no doubts about my feelings for Kate. The more time I spend with her, the more I want her in my life and not just my bed."

"So I'm way off with the Lauren part?"

"Yes," I bite out.

Kate isn't like Lauren; I know she isn't. We're meant to be.

"It's just that for years you've said love, marriage, and commitment are a waste of time and bound to end in heartbreak and—"

"I know what I've always said." I cut him off, my uneasiness growing as he edges too close to the insecurities I've fought to hide.

"I'm not saying she's not the one for you. I'm just saying if you aren't for her, then it's not a reflection on you. You're a good guy, and Lauren was in the wrong. That shit is bound to leave scars."

I grip at the roots of my hair. "Okay, I think I'm done with this conversation."

"I'm not trying to upset you, man; I just wouldn't be a great friend if I didn't ask. It feels like you're pushing so hard to get the girl, and yeah, I get that, but also to prove a point that Lauren was a one-off. You haven't thrown your hat in the ring until now."

"I haven't up until now because until she started carrying my babies, I was convinced I didn't stand a chance with her." My shoulders slump in defeat. "I probably still don't."

"What are you going to do if it doesn't work out?"

That's one thing I am dead certain of. "Easy. Love the shit out of my kids and try not to bury any guy who fucking looks at her."

He snorts a laugh. "You're borderline unhinged, you know that?"

"And this is news to you? I make a living out of stopping hundred-mile-per-hour slapshots."

CHAPTER TWENTY-FOUR

KATE

Numb.

That's the way I've lived my life. The way I've survived as a child and teenager and, consequently, the only way I know how to function as an adult.

Peeling myself out of bed, I poke my head out of my bedroom door. All is quiet and dark; Jensen must've finally finished his call with whoever was on the other end.

My latest pee over with, I pad back to my bedroom when a muffled groan stops me in my tracks. "Hello?" I whisper.

No response until another groan echoes from the living area.

"Jensen?"

My curiosity wins out and I turn and head toward the sound. Moaning lightly in his sleep, Jensen lies sprawled out across the air bed, the sheets resting dangerously low on his naked waist. In the soft moonlight filtering through my sheer curtains, I can easily make out the glistening sweat across his chest. His hands are clenched tightly by his sides, but it's what lies beside him that has my heart tripping out.

Picking up his brown leather wallet, two scan photos are tucked inside and on display. After the first scan, he asked if he could have a couple of the photos, and this is where he put them.

He went to sleep like this, with his unborn children lying next to him.

I set the wallet down, realization washing over me.

He's right, and so is my gut—I know absolutely nothing about the man lying in front of me. But he knows me inside and out.

He groans again and thrashes to the side.

"Jensen?" I whisper. But he doesn't wake.

My heart racing and pulse beating in my veins, I slowly lower myself onto the mattress beside him. I don't know what's going on with him, but he's offered me kindness and defended me to two people who never once showed me an ounce of it, only ever with strings attached.

He stirs and rolls towards me as I settle with my back to his overheating body.

"Kate?" he groans.

Tipping my head over my shoulder, I bring my pointer finger to my lips. "Shh, it's late, and you were having a bad dream." I look over at his wallet, which I set on the coffee table, still open on the scan images. "You put them in your wallet."

"Hmm?"

"The twins. They're in your wallet."

He lifts his head to see what I'm referring to, his cologne surrounding me from all angles. "Yeah, they're always with me that way."

Warmth floods my chest. "You're a good person, Jensen. I just want you to know that. I'm sorry we got off to such a bad start."

He smiles sleepily. "Everything that's happened between us was meant to be this way. I don't regret anything."

"Me neither," I sigh.

A few beats pass as he relaxes around me, the tension between us so charged that it could spark a fire with the single strike of a match.

"Come here." He kisses just below my ear as his huge hand splays out across my hip, tugging me back into him.

"Tell me to stop," he whispers.

I stay quiet. I don't want him to stop. The closer he is, the safer I feel.

"Words, Princess. Give me your words and tell me to stop."

I say nothing.

Lying back down on the pillow behind me, he pulls me so close that I can feel his hard bulge. He's completely naked, and I have a feeling that at any moment, I will be too.

"If you don't tell me what you want, then I'm going to go ahead and take what I do."

"Take it then," I finally whisper.

His lips caress the side of my neck. "Do you have any hard lines when it comes to the bedroom?"

Looking back over my shoulder, his dark brown eyes are blown wide. "Like things I won't do?"

He nods slowly. "You asked me to take what I want. That's like a red rag to a bull when it comes to my need for you."

I smirk. "There isn't anything you can do that I haven't done already."

"Oh, there is."

"Wanna bet?"

"Yeah, I do." Hauling me up off the bed, he carries me into the bathroom, setting me down on my feet in the walk-in shower. I take in his chiseled body and huge erect cock, and my mouth waters as memories from that one night take over my body.

It's then I notice a small string of words down his left rib cage. Did he have it before? I can't remember ever seeing him with a tattoo.

"What does that say?" I ask, pointing to what I think is a phrase in Latin.

Pulling off my cami top, he takes in my full breasts and peaked pierced nipples. He wets his lips on reflex. "I'll tell you when it's time."

"Time for what?"

Next, he yanks down my matching sleep shorts, and I step out of them. Throwing them behind him, he bites down on his fist. "Goddamn, your body is a fucking palace, definitely fit for a princess."

"Time for what, Jensen?"

"Time for patience but also to let me have my way with you."

Stepping in behind me, he pulls the detachable shower head off the wall and sets the warm water running. Steam begins to fill the dimly lit bathroom.

"Bend over, palms on the wall in front of you."

"I've done this before," I goad.

His eyes flash with annoyance. "I never want to hear you talk about another man again."

Dropping to his knees, he pulls my ass cheeks apart, swiping his tongue over my tight hole. Then, he spits straight into me, teasing me with his finger. "This ass." With the shower head in his other hand, he points the jets of warm water towards my pussy, finding my clit instantly. "This cunt." One more swipe of his tongue over my ass. "Your entire body belongs to me and no one else. Hold the shower head."

Taking it from him, he angles my hand so the water continues to power against my clit. God, it feels so fucking good.

"Tell me no man has ever touched you like this." His tongue finds my asshole once more as he circles it, making me cry out with pleasure. His fingers play with my pussy before he pushes two inside, curling them until they find that delicious spot, and I begin to unravel, my release rolling down the inside of my thighs.

"Tell me."

"No, they haven't."

"Keep coming for me, Princess."

"I can't." I begin to shake, but he doesn't let up, only pumping me harder.

"You fucking can, and you will."

The shower head clatters to the base as it slips from my grasp.

"Oh fuck me, Jensen...I'm coming again."

"My fucking pleasure."

My back is against the wall in a split second, my legs wrapped around his muscular waist.

We're face to face as his feral eyes soften and then fall to my mouth. "What about letting you taste your sweet ass?"

My eyes widen in shock. "Taste my ass?"

"Yeah, your ass is so fucking sweet. Do you want to taste it? Seems selfish to keep it all to myself."

My gaze falls to his full lips. "Will I get your cock afterward?"

"What do you think?"

"I think you can't wait to put it in me."

"Finally, something we agree on." His lips find mine as he kisses me, sending chills throughout my warm body. "Part for me, Princess."

Opening my mouth, he glides his tongue against mine, moaning into me as he lets me taste myself. "See what I mean? Fucking delicious."

My release continues to trickle down my thighs, my pussy throbbing hard. "I think I'm still coming."

"It's begging for my cock."

Slowly, he lowers me down and keeps one hand under my ass, guiding himself inside me. "Daddy's home."

"Yeah, JJ, you are."

His hips roll into me, and I moan. "Say it again."

"JJ."

"Again."

"JJ."

"Again." Each time in perfect synchronization with his thrusts.

"JJ!" I cry.

"That's right, Katherine."

"What are you doing?" I gasp as I feel his hand inch towards my tight hole.

"Tell me, did Tom only fuck you in missionary?"

"I thought you didn't want to talk about other men."

"Tell me." He thrusts into me.

"Yes. I told you it wasn't spicy."

Jensen's fingers tease me as he continues to fuck my pussy with his cock. "You're going to have so many firsts with me, Princess."

For once, I think he might be right.

"I'm already carrying your babies."

"Hell yeah, you are." His hips roll against me. "I know I said I didn't have any, but I do have one regret with you," he says in a breathy voice.

"Which is?"

"The day I came inside you and got you pregnant, I had no idea. So I guess I'm going to have to make up for that."

"Well, you can't get me pregnant again," I laugh.

The tip of his finger eases gently into my ass. It doesn't take much since it's so wet with my own release. "Ohmygod that feels so good."

"Mmm-hmm. I fucking love to play with you."

His tongue finds mine once more as he continues to dominate my body.

"You're the best I've ever been with," I admit.

He laughs against my mouth. "Oh, I know. Your body screams it."

"So cocky."

"Tell me, do you feel sexy carrying my babies while I fuck you and fantasize about giving you more? Does it turn you on?"

"Yes."

"Good. Because it drives me fucking wild. I didn't stand a fucking chance from the moment you told me."

Shaking, I collapse against him as we both come together. "Wow, that was, that was like nothing—"

"You've ever done before?"

Yielding for once in my life, I nod my head. "Yeah, that was wild."

The look of victory that spreads across his face is comical. "Does this mean you'll be back for more?"

"I'll think about it."

"You make sure you do." Still inside me, he rests his forehead against my chest, blowing out a long breath.

"What's wrong?"

"I just want you to know that I'm here. I'm patiently waiting, and you absolutely deserve to be loved in the way I'm going to love you. If you'll give me that chance."

My fingers tease his wet, dark strands of hair. "All love comes with conditions, with expectations."

"The only condition I have is that you breathe, and you're mine. Just like with my babies, and just like your parents should've been with you."

"I don't do serious relationships, Jensen."

"JJ. And you did with Tom...you gave him a shot."

I shake my head, although he can't see it with his face pressed against me, gripping me tightly around the hips. "Being with you is very different than Tom."

"Tell me how."

"You know how."

"I want to hear it."

"I can't—"

"Say it. I need to hear how it's different."

Resting my chin on top of his head, he slowly plays with one of my nipple piercings, almost absentmindedly. "Because if anyone is likely to make me feel, it's you. I can't hand my heart over to you when, in the end, you'll just break it. It's not a risk I'm willing to take. I can't be that vulnerable."

Picking his head back up, we're face to face and still connected, his cock still hard and inside me. "I'm scared too, but you should know you have nothing to fear. I'm your protector, your keeper, and your man. Give me your heart and trust me with it, Princess."

CHAPTER TWENTY-FIVE

JENSEN

I think I'm growing soft.

From a table at the back of the reception hall, I sit alone in my tux and watch as Hollie and Ed move across the dance floor and underneath the twinkling lights, their faces lit with love. I quickly reach up and swipe a tear from the corner of my eye.

She deserves every bit of happiness that's coming to her.

"Hey, it's been a while."

I look up to see Chloe, Hollie's best friend and the redhead from that night in Riley's bar.

"Hey," I say, smiling and sipping my bourbon.

She sits next to me, crossing her legs under the table and leaning forward slightly, the low-cut neckline of her pale pink bridesmaid's gown falling forward. I avert my eyes quickly. Something about this feels intense, and I've been avoiding her all day, trying to stay out of the same photos.

She gently taps her fingernails on the tablecloth and rests her chin in the other hand. I can tell by the look in her eyes that she's had more than enough to drink.

"How come every time you see me, I'm a little tipsy?" she giggles.

"I'd say a little more than tipsy, but you're better than you were that night."

"I never did get a chance to thank you for walking me back."

I look at her properly for the first time since she sat down. "You just did, and you're welcome."

She looks around the room, taking it all in. "Do you not have any friends with you? I thought you'd be the most popular guy in the room?"

I lean back in my chair and push my empty glass away. "Nah, keeping a low profile."

"Congrats on the Stanley Cup win."

"Thanks."

This whole exchange feels stilted and awkward, as if she's pushing for something to say to me.

"Are you in town for long? Preseason has to be starting up soon?"

I think about how much I want to be back in Seattle, curled up on Kate's couch with her wrapped around me. "I'll be heading back tomorrow; preseason starts the day after."

Just then, my phone that's lying face up on the table illuminates with a text, and Chloe's head darts in its direction.

It's a picture from Kate.

PRINCESS

This one is probably your best so far...

picture of her cleaned plate held up next to her face

I quickly type out a response, keeping my phone close to me and the screen out of view.

ME

Oh yeah? Which one did you have tonight?

The veggie lasagna.

I continue staring down at my phone, forgetting my surroundings entirely.

"Wait, is that the girl from Riley's that night? The blonde?" Chloe clicks her fingers as if trying to remember Kate's name. "She hangs with your group, right?"

At least, I thought my phone was out of view.

"She does," I reply, locking my phone and placing it face down and out of sight.

Knitting her brows together, she ponders over what she's clearly just seen. "Are you guys dating? You call her Princess..." she trails off.

I fucking wish.

"No. She's just a really close friend who hates being called that, so I deliberately do it." I force out the whole sentence, which feels entirely unnatural. I'm also surprised she didn't see or remember Kate sprawled on my lap that night I walked her home. She must've been drunker than I thought.

"Aww, well, that's cute that you cooked for her."

"Chloe, are you hitting on my brother?" Hollie comes to stand beside me. No, to save me.

Although Hollie is clearly winding her best friend up, I don't miss the flush across Chloe's cheeks. In another world, and even though she's several years younger than me, I might be tempted to see how far that flush travels. But there isn't another woman on the face of this planet that interests me.

I want my blonde princess, just like I did that night. Nothing has changed, and it never will.

It's like Chloe's presence reminds me that while my sister's best friend might have the hots for me, there's only one woman who will ever turn my head.

Chloe stands and brushes down her gown. "I'm going to get

another drink."

My sister squeezes her huge dress into the now vacant seat beside me and narrows her eyes straight in my direction, studying me. I don't like that look. "When were you planning on telling me?"

I snort and shake my head. "She just couldn't wait, could she?" My eyes scan the room until I find my mom standing at another table, talking to some family friends. I turn back to Hollie. "I planned on telling you after your big day."

"I'm still in shock. You, a dad to twins."

I nod. "Yep."

"Mom says you're in love with her."

I throw my head back and laugh. "I'm a lot of things about her."

"She's not in love with you?"

"What is this? The Spanish Inquisition?" I wave a hand around the room. "Haven't you got guests to talk to?"

She flicks her long dark hair out to the side and pins her brown eyes on me again. The shade is almost identical to mine. "Technically, you are a guest. Plus, I'm a huge heap of love today." She straightens my bow tie, which I've yet to take off. "You look, I dunno, sad?"

"I'm not sad, Hollie. I just have a lot on my mind."

"Like what?"

How I'm going to transition from the friend zone where we occasionally fuck to being married.

I don't say anything.

"I think you should bring her to Alberta. Mom says she's been working, so she couldn't come." She sighs. "That's the trouble with a weekday wedding, but this was the only time Ed could get off from his hectic surgery schedule."

"I know Hollie. But I don't think she'd want to come. She'll meet my family as the mother of my children, but she isn't looking for anything with me."

"Well, I think you're a catch."

I nudge my shoulder against hers. "Thanks."

"Seriously. You need to bring her to meet us."

"I'm working on it, trust me. But I am running out of ideas."

"Just straight up tell her you're in love with her. Lay it all out there."

I wince. "I think I already did."

"Have you actually said the words, though?"

I shake my head. "No. Look, it's complicated. She knows what I want, and I'm just trying to hang in there."

"I still can't believe you're gonna be a dad! Will you find out what you're having?"

"Yeah, I think so. But she's only nine weeks. We haven't decided yet, but I fucking hope so. I need to buy all the baby shit, and yeah, I'm going for blue or pink."

She throws a palm to her chest in surprise. "Oh shit, I'm going to be an auntie! Twice!"

"You've only just worked that out?"

"Mom told me the news this morning, and I've only just processed it." She turns to me. "I want to meet her, Jensen. If you love her, then I know I will, too."

I raise a concerned brow. "Why does this idea worry me?"

"Well, it shouldn't." She taps her fingernails against her chin in thought. "I can take her baby shopping for clothes and things. Yes, I can come over one day to watch a game, stay at your place, and then take her shopping the next day."

Scrubbing a hand across my face, I know arguing is pointless. "You're not going to back down, are you?"

"Nope," she sings.

"Let me talk to her."

Hollie squeaks in delight.

"But!" I caution her. "Let me talk to her in my own time."

She claps excitedly. *Christ, was I this excitable at twenty-eight?*

"Okay. And just so you know, only Ed and I know, and obviously Mom and Dad. When do you think you'll tell the media?"

"They don't need to know anytime soon." I pause and side-eye my sister. "And when I let the pregnancy go public, I plan to do it as a couple."

I SHOULD BE DRIVING BACK to my apartment, ready to start preseason tomorrow. At least, that was the plan. Instead, I'm pulling into Kate's apartment parking lot and taking the stairs three at a time. It's been too long since I saw her. She's not expecting me tonight, but like that's ever stopped me.

Pulling out my key to her apartment, I know I'm pushing boundaries I shouldn't, especially since it's eleven at night and she's likely asleep.

But fuck, I can't stop myself as I turn the lock and walk into the darkened living room.

Shrugging off my jacket, I dump it on the couch. Next to go are my sneakers, which I leave in the hallway.

Her bedroom door is slightly open when I step inside and close it behind me.

The entire room smells of Kate, her shampoo, her detergent, her perfume. Just Kate.

Sitting at the foot of the bed, I watch her sleep, but I have no idea how much time passes. Five minutes, maybe ten?

What the fuck am I doing? She gave me this key just in case she needed me, not so I could sit and agonize over making her mine. Not so I could fantasize over what it would be like to finish a game or practice and head back to her bed rather than my own. Or better still, ours.

Resting my elbows on my knees, I hold my head in my hands.

"Jensen?"

Kate sits upright in bed, holding the covers over her chest.

Is she naked?

She reaches across and flicks on a soft green light on her nightstand. "What are you doing here?" she asks, confused.

"I—I, I came to check that you were doing okay."

Cocking her head to the side, she eyes me. "You spoke to me just before your flight. I've been a bit nauseous again, but I'm okay." She leans over to check the time on her phone. "Jesus, it's almost midnight."

"I can't stop thinking about you. About what we did in the shower. About how fucking awesome it was," I blurt out. My mouth is way ahead of my brain. "I had to see you."

"Jensen."

I hold up a hand. "I know. I get it."

Standing from the bed, I walk a couple of paces toward her door before her palm wraps around my forearm. Her touch awakens all my senses.

Staring straight at her door, I shake my head. "Am I just wasting my time, or will you ever be mine?"

"I don't know," she whispers.

I turn to look at her; that's the most she's ever given me. "It's killing me. This. Being near you, around you. I'm addicted to you, but I can't keep surviving on a hit here and there. I need it all."

Her eyes search mine in the warm glow of the room. "If I invite you into my bed tonight and ask you to make love to me, to make me feel something, will you do that?"

I bite the inside of my cheek so hard it draws blood, and I slide her hand down my forearm until our fingers intertwine. "You've been worried about me breaking your heart. But I've got a feeling you might shatter mine, Princess."

"I'm asking you to help me feel, to help me lower my walls."

"And then what?"

"And then there's a chance that I can be yours."

CHAPTER TWENTY-SIX

KATE

Peeling off his black sweatshirt from behind his back, Jensen stands next to my bed in only black low-riding jeans, the gray waistband of his boxer briefs peeking just above.

My body trembles as I take him in. He walks around to the other side of the bed, pulling back the duvet.

Unzipping his pants, he steps out of them, our eyes locked the entire time.

This feels like so much more than just sex. This isn't friends who are fucking.

He pushes his boxers down to the ground and slowly kneels on the bed in front of me, pumping his hard cock.

I lean across to switch off the lamp and plunge us into darkness.

"No," he rasps. "I want to see every way your body responds to mine."

"I'm nervous," I admit.

His dark eyes soften. "Me too, Princess." He flips his free hand towards him. "Come here."

Rising from underneath the sheets, I'm completely naked.

His eyes drop to my stomach. "You're starting to show."

Within a second, I'm wrapped in his arms as he lays me down on my back and hovers over me, bracketing me in with his forearms.

"My clothes feel tighter."

Moving between my legs, he tucks a piece of hair behind my ear. "Watching your body change and grow my babies does things to me I'm struggling to control. You make me wild."

Trembles continue to shudder through me. "You're going to make me fall in love with you, aren't you?"

He smiles against my mouth, kissing me once. "I'm going to really fucking try. I am pretty irresistible after all."

"Cocky bastard."

"I don't care how long it takes you to get there. I'm going to dismantle your walls brick by brick until there's nothing left to stop me from making you mine."

"Give me your cock," I say, holding out my hand.

Trailing up my body, I stop him when his dick aligns with my nipple. "Rub the tip on my piercing."

Raising a brow, he looks unsure, but I can see the way the tip glistens with pre-cum in anticipation.

"It's time for me to give *you* a first."

"Is that so, Princess?"

"You've been with a pierced woman before?"

Instantly, I regret my question. I know Jensen has been with a lot of women, probably multiple at a time. *Of course,* he's experienced this before.

"No," he replies, surprising me again.

Gently, I rub the tip of his cock over the bar piercing through my left nipple, and he gasps with pleasure. "Jesus, that's so fucking good. The cold metal against my dick."

It feels great for me, too. So amazing and worth every bit of pain getting them done.

Just as I think he's about to blow from the sensation alone, he slowly moves down my body, this time taking my nipples into his mouth in turn, teasing the piercings with his tongue. My hips shoot off the bed. "Oh, fuck yes."

Continuing his descent, he stops at my navel and then looks up at me, a proud smile on his face that warms me through. "I think it's one of each."

"A boy and a girl?"

"Yeah." Smoothing a palm over my stomach, he presses his lips to my soft skin twice, sending tingles of need throughout me. "They're gonna be beautiful, just like their mama."

Jensen continues down to my pelvic bone, placing another kiss just above the small strip of hair I leave.

He lifts his eyes to me once more as he brings two fingers to his mouth and sucks on them. "Speaking of beautiful."

His damp fingers slowly enter me as he works his body slightly lower until his mouth is hovering over my pussy. "Tell me how much you want my mouth on you."

"I want it," I whisper, needy and desperate.

"Not good enough. Give me more."

"I really want it," I say louder, plowing my hand through his tousled dark hair.

"Say 'you're the best I've ever had, JJ.'"

I cock my head to the side. "Seriously?"

He smirks, loving how he pushes all my buttons. Then he bites down on his lip and curls his fingers, pumping me a couple of times.

I whimper with need.

"Say it."

"You're the best I've ever had, JJ."

"Good girl."

His mouth is over my pussy as his hand works me into a frenzy. I can hear how wet I am and how much my body responds to him.

As I start to orgasm, my release threatens to soak my sheets, but Jensen swipes it up, taking every drop I have onto his tongue and swallowing me down with a satisfied smirk.

"You want me to take it slow with you tonight, Princess?"

I nod slowly, unable to form words, as he crawls back up my body until we're face to face.

Reaching down between us, he guides himself inside me while he strokes his fingers through the hair on top of my head.

My jaw hangs open at the way he stretches me out. There's no urgency to the motion of his hips, it's slow, languid, and incredibly sexy.

He squeezes his eyes shut. "This is a risk for me, too. Doing this, taking it slow. Allowing my heart to believe it has a chance to be loved by you."

There's no need for me to say anything because I know he's right. Going slow, drinking each other in, being vulnerable together. I might've avoided it my whole life, but something tells me Jensen has, too.

Sitting back up, he pulls me until I'm straddling him, and we're in the lotus position. He looks down, smiles at my stomach, and then returns his brown gaze to mine. "I'm so deep inside you right now, baby."

"So deep, JJ."

"You gonna let me come inside that sweet princess pussy of yours?"

"Yes."

"Tell me you want me to come inside you. Tell me you want my cum."

Chest to chest, I'm not sure whose heartbeat I can feel as we move together slowly, my legs spread so wide for him, opening myself up as far as I can go. "I want you to come inside me."

"I could take your body all day long."

He kisses the underside of my jaw. "Just stop sleeping on your feelings for me. Let me in."

I really want to try. The more Jensen Jones shows of himself, the more of myself I want to offer in return. "I'll try, but you have to give me time."

"Anything you need, it's yours," he rasps.

When he hits a spot so deep inside me, I come. Hard. So hard my nails dig into his back. "Ohmygod, I'm sorry. That was just—"

"Mark me. You've already taken over my mind, so go ahead and imprint my body too."

Jensen thrusts up into me once more, and I grip his shoulders, letting my nails sink into his toned muscles.

"Fuck, that feels so fucking good, baby. So fucking amazing."

"So amazing," I repeat.

"I'm so close, Princess. So close to giving your pussy what it needs."

He thrusts up into me over and over as we both come together, moaning into each other's mouths and then slowly coming down from the incredible high.

"Lie down for me. I need to clean you up."

Lying back on the pillows, Jensen brings his hand to my apex and pushes any leaking cum back inside me. Leaning down from where he's on his knees between my legs, he lifts me by the hips and swipes his tongue over me, lapping up my release.

Licking the last drops from his lips, a sexy smile pulls at them. "Some men use washcloths; I use my tongue."

So fucking hot.

He lies on top of the covers next to me and pulls me into his chest. Tipping my chin up with his forefinger, we share a kiss that ricochets through me, making me dizzy.

Fucking Jensen Jones is one thing, having him slowly is another, but when he makes out with me like this? I'm powerless to hold back. I'm needy for him in every way I promised myself I would never be when it came to men.

Pulling back from our kiss, the back of his hand lightly strokes my face while his breath tickles my cheeks.

He looks like he wants to say something and takes a deep breath, steadying himself. "When I was in my early twenties, I was engaged to a girl named Lauren. We'd been childhood sweethearts for as long as I could remember. Her family was friends with mine. You get the picture." Keeping his left arm wrapped around me, he rolls onto his back, his stomach muscles rippling.

I rest my head against his chest, my heart breaking for him. I knew there was something in his past. "You didn't get married?"

Shaking his head, he blows out a humorless laugh. "No. She did, though, about six months later, to my former best friend."

"Oh shit."

"Yeah, shit. They'd been involved for a while."

"When did you find out?"

He turns his head to look at me, and I'm not sure what I see in his eyes: hurt, fear, anger. None of those emotions fit as well as vulnerable. "At the altar."

My heart rises into my throat. "She...she didn't show up?"

"Humiliating, right?"

"I'm really sorry."

"The thing is, I knew deep down that something wasn't right. But I didn't trust my gut. I played along with what I thought I should do. Follow the crowd, get married, have children, settle down."

I nod but don't speak, bringing my palm to his cheek.

"When Lauren left me, I made a conscious decision that I was done with relationships. I decided messing around with women was the best way to go. Don't go in too deep, then you don't have far to swim to the shore. It was also a great way to bury my feelings of rejection and mask the fact that I wasn't enough for her. For years, my theory worked great." He laughs softly and runs a hand through his hair.

"Until me?" I ask cautiously.

Smiling, he hauls me up so I'm straddling his hips. I look down to see his cock stir into life.

"Until you. You and your smart-ass mouth and brattiness came and blew me straight out of the water. *Then* you decide to go and date someone else, bring him to events like galas and wave him in my face. No matter what you did and how I fought them back, my feelings for you continued to grow. That night in Riley's set the wheels of this train in motion."

I think back to the annual charity gala for Zach's foundation last summer. I took Tom with me. Guilt washes over me. Yes, I wanted Tom there, and no, I wasn't using him; I was genuinely dating a man I liked. But I also knew it could and maybe even hoped it would bother Jensen—such a shitty thing to do.

I lean down and kiss his chest. "For what it's worth, Lauren is an idiot."

Jensen sits up on his elbows and raises a brow. "Do I feel a compliment coming on?"

Pointing at him, I laugh. "Don't get ahead of yourself, buddy."

Reaching one arm out, he smooths his slightly calloused palm down my arm. "I think it's a bit late for that," he says.

"Thank you for telling me that, sharing what happened, and trusting me." So much makes sense now that I know why he avoided commitment for so long and perhaps why he'd come off as cold and uncaring so often. This is my lesson in judging without truly knowing what's going on behind closed doors.

"Come here." He takes my chin and pushes up on his arm, brushing his lips over mine. "I want you again."

My core pulses at the thought. "Don't you have preseason starting tomorrow?"

"Gym work, and I couldn't care less about fucking hockey right now. I want you to ride me all night."

CHAPTER TWENTY-SEVEN

JENSEN

I made it to light conditioning with five minutes to spare.

But it was totally worth spending the entire night in my girl's bed. Christ, she's amazing.

Pounding the treadmill, I increase the gradient and switch the setting to interval training. I'm full of energy despite zero sleep.

Zach comes to stand next to me and side-eyes me, setting his pace to a slow walk. "All good, man?"

"Yeah. I just have energy, you know." I keep looking straight ahead, grab my drink, and take a gulp before setting it back in the holder.

"Yeah, well, pass me some. I'm fucking spent."

My treadmill automatically slows as it hits the next stage in the interval program, which gives me time to look at Zach.

"What's eating you?"

He scratches the back of his neck. "The Captaincy. Becoming a dad. All the responsibility looming this year."

"Well, we can freak out together since I'm going to be a dad, twice. But you know I got you, right? I'll always be there to support you and the team."

He nods. "You know if the rules allowed, I'd have you as my AC any day. You mean everything to this team." He pauses and blows out a long breath. We don't say anything for a few seconds as I let his words sink in; they mean a lot to me.

He breaks the silence first. "How's Kate?"

"Already starting to show. Sickness has stopped, though, thank fuck."

He nods. "I'm putting our place up for sale and finding a house with a yard and a pool for Luna. She's really missing the ocean."

Catching my breath a bit more, I swipe at the sweat on my forehead with my towel. "I don't blame you. The city isn't really the place for bringing up children. If you can get a yard, then why not?"

"How are things going with Kate? I'm assuming better with the way that photo leaked online looked."

"They're...going. At this point, we're just friends."

With insane benefits that I want to turn into a whole heap more.

I don't know how much he knows from Jon or Felicity, but if I get my way with Kate, he'll know everything soon enough.

He nods, but I think he's worked out we're at least sleeping together. I'd tell him everything if I wasn't unsure of where Kate's head was. "Luna said you're getting along better."

"Yeah, we're making progress. I'm back at my place now, though."

"Alright, ladies." Jessie joins us on the other side, setting his treadmill to a bare walk.

Zach looks at him, only wearing his athletic shorts and sneakers. "Are shirts now illegal?"

"Why hide this incredible physique?" He waves a hand up and down his body. "Jealousy isn't a good look on you, Captain."

"I'm never going to get used to that," Zach murmurs before bringing his treadmill to a complete stop and grabbing his drink.

"I'm heading to the bench press; I've got some strengthening exercises I need to work on."

Once out of earshot, Jessie turns to me. "Are you with baby and girlfriend yet or just baby?"

"Still the babies, but I'm making progress."

"Progress...how?"

"Progress, as in I came straight from her bed to the gym this morning."

"Oooh, that kind of progress," he chuckles. "I thought you looked a bit flushed."

"Yeah, well, I was beginning to break through, and now that the season's started, I'll barely get to see her. I've gone from hated to tolerated to sort of liked to now being given half a chance, and guess what? I'll be gone a lot."

"Ask her to move in with you."

I look at him like he's from another planet. "Did you hit your head on the Olympic bar?"

My best friend shrugs. "I've been thinking about it. You're having babies together, and her place is fucking tiny compared to yours. Just ask her to move in with you."

Lightly jogging, I consider asking Kate to shift her life across town and move to mine. Logistically, it would make a lot of sense; emotionally, she'd freak the fuck out for sure.

Jessie speaks again. "You're having twins. That's a whole lot more than just one baby. Double of everything. I don't think co-parenting from the other side of the city is going to work, personally." He clicks his tongue. "But what do I know? I might be talking shit."

Would Kate go for that? Fuck that would be awesome, having her in my apartment. Driving back from games or the airport and finding all her stuff in my place. Hell, I'd even take all her houseplants and chipped mugs.

"I think a lot of this hinges on how you deliver it to her. If you say, 'Hey babe, how about you move in with me this week and get married the next?' you might have an issue."

I snort a laugh. It's like he just said out loud my ultimate fantasy.

"But if you sell it as a practical solution, I think you'll have a better shot. It's easier to woo her from the same apartment."

I quirk a brow. "I'm having no issues there. Last night was fucking awesome. It's just her fear of commitment. Not believing she's loveable."

I stop the treadmill and check my stats. "I told her about Lauren last night."

"No shit. Only your family and I know about that. Good for you, man."

"And now Kate Monroe," I add.

"What did she say?"

"I think she was pretty shocked. I wasn't planning to tell her, but whenever we're together, I just, I dunno, my guard comes down, and so does hers. It used to be the complete opposite between us, but everything's shifted. She's starting to let me see her in some way, so I wanted to show her a piece of me, you know?"

He nods. "I do. I'm also even more convinced that you need to talk to her about moving into your place."

"I'm just worried I'm going too fast, and she'll slam the door in my face."

"Dude. You're in love with her. Where you're concerned, there is no 'too fast.'"

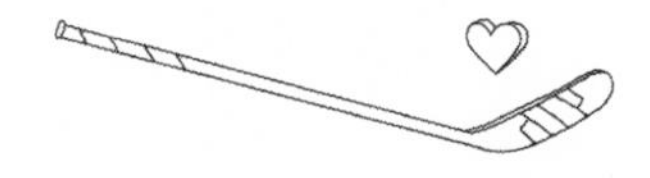

KATE

EASTON

So I just got off a call with Mom, and then I picked myself up off the floor. She just told me you're pregnant with Jensen Jones' twins and that he came over to the house and insulted their integrity.

Fuck!

This is not how I wanted my brother to find out. I've had my head so far up my ass I didn't think about my mom spilling everything to him.

Think again, Kate.

Sitting at my desk, I hit dial on his international number and head for the kitchenette.

"Hi." His tone is clipped.

"Hey. Look, I'm really sorry you found out this way. I wanted to wait until after I hit twelve weeks, and I needed to figure out what I was going to say. Then she goes and blurts it all out anyway," I rush out in a panic.

"How did Mom and Dad find out? Did you tell them?"

"There was a picture posted online. It didn't get far. Jensen's agent had it taken down quickly. We were getting close, and his hand was over my stomach. It was questionable at best. Next thing I know, I've got a barrage of texts from Violet telling me my career is over and I'm 'cheap.' Jensen was pissed and had it out with them."

"Wow."

"Yeah."

"Was this planned? I saw you only weeks before, and you didn't talk about him."

I lean back against the kitchen counter. Propping my phone between my ear and shoulder, I undo the button on my pants using both hands and instantly feel the relief. I'm going to need new clothes.

"No," I laugh. "Back in June, I hated him. It was a one-night-to-see-what-happens kind of thing." I do *not* need to tell my brother it was also hate sex.

"Yeah," he drawls. "Mom would love that." There's no judgment to his voice, but he totally gets why she'd go crazy.

"I thought he'd run, but I misjudged him, East. He's..." My body tingles as I recall last night. "He's nothing like I thought he was."

"So you guys are dating?"

"No. We're just friends. He wants more. I know he does, but I don't think I can give anyone that." He's wearing me down, though; I know he is.

Silence.

"East?"

"Yeah, I'm still here."

"Oh, okay," I chuckle. "I thought the call had been cut."

"How much does he know about our home life, you know, about when we were kids?"

"He's met our parents, so I'd say a pretty good idea."

"Did you tell him about the lock on your door?"

An ice-cold trickle runs down my spine. "No."

"Kate, do you like this guy?" he asks, his voice soft.

My stomach knots. "Yes, I do. But you know how much I struggle."

He sighs. "For once, just let him in and talk to him. Give him a chance. He sounds like he's good for you."

I scoff. "How do you know that? Just because he's the goalie for the Scorpions."

"You just told me that he sat in our parents' house and took them on. From the way Mom was fuming, I'd also say he put both of them in their place. He's clearly fucking crazy about you. To walk into the snake's pit and do that."

"I'm trying," I whisper.

"You trust me?"

"More than anyone."

"Well, I'm telling you. Let him in, tell him what you went through, and give him a shot. You can't close yourself off forever, Kate."

Jensen might see straight through me and know the real Kate of today, but my brother knows my past. He knows what made me this way and why I closed off to those around me.

Standing in the tiny kitchenette and thousands of miles from my brother, I feel a lone tear trickle down my cheek. "I'm already scared I won't be able to do this—to be a mom, East. Everything is spinning out of control and changing so rapidly. My life, my emotions, even my body."

"Are you kidding me? You're going to be the greatest mom there is. They'll never take any shit, that's for sure."

"I wish you were here." My voice cracks just as Felicity walks into the kitchenette and stops in her tracks at the sight of me crying in the office. I don't think she's ever seen me upset like this before, let alone at work. She's seen me puke on myself but never cry.

"I know. Look, I have to go, but all I'm saying is, I've never met this guy, but a man who defends my sister like that is a man I want around her."

"Yeah, he's a good person."

"Let him in, Kate. Talk soon. Love you lots."

The call ends, and I look up to see my best friend hovering over me. "Was that Easton?"

Hearing his name and her concerned look is the final act that sends the walls of my dam tumbling. I lean into her, my head on her shoulder, as she takes my phone from my hand and sets it on the counter, wrapping her arms around me.

"Hey, hey, it's okay. It's all okay."

"Why is this so hard? No one ever told me this would be so hard," I sob, knowing co-workers can probably hear me in the office.

"Being a mum is hard, babe, and from the moment you conceive, it feels like every day is a new challenge. But the way you've taken all this in stride, you should be so proud of yourself."

"I hope I can be half the mom you are."

"Oh, trust me; you'll smash this whole thing out of the park."

I pull back and look at her, mascara no doubt smeared around my eyes. "I really like him. But I'm scared. I have real feelings."

Felicity strokes my hair and wipes under my eye. "I know you do; you have for a very long time, but you're now only seeing them, and that's okay. He's waited for you. But it's time to explore them."

"How do I do that?"

"With how strong he feels, I don't think you need to do much. Let him take control."

I half scoff, half sob. "Ha, yeah, not sure I can do that."

"This isn't a legal case, babe. You can't file it away. This is your heart, and it won't relent until you give it what it wants."

"And you think that's JJ?"

"Yeah, it really is."

CHAPTER TWENTY-EIGHT

KATE

Wow, that was stressful.

Turning from side to side in my full-length mirror, I take myself in. Yep, twelve weeks and definitely showing. I should've listened to my gut weeks ago and gone shopping for some clothes. Then I got sidetracked with work—*what's new*—and now I've spent the past fifteen minutes squeezing myself into an A-line dress that is not thanking my ever-growing stomach and cleavage right now.

I can't hold it off any longer. I have to tell my boss. I've been at Preston & Preston for years, but that still doesn't make it any easier. Violet is probably right; they will find a replacement who's likely way better than me at my job.

Stepping over to my dresser, I check my makeup again and pick up my favorite rose gold necklace—a thirtieth birthday gift from Easton. Clasping it around my neck, I look at my reflection in the round cosmetic mirror. Pregnancy is changing me, not just externally but internally, too. Yes, I'm freaking out about maternity leave, but deep down, I care far less about the impact it could have on my career than I ever thought I would. I've switched up legal journals for mom and baby books, and you know what, I'm enjoying them. Jensen annotated all the parts he thought were especially important with little notes and tabs.

I haven't seen him much the past couple of weeks, just as he warned me. He's back in his apartment, and training is in full swing, ready for preseason games to start and then for the NHL regular season to get underway on October first.

I miss him for more than just the sex. But I told him I needed time, and while he messages me every day, he's clearly giving me space to process.

There's a part of me that wants to head over to his place now and tell him I'll give us a shot. But the larger part still holds me back. Not that I could go over anyway since I'm headed to Marissa and Brad's engagement party tonight. It's the first time I'll see Tom since we split, and uneasiness settles inside me.

Grabbing my jacket and clutch, I head for my front door but stop dead in my tracks when I almost collide with Jensen.

"Hi," I squeak.

God, he looks amazing in his post-practice training gear, complete with gray sweatpants.

He slowly scans my body, from my black patent heels to my low-cut sweetheart neckline, and he finally meets my eyes. "Where are you going?"

"To an engagement party for my friends." Heat thrums through me from the possessive way he's staring.

"I was just heading over to restock your freezer." He tugs on the strap of his backpack, indicating the meals he's made are in there.

"Thank you. You can still do that; I just need to head out."

He doesn't move from the doorway. "Who's engagement party?"

"No one you know. Just some old college friends."

And Tom.

His eyes widen. "Old college, as in the same college Tom went to?"

"Yes." I prop a hand on my hip. "But it's just a party, and I'm not even sure he'll be there."

I'm ninety-nine percent sure he will be since he texted me about it.

"Come back inside." He points to my living space.

I check my watch. "I'm going to be late."

"I want to talk to you."

"Jensen, I'm going to be late. It's right across town, and I—"

In an instant, my back is against my closed apartment door, and he's pressing against me, his mouth hovering over mine. The move was soft and gentle but so fast, and it has my knees going weak especially when his breath fans my lips.

"There's no way he gets to see you like this." He scans down my body once more. "Not looking this fucking stunning and not without me by your side."

I'm single, and no one has ever owned me, but right about now, Jensen Jones is the closest any man has ever come. And I hate that I like it.

"Did you get all dressed up for him?" he asks, pushing my long hair behind my ears.

"No, I got dressed up for me."

"Is that so?" His right hand slowly travels up the inside of my thigh, and I squeeze them together as I fight to control my reaction.

"I need to head out. My Uber will be here any second."

"Mmm-hmm..." His lips find my neck as he moves my hair to one side. "But the thing is, my babies are showing in that dress, and now I want you to have my cum, too. I want it dripping down your thighs when you walk into that party."

"Has anyone ever told you that you're a caveman?"

Placing one palm above my head, with his other hand, he slowly pulls down my panties until they hit the floor. His sweatpants and boxer briefs are the next to go.

"No. You. Only you. Only ever you."

Picking me up in his arms, I wrap my legs around his waist, my lacy thong dangling on the end of my heel.

I giggle. "My thong is still hanging from my foot."

Setting me on the kitchen counter and standing between my legs, he looks over his shoulder at my outstretched leg. Grabbing the thong, he tosses it across my apartment, and it hits one of my floor plants, now hanging off one of the leaves.

"Fucking plants," he part grumbles, part chuckles.

"Hey, that's Howard. He's one of my oldies."

Turning back to me, fire swarms his eyes. "Now, where was I? Oh yeah, that's right. Fucking you."

His mouth crashes against mine as one hand cups my face, his long fingers tangling in the hair at the nape of my neck.

Taking one of my hands in his, he wraps my palm around his hard length as we both pump him. "You feel how hard you make me, Princess? Are you already dripping for me?"

"What do you think?"

Pushing my dress over my hips, he swipes a hand through my pussy as he smirks. "I think when you sit down next to him at some fancy table tonight, all you'll be able to feel is me."

He enters me fast, and I gasp from the way he stretches me out so fully.

"So good. Your pussy is so good."

"You feel so big," I gasp.

Pumping into me, his black training top strains against his flexing abs and biceps. The sight from this angle is fucking glorious.

Jensen Jones is glorious.

"Come for me, Princess. Let go with me."

His slick hair falls over his darkened eyes as he fucks into me on my kitchen counter.

"I'm so close, JJ. I'm so fucking close."

"Yeah, you are, baby."

I crash over the edge, my hips losing control as I cry out so loud; I know everyone around us can hear the way this man has just owned every part of me.

Pulling me back into him so he's as far seated as possible, he holds me dead still as he brings my lower lip between his teeth. He shudders and jerks, and I know he's coming; I can feel his warm release as it shoots deep inside.

He pulls out and takes a step back, opening my legs wide as he drips from my pussy. A satisfied smile pulls at his lips. "You're mine—all fucking mine."

I want to argue, give him back talk, and be the brat I always am. But this time, I don't. Instead, I simply lean forward and kiss him.

"THANK you so much for coming tonight." Marrisa kisses me on the cheek.

"It was a beautiful evening." I wrap my arms around her. "I'm so sorry I can't make the wedding but, you know..."

"I know, I know, work."

Well, actually, no. I'll likely be in labor, but she doesn't need to know that.

Walking toward the hotel exit, I hear footsteps behind me and turn around to see Tom rushing to catch up to me.

"Were you going to say bye?" he says, looking hurt.

I've avoided him all night. I don't want to hurt him anymore, and I don't want to get into the conversation of my last text telling him I slept with someone else since we split.

"Sorry, I thought you were busy talking, but I'm exhausted anyway." Which isn't a lie.

"Yeah, pregnancy is tiring," he says, low enough so no one else can hear us.

My eyes flare as he stands there, his hands tucked in the pockets of his black dress pants. "I'm sorry?"

He steps closer. "A lot of people here haven't seen you in a long while, but I know your body like the back of my hand. How many weeks are you, and I assume it isn't mine?"

I prop a hand on my hip, trying to shrug off my shock. "Well, wouldn't it be really awkward for you if I told you I wasn't and I'd just had a few more cakes?"

"But you are. You're glowing. You look..." He sucks in a breath. "You look beautiful."

I drop my eyes to the ground. "I'm twelve weeks." Looking back at him, I cast a tentative glance around the lobby. "But I would ask you to keep this to yourself. It isn't common knowledge."

"Yeah, especially when the dad is Jensen Jones."

I balk. "H-how do you know this?"

"Oh, come on, Kate. I'm a lawyer. It didn't take my analytical brain long to put the pieces together. The way you looked at each other at the gala, the obsession in his eyes." He looks over my shoulder toward the main entrance and huffs out a laugh. "Why am I not surprised?"

I turn around to see Jensen stalking toward us. But he isn't looking at me; he's looking at Tom, murder in his eyes.

Oh. Shit.

Registering Jensen's glare, Tom raises his hands. "We're just talking here, man."

At first, I think Jensen's going to grab him by the throat, but then he stops right in front of him, his hands in fists by his side.

How the fuck did he know where I was?

"Just can't take a hint, won't you?" Jensen hisses.

Tom shakes his head and looks up at the ceiling. "What the hell is wrong with you?"

"I knew from the minute I found out she was coming here tonight that you would take any opportunity to make a move."

I put a hand on Jensen's arm and look around the lobby. Thankfully, nearly all the guests have left or are back in the party. "It's okay. He was just asking me about—"

"I was asking her about the baby," Tom cuts me off.

Turning to look at me, Jensen thumbs at Tom. "You told him?"

"No, I guessed."

Jensen turns back to Tom. "That's our private business."

His hands are back in the air, and Tom shakes his head. "I've got no intention of saying anything. If you want to hide it from the world, that's your prerogative."

I swear to God, I see flames in Jensen's eyes. "Hide it?" he scoffs. "I'd marry this girl in a fucking heartbeat. She and these babies are everything I want. *She's* everything I want, and one day, when she's ready, she'll be my wife."

Taking my hand in his, he leads me away from Tom and toward the exit where his white Tesla is parked outside. The lights are still on, and the driver's door is swung open.

Opening the passenger door, I get in without argument, and he leans over to buckle me in.

"How did you know I was here? And why did you go off at him like that?"

Gripping the car door frame above his head tightly, he squeezes his eyes shut. "I'm here because I can't stay from you. I knew where you were because the hotel's name was on your wall calendar. And I went off at him because he accused me of hiding you." His hand flies out to tip my chin as he leans in and kisses my lips. "I want to yell about you to the whole world, Princess. You won't let me, so I'll wait. But like hell am I having another man, let alone your ex, tell me I'm anything but gone for you."

CHAPTER TWENTY-NINE

JENSEN

It's the final game of preseason, and when I walk into the locker room, all heads turn my way. "What? Do I have something on my face?"

"No, just good of you to join us," Zach drawls.

Zach has always been annoyingly early to each game, and now that Jon has retired, he's definitely stepped it up a gear as captain.

I'd be extra early if I wasn't fucking Kate's brains out half the time. And that's what it's been for the past three weeks.

Eat, sleep, sex, more sex, hockey, repeat.

She's insatiable. The thing is, I'm freaking out that she still hasn't committed to me. I thought that night in the shower was the turning point when she said she'd try, told me I was a good person, and called me JJ. I thought she was letting me in when she asked me to take it slow with her.

But now it feels like more friends with benefits who are going to raise children together.

Fuck. That. Shit.

So I might be late to today's preseason game, but I'm ready to take out anyone who pisses me off, including the opposition.

"You look like you've lost a dollar and then been slapped multiple times." Jessie comes to stand beside me, his arms crossed over his chest.

I say nothing but groan and start suiting up.

"I'll take that as a yes then. Have you asked her to move in?"

I shake my head, my mood getting progressively worse.

"Why not?"

"Because she doesn't love me, okay?!" I snap. My voice is way louder than I want.

"Fucking great, now the entire fucking team knows I'm down bad for a girl that doesn't want me in return," I grumble to Jessie.

"She does." Zach comes up behind me.

"She wants me in some kinda way, yeah," I huff out, not caring what he does or doesn't know about us at this point.

Zach props his skate up on the bench. "You know Luna was scared to make the jump, too, right?"

"This is different. That was logistics and lifestyle. This is about me. This is about her past, but fuck if I can't get her to open up to me fully. It's like two steps forward, one or sometimes several back."

"What about her past?" Jessie cocks a brow.

Shit, I've said too much.

"We've got a game to play," I deflect.

"True that." Zach claps me on the shoulder and makes for the exit, but Jessie lingers behind as I continue to pad up.

"What do you mean her past?" he presses.

I should've known he'd latch onto that and run with it. This guy has been through more shit as a kid than most humans experience in their entire lives. His heart is as big as an ocean, and anyone he can help fix, he's right there.

"I told you; I don't think her parents were good to her. She's damaged, man. She's so fucking beautiful, but she can't see it.

She's kept everyone but her closest friends at arm's length. The thing is, I know her heart wants me." I tap my finger against my temple and look him dead in the eyes. "But her head has thirty-six years of shit to wade through."

He nods, and I know he gets it.

"I know I'm it for her. I know I'm the one, and fuck if she isn't the only girl my head, heart, and dick wants. But I'm going backward, man. I'm now firmly a friend with added benefits. But I can't fucking stay away."

"You just need to keep telling her."

Finally full-kitted, I grab my stick and helmet and point to the exit, but not before I've given my best friend one last look. "Even if I wanted to pull back, I couldn't. She is my north. No matter which way she twists, turns, and tries to evade our truth, I'm pointing straight at her. We are meant to be together."

I AM PLAYING like total shit. Like a rookie caught in the headlights.

We're three goals down, and every single one has been my fault.

She's there, in the box, looking like a fucking dream, and I can't stop staring.

The game is passing me by with Zach shooting fucking daggers at me, and I know Coach Burrows is going to ream me out at the end of this period.

Like I give a shit.

"Where is your head at, man?" Zach screams at me when a fourth goal hits the back of the net.

I turn away from him and take a deep breath. Our fans are loyal to a fault, but I can sense the frustration and concern building. We've got one more period to prove to them that we're ready for the first game of the season.

"Did you hear me? Where is your head?"

"Not here," I say under my breath, the arena noise drowning me out.

"You're fucking this up!"

I whip around. "Do you think I give an actual fuck?!" I point at my chest. "Right now, I don't give a shit. I don't care."

"You do, man." His voice softens as the ice clears around us.

I laugh sarcastically. "I'll care when the more important things in my life are here. I'll care when I can't feel the palpable pain I know she's feeling. I'll care when the agony stops for me, too."

He drops his shoulders. "You really are in love with her, huh?"

"I've cared for and protected her for two years, but my heart fully fell when she told me she was carrying my children."

His eyes widen. "Wow."

I look around. "Can we not do this on the ice?"

"Yeah, sure." He props his hands on his hips. "Look. Why don't you just tell Burrows you're sick? I'll cover for you. Head home, get your shit together, and come back to an early morning skate on Saturday with a clearer head."

Fuck me, but that sounds like everything I need. "I can't do that to the team."

"You can and you will. I'm making the call."

I purse my lips, hating that I'm about to duck out of a game but knowing I've got no choice. "Alright."

Walking off the ice, Zach strides out in front of me on his way to sort out my mess with Coach Burrows, no doubt.

"Jensen?" My hand is on the locker room door handle when I hear her voice.

"Yeah." I keep my head straight forward, not wanting to look at her. Right now, I'm weak and vulnerable, and this time, I don't want her to see.

"Are you okay?"

Taking in a huge breath, I finally turn her way. She's dressed in black leggings and a long white sweater, and our bump is really starting to show.

Christ is she beautiful.

"Yeah, just sick. Maybe keep your distance for a while," I lie.

"Can we talk?" she says softly, taking one step toward me cautiously. I know she can read that I'm making excuses.

"Not right now, Princess."

"I need to tell you something." Her voice shakes.

Instinct kicks in. "Are the babies okay?" She's nearly sixteen weeks, so we should be out of the danger zone.

"Yeah. It's not about that."

"Okay, that's good," I nod. "But I need to head home."

"Don't close off, please."

"I'm not closing off, Kate. I'm just out of ideas with you. I need to reset and take a minute for myself."

"I'm trying. I know whatever happens, we'll make the best parents; you'll make the best daddy."

Holding up a hand, I drop my eyes to the ground. "Please, Princess. Not now. Not fucking now."

She steps forward again. "I was wrong about you."

"I know. You've told me this, and it's good. We're good."

"I can't bear to think you're hurting."

"Not now," I repeat, pushing the door open.

"When will you be ready to talk?"

My vision blurred, I finally show her my eyes. "When you're ready to admit you're in love with me."

"I feel so much for you."

"Yeah, I know." I grip the handle so fucking tight.

She stands there, this woman with so much strength who has been through so much. For the past two years, all I've seen is a hardened shell, yet today, she looks exhausted. But I can't keep forcing the issue. I can't keep letting myself into her apartment. At some point, you need that person to come to you to show you that she's ready to hold your heart in her hands and keep it safe. To give your feelings validation.

"You're still coming to the mid-pregnancy scan, right?"

How could she even doubt that? Whatever happens between us, she will never be without me by her side, raising our perfect babies.

My stick clatters to the floor, followed by my gloves, as I stride over to her.

Still in my full pads and skates and her in sneakers rather than heels, I tower over her. "You will never need to doubt my devotion to you," I say, placing a hand on her growing bump. "And my family. Hockey is a distant second to you and this pregnancy."

Looking up at me, she brings her palm to my cheek in response.

Fuck, I want to kiss all that doubt and worry right out of her.

"Do you want to see me before then?" Kate asks.

Leaning into her touch, I don't want her to go right now, never mind waiting two weeks for the scan. But I'm at that point where sleeping with her is killing me. Every time I slide inside her, my body is fucking, but my mind is making love.

I place my palm over the back of her hand. "As your Baby Daddy, no. As your boyfriend, absolutely yes. If you need me, I'm there, but the next time I put my hands on you, it has to be as your man."

CHAPTER THIRTY

KATE

LUNA

Okay, I've collected everyone's guesses and only Jon thinks you're having one of each. The rest of us think you're having twin boys or girls.

JJ

Hey, woah. I've always said one of each.

LUNA

You don't count. You're the daddy.

JJ

Yeah, I fucking am.

FELICITY

Oh the maturity in this group chat is palpable.

JON

I thought it was pretty smart actually.

FELICITY

I rest my case.

JON IS TYPING...

ME

Jon, if your next message in this chat concerns punishing your wife for her snark, then I'm leaving and withdrawing your entry.

JON

Fuck.

JESSIE

Withdrawing his entry...there's still a joke in there somewhere.

LUNA

ANYWAY. I personally would like two girls, please. That would counteract the two boys I'm to live with come March.

ZACH

We aren't done with babies, Rocket.

JON

I am LIVING for this.

JJ

I'm going to be the mature one here and say everyone be at my place at seven tonight. Dinner will be served at seven-thirty.

JJ

And Jon, prepare to taste and weep.

JON

Wifey, when can we arrange a dinner at ours?

ADAM

As long as it doesn't affect my weekly dinner nights with you.

ME

I'm going to go and be pregnant now.

JJ

Pick you up in an hour.

JON

(Princess)

JESSIE

Ooo...He's had you there.

I roll my eyes and close out the group chat. Nothing short of chaotic.

Standing up from my desk at work, I'm about to head to the bathroom for what feels like the fiftieth time this hour when an email from Mark Preston pings into my inbox. I take a seat as I process all he has to say.

From: Mark Preston

To: Kate Monroe

Cc: Nina Higgins

Kate,

Once again, congratulations on your news. We are delighted for you and wish you all the best with your pregnancy.

I have now had the chance to speak with my HR department in preparation for your six-month maternity leave, and I can confirm Nina Higgins will be stepping in to work on your cases during your absence.

I trust I can leave you to communicate and hand over all the work and details quickly, but if you have any issues, please let me know.

Kind regards,

Mark

Nina Higgins is a top-performing litigation lawyer in

Washington. She's formidable and has an incredible client retention rate.

Panic races through me when a response comes through from Nina herself.

From: Nina Higgins

To: Mark Preston

Cc: Kate Monroe

Thanks, Mark.

I'll be delighted to take on your cases, Kate. I know they'll be in excellent shape for me to pick up and continue working with your clients.

Let me know when you have time in your schedule to begin the case familiarization and handover process. Might I suggest not leaving it too late, perhaps a month to six weeks before your departure.

Regards,

Nina

UGH, NOT EVEN A FUCKING "KIND" before the regards, and who the fuck does she think she is? Of course, I wouldn't leave it "too late" to hand over my cases.

Moody, irritable, and now desperate to pee, I make my way to the bathroom and almost get taken out when the door swings toward me.

"Oh shit. Sorry, babe," Felicity winces.

"No worries." My tone is flat, like my mood.

"What's wrong?" She reaches out, placing a gentle hand on my arm.

Getting antsy to make it to the bathroom, I whisper-hiss. "Nina Higgins is taking over my caseload."

"What?? *The* Nina Higgins?" Her eyes flare with surprise.

Not helping Felicity.

"Yes. There's only one. She'll make me look like an amateur."

"Well, that's not true. And you never put yourself down, so don't start now."

"I'm not putting myself down. I'm just saying I can't live up to her." I glance around to make sure no one's listening.

Felicity looks down at my crossed legs and smirks. "Let's resume this conversation when you aren't about to pee yourself, shall we?"

She steps to the side, and I dash in, thankfully making it in time.

Nina Higgins nearly made me pee myself, *literally.* Ideally, I should wait and have a full bladder for the scan I'm about to have, but with the way I'm peeing lately, I'll no doubt be desperate again in a half hour.

Returning to my desk, I check my email for more delights, but this time, my phone screen lights up.

JJ

I'm outside. Do you want me to come up or wait here?

ME

I'm coming down now.

Grabbing my jacket and bag, I smile at my best friend as she says, "Two girls," and gives me a matching thumbs-up.

There's been a lot of speculation around the office, but no confirmation about who the father is. I've heard whispers in the kitchenette, where some have said it's Tom's. At one point, I almost choked on my coffee when I heard one of the receptionists claim I've been having an affair with Mark Preston.

The truth is, Jensen and I will announce the twins when we're ready. Just because he's thrust into the limelight doesn't mean every member of the public is entitled to every detail of his, or now my, life.

Jensen's parked along the sidewalk, and when he sees me approach, he quickly climbs out and hurries around to open my passenger door.

"Hey," I say, smiling sweetly at him.

He looks killer as always in black jeans, gray sneakers, and a cream long-sleeve designer shirt, the sleeves rolled up in the way he always does. He looks tired, though. His eyes are slightly puffy and red.

"Hey."

My heart drops when I see the deflated way he takes me in. Things have been only slightly better than really awkward since I saw him outside the locker room. We're talking, but only about the babies and when we're going to start ordering furniture, which we finally agreed would be after this scan.

He jumps into the driver's side and takes off toward the hospital, not saying another word.

"Are you excited?" I turn to him.

"Of course. This is huge." He throws me a quick smile but concentrates on the road ahead.

"Felicity wants two girls."

"I bet she does," he responds, taking a left.

"You still think one of each?"

"Yeah, I do. You?"

"Boys." I'm bound to be outnumbered for the rest of time.

Jensen looks at me and then back at the road. He opens his mouth but closes it again, clearing his throat.

"What were you going to say?" I push cautiously.

"Nothing."

"Tell me."

"It's fine."

"It's not fine," I argue as we pull into the hospital parking lot.

Putting the car in park, he rests his forearm over the steering wheel and blows out a long breath. "Just inner thoughts, Princess."

The nickname I once hated washes over me in a wave of relief—it's the first time he's called me that in a couple of weeks.

"Care to share them with the class?"

He shakes his head, and I deflate further. "Nah. Not class appropriate."

"Okay, fine. Let's get going." I grab my bag from the floor and open the door when he stops me with a hand on my thigh.

"Are we definitely going to find out today and know what we're having?"

With hope in his eyes and the way our group is so excited, I can't say no. I place my hand over his. "Yeah. Let's do it."

JENSEN

"Alright, let's see what we have." The sonographer pats the bed for Kate to lie on.

Getting the probe ready, I stare at the screen, waiting for the moment she places it on Kate, and I'm reunited with the two bundles that haven't left my mind since July sixteenth.

"Okay," the sonographer chimes, making some adjustments and pressing a few buttons. "Ah, here we are."

She stops over two much clearer heartbeats than the previous scan, and I hear Kate pull in a sharp breath.

Reaching out, I place my hand over hers as emotions overwhelm me. "There they are," I whisper.

"Amazing," she responds, wonder lacing her tone.

"I have in my notes that you declined the blood tests to find out the sex of the babies. We can confirm genders right now if you would like to know?" the sonographer asks.

I look to Kate to give the final word. I'm fucking desperate to know so I can start buying the shit out of every baby store I can find. "We still good?" I ask.

She doesn't hesitate. "Yeah. Hit me with it."

I chuckle, and without being able to stop myself, I lean across and kiss her forehead.

Yeah, baby daddies and friends don't do that, Jensen.

Kate's eyes flare wide, but the flush of pink painting her cheeks tells me she loves it. It gives me hope for everything I'm waiting, praying, fucking dying for her to admit.

"Well," the sonographer points to one baby on the screen. "First, everything looks perfectly fine, and you are right on schedule with your due date. Although, we may only take you to thirty-six or thirty-seven weeks. I'm sure your doctor has discussed all of that with you."

Kate nods. "Yes, since it's twins."

The sonographer nods back. "That's right. But that decision will be made by your primary care team. From my point of view, though, everything looks perfectly normal."

Every ounce of tension leaves my body. Fuck me having a baby is stressful, never mind having two.

"Now for the exciting part." She adjusts the probe and presses a couple more buttons.

"Wait, that's a dick," I blurt out.

"Jensen!" Kate hisses.

I snort a laugh and point. "It is! It's...sizeable."

"Well, yes, you're right. You are having a boy."

"Holy shit," Kate responds, then throws a hand over her mouth.

"And..." The sonographer moves the probe once more and then freezes the screen. "A little girl." She points to the image. "There she is, hiding behind her brother, but she's there."

Dropping my head between my shoulders, I fucking lose it. This fucking hard ass six-foot-three NHL goalie loses it right here in this tiny white room.

"Are you okay?" Kate reaches out, takes my hand from my lap, and places it into hers.

"Yep." My voice shakes, and I lift a finger. "Just one second."

Taking a moment and a huge gulp of air, I center myself and then turn to the sonographer. "Can we have a couple of minutes?"

She smiles and nods. "Sure, I'll get your images sorted." She hands Kate a paper towel to clean herself up and then closes the door behind her.

I move Kate around to face me, her lower legs dangling over the bed. Standing between her parted thighs, my hands tangle in her thick blonde hair.

I half expect her to protest at the way I'm touching her. But she doesn't. Instead, her body relaxes against mine. She wants this—us—as much as I do. I can feel it in my soul.

"Fuck it," I whisper into her hair.

Tipping her head up, I brush my lips over hers, causing her eyelids to flutter shut. "Kiss me," I plead.

"Baby daddies don't do this," she whispers back, a sly smile pulling at her lips.

"If you don't want me, don't want us, then pull away. But if you do, just like I know it deep down in my gut, kiss me. Let me put my mouth on you and finally make you mine."

Fuck, this is it. The emotions from the scan, seeing this incredible woman carrying my whole world. I can't hold back; I have to know which direction she's going to choose. My hands tremble as I hold her.

We're nose to nose, eye to eye, when her hands come to my waist, pulling me close, and my cock stirs at the contact.

"Just to be clear, if I kiss you, then we're doing this, you and me? We're going to give it a shot?"

"You still don't get it, do you, Princess? I'm not giving anything a shot with you. This is it. Forever."

"I'm scared."

I shake my head softly. "Don't be scared. Be mine."

Come on, Katherine. Hold my hand and jump with me.

My whole fucking soul lights up when she slowly presses her mouth to mine. Bringing my hands under her ass, I pull her into me as far as she will go, desperate to make us one. Her rounded stomach presses against my body, and automatically, my hand shoots down between us to smooth a palm over it.

But that's not enough. Pulling up her soft white blouse she'd only just tucked back into her black work pants, I roll it until it's just below her breasts.

"I don't think I've ever seen a more beautiful sight." My eyes find hers again.

Crouching down slightly, my mouth finds her navel as I press gentle, closed mouth kisses across her beautifully soft and perfect complexion, marks already beginning to show where her body is accommodating our children.

Kate gasps at the contact. "JJ, we're in the hospital. You can't fuck me here."

"I don't plan on fucking you," I say between kisses. "I plan on taking you back to my apartment, having dinner with our friends, and then making love to you in my bed."

"Oh." Kate's hand flies to her side.

"What? What's the matter?"

"Shhh. It's okay," she says in a hushed tone. "I just felt a kick."

"What?" I marvel, my voice cracking.

Taking my hand, she places it where hers was a second earlier. "Maybe they'll do it again."

Silently, we stare at each other while we wait, and I fucking pray I get to feel what my girlfriend just did.

Girlfriend.

That's fucking right, my girlfriend.

"Woah." A laugh bursts out of me as I feel movement.

"Crazy, right?" Goddamn. She looks so happy in this moment.

"Incredible." My voice is full of wonder.

"It's definitely the boy. Awkward, like his father."

Pressing my lips to hers, I smile against her mouth. "Well, you're my doppelganger and girlfriend, so what does that say about you?"

"It says I'm a very lucky girl."

CHAPTER THIRTY-ONE

KATE

Sitting at Jensen's kitchen island, I watch and swoon at how he moves around preparing dinner.

This man knows what he's doing in the kitchen. He wasn't kidding when he claimed he would make Jon weep.

"Can I help?" I ask.

"Nah, Princess." He rounds the counter with two bell peppers in hand. Spinning my chair around, he places them against my stomach and kisses me. "According to the book I was reading last night, at eighteen weeks, our babies are the size of bell peppers."

"And by the time I push them out, they'll be pumpkins." I wince. "I'll never be the same again—my pussy will never recover."

"Your pussy." Kiss. "Is fucking stunning." Kiss. "And always will be." Kiss. "And I really need to stop talking about it because all I want to do is slide inside you when I'm against the clock to get this food done."

"It's all in the prep." I cast a hand across the kitchen, offering a bratty smile. "You could've had some of this done already."

He huffs and gets back to chopping vegetables. "But someone needed to head home and change."

"I felt icky after that jelly and all day in my work clothes."

Throwing some potatoes into a pan, he smirks. "Sure, Princess. Not a diva at all."

I look him over, my nonalcoholic cocktail he made me to my lips. "Doppelganger, remember? Works both ways."

Sliding off the stool with sass for yet another bathroom break, I feel an arm come around my waist. Jensen's lips find the shell of my ear, sending shivers throughout me. "Are you doing anything tomorrow? We don't have a game or practice, and I assume you don't have work since it's a Saturday?"

I was going to spend some of it starting my preparation for Nina's benefit, but I find myself shaking my head. "Nothing."

"Here's the plan. Tonight, after everyone's left, I'm going to lay you on my bed and show you what the best night of your life looks like. Then tomorrow, I'll show you your greatest morning before we head out shopping for our babies *and* my girlfriend."

Girlfriend.

I keep waiting to freak out every time he says it, but I don't. Instead, warmth washes over me like it's the most natural feeling in the world. The moment I placed my mouth on his at the scan, it was like I finally decided to let go. To let him take control just like Felicity said I should. Trusting Jensen Jones with my heart and putting it in his hands is everything I want—*and need.*

"Shopping for me?"

He spins me around in his arms like we're dancing. "Well, I only have one girlfriend, so yeah, something for you."

Oh, here we go with the hockey player gift-buying malarky. I should've seen it coming, given all that happened with Felicity and Luna.

"I don't think I need anything. I have all I want."

I have you.

Narrowing his eyes, he quickly glances over his shoulder at the burner and then back at me. "I'm spoiling the shit out of you. Period. I don't want any bullshit 'Oh, I can take care of myself,'" he repeats in a mocking tone. "Yeah, I worked that one out a while back, Princess. But you belong to Jensen Jones now, and when that happens, even Princesses get an upgrade."

"WAIT, Kate, do you not want some pot roast?" Zach points to the huge dish set out in front of us.

I screw up my nose.

"She's off meat," Jensen answers, edging his chair closer to me.

"It's just the smell makes me want to puke."

"I told you we could've gone vegetarian tonight," Felicity says.

"It's fine," I say, waving a hand in front of me. "It's not as bad now that the morning sickness has worn off, but I'm good with my ratatouille and bread selection."

Jensen smiles at me, his fork halfway to his mouth, and I melt at the sight. I've spent way too long trying to make him scowl, and it's criminal when he has a smile like that.

Jon's fork clatters to his plate. "Right, I'm gonna step in here and say we've all congratulated Zach and Luna and Jensen and Kate on having babies. But is anyone going to congratulate me on guessing the genders correctly on not one, oh no, but all *three* babies?"

"No," Zach shrugs.

"Charming," Jon retorts.

"You're such high maintenance," I drawl, when suddenly, I feel a kick much harder than the previous ones, and my hand flies to my stomach.

Jensen is straight after it. "All okay?"

"Yeah, stop worrying." I giggle flirtatiously. I'm so fucking giddy at the thought of what he promised later.

Jensen's lips find the top of my head.

"*Knew it*. I fucking knew it!" Jon exclaims.

"Wait, are you guys..." Felicity motions between us with her fork.

He brings my hand to his mouth and kisses my knuckles, never taking his eyes off mine. "Finally, yes."

"Hell to the fucking yes!" Jessie shouts.

All heads turn his way, and he winces. "That was a bit loud, wasn't it?"

Zach narrows his eyes at his almost closed thumb and forefinger. "A touch."

"Just need to marry *you* off now." Jon waggles his eyebrows at Jessie.

He scoffs, pushing his food around his plate. "Not a chance."

The table falls silent as we take in Jessie's demeanor. Taking a deep breath and pushing his hand through his sandy blond hair, he throws his napkin on his plate. "That was fucking awesome, man. Thank you."

"Don't mention it," Jensen responds.

"I would suggest an eight out of ten." Jon shakes his hand out in front of him as if reconsidering his score. "Maybe eight point five."

"Please forgive my husband's lack of manners," Felicity jibes.

"Always so competitive," Zach shakes his head. "I can see it now when you're coaching, poor guys," he laughs.

"All I'll say is we're top of the league, and Jack is absolutely smashing it."

"He's a forward, right?" Jessie asks.

"Yeah. And an awesome one at that." Jon shakes his head in awe and leans back in his chair, crossing his arms over his chest. "I'm pushing him for the NHL. There's a place for him for sure."

"He was a free agent when he went to college, though, yeah?" Jessie responds.

"Yep. But Jon thinks he's got a chance at a team picking him up. With his contacts and everything." Felicity looks to Jon, hope in her eyes for her son's dreams.

"I do, Angel." He smiles back at her. "I'm talking with my former agent. We think he has a shot."

"What I would give to have had a dad like you." Jessie drums his fingers on the table, and we all look at him, wondering if he'll elaborate, but he doesn't.

"He started late, and being from the UK, he's had few opportunities, but he's talented, and now his technical skills are catching up with his skating. He's..." Jon gives a chef's kiss.

"That good?" Zach's eyes bug out.

"That fucking good," Jon confirms.

"Talking of good," starts Jensen, whose eyes haven't left mine all night. "Dessert? I made a Madagascan vanilla cheesecake."

"Can't you just buy those?" Luna asks.

"Yeah. But they're way better when you make them."

I stand as Jensen's hand trails around my waist, and I smile at the way he can't keep his hands off me.

I love my friends with all my heart, but right now, I just want to be alone with him and make up for all the times I've told him to fuck off.

Yet here he is, still obsessing, still wanting me.

"I'll serve it," I say, walking to the kitchen.

With my head in Jensen's refrigerator, my body leaves my skin as I turn around and find my boyfriend standing right behind me. His hands are in his pockets as he watches me swoon over everything he has in his fridge—all without meat.

Setting the cheesecake on the counter, I look up at him. "Go be with everyone. I've got this."

"I'm just watching you."

"What, like a stalker?" I jibe.

"Why does everyone think I'm some kind of stalker? Can't a boy be obsessed?"

The way I want to march him into the bedroom and let everyone else help themselves to dessert while I take a piece of my own.

Leaning against the fridge, I smile playfully at him. "Is that so?"

He steps closer, and I feel him all around me. He's intoxicating. "Yeah. I don't think there will ever be a day you don't drive me a little crazy."

Looking over my shoulder and to the living area, I hear laughter filtering through. "You have guests."

"*We* have guests."

"Are you going to fuck me right now?" His weighted look steals the breath from my lungs and promises he might just bend me over right here.

I sure hope so.

He bites down on his bottom lip. "Do you want me to?"

"Maybe."

He leans across and takes a spoon from the drawer in the kitchen island. Digging right into the cheesecake, he offers me a bite. "Don't take it all."

Leaning forward, I bite around half and slowly swallow. God, that tastes good.

Jensen slowly eats the rest but deliberately leaves some on the spoon. "Lick it clean, Princess." His tone is sultry and oh-so-sexy when he offers it to me.

I do just that, wrapping my tongue around the underside, keeping my eyes pinned on him. "Tastes so good."

His eyes hood. "Does it? I've already forgotten." Pressing my back against the refrigerator door, Jensen places his mouth over mine, swiping into me with his tongue. Pulling back, he licks his lips. "Yeah, so fucking sweet."

The way I'm obsessed with his dominance, the possessive way he watches and touches me. I want to stand in the mirror and scream, *'Who are you, and what have you done with Kate Monroe?'* But feminism has left the building, and in its place is the man I loathed for all the wrong reasons.

"Where did you go there?" He caresses my cheek with his palm.

"Somewhere nice."

"Yeah. Care to share?"

"I'm just thinking about us and the journey we've been on to get here, to this moment."

"Are you happy, Princess?"

My eyes sting. For the first time in my life, I am. "Yes. Are you?"

"I'm on top of the fucking world—no, universe. Nothing, and I mean nothing, could top my love for you."

"Y-you love me?"

He throws his head back and laughs softly. Looking at me, he tucks a lock of hair behind my ear. "I don't think love is enough. Four letters could never do justice to the way I feel. I guess I'll just have to spend the rest of my life showing you."

My heart thunders in my chest uncontrollably in the silence as I take him in.

That's until Jessie sighs heavily. "For fuck sake! Who's had a bite out of this?"

CHAPTER THIRTY-TWO

JENSEN

"So happy for you, man." Jessie, the last person to leave my apartment, pats me on the shoulder. "You really have it all now."

I nod. "Yeah, I do."

Standing by my apartment door, he looks down the hallway and then back at me. In a low voice, he asks, "Have you asked her to, you know, move in yet?"

"Nah. I only made her my girlfriend six hours ago."

"Yeah, yeah. Gotta give it some time."

"Maybe later tonight or possibly tomorrow morning."

His head whips up to mine, and he snorts a laugh. "Yeah, that doesn't fucking surprise me."

"Jessie?" I ask. We haven't spoken about it in a long while, but good friends check in every now and then.

"Yeah?"

"How you doing? Have you heard from her?"

He grips the back of his neck. It's been a long time since he told me about the reason for the trade from Dallas, and it had nothing to do with hockey and everything to do with a girl. He rarely talks about it or her, but I've also never seen him with anyone else. I don't think he ever moved on.

"No," he exhales heavily. "I don't expect to either." He looks away and then down at the floor.

"Go after what you want, man," I say. "And if it's still her, then don't let anyone stop you, least of all him."

He shoves his hands in the pockets of his jeans. "I still want her."

Thought so. "Then you know what you have to do."

He blows out a humored breath. "Stalk her? She's back in Dallas under *Daddy's* watch," he mocks.

"Who gives a fuck?" I shrug.

"Uh, me, my career, the Scorpions."

"Still waiting for a real reason."

He smirks and turns to head down the hallway, throwing a wave over his shoulder. "See ya, buddy, and congrats again."

Shutting the door, I think about how lucky I am to finally get my girl when I hear water running in the bathroom.

Shower sex...my favorite.

Walking through the living space and then down to my bedroom, I begin unbuttoning my shirt and then unzipping my pants, leaving a trail of clothes behind me and a shit-eating grin across my face.

Steam fills the room when I step inside, but my girl isn't in the shower. She's made herself comfortable in my huge tub, which, thankfully, is easily big enough for two.

Humming happily, she begins rinsing herself, squeezing the sponge over her shoulders and letting the warm water cascade through her hair and down her back.

I don't know what's more beautiful right now, her body or the happiness radiating from it.

I'm not even sure she knows I'm watching, and I want to keep it that way, so I bite down on my fist as my rock-hard dick leaks pre-cum at the sight alone.

Pulling her hair up, she twines it around her fingers and then pins it on top of her head with a black clip resting on the side.

As she continues humming, I recognize the tune—John Legend's "All of Me." And as I place my hands on her shoulders, slipping in behind her, I quietly sing the lyrics to the chorus.

She turns to me, her eyes wide. "Y-you can sing?"

I smile. "The surprises just keep coming, don't they, Princess."

"Like *really* sing."

Pulling her body into my chest, my cock rests against her ass under the water, and I begin to kiss up her shoulders towards her collarbone. "Yeah. I can. I just never sang for anyone until now. Until you."

"Did you take lessons?"

Reaching around, my palm is flat against her stomach as I stroke our babies softly.

"No. Just another of my many talents."

"Mmm-hmm." Tipping her head over her shoulder, she places a soft kiss against my lips. "What other talents do you have?"

"Let me show you." My hand travels from her stomach down to her apex, and without hesitation, she parts her legs for me.

"That's a good girl."

She whimpers as I slowly stroke her needy clit. Even under water, I can tell how wet she is for me. "Is this for me, Princess?" I say, burying my face in the crook of her neck as she sits between my open thighs.

"Yes."

"This pussy of yours is so fucking gorgeous and desperate and absolutely ready for me. Are you ready for my cock?"

"I want it."

"Okay, but I'm gonna need you to answer something for me first."

"Anything." She gasps as I push two fingers inside her and stroke.

"How can I put this?" I pause and stroke her again. "You see, now I have you as mine, and as I feared, it's still not enough. I need more."

She blows out a breath. "You're never going to stop, are you?"

"Being obsessed? Wanting everything you have to give? Probably not." I kiss her collarbone, and I feel her release over my hand. "Are you coming for me, Princess?"

"Yes."

Withdrawing my fingers, I lift her up, pressing my fingertips into the soft flesh of her ass. Seating her on my cock, she gasps as I stretch her out and then rock her over me by the hips. The bath water splashes over the sides, but I couldn't give less of a fuck if I tried.

"What do you want from me?" Kate asks, her head tipped forward as she rides me in reverse.

"I want you with me, every day, night, every goddamn minute. Bring all your houseplants, even Herbert, and let me have you all to myself."

"Jensen—"

"JJ."

"JJ," she corrects. "We've been together for only a few hours, and now you're asking me to move in with you. That's a huge deal."

She gasps again as I tilt her hips and hit deeper.

"Not really, Princess. It's just a step towards the rock I have in my dresser drawer."

"Wait. What?"

"You can try it on for size if you like. But judging by the way my cock fits you, I know it's going to be perfect."

Rocking her faster, she begins to unravel for a second time.

Bath water splashes everywhere as I reach up and unclip her hair, tossing it to one side.

"Yes, ohmygod, that's fucking amazing." she cries.

"Tell me you want me to give you another baby."

"Yes, I do. Come inside me."

And I do, over and over again. My entire body shakes and

shudders as I empty myself into my girlfriend. "I love you," I whisper.

Rising off me, she spins around and then sits back down on my still-hard dick. Being face to face, eye to eye with the most beautiful woman in the world as I enter her is everything.

"You gave me your cock before I said yes," she jibes.

Leaning her back, I take one of her nipple piercings into my mouth, biting down gently and tugging it. She writhes in pleasure, so I move on to the next.

Popping off her breast, I stare up at her as she continues to take what she wants from me. "Move in with me, Kate. I want you and our babies under the same roof permanently."

Her head falls back as she comes again, and her pussy tightens around my cock, drawing another orgasm from me.

"Okay," she squeaks out. "I'll move in with you."

LAYING her down on my bed, her towel dried hair is still wet when I run my fingers through it and lie down beside her, stroking her stomach.

"Ooof." She winces, her hand flying over mine.

Wow, that one was strong. "I felt that too."

She nods, but her face twists in pain. "Yeah, but this one actually hurt."

Kate winces again, and I feel another hard kick, almost like they're unsettled. "Wait here."

When I get back to the room, she's lying on her side facing me. Like a fucking angel or something.

Her eyes go wide when they drop to what I'm holding. "Wait, do you...play the guitar?"

I walk over to her in just my gray boxer briefs and sit next to her on the bed. "Come sit in my lap."

For a confident woman in public, Kate Monroe sure is tentative behind closed doors. She hesitates and then winces again. "They're definitely strong." She laughs. "I also think one of them has the hiccups."

"Come here."

This time she follows and sits in my lap. Placing the leather strap around her neck, I rest the Spanish guitar over her belly and slowly begin to strum.

"Is that 'Pappa Don't Preach' by Madonna?"

I chuckle softly and kiss her neck. "Yeah. Probably not my best choice, all things considered."

My dick starts to harden.

Not fucking now.

"Are they calming?" I say, strumming the guitar.

She nods. "Not one kick since you started playing. They like music like their Daddy."

Strumming out "Twinkle, Twinkle Little Star," my girlfriend melts into me, and I can feel the way her breathing slows and relaxes.

A couple of minutes later, she takes a deep breath. "Did you teach yourself to play?"

I nod over her shoulder. "Kind of. My dad is Welsh, and music and singing are a big deal over there. He taught me the basics, and I carried on. It helps me relax before and after games."

"You're Welsh?" She sounds surprised. *Again.*

"Half Welsh."

"Jones is a common surname here, so I just assumed you were fully Canadian."

"Nah. Mom and Dad met at Cardiff University. Mom was an international student."

"Can you do a British accent?" she croons.

I clear my throat and give it my best shot. "Good evening, your Royal Highness."

She barks out a laugh. "Finally found something you aren't good at."

"Oh, game on. Just watch me morph into Daniel Craig."

"Oooo, now that would be something."

"Dating me for all of ten hours, and you're already fanaticizing about another man."

"Well, you know, gotta keep my options open."

Pulling the strap from her neck, I lift her off me and lay her down on my soft white duvet, hovering above her. "Tell me I'm the one."

Her eyes flare.

"Go on, Princess. Say out loud what I know you've been thinking. That you and I are forever."

She smiles, and I know she loves how I test her boundaries like this.

Twining her dark blue fingernails through my hair, she nods slowly.

"Say it, baby, please."

A few beats pass in the silence of my bedroom before she whispers. "Forever."

CHAPTER THIRTY-THREE

KATE

"I'm one hundred percent waddling, aren't I?" I say to Felicity as we enter the family box, ready for the game.

"Hmm, I'd say less of a waddle at this point, more of a wallow from side to side," she responds as she takes her seat, and I do the same.

"Well, that's even worse!" I exclaim.

At twenty-two weeks pregnant with twins who are fighting to be the largest, I am freaking huge. Well, so it feels anyway. "Ugh, I'm so uncomfortable."

"Well, on the plus side, it's mid-November, so at least we won't be heavily pregnant in the summer." Luna balances her popcorn on her ever-growing stomach. She points to her bump. "This makes a great shelf."

"At least there's only one in there fighting for attention." I shift awkwardly in my seat, desperately trying to get comfortable. The kicking is non-stop, and the only way to calm them is when Jensen sings.

Right as my mind wanders to him, the players skate onto the

ice for warmups. I clock him straight away as he leisurely slides over to the crease, ready to begin his routine.

"Would you like me to wipe that drool from your chin, babe?" Felicity leans into me with a smirk.

I swipe at my chin, and she laughs. "Look, at least I can freely stare at him now." How the hell I kept up the persona of being unaffected by Jensen Jones for so long is beyond me.

When he drops down into the splits, I simultaneously cross my legs on instinct.

Jesus, I could go into early labor right here.

Luna barks out a laugh. "I mean, I like hockey and all, but you could argue this is the best part of the show."

"I'll say," Felicity agrees.

"Christ, don't tell Jon you're eyeing up other players while he's busy coaching," I drawl. "That boy is as possessive as they come."

She balks. "You are kidding me, right? Your boyfriend is a Rottweiler. It's hilarious, really, all the talk of you never falling in love or being possessed by a man, and here we are." She points to Jensen, who's started blocking Jessie's slap shots. "You two are the worst."

"I have to agree," Luna adds.

The lawyer in me would love to argue back and count all the reasons why they're wrong. But they aren't. He's everything and the total opposite of what I ever thought I would want—possessive, obsessive, borderline stalker, and oh-so-loving.

When I moved into his place two weeks ago, he had everything moved across town and into his apartment while he took me away for a mom-to-be spa break. Massages and pampering were what he said I needed, but that's questionable since he spent the entire forty-eight hours making love to me. We barely left the hotel bedroom, and when he wasn't inside me telling me all the ways he loved breeding me, he was cuddling me as I drifted to sleep, only to be woken up with him between my legs, tasting me.

Heat pools in my core at the memories, and this time, I know I'm drooling, so I quickly wipe away the saliva before anyone notices.

Jensen tells me he loves me every time he sees me; the last time was when he brought me breakfast in bed, just like he does every morning.

I need to tell him how I feel, but even when it involves arguably the most perfect man to walk the earth, I'm scared of saying the words out loud. I don't even know that I can. Other than to my girlfriends, I haven't used those three words in a very long time.

"All okay there?" Felicity taps me on the arm, breaking me from my daydream.

"Yeah," I bite down on my bottom lip to center myself and fight back the onslaught of mixed emotions.

"How are things coming on with the nursery?" Luna asks just as the boys skate off and back to the locker room, ready for the start of the game.

I shrug. "Actually pretty slow going. We have all the furniture built, but I'm worried about having them in the same room. What if one wakes the other?"

"Then put them in separate rooms. Jensen's place has four bedrooms," Felicity offers.

I scrunch up my nose. "I wanted them to be together. Then there's the choice of colors. Jensen wants to go with blue and pink, but I'm saying sage green. It's a good gender-neutral color. He doesn't care for it."

"We've decided not to do anything just yet. If the apartment sells, we'll be out and waiting for the new place to be ready."

Luna and Zach submitted an offer on a suburban home with a pool just outside of town, and it was accepted yesterday.

"It needs a lot of work, but you know us—renovations are our specialty," she giggles.

"It's a bit bigger than the beach house, babe," Felicity laughs.

"Plus, didn't you just spend that entire summer having sex and little else?"

She throws her hand to her chest in mock hurt. "We did *not*." Twisting her lips to the side, she reconsiders her response. "Okay, maybe, but the beach house was complete by the end." She pauses. "I just hope everything is finalized in time so we can at least move in before Aster arrives."

"God, I love that name," I say. It's beautiful and totally appropriate for star gazing Luna.

Names are one thing that Jensen and I have agreed on. Well, I say agree, we haven't actually picked them out yet, but the agreement is I get to decide the girl's and Jensen the boy's. I'm struggling to narrow mine down from ten possible options, but I'm pretty sure he's got his. He won't tell me, though. *Bastard.*

Felicity clears her throat. "Are you nervous about later?"

I assume she's referring to the fact that later on, Jensen plans to go public about our relationship. With my baby bump and the various pictures posted of us online, the rumor mill has gotten so intense that his agent and the Scorpions media team are fielding calls from all over America, and the speculation is becoming comical to deny.

"A little," I admit. "I'm a private person."

"They're just a pack of wolves." Luna bites out, and I know she's recalling the way they hounded her and Zach last year.

"I guess I'll lock myself away in the apartment and at work until the storm dies down," I shrug. "I can't control what they choose to say."

"Healthiest way to deal with it," Felicity agrees.

Butterflies swarm my stomach as the boys retake the ice under the flashing lights and blaring music, and Jensen skates over to take his position.

Tapping the goalposts with his stick a couple of times as he always does, he tips his head over his shoulder and looks up. I know he's looking for me, just like I've been watching him this entire time.

At this point, I don't think there's anything I wouldn't do for this man. On my knees or otherwise.

I HAD the option of being present in the media room when Jensen had his post-match interview. The Scorpions media team knows he plans to confirm our relationship status when the question inevitably arises.

But I declined, and straight after the game, Felicity dropped me off at the apartment, where I've been sitting on the couch watching the post-game analysis and waiting for the interview to start. I wanted to be alone for this and not make a big deal out of it, but right now, I'm regretting not having my girls with me.

Twisting my hands around in my lap, I decide to busy myself with my latest calligraphy project when my phone vibrates on the arm of the couch.

JJ

Listen for the door, Princess.

I frown at the message in confusion.

ME

What do you mean?

Just listen. I've asked security to let her pass.

Who?

Hollie, my sister. She showed up after the game today and then caught up with me outside the locker room. She's heading over now. Ideally I'd like to have been there when you met, but something tells me you'll hit it off and I'll just get in the way.

Panic races through me.

I'm sitting here in your sweatpants, t-shirt, and no bra!

JJ: Fucking hell. Don't tell me things like that. I'll have a boner for this interview.

I snort a laugh just as there's a knock at the door.

She's here. I'm nervous.

Don't be. She's just like me. But female.

Not selling it.

Desperately trying to smooth out my hair, I open the door and face a stunning dark-haired beauty. She's a similar height to me but with delicate features and the deepest brown eyes.

"Hi!" she squeaks.

"Hi," I smile. "Hollie, right?" I ask awkwardly, but I know who she is since she's been at the occasional game in the past.

"Yes!" Her eyes fall to my stomach, which, even beneath the baggy training top I'm wearing, it's clear I'm pregnant and haven't just had an overly large meal. "Oh wow, you really are showing now."

She steps inside and looks around at the apartment before setting her bag down on the kitchen island. "He hasn't done much with this place, but the houseplants definitely make an improvement."

"They're mine," I say, still trying to make my hair look presentable.

"Yeah, I guessed. My brother has never been good with living things."

She's funny and reminds me a lot of Luna, not just because of her eyes but because of her sing-song voice and sunshine personality. She makes me feel at ease, and I like her.

Hollie points at the TV in the living area. "I think the interview is about to begin."

I take a seat on the couch, but instead of taking the one opposite, she sits right next to me and turns up the volume.

"It's really good of you to fly in to see him like this."

She shrugs and sets down the remote. "Don't get me wrong, I like watching him play, but I didn't come for Jensen and missed most of the game anyway." She looks at me then, warmth in her eyes. "I came to see you."

"You did?"

"Of course! You're the woman who has my brother on his knees. That alone tells me it's worth getting to know you better."

I'm tempted to tell her I'm mostly on mine, but I figure she probably doesn't want to hear how filthy her sibling is in bed. I know I wouldn't with East.

Walking up to the microphone and taking a seat behind it, Jensen smiles at the flashing lights and cameras. It's not all that long since the game ended, but his dark hair still has a wet shine to it, and he's wearing his post-game dark blue suit.

"He looks so happy," Hollie croons.

"Firstly, well played out there. Talk us through the win today, Jensen, and the main targets you have for this season as a team." the off-camera reporter says.

Jensen sips his water and nods, setting the bottle down. Running a hand through his hair, he leans back and relaxes, like talking to millions of people is an everyday thing. I guess it is for him. "Thanks, it was a good game, and this season is like all the rest. Push hard, practice hard, play harder, and see where we wind up. The minimum has to be making the playoffs."

"Without Morgan on the team, do you think that will hinder your chances?" the reporter asks.

Swiping a hand across his mouth, Jensen leans forward on his elbows. "The absence of a player like Jon would be felt on any team, but we've started the season strong. We have no reason to doubt our ability to continue our winning form."

"And what about personally? What are your main goals this season?" a female reporter asks.

Jensen narrows his eyes her way. "Are we talking about my personal performance or personal life?"

My breath catches in my throat.

"Both," she confidently confirms.

Silence falls across the room as the media await a response.

Looking directly into the camera, I almost forget I have company or that viewers are watching this across North America and Canada. He's looking at me. I know he is.

"Professionally, I simply want to build on last season. I have a few technical elements to my game I want to refine." He pauses and blows out a breath. "Personally, I aim to be the best daddy I can be and finally marry the girl of my dreams, not necessarily in that order."

Muted conversation rumbles around the room as Jensen leans back and takes another drink.

"Oh, my God." Hollie gasps. "My brother is an actual swoonbucket."

"That he is." My drool is no doubt making another appearance.

"The girl of your dreams being Kate Monroe?" a different reporter asks.

My boyfriend smiles wide and winks at the camera. "Yeah, my girlfriend and mother of my two babies."

"Wait, two?" another voice shouts from the back.

"Absolutely. Kate Monroe and I are dating, and we're expecting twins in the spring, right after we get married."

My jaw hits the floor. I swear it does.

"Oh. My. God." Hollie elongates each word. "I came over here to help you pick out baby clothes. Now I'm thinking wedding dresses!"

Throwing herself into my arms, her black hair sticks to my cheeks. She pulls back, looking concerned. "Wait, are you okay?"

For the second time since I started dating this man, I sit and wait for me to freak out. For the panic to rise and the urge to run to kick in. But...these tears aren't anger or hate or anything else I've felt for him in the past.

These are tears of relief. To finally know what it feels like to love and be loved in return.

CHAPTER THIRTY-FOUR

JENSEN

HOLLIE

I left about a half hour ago. I thought you guys might want some privacy. I had planned to go baby shopping tomorrow, but maybe it should be dress shopping?!

MOM

Did you just propose on live TV?

DAD

Way to go, son.

JON

I'll be over tomorrow with the spare wedding planner I have.

JESSIE

Classic Jensen. Can I say congrats yet?

PRINCESS

When will you be home?

Right about now.

I walk into our apartment. Everything has been cleaned and wiped down, and I smile when I see Kate's sketchpad and pen set on the side.

Slipping off my loafers, trepidation overtakes me, wondering what I'm going to be faced with when I walk into our bedroom and see her.

I want to marry Kate desperately, but my eager brain decided I might as well announce it in front of the entire fucking population.

And once I did, a circus ensued, leaving me no time to check in with anyone, even Kate.

I toss my phone on the couch—everyone can wait. There's only one person I need to be with right now.

A soft glow greets me when I enter the bedroom, and I spot Kate sitting up in bed, looking like a fucking dream in a white silk cami nightdress. Her bump shows underneath the duvet that rests over it. Her blonde hair is down and around her shoulders. She's reading one of the baby books I bought her, and my heart squeezes so hard in my chest.

As I stand at the foot of the bed, she looks calm and collected—not the Kate I was half expecting to see.

Maybe we surprise each other sometimes.

"Hey," I say, pulling off my tie.

"Hi," she whispers.

Shrugging off my jacket, I start unbuttoning my white dress shirt. "Did you watch the interview?"

"I did."

I know she did.

"And?" I ask.

She replaces her bookmark and closes the book, resting it on her cute bump. "And nothing about what you say or do surprises me anymore."

"Are you pissed at me?" I ask, pushing the stress lump down in my throat.

She shakes her head. "No."

I narrow my eyes playfully at her as I unzip my pants. "What are you then?"

She sets the book on the bedroom floor and pats the bed beside her. "Waiting for you to come fuck me."

Barking out a laugh, I throw my head back as a mixture of happiness and relief hits me.

Fixing her with my eyes again, I push my pants down until they pool around my ankles, and I step out of them, holding out my hand. "Come here."

Slowly, she climbs out of bed and then takes my hand as I pull her toward me.

Wrapping an arm around her waist and raising our joined hands into the waltz position, I slowly start turning us around in a circle.

She chuckles. "What are we doing?"

"Dancing, Princess."

Clearing my throat and against the silence of the bedroom, I start singing out the lyrics to ABBA's "Dancing Queen."

She looks up at me, her swollen stomach rubbing against my body. "I need you to know that I...I love you."

I already know she does. I didn't need her to say it out loud for me to know. But the fact she did tells me she's ready.

Placing a soft kiss on her forehead, I close my eyes and leave this moment to fate. "Marry me, Princess. Be my wife. Let me dance with you in our bedroom when we're old and gray in our underwear. Give me that honor."

Keeping her beautiful blue but now slightly glassy eyes on me, she nods slowly. "You've blown every theory I had about you completely out of the water. You've proven me wrong at every turn. You've proven to be my soulmate, JJ. So, yes."

Taking her mouth with mine, I kiss her in a way that tells her she's my world.

"Hang on a minute."

Stepping away, I move to my dresser and pull out the small

black box I buried in there when I bought it right after Kate told me she was pregnant.

Standing there in her silky nightdress, I slowly spin around to face her and drop to one knee.

"I can't believe you bought a ring in advance." She props a sassy hand on her hip. "No, wait, I absolutely can."

Still on one knee, I cock my head to the side. "You going to let me put this on your finger or what?"

"I will, but once you get off your knee."

I laugh and come to a stand.

Popping the lid on the box, Kate's eyes go wide. "A black diamond?" She reaches out and touches it. "It's really beautiful."

The ring is set on a platinum band, and when I saw it sitting in a jeweler's window as a "one-off" piece, I knew that it was made for one person only.

My girl.

Slipping it onto her finger, it's the perfect fit and needs no adjustments.

"JJ, it's amazing." She looks at it in awe.

Resting my forehead against hers, I look down at the ring and place a hand over her stomach. "I want our wedding to be small and intimate. Just you, me, close family and our friends. What do you think?"

She palms my cheek and nods. "I know how much of a big deal this is to you after everything that happened last time. I never pictured myself having children or getting married. But now I do, and it's entirely because of you and how you've turned my life around. I'll happily marry you alone and in some dingy bar."

Kissing her gently, I smile against her lips. "I was thinking of my hometown."

"Perfect. And only East, Layla—his wife—and Ava. I want my parents nowhere near." She laughs darkly. "Not that they would anyway."

"Princess, you're my family now. I promise they'll never hurt you again."

Slipping her left hand, complete with my rock, into the waistband of my boxers, she palms my already hard dick. "I want you."

KATE

Walking to the bed with my legs wrapped around his waist, we kiss passionately, his tongue sliding against mine.

As he lays me down on the bed and lifts my nightdress, a satisfied smile spreads across his face. "No underwear."

"You like me bare, right?"

"Damn right, I do." Pushing his boxers to the ground, he drops to his knees on the floor and then pulls me towards him.

"I want to know if wife pussy tastes any sweeter."

He licks me from my ass to my clit, circling his tongue until my hips rocket off the bed.

"I never thought it could be sweeter, but it fucking is." He licks his lips. "You've always tasted like mine, but now you taste like forever."

"I want you inside me," I cry as the first orgasm hits me hard, melting me into the mattress.

Crawling over me, he positions his huge cock at my entrance.

"Please," I beg.

"Please, what?"

"Please give me your cock."

"That's a good girl." He pushes in halfway but then stops, leaving me more desperate than before. "Tell me you're in love with me."

This moment feels bigger than when he put a ring on my finger a few minutes before. But big doesn't necessarily mean scary, and I'm not scared anymore. I'm nervous about what my future as a mom and wife will look like for my career, but mostly, I'm excited. I know he's what I want.

He's the only one that's made me feel this way.

"I'm in love with you."

He smirks. "Yeah, you are. But remember, friends don't do things like this."

I smack his chest lightly. "You told me you'd remind me of this moment."

"I know I did, and one thing about me, Princess—I always keep my promises."

Sliding all the way in, I gasp at the way he fills me. "Friends don't do this, Kate. I've never been your friend. I've only ever been your endgame."

In the soft light of our bedroom, I let my fiancé make love to me, and I feel it all. All of the emotions I've been fighting back from the moment I sat on his lap and convinced myself he was an asshole.

Kissing me gently as he brings me to the edge of utopia, Jensen looks me in the eyes. "You gonna go find a dress tomorrow with Hollie?"

"Yes, I think so."

Tipping my head up, he begins kissing down my neck while moving inside me in languid strokes that set my body alight.

"Do you know how hard it's going to be for me after you have our babies not to put another inside you right away?"

I fall apart and come so hard my vision blurs. I would cry out, but every muscle in my body contracts, and all I can manage is a needy whimper.

"My girl has a breeding kink." He continues to move inside me, going deep and hitting that spot. "See, we're the perfect match. You love to be full of me, and I love to watch you take it."

He withdraws and slowly flips me onto my hands and knees. Spanking my ass, he re-enters me. "You'll always be my naughty girl with a pretty pussy and a wicked tongue."

Even if I could summon the energy to argue or respond, I

wouldn't. And as I comply with his commands, he fucks me so good from behind, his head back and his hands on my hips.

"I'm going to come inside you, Princess. Are you ready for my cum?"

My plea is a desperate, muffled one. "Yes."

As he empties himself inside me, he withdraws and then leans down on one forearm and kisses the back of my hand, now wearing his ring. "I fucking love you, Katherine Jones."

CHAPTER THIRTY-FIVE

KATE

JON HAS ADDED KATE, JJ, FELICITY, LUNA, JESSIE, AND ZACH TO THE GROUP CHAT.

You are joking, I think to myself as I stir creamer into my decaf coffee, which incidentally tastes like shit. At this point, I'm not even sure why I continue to have it.

"Did you just get this?" Felicity stands at the entryway to the kitchenette, her cell in hand.

"Yep," I say, leaning back against the counter and resting my mug on my twenty-four-week pregnant stomach.

She looks down at her phone again and rolls her eyes. "He just changed the name of the group to Operation Kate and Jensen's Emergency Wedding."

I fight back a smirk.

"Do you want me to message him and ask to rein it in? He's getting carried away again, just like he did with getting Zach and Luna together."

"I think it makes him happy," I shrug nonchalantly.

"It drives me insane. Apparently, he dropped one of his wedding planning folders off at yours the other week?"

"He did." Dumping the rest of the coffee down the sink, I turn to her. "But honestly, the venue is booked. I have my dress, we have the rings, and the officiant is happy to marry us on Christmas Eve. I don't see why we need to overcomplicate it. We just want a simple wedding."

"Now there's a sentence I never thought I'd hear come from your mouth, let alone the groom-to-be Jensen."

"Girl, I'm standing here twenty-four weeks pregnant with twins. I'm being told that they want to deliver the twins at thirty-six weeks, and I'm about to meet with Nina Higgins about handing over my entire caseload to her in eight weeks. And I'm not in the least bit phased. All I can think is that the shade of sage green I finally convinced JJ to use had better be drying lighter than what it looked like when I left this morning."

Okay, maybe I am panicking a bit about what my job will look like when I return to work.

She snorts a hard laugh. "Jesus, in a matter of weeks, you'll be Mrs. Jones. I keep thinking I've died and stepped over to some parallel universe or something."

I fill my glass with water from the cooler and turn back to her. "The only thing I'm nervous about is meeting his parents. Sure, I've met them briefly at games but never to talk to and never as the mother of their son's children and now fiancée."

Hollie is amazing. We hit it right off from the moment she walked into our apartment until I dropped her at the airport the next day. The wedding dress and bridesmaid colors were all picked out and in hand.

"I don't think you need to worry about that babe."

"No?"

She shakes her head. "Not everyone is like your parents."

"East called me last night and said they wouldn't even acknowledge the wedding or my existence at this point."

The scowl that crosses my friend's face is enough to sink a thousand ships. "They really are disgusting."

I nod, but I can't find the words to describe how truly awful they can be.

"Do you think you'll ever see or speak to them again?"

A lump forms in my throat. Despite the people they are, they're still my parents and, ultimately, grandparents to our children. "I don't know," I say in a shaky voice. "I think it's doubtful, and I don't want to expose anyone, let alone my own blood, to their mean-hearted ways."

Slowly, she nods. I know she doesn't have any words to console me because, honestly, saying anything other than acknowledging this shit situation would be a lie.

Her cell buzzes in her hand again. "Jon's concerned that you haven't arranged a cake."

I pick up my phone and start scrolling through the messages when I land on the one Felicity is talking about.

JON

Let's discuss cake options. I vote for some kind of buttercream, but avoid lemon. I think that was my only mistake at our wedding. Otherwise the organization and choices were perfection.

JJ

Jon Morgan—humble as ever. Princess, do you want a cake? Personally, I'm happy to take my dessert later on.

My cheeks flush. I know exactly what dessert he has in mind.

JESSIE

Annnd I've just puked in my mouth.

JON

I'm reaching suppliers in Alberta right now. You cannot get married without a cake.

ME

Let him organize the cake if it makes him happy.

FELICITY

For the love of God, Jon. Haven't you got a practice to get to? Maybe another season in the NHL wouldn't be a bad thing. Keep you busy and out of trouble.

ZACH

I'd be so down for bossing him around as his captain. Payback.

JON

Hockey was fun and all. But I've found my calling.

I look up at where she's still standing in the entryway, and we both laugh.

I wave a hand in front of me. "Let him have his cake and eat it too." Checking the time, I realize I've only got ten minutes before I meet with Mark and Nina.

"Since the boys are on an away series, I invited Luna around to ours for a movie night. I actually came in here to ask you if you want to join. Jon's at a late-night practice and, knowing him, won't be back much before midnight."

Walking toward her, I plant a kiss on her cheek. "Yeah, that sounds perfect. Just don't drink wine in front of me, and I'll be good."

"So these are currently your open cases?" Nina pulls the folders towards her and begins flipping through the pages.

"Yes, that's right," I reply confidently.

"I assume the Plaintiff has filed a complaint in all these?"

I sit up straighter. Is she trying to look for holes in my work or simply understand the cases better? "Yes, that's right." I repeat.

Nina nods but doesn't look up at me as she takes another folder and flips through the paperwork. A lot of my files are paperless, but she insisted that she wanted them in front of her so she could make notes on each one.

Mark Preston folds his hands together on the table and offers me a warm smile. "Are you still aiming for a six-month maternity period, Kate?"

"I am, yes."

"My sister-in-law had twins," Nina pipes up, never once taking her eyes from the file. "She's a professional too. Initially, she anticipated a six-month leave, but that soon turned into twelve." She closes the files and looks at me for the first time in several minutes. "Then she returned part-time." Her tone is icy and judgmental.

I feel one of the babies kick and I inwardly smile.

That's right, Bubba, sock it to her.

"I'm pleased she got the time off she needed. It sounds like your sister-in-law made all the right decisions for herself as both a mom and a professional."

I don't miss the slight narrowing of her eyes. I'm sure Mark missed it, but this woman clearly has an agenda, and I fear I'm the potential victim. Who the hell does she think she is judging others?

Mark clears his throat. "We also need to discuss what your return to work will look like, Kate, including updating all the correspondence since I assume you will be taking Jensen's surname."

I fight back a smirk, imagining his response if I kept my maiden name for work purposes...*tempting*.

"Yes, Kate Jones." It's the first time I've said it out loud. Again, I wait for my panicked response, but there's nothing—only warmth.

"We will also need to discuss client generation for you on your return," Mark adds.

"Well, we have many referrals, and as long as new clients are aware of my return date, I can start taking on inquiries."

Mark shifts in his chair and then looks across at Nina. "Do you have any more questions for Kate?"

She taps her pen on the table. "Has the judge for each of these cases issued schedule orders?"

"For some, yes." I lean across and point at the tabs. "Each file labeled green is at this stage. You will then find a detailed breakdown of the timelines and dates on each page."

I can tell my response is both satisfying and annoying to her at the same time.

That's right. I know my shit too.

"Okay, no more questions." She gathers the folders up. "I'll let you know when I do."

I'm sure you will, Nina.

"No problem." I smile sweetly up at her as she turns to leave the meeting room.

But the moment I look back at Mark, my smile disappears.

The door closes behind Nina, and it's at that moment my stomach drops. I know whatever is going to leave his mouth next is not good.

"I wanted to talk to you about the referrals, Kate. Yesterday, we heard that Monroe & Co. is withdrawing from our arrangement. I was on the phone with Henry this morning, and he explained that, at this point, they have a better and more appropriate firm in mind. They also explained that their fees were more competitive than ours." Mark twists his lips together. "Don't get me wrong, the majority of our business comes from new client inquiries, but our referrals are also a main source of income to the business. Monroe & Co. are one...were one of our biggest introducers."

I've been waiting for something to go wrong, for them to follow through on all the promises and threats they made when they paid for all of my tuition, when they got me opportunities using their contacts, as they would always remind me.

"Just follow our rules, and don't let us down."

Words fail me as the room begins to spin.

"Did something happen, Kate? Your parents are ordinarily very supportive of your career and our firm; likewise, we are of them and their exemplary practice."

Bile rises in my throat; this might be the second time I puke at work. I don't know how much to tell him. The temptation to reveal that they might be kick-ass lawyers but asshole parents is strong, but I know that will only end badly for me too.

"I don't know what's happened, Mark. I wasn't aware of an issue until you raised it."

He flattens his lips together. "It's just come out of left field, and to be honest, David and I are left confused and, well, reeling."

My eyes sting with tears, and I blink hard to push them away. "I can have a word with my parents if you like?"

I know that's what he's getting at, even if he doesn't say it out loud.

A relieved smile spreads across his face. "Would you?"

"Yeah. Of course."

Standing to leave, he pushes his chair back. "Is the plan to deliver at thirty-six weeks?"

I nod. "Yes, I'm moving to check-ups every two weeks after Christmas, but I'll be in the office as much as possible."

Mark smiles at me, although I can tell he's stressed. "You've been one of our finest lawyers, Kate, and I'm sure we can expect many great things from you in the future. Just..." he scratches the back of his head. "Just let me know the outcome with Henry and Violet, would you?"

"Thank you. Yes, I will."

He steps out, and I begin gathering my things, tears running down my cheeks. My biggest fear has always been that my last name means more to David and Mark than what I can bring in my own right. I wonder if that's why he asked if I'd be changing it. I wonder if that's why he thinks my parents are pissed.

I wonder how much of what I've achieved in my life has really been them in the background pulling the strings.

CHAPTER THIRTY-SIX

JENSEN

Multiple days of "I'm fine" has driven me to the brink of insanity. At one point, Jessie sat with me in my hotel bedroom to make sure I didn't catch the next flight from Dallas back to Seattle and completely miss the rest of the away tour.

She's not "fine," and I know that. She can't hide anything from me. Her being upset for whatever reason devastates me, but the fact she won't say tears my fucking heart out.

I might as well be on the bench watching the game playing out in front of me. I've been God awful, and we're down one-three in the final period.

The Dallas winger flies down the ice, heading straight for me. Zach has saved me several times tonight, but not right this second when he passes the puck off to their center, eliminating our captain from the defensive line.

Barreling toward me, their center wastes no time in sinking the puck in the top right-hand corner. I failed to track his movements or recall his favored approach from the hours of game tape I've watched and apparently memorized.

"Fuck, this game is totally buried." Zach skates past me, shaking his head, his hands on his hips.

Circling around, he skates over to me. Whatever he or Coach has to say at this point makes no difference to me. I just want back on the team plane and back to my fiancée.

"Your head has been in the toilet this whole away series, man. We can't do this without you."

"Yeah, well, there are bigger things in life than just hockey," I respond.

Fire swarms his eyes. "Not when we're on the ice."

He skates away, ready for the re-start, and I know we'll probably concede again between now and the final five minutes of this game.

"FUCKING SLOW DOWN, WILL YOU?" Jessie races up to me, his carry-on trailing behind him as I make for the parking lot in the private airport.

"Your little legs struggling to carry you?" I jest, looking over my shoulder.

He scoffs. "I'm six-two and hardly small!"

Picking up the pace, he finally catches up to me as I pop the trunk on my Range Rover, a new car I bought to get ready for the twins' arrival, and throw my case inside.

"She'll be okay, you know. She's a big girl."

"Something's bothering her, and she won't tell me. It's freaking me out, to be honest."

"You think she's..."

"Getting cold feet?" I finish for him.

This is exactly how Lauren was in the weeks leading up to our wedding. I told myself she was just nervous. In reality, she was fucking my best friend. Not for a second do I think Kate's cheating on me, but something's off.

"I don't think that's the case." Jessie leans against my car, the streetlamps our only source of light at ten p.m. on a cold December night.

"Something's eating at her." I squeeze my car key in my hand. "Fuck me, man, if she says she can't marry me, I'll...she's fucking everything to me."

He rests a palm on my shoulder and squeezes. "Get back to her."

I look at him. I've been so out of it this past week that I haven't spent much time with him, but he hasn't been around much, either. "Where were you last night anyway? I didn't see you at the bar."

He flushes slightly, and I notice, even in the dim lighting. "Out."

"With..."

"Yeah." He shoves his hands in his pockets. "But for fuck's sake, keep it to yourself."

I nod. "Are you two?"

"Sleeping together?" He laughs. "No. But I did take her out."

"And?" Jesus, it's like pulling teeth.

He runs a hand through his dark blond hair. "And...I want her, and I think she wants me."

I hold out my fist to bump him, but he leaves me hanging.

"Yeah, I don't feel like celebrating right now. Just head back to your girl and let me know you're okay." He taps the hood of my car on his way over to his.

"You're all set for Banff, right?" I shout.

He waves over his shoulder. "Yeah, your mom texted me last night to confirm my measurements."

When I get home, Kate is asleep on the couch, the soft blue blanket she brought from her apartment half draped over her ever-growing stomach. Even when she snores, which she absolutely does, she looks stunning.

Kicking off my shoes, I approach her. But before I slide in behind her on our huge couch, I pull out my phone and snap a picture of her sleeping peacefully. No worry or stress etched across her face. No concerns about working or thinking of the next thing she needs to do—she's content and comfortable to live in this moment.

Pulling my top over my head, I slide in behind my fiancée, who, thank Christ, is still wearing my engagement ring. She's answered my calls and texts while I've been away, but her spunk has gone, replaced by a shadow of her sassy self.

She stirs as her familiar citrus scent spreads warmth throughout my chest.

"Hey, Princess. I'm home," I whisper into her ear.

She groans as I barely make out a "Hey."

Reaching around, I palm her stomach, but she turns over to face me, opening her beautiful eyes slowly. "I missed you," she says.

Relief washes over me. "Yeah?"

"Yeah. It's been a shit week."

Pushing her hair back from her face, I tuck it behind her ear. "What happened, and why didn't you tell me before?"

"Because I knew you'd go off and because I'm a big girl who can fight my own battles."

"Battle? Who's giving you shit?" I growl.

"It's a long story."

"I've got time. Our whole lives, in fact." I kiss her forehead.

She huffs out a breath. "In a nutshell, Violet and Henry have cut off referrals to Mark Preston. He wanted me to speak to them. So I did."

Every fucking nerve fires off in my body. "You went to see them?"

She nods. "Yep."

"You should've waited for me to come home."

"I can take care of myself. Not that it would've mattered anyway. They were home but refused to answer the door."

I pull back. "They left you standing on the front porch of your own family home. In the freezing cold December weather? Fucking pregnant?" Each word gets harsher as it leaves my tongue.

Placing her hand on my chest, I know she can feel my racing heart. "Yeah, it's shitty of them, and yeah, it makes me think that Mark and David are more interested in my last name and how it benefits them than they are in me as a lawyer. But trust me, they've done much wor—"

She clamps her mouth shut like she didn't mean to go that far.

"What?"

"Nothing." She strokes my cheek, trying to soothe me.

Not happening.

"What the fuck did they do to you, Princess?"

"It was a long time ago."

"Doesn't matter, tell me, I need to know everything about you." I press my forehead against hers. "Just like I'll give you every part of me."

Pressing her lips together in a thin line, she squeezes her eyes shut, almost like it pains her to recall the memories, and that breaks me in fucking two.

"When East left to go to college, I had two years remaining in high school. They were two key years to get me into the best schools and get the best grades. I was already achieving those things, but that wasn't enough for Violet and Henry—they wanted their daughter to be the country's top-performing student. You were right with what you said that time—my success was an extension of theirs." She pauses and inhales slowly. "They pretty much locked me away for that period—no friends, no social life, definitely no parties. I tried to sneak out from my window once or twice, but they installed a lock. They said it was for my own good and 'time spent partying was time lost studying, leading to mediocrity.'"

I pull her into me, burying her face in my chest. Her shoulders start to shake. Kate barely cries, and fuck me, does it tear me limb from limb to hear those words and then the pain in her cries.

"That's all I've done my entire life. Expect perfection and never take a minute to sit back and relax or acknowledge what I've achieved. If I did, they'd be onto me, reminding me of how I might be at the top right now, but one slip and someone would take advantage of my weakness. Decades of that weight of expectation is enough to break someone," she sobs.

"If you weren't pregnant with my babies and I wasn't about to be a dad, I would be hauling ass over there right now to bury them in those fake-ass manicured gardens. No one would miss them."

She shakes her head against me. "They aren't worth it, and a lot of people would miss them. What the public sees and thinks about my parents is far removed from who they truly are."

"Yeah, I worked that one out already."

A long stretch of silence passes between us as I embrace my broken girl and run over the options in my head, debating whether to grab my keys and do exactly what I want.

But those babies and Kate hold me back.

"Come here."

Sitting up, I pull her to straddle me on the couch, wrap her blue blanket around her shoulders, and focus her attention on me.

"Is six months really what you want?"

"I don't know. I'm scared that taking longer will be too much, that I'll lose touch and be left behind."

Smiling warmly at her, I place a soft kiss on her hair. "It's not about being 'left behind,' Princess. It's about embracing life and how it changes for us. Everything happens for a reason."

"You really believe that?"

I nod slowly. "Everything about you, our babies, and the fact that in a couple of weeks, we're going to fly to Banff and get married is all part of the plan. Our plan. What was meant to happen for us. I've been falling for you for so long now, even before that night at Jon's and Felicity's wedding. I've just been waiting for you to catch up, and now that you have, I just want you to trust the process. Trust what your heart is telling you and work to eliminate all that bullshit your parents fed you when you were younger. They're toxic. They're fucked up. Not you."

She swallows thickly as she digests my words. "I'm officially rescinding my previous comment. You aren't a prick; you never were. You are, in fact, my prince."

CHAPTER THIRTY-SEVEN

KATE

Banff is a place I've always wanted to visit, especially at Christmas. But did I actually think I'd be getting married here?

Hell to the no.

Did I think I'd leave my future sister-in-law to make all the arrangements alongside my fiancé's ex-captain? *Also no.*

But here we are, on the morning of my wedding, as I look out over the snowy mountainous landscape of one of the prettiest places I've ever seen.

Jensen said he wanted to marry me in Alberta, so when Hollie suggested a chic hotel set in the heart of the town, I knew it was perfect. How they managed to get availability at such late notice remains a mystery, but I guess anything is possible when your man is the resident hockey star.

Hollie asked me if I wanted a beautician this morning, but I declined. I've been doing my hair and makeup for as long as I can remember. Sometimes, when I was alone and stuck in my bedroom as a teenager, I'd kill time by teaching myself the latest trends, pretending that I was going out with my friends and not being held prisoner in my own home by my own parents.

But this morning wouldn't be complete without my girls next to me.

The door to my bedroom creaks open, and a huge smile breaks across my face as Luna and Felicity enter, dressed in gorgeous sage green, the same color as the twin's nursery. Their long, flowing, silky dresses hug every curve and line of their womanly figures, taking my breath away.

"Holy hell." Luna's hands fly up to cover her face.

"You've seen the dress before," I say.

"We have, but not like this. The finished article." Felicity waves a hand up and down my body. "I'm really glad Jensen managed to convince you he was the one because, wow, you make the most beautiful bride."

"I can't see my feet, as predicted," I say.

My dress is an ivory corset lace bodice which then flows straight out from just below my breasts, leaving plenty of room for my huge bump.

"I don't think I have another nine weeks in me, you know. How the doctors think I'll make it to thirty-six weeks is beyond me."

Luna sighs. "I'm gonna be honest. It was a struggle this morning. My bump is getting out of control, and this dress only just made it." Her long, auburn hair curls around her shoulders as she breathes in and then back out.

"Yeah, I don't think you can breathe in the baby," Felicity laughs.

"Ugh, I have such bad water retention. Everything is swollen." Luna throws her head back and groans. "And all I can think about is pickles."

"On their own or as part of a wider meal?" Felicity laughs.

"No, on their own and straight from the jar. Zach tried to steal one the other day for his burger. I nearly impaled him with my fork."

"I don't think I have any cravings."

"Just JJ's cock," Luna croons.

She's not wrong.

Right at that moment, a knock on the door sounds, and a familiar female voice calls from the other side.

"Shit, that's Claire, Jensen's mom!" I whisper-shout. "Do you think she heard that last bit?"

"I don't really think it matters if she did, babe." Felicity points to my bump. "She already knows you're not averse to his dick."

"Shhhhh!" I exclaim, which draws a laugh from my two best friends.

"Come in!"

Claire steps into the room wearing a sage green two-piece suit and a cream hat. She looks stunning with her dark hair and striking features. I can certainly tell where her son got his looks.

"We'll give you a moment." Felicity and Luna step out of the room, closing the door behind them.

Since our engagement, I've spoken to Claire on Facetime and the phone more times than I have my own mother in a lifetime, but I've only met her a handful of times at games. At that point, I hated her son, and I'm pretty sure she knew it as well.

So, naturally, this feels more nerve-wracking than the thought of standing at the end of the aisle in an hour and exchanging vows I'd convinced myself I never would.

She steps closer, her eyes wide as she takes me in from head to toe. "Kate, you look...well, you look absolutely incredible." She reaches into her purse and pulls out a tissue. "I've got a few of these on hand for today."

"Thank you." I pause. "I'm sorry we haven't had much time to plan or speak before we got to this point. This entire six months has been surreal, but in the best way."

She smiles warmly. "Kate, it really doesn't matter if you've been dating my son for months or years. Couples move at their own pace, and when feelings are as strong as they are between you and Jensen, you just have to go with it."

I huff out a laugh. "My feelings have always been strong, if not misplaced at times."

She chuckles and steps closer, taking my engagement hand in hers. "I actually found the whole thing entertaining."

"Wait, you did?"

"Yes! Here's my cocky, flirtatious boy being brought to his knees by the one woman who couldn't stand the sight of him. I don't know what happened between you two, but it was sure funny to watch you put him through the wringer. I appreciate a strong woman with values, and that's all I needed to know about you."

I consider telling her what happened in Riley's that night. But really, what's the point? It's just another part of our love story and journey to how we got here.

"Well, I hated that I wanted him too. I was convinced I had him all figured out."

"Jensen Jones is for sure an enigma. Just like you, he takes a long time to figure out, but when those special few take the time to peel back the layers, they are often surprised."

"Well, I sure am."

Claire lowers her voice. "I'm really sorry your parents couldn't be here today."

I shrug. "I'm not sure I am."

I've shared a little bit with Claire during phone calls, but the only people who know the whole truth are Easton and now Jensen. But like her son, Claire is perceptive, and I can tell she's read between the very painful lines.

"Hollie has everything pretty much ready down there," she laughs. "And Jon is following her around, checking items off in his folder."

I smirk. "He's in the wrong career, that boy."

She squeezes my hand. "Let's go get you married because I, for one, cannot wait to have you as part of our family, and also,

I'm a touch concerned Jensen is going to murder Jon if we don't get everything started soon."

STANDING on the other side of the doors to the room where I'm about to be married, I wait once again for the reality of my situation to hit me—for the one-eighty my life has taken to come barreling towards me and hit me square between the eyes. But it doesn't. If anything, I want to be back and near Jensen, given I haven't seen him since we flew in yesterday.

John Legend's "All of Me" starts and filters underneath the doors as they open, and Felicity turns over her shoulder where she's standing next to Luna and offers me a reassuring wink.

Since I'm standing around the corner and out of sight, I watch as both of them disappear and turn to head into the main room, where Jensen is standing alongside his best man, Jessie.

I can't imagine how nervous he must feel. Memories of the last time he was in this position must be flooding his mind.

But I'm not going anywhere.

The moment he sets eyes on me walking up the aisle alone, which I wanted, he covers his face with his hand, and I know he's hiding the emotion also building behind my eyes and in my throat.

This is it. Our forever.

The chapter neither of us saw coming, or at least I didn't, and with the very last person I expected.

As I hand my small white bouquet to Felicity and come to stand next to him, he reaches out and slowly intertwines his fingers with mine.

Leaning into me slightly as the officiant begins her introduction, I get a waft of his familiar cologne, a sure sign that no matter where I am, I'm exactly where I need to be.

"I want you to know that I've longed for this moment.

Whether you were carrying my babies or not, it was my ultimate fantasy to hold your hand at the end of an aisle, any aisle, and exchange vows with you. Thank you for making my dreams come true."

I squeeze his hand tightly as the tears begin to tumble. "I know. Thank you for believing in us."

CHAPTER THIRTY-EIGHT

JENSEN

I've been married for exactly five hours but already have zero recollection of our vows. All I remember is the way she looked walking towards me down that aisle and how she felt pressed up against me when we took our first dance in front of the thirty friends and family we invited.

"You know, if you remove your eyes from her, she won't suddenly vanish," Jessie tells me from our position at the bar.

It's true; I've been standing against this bar in my black suit pants and white shirt for the past half hour, watching my wife mix and socialize with our guests.

"Fuck socializing," I reply. "I've only got one priority tonight."

"Say less," he drawls.

"Well, I think that went fucking great." Jon sidles up next to me as he orders another round for everyone, no doubt.

"Yeah, great job, man." I bump his fist.

"I'm serious. Coaching is great and all, but I am considering a wedding planning business as a side hustle."

I turn to him, my eyebrow raised. "You *are* joking, right?"

"Felicity thinks it's a ridiculous notion, but I can see me nailing it." He lifts his hands in the air, imitating the name up in lights. "Morgan's Magical Marriages."

"Fuck me," Jessie laughs as he types something out on his phone, and I have no doubt who the recipient is.

"I support the idea. I'm also happy to make an investment; I'm always looking for start-up businesses, especially ones with a great concept."

I look across at my new brother-in-law, who's standing on the other side of Jon, and shake my head slowly. Half an hour in Easton's company this morning told me all I needed to know—neither he nor my wife inherited their parent's asshole genes.

Thank Christ.

"Don't encourage him." I wave a hand at Jon and take a sip of my beer. "It's easy investing and then running back overseas to leave us with his crazy ideas and non-stop bullshit."

"Hey, do you mind?" Jon protests. He gathers the drinks onto a tray and then turns back to Easton. "And who's to say I wouldn't be in touch with him? I'd provide regular updates and at least twice monthly meetings, so he knows his money is being invested wisely." He pats Easton on the shoulder.

The panic immediately rises on his face, like he hadn't considered that, and I offer him a satisfied smirk.

As Jon walks away and with Jessie now on a call and walking toward the exit, I take what could be my only opportunity since he's flying back to Dubai tomorrow morning.

"Have you got a couple of minutes?" I point to an empty table at the other end of the room.

Easton is a smart guy, just like his sister, and I can tell he knows exactly what I want to talk about.

He looks over at his daughter, who's dancing with Kate on the dance floor, and then at his wife, who is busy talking with family, and nods his head slowly. "Sure thing."

Taking a seat on the plush black velvet chairs, he surprises me when he speaks first. "First, I want to know what she's told you. Don't get me wrong, I like you and all, but I'm not about to divulge details that are hers to share."

I nod. "Fair enough. I know they're assholes, I know they want nothing to do with us or the babies when they arrive, and I know they don't approve of this marriage." I take another sip of my beer. "I also know they locked her in her bedroom for hours on end to prevent her from going out and to keep her studying in the final two years before she left for college. She said you'd already left home at that point."

"Yeah, that's right. I swear I didn't know anything until maybe two years ago when Kate had too much to drink one New Year's night and spilled her guts to me." He winces. "They were kinder to me, but I wasn't planning to go into law."

"They're trying to sabotage her career by cutting off referrals between Mark Preston and the family business," I say.

You'd think I just told him it would get dark tonight by the unsurprised way Easton leans back in his chair. "Let me tell you something about my parents, Jensen. There is very little, if anything, they care about other than their firm and reputation, and they both go hand-in-hand. The circles they run in and the people they associate with are cold and calculating, just like them. You won't ever change their minds once they've made a decision." He points to me. "And they've decided you aren't a good image for their daughter, and neither is having children good for her career. Total bullshit, obviously, but all I'm saying is this is the start of them cutting contact and association with their daughter."

"Because my face doesn't fit?"

"Yep. Tom was largely acceptable because he did fit the image they like to portray, not that they cared about him. But he was less likely to march into their study and give them some hard truths."

"You know about that?"

He smirks. "Oh, yeah. Mom was livid."

I bite the inside of my cheek so hard I'm close to drawing

blood. "My turn now. Let me tell you something about me, Easton. Since I've known your sister, I've been gradually falling in love with her, whether I wanted to admit it or not. My obsession with her is real, and I will set the fucking world on fire to protect her at all costs. I'll burn myself to ashes in the process if that's the cost of safety for her and our children. So like hell am I going to allow them to drag Kate's name through the mud. Whether they change their minds about me and our marriage or not, it really doesn't matter. My wife will never shed another tear over them. Period."

Easton runs a palm over his mouth. "For what it's worth, I think you're the best thing that's ever happened to her."

Clamping a hand on his shoulder, I leave my half-finished beer on the table and stand. "Cheers, bro, and welcome to the family. I'd love to stay and talk to you all night, but right now, I have something I need to take care of."

He holds up a hand, clearly not wanting any more details on how I plan to slide inside his sister in the next five minutes.

KATE

JJ

Come next door.

Looking around the room filled with loved ones, I notice one absence: my husband.

ME

As in the room next door?

Yes, Princess. Just slip out and don't tell anyone where you're going.

Still fucking bossy, you know that?

Tell me what part of that you have a problem with...

None of it.

Excitement charges through me as I quickly slip out of one of the two doors into the hotel hallway. Taking a chance on the room to the left, I twist the metal handle and open the door.

The room is empty, and a slight chill hits me, the cold Banff air having infiltrated the dark space. Chairs and tables are stacked, but to the right of me is a raised stage, making me think the hotel uses this area for performances.

"Princess."

Pushing my hair to the side, I don't even flinch when my husband sets a kiss on the side of my neck. Instead, goosebumps travel down my arms and across every inch of my skin.

Spinning me around so I face him, his brown eyes are blown with more than just lust...need, desperation. Devotion.

Taking my hand, he guides me over to the stage and then picks me up, which is no mean feat given my size, and sets me on the edge. I lean back on my elbows as he lifts my legs and rests my feet on the edge, spreading me wide.

Without saying a word or taking his eyes off me, he gathers up the skirt of my dress and licks his lips as the moonlight shines through the windows, providing him with enough to see my white lacy thong, stockings, and light blue garter.

Hooking his fingers through the straps, he peels my thong down but makes sure my stockings and garter remain exactly in place.

"Your pussy is shining in the moonlight for me, Princess. Are you desperate for my tongue?"

I nod and whimper at the same time.

He walks a couple of paces to the right, and that's when I see it: a piece of the wedding cake we cut earlier, complete with a stack of vanilla buttercream.

Running his fingers through the frosting, he drops to his knees in front of me. "Wider for me, Princess, but make sure you're still comfortable. I may be a while."

Heat pools, and I swear I feel my release trickle down.

Running my feet along the edge of the stage, I go as wide as I can.

"Since Jon insisted on having a cake, I think it's only fair that I get to eat it from my favorite plate."

He smears frosting on the inside of my thighs, trailing his fingers toward my apex, where he rubs it over my clit. The sensation makes me want to cry out, but I bite down on my bottom lip.

"It's okay, Mrs. Jones. You can scream. In fact, it's compulsory that you scream my name so loud that our family and friends hear it over the music."

He nips at the inside of my left thigh, then runs his tongue towards my center.

"You want them to know what we're doing?"

"No, Princess, not just them. I want everyone on this earth to hear that I lick your pussy better than any other man."

Circling his tongue over my clit, he laps up the frosting, licking his lips as he does. "You want to try some? It's fucking delicious?"

I nod as he gets to his feet and hovers over me.

"Open up for me."

I open my mouth and take two of the fingers he swiped through me, sucking on the taste of myself and the frosting.

"Atta girl."

But he's not done as he removes his fingers and leans closer, bracing his hands on either side of my elbows. His white shirt is partially undone and open at the neck, offering me a glorious view of his pecs.

Teasing me with his tongue, the sweetness of the frosting mixed with the taste of him sends me into a spin.

"This stage is the perfect height to get you on your hands and knees. Do you think you can do that for me?"

"Yes," I breathe out, still dizzy from his effect on me.

He stands up and unzips his pants, letting them hang open at the front. His platinum wedding band matches mine and shines as he works to free himself.

On all fours, he wastes no time pushing into me, stretching me, toying with me, hitting parts of me I didn't know existed.

His hard cock slowly undoes me as he pumps in and out. With one hand on my hip, he reaches forward and trails his fingertips down the back of my neck, the sensory pleasure causing me to fully unravel.

Fighting to stay upright, he knows I can't hold this position long when he empties himself inside me with a possessive growl that kicks my orgasm up another notch, and I scream his name just like he wanted me to and definitely loud enough so everyone in Banff will hear.

Withdrawing, he wraps his arms around my waist and sits on the edge of the stage, pulling me onto his lap.

I feel the way his cum trickles down the inside of my thighs. "Can you feel me dripping from you, Mrs. Jones?" Jensen whispers into my ear.

"Yes."

"Do you want me to do it again when you've had our babies? Do you want me to breed you again?"

My pussy throbs in response to his dirty mouth. "I want you to breed me all the time, JJ."

He kisses my forehead. "Let's get back to our guests and spend some time. The faster we do, the sooner I can take you again, but this time, we will be in our wedding bed."

CHAPTER THIRTY-NINE

JENSEN

"You know you'll need to take that off, right?" Zach points to the ring on my left hand as we gear up for a home game.

"Not if I hide it."

He rolls his eyes. "Come on, man. You know the rules. It's not going anywhere, and neither is she."

Jessie snorts. "He's like a dog in heat or something—humping his owner's leg every chance he gets, but instead, it's his wife's."

"Listen," I say, sitting on my bench and inspecting my stick. "I would hump my wife anytime, anyplace, anywhere."

Goddamn, now I get why Jon has the obsession with saying "my wife." It feels good.

"Like on the stage in the room next door to your wedding?" Zach asks, not lifting his head from where he's examining his blades.

We almost got away with it that night, but the flushed look on Kate's cheeks told the story. For the past four days, Zach, Jessie, and Jon haven't shut up about it.

"You know, you could just take your woman and have a good

time yourselves. You don't need to live vicariously through me," I muse. "Albeit I'm not complaining about the reminders, and neither is my dick."

"What's that about your dick, Jones? Still tiny?" Coach Burrows interrupts as he barges in and stands in the center of the room, his hands on his hips as he glances around at everyone.

"Tonight is big. If we get the W against Nashville, then we leapfrog Calgary and head into second." He points at me and then thumbs over his shoulder. "Perhaps now that you put a ring on it, you can stop obsessing over your personal life and actually give me your best out there."

"Always my intention, Coach."

"Intention and execution are two very different things. I want a shutout tonight. We're three months deep into the season, and your shutout stat is the lowest it's ever been at this point."

Bringing my hand to my forehead, I salute him, and he narrows his eyes at me in response. He knows shutouts are my priority and I'll be working on that stat, ASAP.

"We got this, Coach," Jessie reassures, slapping his thigh in motivation.

He pins him with a glare in response. "Talking of distractions..." He trails off, and I watch the way my best friend's face falls.

Does Coach know something?

Burrows throws one last glare our way, and I turn to Jessie. "What's up his ass?"

He shrugs. "Fuck knows, but whatever he thinks is going on, he has it wrong. She's ghosting my calls and texts."

"Fuck man, I'm sorry."

He shakes his head and grabs his stick. "You coming to Riley's after the win?"

"Nah, got an evening check-up with Kate's doctor. Now that she's twenty-eight weeks, they want to keep a closer eye on her and get the birthing plan all straight."

"It won't be long now. Have you spoken to Coach about how much time off you'll get after the birth?"

I grit my teeth in frustration. "Yeah. Next to nothing, but thankfully, her due date doesn't clash with a game. If she goes either side, though, there's a chance I'll be fucked."

And if I'm on the ice at the time, best believe nothing will stop me from getting to my girl. I'll leave the goal wide fucking open.

"ALL LOOKS to be great and coming along well. The plan is to take you to a maximum of thirty-six weeks. You're twenty-eight now, so we really are in the home stretch. Is everything set at home?" the doctor asks.

"I'm building their bookcase and toy box tonight," I reply, keeping one eye on my wife, who has been withdrawn and closed off since the game ended, which we won, and then we made our way to the hospital.

"And your overnight bag? Have you got all of that ready to go?"

Kate nods. "Yeah, breast pads included."

The doctor chuckles and removes her latex gloves. "Do you have any questions at this stage?"

Kate chews nervously on the edge of her thumb, and the urge for me to reach up, grab her hand, and kiss it is overwhelming.

I got you, Princess. It's going to be okay.

"I guess as I get closer, I'm starting to think about the birth more and more. My friend is having a baby at a similar time to me, and she's been going through pain relief options. I'm hoping to do it without too much medical interference, but it got me thinking: what are my chances of having a natural birth?"

The doctor takes in a deep breath. "As we discussed in the

previous appointment, birthing twins can bring more complications for obvious reasons, but everything I'm seeing right now tells me you can still hope for a vaginal birth. We can provide pain relief options and have everything available since you don't have any allergies."

Kate bites on her thumb again, and this time, I reach up to her as she sits on the bed. I take her hand in mine, brushing a kiss across her knuckles. "Nothing bad is going to happen to you, Mrs. Jones. It's just not possible."

The doctor looks over at me and smiles. "We have some of the best trained staff and most equipped delivery suites available to us here."

"And there's not a fucking chance I'm going to let anything happen to my wife or babies. Anything you need, it's yours. Anything. All of it."

"Well, it sounds like you have the best support available." The doctor finishes up and signs off on some paperwork.

Kate climbs down off the examination bed and shrugs on her coat. Stepping over to her, I pull on her cute black toque and hold out her matching gloves.

"I can still dress myself, even in pregnancy," she jibes.

Shoving my hands in the pockets of my post-game pants, I lean down and whisper in her ear. "Are you being a brat, Mrs. Jones? Pregnant with my babies doesn't mean you're exempt from a spanking."

She flushes and side-eyes the doctor, who's already halfway out the door.

"Like I give a fuck if she heard."

She rolls her eyes as she reaches into her bag for her cell, and it's at that moment that I start to piece together why she's been off today.

I nod at the phone in her hand even though I can't see the screen. "Who's that?"

She quickly locks it and throws it back in her bag. "No one."

Wrapping my arms around her, I breathe in her citrus

shampoo and kiss her hair. "You're not keeping secrets from your husband now, are you, Princess?"

"Leave it alone," she snaps, but I know it's not at me, and that pisses me off even more. Who the fuck is bothering her?

As she turns her back to head to the parking lot, I catch her arm and pull her back into me again. Pushing her toque up on her forehead, I breathe out, trying to keep myself calm. "You don't have to fight battles alone anymore, Kate."

"I can handle it."

"Is it work?"

She shakes her head. "Really, it's nothing."

"Is it really 'nothing,' or are you choosing not to tell me because you're worried whoever it is, I'll tear them limb from limb when I eventually find out who's giving my wife shit?"

She brings a gloved palm to my cheek. "You can't protect me from everything and everyone all the time. Just let me work through this."

The hairs on the back of my neck bristle. "You're so fucking stubborn, you know that?"

"What was it I said all that time ago? Ah, that's right! It takes one to know one."

I narrow my eyes at her. "Let me take you out tonight. We can stop at our favorite Italian place on the way home."

She sighs and checks her watch. "It's past seven, and I'm so tired, baby. Rain check?"

Buttoning up her jacket, which only just fits over her bump, I try to push past the fact that she won't tell me, and neither would she appreciate me going through her phone. "Okay. I'll make your favorite. Ratatouille."

She smiles up at me and then plants a kiss on my lips. "The best."

CHAPTER FORTY

JENSEN

Kate's phone sits on her nightstand as I sit beside her and read my latest birthing book. This one is okay, but the previous read definitely offered more.

I look at her phone again. I know I shouldn't; it's her privacy I'd be invading, but I *need* to know who's been bothering her. My wife is tough and doesn't need me to fight her battles. But that doesn't mean I can keep away. I *can't* keep away.

As she sleeps peacefully beside me, I try to keep my busy mind from wandering, trying to work out who is trying to hurt the woman I love. The woman who's saved me in ways she doesn't even know. I no longer wake up in cold sweats, nor do I toss and turn in the night, trying to fight back nightmares of rejection.

She's cured that. She's cured me.

I'm ten seconds away from reaching for her cell when mine starts buzzing on the side, and I snatch it up before it wakes Kate.

EASTON

Are you around for a call?

He never texts or calls me.

Fuck.

Hitting dial, I throw on a pair of sweats and stride through to the kitchen. Pacing the floor, I wait for the international dial tone, and Easton picks up on the second ring.

"Jensen?"

"Yeah, all okay?" I get straight to the point.

"Is Kate okay?" he asks in a concerned tone.

"She's been...off. Why? What the fu—"

"Violet and Henry have been sending her shit again, you know, since the wedding a few days ago. I just got off the phone with Mom, and she sounded livid that they hadn't been invited to the wedding." He laughs darkly. "Even though they said they wanted nothing to do with you both, they still expect an RSVP to decline." He draws in a deep breath. "They cut her out the will and told her she isn't welcome back at their house ever again."

Silence.

I say fucking nothing because the only thoughts I have right now are murderous ones, and I doubt Easton wants to hear in which end of the garden he can find his parents buried.

"Jensen?" he breaks the silence first.

"I'm here," I push out, my blood boiling. "But I'm heading over there right now."

"I was afraid you'd do this," he puffs out.

"Afraid I'll go tell your asshole parents where to shove it? Glad I haven't disappointed."

"You won't change their mind, Jensen. I told you that at the wedding."

Snatching up my training hoodie and shoving my feet in my black Nike sneakers, I grab my car keys and head for the front door. "And I told you I'd do anything for her. I might not be a hotshot professional with degrees coming out my ass, but I am her warrior, and like hell am I standing by to watch them walk all over my wife. I couldn't give a fuck if I change their minds or not. This is about my girl and her alone."

IT'S past eleven p.m. when I pull up along the sidewalk outside their house.

Almost immediately, the front bedroom illuminates, and I watch as a silhouette crosses the room and stands at the window, checking to see who's there.

That's right, Violet, it's your favorite son-in-law. Come let me in for a cup of cocoa and a friendly catch up.

I waste no time pushing past the black iron gate that leads through their front garden and up to the grand white porch. I'm surprised it's unlocked. Perhaps they were expecting me.

Raising my hand to knock once, I'm saved the trouble as the door swings open, and Henry stands there in his tartan nightwear and robe.

"Nice pants," I say, taking in the red and green checkered print.

"What the hell do you want?" he bites.

Leaning back slightly, my hands in the pockets of my sweatpants, I check out the neighborhood. "That's not a very nice way to greet your new son-in-law, especially out in public."

He leans into me, a sneer right across his face. "You're no family of mine. Now, fuck off."

I shake my head. "Nah. I guess you'll have to keep me on your porch, bringing down your image, until you let me in."

His hand shoots out as he shocks me and grabs me by the forearm, pulling me into the entryway before shutting the door behind him.

The house is just as I remembered it when I last 'visited.'

The one photo they had of Kate at her graduation has been replaced by a recent shot of them meeting the governor.

Fitting.

"Take him through to the study, Henry," Violet bites as she makes her way down the stairs in nightwear, her long blonde-gray hair in overnight curlers.

Shaking my head, I stay rooted to the spot. "Nah, no need. What I have to say won't take too long."

"We don't need you to say anything. We heard enough the last time you paid us a pleasant visit. I think enough insults were slung at us then." Violet takes the last step and comes to stand next to her husband. Both of their cold faces are twisted with anger.

Looking up at the ceiling, I nod a couple of times and smile.

Dropping my head, I look them both in the eyes. "I've spent the last six months proving to your daughter that I'm not the man she thought I was. She made assumptions about me based on my reputation and an incident one night in a bar. On the outside, she comes across as guarded and reserved. I've been obsessed with your daughter for way longer than you know or probably care about. Despite the fact she knew nothing about me, I'd worked everything out about her. The only thing to evade me was why she was the way she was." Offering a pitiful smile to them both, I press on. "Tell me, do you still have the lock on her bedroom door?"

They look at each other, clearly surprised that I know. "I have no idea what you're referring to, and I think it's best you leave," Henry rushes out.

"I know I annoy you, so I'll go," I reply, turning to head out. But then I flip back around and snap my fingers. "Oh, yeah, I nearly forgot..."

Finally, after months of holding in my rage, I show the colors in me that my family will never see. Their faces drop as I sneer at them in a way I know they've never seen before. "So this is how it's gonna go from now on. You're going to do exactly what your daughter wants, and that's to leave her the fuck alone. And in return, I'm also going to do what she wants, which is to allow you to retain the air circulating in your lungs."

"Are you threatening us?" Henry asks, his voice filled with fear even though he tries to hide it.

"Hmmm." I scratch my chin. "I guess I am, yeah. You see, I'd die for my wife and her honor, but I'd also kill for her happiness. And you two—" I point between them. "You make her unhappy. My wife and I are the same. We think the same and operate in the same way. Internally, she's my dead ringer—she laughs, I laugh; she cries, I cry. She gets hurt, well, that's the only area where we differ, because I get even."

CHAPTER FORTY-ONE

KATE

"Want me to come upstairs and give Nina my best death glare?" Jensen playfully narrows his eyes at me as he pulls into my office parking lot.

I tap my chin. "Let me think about this...no?"

He laughs and reaches over, placing his palm behind my head and pulling me in for a kiss. His soft, full lips move over mine, reminding me of the way he made love to me all morning in our bed, and I feel myself begin to unravel again at the memory.

Now I'm thirty-two weeks pregnant, and I'm huge, so we've had to be more inventive with positions. Not that I'm complaining.

The more heavily pregnant I get with his babies, the hornier he becomes. It's to the point where he's feral. I thought he was going to leave the ice at last night's game, march up to the family box, and fuck me right there, and then when he realized I wore his jersey with "Mrs. Jones" stamped across the back...

Let's just say I got next to zero sleep last night.

There are downsides to being heavily pregnant with twins, though—pelvic girdle pain. Wow, it's intense. Half the time, I want to cry out when I take even a few steps, and the other half, I'm asking Jensen when I can have my next dose of pain meds.

He's done everything to try to ease my discomfort. At one point, he came home with two exercise balls—one for me and one for him so he could help show me the best ways to relieve the grinding. His entire home gym is now a pregnancy fitness and wellness center. I swear to God he worships every painful bone in my body.

But I finally gave in last week and conceded that I can't continue working. I'm exhausted and can barely focus on anything other than how many more weeks I have to endure. Being pregnant is a blessing I'll never take for granted, but that doesn't mean the pain gets any easier.

"You aren't having second thoughts about this, are you, Princess?" He pulls back from our make-out session and tucks a lock of hair behind my ear.

"No. I know I need to finish now. I just...I don't know what I'm going to do with myself for four weeks. The babies won't be here until then, and I—"

He stops my rambling with another kiss.

Speaking against my lips, his breath fans my face, and my body tingles with need for him. Need for his proximity, need for him to be inside me all the time. "I'll tell you exactly what you're going to do while you're on maternity leave. Nothing. Relax, read, do your calligraphy shit, let your husband take you out." He kisses me again. "Speaking of, when can you finish today?"

I shrug. "As soon as I'm finished passing everything across to Nina, I guess. That shouldn't take long since we did the full handover a while back. It's just an opportunity for her to ask questions."

And my cases are watertight.

"Let me know a time. I have morning skate, but I can get you any time after that, and I'll be waiting."

"What do you have planned?" I ask suspiciously as I open the passenger door to climb out.

"Something fit for a Princess." He sees that I'm about to leave and quickly unclips his belt, pushing the driver door open and rounding the new silver Porsche Cayenne he bought me and decided I needed.

Helping me out of the SUV, he takes my hand and walks me to the elevator.

"Sure you don't want me to come up with you?"

I gently push him away with a palm to his chest as I enter and hit the button to my floor. "I'll see you later, crazy boy."

"I'M GOING TO MISS THESE." Felicity sidles up next to me in the kitchen as she pours herself her third coffee of the day.

Caffeine, how I miss you.

"You know there's always the option of stopping by our place and having a coffee there."

"Obviously, but you know I won't be stopping by to see *you* anymore. It'll be my bundles of joy. I've already made it clear to Luna that I will be your and her babies' favorite aunty."

I quirk a brow. "You're getting just as bad as he is, you know that?"

"Who?"

"See, you don't even notice it anymore. Your husband, Jon. So damn competitive with everything."

Her eyes go wide. "I am *not!*"

"You are."

She props a hand on her hip. "Yeah, well, all I'm saying is, I will miss you these next six months."

Pulling the smoothie Jensen made me from the fridge, I twist the cap and close the door with my hip.

Ouch.

"I'm thinking of taking longer than six months."

My best friend looks as shocked as I feel saying it. "What?"

"I've been thinking about it for a while, and I don't know if it's going to be enough time."

Setting down her coffee mug, she pulls me into her arms. Even in my flat boots and her in heels, she's still smaller than me. "I know how big a decision this is for you, babe. But I really think you're being smart, and I'm so proud of you for thinking about what *you* need, not your boss or clients."

I laugh. "It's not like I have Violet to keep happy anymore."

She scoffs. "I'm struggling to work out who I hate more: my ex-husband, your parents, or Amie. There's still a part of me that really wishes Jensen had punched your dad that night."

"Oh, no doubt! He was desperate to land one on him. When he got home, he was pacing the apartment for hours. He wanted to go back and finish the job, I think."

She smirks. "Have you heard much from them?"

Shaking my head, I take a sip of my smoothie. "Nada. East tells me he's not even allowed to mention my or JJ's name in conversation. So I guess I really am dead to them."

"I'm so, so sorry you have to go through this. A woman should have her mom and dad by her side right now, not against her."

"They've never been by my side, babe. Apart from when I opened my exam results." Replacing the cap on my smoothie, I offer my trademark unaffected smile.

"How much longer until you can officially say you're on leave?" Felicity checks her watch.

"Anytime. I've finished my final meeting with the wonderful Nina, and I'm all set. Feels kind of weird to be finally at this point."

Felicity takes a couple of steps backward and casts a quick glance out into the main office area. Turning back to me, she smiles. "Best we get you seen off then!"

I narrow my eyes and head towards her. "What are you hid—"

As soon as I peek around the corner, I see it. Well, him.

With my box of desk items resting on his lap, he swings around in my chair, clearly waiting for me to get back.

Jensen doesn't often wear a baseball cap, but when he does, my knees go weak, and today he wears it backward. And that, combined with his post-practice training gear and sweats, has my mouth watering as I walk towards him.

Other than that time he turned up at my office and asked me to go to lunch, he hasn't been here. The way my colleagues all stare at him reminds me that my husband is super famous and our relationship is the object of everyone's interest.

"Princess." He offers me a smirk as he pushes up from the chair and holds my box under one arm. The other hand immediately tips my chin and plants a kiss on my lips.

I don't take my eyes off him as he pulls back, swiping his tongue across his bottom lip, clearly enjoying my taste.

"You know it's frowned upon to make out in your office, right?"

He shrugs and interlaces our fingers. "Come on now, Mrs. Jones, since when have I ever given a fuck about what anyone else thinks."

I giggle. *Like a fucking schoolgirl.*

"What are you doing up here? I said I'd call you," I say, picking up my bag and jacket.

"Here to carry your things and take you out like I promised." He indicates to the box he's holding. "Put them on here."

I don't argue as I balance my bag and jacket on top.

Pulling me by the hand, he leads me toward the reception area where Felicity's standing with Margo.

"I'm going to miss you so much. You know that?" Felicity throws her arms around my neck, her voice shaking.

"Babe. I'll probably see you more when I'm on leave than at work."

She smiles and then looks at Jensen, her grin turning mischievous. "Have a good afternoon."

Hmmm...

With a final goodbye to Margo, we head into the elevator and down to the parking lot. My thoughts are overcome with emotion.

This is it. One door is closing and another opening, and I know from this moment on, my life will never look or feel the same way again.

As if he knows exactly where my brain is, Jensen leans his head down towards me as the elevator descends. "This moment right here is where you start calling the shots on your life. This is your time, Princess."

CHAPTER FORTY-TWO

KATE

I expected us to head straight home, so when Jensen takes a left turn and pulls up outside one of the most exclusive jewelers in the Seattle area, I turn to him, my jaw hanging open.

"What are we...doing?"

"Doing princess things."

Butterflies dance around with excitement, but I narrow my eyes at him. "Jensen."

He rolls his. "JJ."

Thumbing over my shoulder. "Are we...going in there?"

"Sure are, Mrs. Jones."

Outside in the freezing late January air, I stand gazing through the window of a store I've stopped to look at a time or two in the past.

Jensen wraps his arms around my waist from behind and places his hands on my huge stomach. Breathing into my swirling hair, I can sense his comforting cologne. "Whatever you want, it's yours. This is from me to you. To my wife and the greatest momma to exist."

He takes my hand and pulls me into Ruby's. The entire place

is decorated in soft red velvet. As I look through a couple of the display cabinets at the stunning necklaces, there isn't a price tag in sight.

My family is wealthy, but besides the money I've earned as a lawyer, I've never seen a penny, and I likely never will.

Not that it matters to me.

"Are you serious right now?" I look at him.

He pins me with a glare. "Deadly, Princess. We have the store to ourselves for the next two hours."

I turn back to the display cabinets as the jeweler, and I assume the owner, hovers around us.

"What sort of item are you looking for?" he asks, clearing his throat.

"Um, well..." I glance at the necklaces again. "I was wondering about a necklace."

The owner nods and begins opening the cabinet.

He guides us over to a plush seating area and begins setting out the displays. "Were you looking at diamonds or a different stone?"

I look over at my husband, who simply smiles at me and quirks a brow. "I'd say diamonds."

He's not wrong.

"Okay, well, that narrows it down considerably." The jeweler looks to me. "Is there something on this display that catches your eye? If you have anything in mind but don't see what you're looking for here, we do have a bespoke service where we can have anything made to your style, preference, size, and general requirements."

"Thanks, but I don't think we'll need that. Will we, Princess?"

Even though I just stepped out of the frigid air and into a warm store, I feel my cheeks flush further.

He knows the necklace I've been eyeing since the moment I stepped in here. The same necklace I've stopped to look at a few times. But I've only ever glanced at it when we've walked past this store together. I've never pointed it out, never stopped when he's been with me.

Looking back at the double-strand knot necklace, it sits alongside two others.

Leaning over, Jensen points to the exact one. "This one."

All the air leaves my lungs in a whoosh.

"Excellent choice. This is a white diamond gemstone set in white gold. Approximately eight carats in weight and a timeless piece."

"So beautiful," I swear I have heart eyes as he removes it from the display and sets it on the large red velvet cushion.

"It truly is. Would you like to know the price?"

Jensen shakes his head. "Nah. The price is irrelevant."

I want to protest that he's about to buy me something I know will cost in excess of a hundred thousand dollars. But like everything with this man, he knows what he wants and won't stop until he makes sure I get everything he has to offer.

Reaching out, I run a delicate finger over it. "Can we have a moment?" I look to the owner.

He nods and takes himself across the other side of the store, giving us privacy.

"What's this for? It can't be for my birthday or Christmas." I look at my husband.

He takes my hand in his. His palms are warm and slightly calloused. "Some people call it a 'push present,' is it? I guess this is, too, but it's also so much more than that. This is the necklace you've always wanted but never bought, just like you've denied yourself what you've truly wanted for most of your life. The family you've been desperate to have." He smirks, points to himself and lowers his voice. "The man you've been dying to fuck."

I swat at his arm and laugh. "Shhh."

"Think of this as a symbol of a new chapter in your life—one where you stop denying everything you are, everything you want, and everything you deserve. Let me buy this for you."

"How did you know about this?"

"Are you seriously going to ask me how I know something about you? Each time we've walked past this place, your eyes have been drawn to it."

I shake my head. "We never stopped, though."

Jensen indicates to the owner that we're ready and then looks back at me. "That's the thing, Princess. I don't need you to spell it out for me to know what you want and what makes you happy."

The jeweler returns to sit in front of us. "Alright, let's talk about sizing and collection of the piece once it's ready."

JENSEN

She's quiet the entire ride home.

Not because she's upset I just dropped a hundred grand on a necklace, but more because of the meaning behind it.

And I'm stoked she's taking my words in, today is the start of Kate Jones putting herself first and ahead of everyone else's expectations.

Walking into our apartment, I take her jacket, walk her over to the couch, and crouch in front of her, removing her boots.

"Do you want a baby shower?"

She shakes her head. "Luna asked me if I wanted to do a joint shower with her since Zach has arranged one, but I guess it's just not my thing. Maybe a meal out with my friends. I just want to lie in bed, drink cocoa, and watch trash tv for a month."

Looking up from where I'm undoing her laces, I see a smile I don't think I've ever witnessed. My wife looks light, free, and like she's finally making decisions for herself.

"You look really fucking beautiful right now, you know that?"

Her blue eyes shine back at me with warmth.

Wasting no time, I toss her boots to one side, kneel between her legs, and undo the button on her work pants.

Pulling them off her legs, she's left in only her black lacy thong and work blouse. As I push that up and over her pregnant stomach, I marvel at her stretch marks. "Your body is a work of art, Princess. Every line, mark, every way you've adapted to our babies. I'm in awe of everything you are."

Her eyes gloss over. "You really mean that?"

Biting down on my bottom lip, I nod a couple of times and hook my fingers in the waistband of her underwear.

I watch as my wife's chest begins to rise and fall more rapidly in anticipation as I drag her already soaking thong down her perfect legs before I hook them over my shoulders.

One small swipe over her needy clit has her back arching upwards. "The grin on my face must be so fucking wide right now, huh?" I croon.

"Annoyingly big." She replies and then gasps as I push one of my fingers inside her.

"How many of my fingers do you want, Mrs. Jones?"

She squeezes her eyes shut as I slowly curl inside her. "More."

"My wife is so greedy," I say, entering her with another and then one more. As she takes me, I can hear the way her pussy sucks on my fingers, and my dick strains against my pants in response.

I want to fuck her so badly. But more than that, I want to watch the way she can come undone from my hands and tongue alone.

I look down at the hardwood. "Princess, you're so fucking wet for me. You're dripping on our floor."

She moans and throws her head back into the couch cushions.

"Want me to clean you up or leave you in this mess?"

"Yes."

"Which one?"

"Clean me up. Please."

"So fucking polite for such a dirty girl."

Eating her pussy like an ice cream cone, I waste no time as I draw my tongue through her cunt, all while moving my fingers at a torturous pace.

But I want more. I want her moans to be louder, her need for me to be unbearable.

Dropping her legs down, she looks heartbroken as I stand and walk to the bedroom, making a beeline for her nightstand.

"Where are you going?" she cries.

Kate's frown turns into hungry need when I return a second later with her purple butt plug and lube.

Dropping back down to my knees in front of her, I make sure everything is ready before slowly pushing it inside her ass. "You thought I didn't notice when you brought this home last week." I slide it in slowly, and she gasps when I push my fingers back into her pussy.

"JJ, that's...I feel so..."

"Full?"

"Yessss."

With the butt plug seated deep inside, I pump her with my fingers. "My mouth wants you too. Can my Princess handle that?"

I don't wait for a response as my tongue finds her clit. I clean her up good, taking every single drop into my mouth, reveling at the way she watches my mouth work.

"Oh my god, I think I'm fucking squirting!" she shouts.

Damn fucking right she is, all the way down my throat.

"Again. I want more," I demand, pumping my fingers harder, the plug still tight in her ass.

"Baby, I can't," she shakes her head.

Fuck this.

Feral need hits me as I pull out the plug and carefully replace it with a finger. "You like that, yeah? Do you like your husband fingering your tight, sweet ass?"

She throws an arm over her eyes. "Give me another."

"Such a bossy little slut for daddy, aren't you?"

"I think I'm going to come again."

My mouth only just finds her pussy in time as she squirts hard onto my tongue. Fucking hell, she tastes even better the second time.

"I want you to fuck me, JJ."

I shake my head. "Nah." Lick. "I'm not moving from my position between your thighs until I'm sure you've emptied everything you have down my throat. I'm thirsty, and your cum is the only thing that can quench my need."

CHAPTER FORTY-THREE

KATE

My heart has never been fuller as I sit in the family box with my two girls to my left and Hollie and Claire to my right.

And neither has my womb. I'm fit to burst, like literally. The doctor told me at my checkup a couple of days ago that they would definitely take me to thirty-six weeks, but honestly, I don't think I can stand another thirty-six minutes.

Sitting next to Luna, I snag a piece of her popcorn. "I still hate this stuff, but the constipation from my vitamins is a killer."

She side-eyes me. "Another tip from Jensen's collection of mom and baby books?"

I wash it down with a sip of water. "Yep." Trying to get comfortable, I kick out my swollen feet. Even though it's mid-February and freezing outside, I opted for flip-flops. "Why is it you can still wear shoes?" I point to Luna's brown winter boots. "And why do you still look cute? I, on the other hand, look like a beached whale."

I feel like one, too.

"Because she's not carrying a whole other baby," Hollie

chimes in. She reaches across and rubs my huge bump. "Beautiful."

"Whale," I retort.

Felicity clears her throat. "All I'm saying is JJ would be pissed if he heard you referring to yourself like that."

"True," Luna nods. "Last week at our prenatal class, you referred to yourself as gross, and I thought he was going to throw you over his knee or something."

He did—later that night.

"Wait." Claire holds up a hand. "My son is attending prenatal sessions with you?"

"Oh, he doesn't just attend. He arranges them. He takes notes and everything." Luna swoons.

"Wow," Hollie gasps.

My attention focuses back on the ice. Home games against Colorado were once full of angst and banter, but since Jon retired, his former team has progressively lost their grudge against the Scorpions.

With the score three-zero, I watch as my husband never takes his eyes off the action, even though he's had almost nothing to do the entire time.

He won't let me out of his sight. He's constantly checking on me. I swear if he could take his cell phone onto the ice and text me for thirty-second updates, he would.

Hollie leans in to break me from my drooling session. "If he wasn't my brother, I would be swooning with you. He's a mighty fine husband, future dad, and everything you deserve."

I quickly reach over and snatch another piece of Luna's popcorn to distract my mind from the tears threatening to pool in the corners of my eyes.

"He absolutely is," I reply on an exhale, my attention fixed back on number eighty-eight.

"Has he told you the name he's chosen yet?" she asks.

Shaking my head, I twist my lips to the side. "Nope, that's

the only secret we have from each other—the names we've picked out."

My eyes return to the ice just as Jessie Callaghan sinks the puck, making it four-zero, and Luna jumps up, punching the air.

What it is to be carrying just one baby.

"Babe, you've spilled your drink all down me," I groan.

Her head whips over. "But I'm not h-holdi—"

"Oh. Shit." Felicity announces as I slowly take in that I'm sitting in a puddle of my own amniotic fluid.

Time moves slowly as I watch the liquid soak through my leggings. "I think my waters just broke."

"Are you feeling any contractions?" Claire asks, slightly panicked.

"Nope. Just really, really wet."

"I think we need to take you to the hospital. They need to check you over because at this point, labor could start at any moment," Felicity adds.

I wince and ask the question I've been putting off for some time. "How bad is childbirth exactly?"

"I'm not going to lie to you, babe. Horrific," my best friend answers.

I look to Claire for some form of reassurance. She shrugs and nods at Felicity in agreement.

"You could've just lied and told me it's uncomfortable like the doctors do."

"It's a mild feeling of discomfort followed by a sharp scratch," Felicity corrects.

I huff. "Now I know you're lying."

"There's still a good chunk of the period left." Luna points to the countdown clock, which indicates that just over fifteen minutes of the second period remains. "He will lose it if he's not told that she's going to the hospital."

I wave a hand in front of me. "I'm not about to have the babies right now. Let him know after the game."

Felicity raises an unsure brow. "If your husband isn't told in the next ten seconds, he will lose his shit, and I'm not being the one to witness his wrath."

"Leave him to the game," I repeat, coming to a stand, and I wince at the way my hips scream at me. I look down at myself. "He'll be too busy worrying about my wrath over the state he's got me into to care."

Luna snorts a laugh. "Why do I get the feeling he's going to be in more pain than you?"

Hollie rubs her hands together with glee at the thought. "Oh, to be a fly on the wall."

WITH A LARGE BLACK Scorpions hoodie wrapped around my waist to cover my very wet dignity, we pull up in the hospital parking lot.

Throwing my head back in the seat, I realize I couldn't be any less organized right now. "Shit."

"What. What is it?" Felicity looks across at me in panic. "Are you in pain? Have the contractions started?"

"No. I just don't have my overnight hospital bag with me, and in terms of pain, I am, but not from the contractions. More the way you've squeezed me into this tiny fucking car." I look around at Martha Mini. "I really hate this thing right now. I'm defecting to Jon's side."

She ignores my jibe and checks her watch. "It's been fifteen minutes since we left. The boys will be heading off the ice. Are you sure you don't want me to make the call?"

"No. I want him to concentrate on his game. I'm not in labor. I just need to find out what I need to do next and if I'm staying in."

Unclipping her belt, she rounds the car and extracts me from Martha, an amused smile on her face.

"Don't laugh," I grit out, trying and failing to look as graceful as possible.

Her shoulders shake slightly as she loops her arm through mine, and we make our way to the entrance. "I'm not laughing," she says.

"I'm scared," I say, coming to a stop in the freezing air. "Promise me it's going to be okay."

Placing her soft, warm palms on either side of my face, she looks me dead in the eyes. "You really think that boy of yours is going to let anything happen to you or the babies?" She casts a glance down my body and smiles. "Especially when you turn up at the labor ward wearing his jersey?"

I twist my face to the side as a wave of dull pain radiates into my lower back and pelvis. Felicity drops one of her hands to my stomach in response, asking a silent question.

I nod. "Call him."

JENSEN

"Easiest period we've had in a while." Jessie stands from the bench and checks the laces on his skates.

"Yeah. But don't underestimate them. They won't want to be totally embarrassed, and I want the shutout for my stats."

"Damn right you do, Jones!" Coach Burrows bellows across the noisy locker room. I swear that guy has radar ears.

He looks at me and then at Jessie, narrowing his eyes at him.

Ignoring the look, Jessie picks up his stick and nods at the exit towards the ice. "More of the same."

The team begins to file out when Zach hangs back, staring down at the phone in his hand. His eyes blown wide in panic.

Shit. *Luna.*

Pushing past a rookie forward who looks like he came out for a Sunday stroll rather than a league game, I stride over to the other side of the room and clamp a gloved hand on his shoulder. "What's up?"

He shakes his head, words trying to leave his mouth but failing.

Eventually, he looks up at me. "She's at the hospital."

"Luna?" I reply. "She's not due for another few weeks, right?"

Shaking his head again, he hands me his phone to check the text.

FELICITY

I'm trying to reach Jensen, but he isn't answering his phone. I'm here at the hospital with Kate. Her waters broke in the second period, and her contractions have just started. They're coming on pretty fast and strong.

The phone leaves my hand, but Zach grabs it before it crashes to the floor. The only few minutes I haven't had my phone glued to my side, and it happens.

"My fucking babies are coming," I whisper.

"Go. Now. I'll deal with Coach and replacing you," my captain instructs.

He doesn't need to finish his sentence. I'm already halfway out of my pads, adrenaline pulsing through every part of my body as I throw on a pair of black sweats, a gray hoodie, and a Scorpions cap to cover my sweaty hair.

Fucking great. I'm going to become a dad looking and smelling like a piece of trash.

"When was the text sent?" I shout, pulling open the door to the locker room, but Zach's already gone.

I run faster than my legs can carry me down the player corridor and into the private parking lot.

Jumping into my Range Rover, I crank the engine and hit dial on Kate.

"He-hello?" She answers almost instantly and sounds breathless.

Exiting the lot, I join the freeway, but fucking traffic is everywhere, and snow is beginning to fall from the sky.

"Princess." My heart cracks clean down the fucking center. She's in pain, and I'm not there. I promised I'd be there. "What's happening? Tell me you're okay."

She blows another breath. "Just peachy, Husband. My uterus feels like it's auditioning for the contortionist of the year award, and I've only puked twice in the past ten minutes."

I switch lanes and hit the gas. "Such a pleasant wifey."

She groans like another contraction is hitting her.

"Put Felicity on for me."

"Hello?"

"How's she doing?" I ask.

"Her waters broke during the second period, and she asked us to hold off calling you since she wasn't in labor. But as soon as I got her to the hospital, the contractions started, and they've been coming on pretty strong and close together. The doctor doesn't think there will be time for strong pain relief."

Fuck. Fuck. Fuck. I promised her I would get her anything she needed.

"How dilated is she? I'm ten minutes away."

"She was checked a few minutes ago, and they said six." She takes a sharp breath. "Hurry, Jensen."

I cut the call and drive like a fucking lunatic towards my girl.

After everything I said and all the ways I promised I'd protect her, here I am, letting her down and running the risk of missing the most important moment of my goddamn life.

My phone rings again, but I'm relieved to see 'Jon' flash on the screen and not his wife's name.

"I'm on my way," I rush out.

"I'm here, in the hospital parking lot."

"What, why?"

"I've got her overnight bag; Felicity asked me to go grab it.

Apparently, it's got everything she needs, including her relaxation techniques, a calligraphy set, and things she needs after the babies are born."

I huff out a laugh. "Bro, my wife's six centimeters dilated and about to give birth to my twins on next to no pain relief. If I hand her that calligraphy set, there's only one place it's going to end up."

"What do you...oh right, yeah. Your ass."

"Yep."

"I'm in my silver Porsche. You can't miss me, right next to Martha," he instructs.

"I'm turning the corner now."

Jon's car comes into view as the snow begins to fall more heavily onto my windshield, and I throw my Range Rover into the drop-off zone. I'll sort that shit out later.

Running across the lot, he hands me the black leather bag. "Have you told her the name you picked out yet?"

I shake my head. "Nah. We agreed to at the birth."

He nods. "Everyone is on standby waiting. The boys will be here after the game."

"Claire and my sister?"

He points at the hospital entrance. "Already here and waiting. I saw them run from their car and inside."

Turning to enter, Jon takes my arm, halting me for a second. "Fucking proud of you, man. Proud of you both."

"Thanks," I reply, my voice thick with emotion.

"Now go. Have your babies, and complete your life."

CHAPTER FORTY-FOUR

KATE

Sweat pours down my forehead as another contraction slams into me, and this time, I can't hold in the pain as I grip the side of the bed and scream.

Felicity jumps to her feet to try and comfort me right as Jensen comes barging through the door, my overnight bag in his hand.

His eyebrows shoot to his hairline as he takes me in.

"I'm a mess," I moan, just as the latest wave of pain subsides.

He drops the bag to the floor beside my bed and takes the hand gripping the mattress in his. "You squeeze my hand, Princess. Let me feel everything you do. I'm here now, and I'm so fucking sorry."

Swiping under my eye, I notice a streak of mascara on the side of my pointer finger. "I wasn't prepared for this. I had everything ready, and here I am. I haven't even removed my makeup. They're coming a week earlier than we planned."

Claire comes to stand next to Felicity. "We'll give you some privacy, but just know we'll be right outside."

She leans across and kisses my forehead. "Love you lots."

Felicity plants a kiss on my cheek. "He's here now. Go ahead and have those babies."

They both leave and close the door softly with a click.

Immediately, Jensen picks up the bag and balances it on the side of the bed, searching through it.

"What are you looking for?"

"Your makeup bag."

I shake my head in frustration as another wave builds. They're coming faster and faster now. "I took it out of my bag last night to grab something and forgot to put it back in."

Like some sort of fucking magician, he fetches it out and unzips the top. "I noticed it on the side when I finished my workout and was showering. I put it back in."

Taking out my cleanser and cloth, he holds them in one hand and lets me squeeze the shit out of his other as he helps me through my latest contraction.

"Let me clean you up."

"I look terrible, don't I?" I whimper.

Smiling, he shakes his head at me. "You're laboring my babies. You couldn't be any more perfect in this moment. But I told you I'd give you whatever you need, and right now, I know you, and I know this is what you want. It's something you have control over."

My dry lips quiver with emotion as he turns my head to him and sets a kiss against them. Then, slowly, he wipes away my makeup. With each pass of the cleanser, I feel a sense of relief.

Another contraction hits, and as it builds in my spine, I know the intensity has cranked up a notch. "I think you need to call the doctor. The pressure to push is starting, JJ."

Bracketing my face with his large hands, he looks me dead in the eyes as he reaches over to press the call button. "You are so fucking powerful. You're going to deliver these babies like a boss, and I'm going to be here for every single push, every whimper, every smile, and every tear. I wish I could take all the pain away, but instead, I'll just make sure you get all the aftercare you need. I worship you, Princess."

He reaches into my wash bag again and pulls out my lip balm. Popping the cap, he smooths it over my lips before setting his against mine. His tongue sweeps out to caress me, and even though I'm in the height of labor, this brief moment feels like the sweetest few seconds of my life.

JENSEN

"Okay." The doctor and a couple of nurses push through the door. "Let's see where we are."

Pulling on her gloves, she pushes up Kate's hospital gown, and a flash of black shows beneath.

I look at her as she relaxes her knees for the doctor. "Is that?"

She smirks through the clear discomfort she's in, which breaks my fucking heart to see. "Your jersey. It survived the amniotic fluid, and it's what I arrived in. They wanted me to remove it, but I insisted, so they let me keep it on. Feels kind of fitting, right?"

My dick twitches as I lean in to whisper, "How many weeks do we need to abstain?"

Another wave hits her again as she grabs hold of my hand, lurching forward and almost knocking me out in the process. "Never fucking again, Jensen."

Goddamn my need to wind her up. "JJ," I reply.

Her head whips to me. "Oh, you better not be correcting me right now."

The doctor finishes her inspection. "We're at ten centimeters and one hundred percent effaced. It's time to start pushing, Kate."

I see the panic as it overwhelms her. "I can't do this."

"You mean to tell me my boss woman can't do something as simple as this? Come on, Princess. You scare the shit out of people for a living. You can do anything." I kiss her knuckles. "Plus, once we have our babies, you get to find out what you've been dying to know."

She narrows her eyes in determination and then cries out when, without a doubt, the biggest contraction ricochets through her body. The way she squeezes my hand makes every puck I've taken to the body feel like a light tickle. I'm not sure I have any fingers left since I can't feel them, only the cracking of my knuckles under the pressure.

"Okay, Kate. We're about to enter the crowning stage. I need you to take some deep breaths for me, and on the next contraction, I want you to push with everything you have."

The wail that leaves my wife's throat is nothing short of terrifying as I leap to my feet and stroke her back, all the while helping her follow the rhythmic breathing she's so desperately trying to use from what she learned in the birthing classes we attended.

The best advice I received was to let her take the lead. I'm not about to do anything other than what she wants.

"Water," she cries after the latest contraction.

"Just enough to wet her lips," the doctor instructs. So that's what I do, dampening her soft lips as carefully as I can.

Inside, I'm a panicked mess, hoping and praying everything goes right and knowing once she's birthed our first child, she has to go through it all over again. But somehow, I keep it together and don't let it show. I need to be strong for us both.

"Here comes another," Kate moans.

"One big push, Princess."

The huge cry from my wife is quickly replaced with a much smaller one as the girl of my dreams delivers the first of our babies into this snowy, wintery world.

My efforts to hold it together almost fail me as Kate falls

apart right next to me. Exhaustion, elation, relief, and the knowledge that she has to do it all over again hit her.

The nurse weighs our crying baby as I hold my sobbing wife, the tears flowing from her eyes mixing with mine. "I'm so fucking proud of you, Mrs. Jones," I whisper into her ear.

The nurse wraps and cleans our baby, and then I catch a glimpse that it's our boy, and a huge lump forms in my throat.

"It's our boy," I whisper.

"Congratulations, Mommy and Daddy." Bringing him around, the nurse places him on Kate's chest. She looks down at the jersey underneath her gown. "I know you wanted to keep it on for the birth, but it would be ideal for you to have skin-to-skin contact. This helps calm the baby and increase your bond."

"I can take him for a second," I say, begging for a hold as Kate sits up and the nurse helps remove my jersey.

This is the only time I'll ever be okay with her taking off my jersey for another man.

Holding my boy in my arms, I look over at Kate. I want to tell her his name, but I also want to wait for one last thing.

He smells like perfection.

Setting him on his mommy, they look like pure perfection, too, as I take in the most incredible sight of my life.

"I think you have competition," she whispers to me, a look of awe in her eyes at our boy.

"The only time I'll ever share my girl."

Kate's face twists again. "I think I'm contracting."

Excitement swirls in my stomach.

She's coming.

The nurse helps Kate by taking our boy and putting him in his bassinet. He is wrapped up in a baby blue blanket and matching knitted toque.

I'll dress him later, and fuck, I can't wait to change his first diaper.

Our daughter arrives with relative ease compared to the first birth, but Kate looks absolutely spent as she's placed onto her chest.

"Do you want your baby boy too?" I ask her.

She nods, tears streaming down her face and onto her chest. "Yes."

The way she holds and nurtures them. Like a fucking duck to water. Kate was made to be a mom, and by the look on her face, as she follows the nurse's instructions for breastfeeding, I know she feels it, too.

With the room quiet, I lie on the bed next to her. It's a tight squeeze, but I don't want a single inch between my family and me.

Not now, not ever.

"There's a few people hovering outside, and I think they might be desperate to meet..." The nurse trails off, realizing we've not provided names yet.

I wave my hand towards me and make sure Kate is covered properly while she continues to feed like a fucking pro.

"I was so worried I wouldn't be able to do this." She looks down at her chest.

"Why? It's great that you can, but it really doesn't matter how anything plays out, you know?"

"It doesn't?"

I shake my head. "No. I want you to promise me something."

"Anything."

Kissing the side of her jaw, I stare at her in wonderment. "That you will never put any pressure on yourself to meet the expectations of others, starting with the way you feed our babies."

Tears reappear for us both as there's a knock at the door.

"Come in," I reply, holding my wife's eyes with mine.

Gasps ring around the room as my mom, Hollie, Luna, Felicity, Jon, Zach, and Jessie all enter the room.

My mom makes a beeline for me as I stand from the bed, and

she squeezes me tight. "Your dad's on his way. His plane lands in twenty minutes."

Luna and Felicity fawn over the babies as Jon, Zach, and Jessie look on with emotion in their eyes. Jessie shifts from one foot to the other. I know he's emotional for us, but I also know this moment right here has to be so fucking hard for him.

"I think it's time."

"Thank f—"

Felicity cuts Jon off with a death stare.

"Sorry." He winces. "Forgot myself."

"Ladies first." I nod at Kate, desperate to know my daughter's name.

Stroking her soft cheek with her finger, she takes a deep breath. "June."

Luna's hands fly to her mouth as she gasps again. "That's so beautiful."

"Wait," I say, knowing the meaning behind the choice. "As in the month we..."

She nods her head. "Yes. And your JJ partner in crime."

I lose it just like I did that day at the scan.

"I need to hear his name," Kate says.

Pulling myself together, I look around the room, hoping this will go the way I truly want it to. He deserves that.

"I...I thought about a lot of names, but honestly, there was only one that felt right. Felt like his name belonged out here with us." I look at Jessie. "Back with you."

Jessie runs a palm over his shaking lips. "You, you named him William."

I nod and walk across to my best friend. "I hope you don't mind, but I wanted to offer you a small part of him right here, back on this earth with us."

Bringing him into a hug, I know the tears he cries against me are happy.

"You named him after my brother."

"I did."

Jon and Zach know Jessie lost his twin brother at birth, but they don't know the whole story or the way his death tore apart his family in unimaginable ways.

That's his business to tell.

"That's everything," Kate sobs. "June and William Jones."

Luna looks over at me. "You have two princesses now. It's good you have Will to keep you from being outnumbered."

Shaking my head, I round the bed and kneel by my wife. "Nah. Only one. Mrs. Jones is my queen."

CHAPTER FORTY-FIVE

KATE

Childbirth is a beautiful, wonderful thing, they say.

Lies. All of it. Lies.

Two days in the hospital on antibiotics for an infection after I was stitched back up, and I can absolutely say that Jensen Jones is never coming near me again.

Okay. More lies.

Because June and Will were born during the season, Jensen gets no time off. He was even fined for leaving the game partway through.

Not that he gave a fuck.

The only saving grace is he isn't due to go on an away series for another ten days.

On the way back from the bathroom, I creep through the dark bedroom and dance around all the places I know where the flooring makes a noise and could disturb either one of our sleeping babies.

We alternate which side they sleep on, and tonight, I have Will next to me. His arms are raised above his head as he rests peacefully in his bassinet.

Lying back in bed, I'm sure my husband's asleep when he rolls over and curls his body around mine. His hard dick presses against my ass, and I pulse in response. Even though I know we can't do anything, I just want to feel him.

Turning in his arms, he opens his big brown eyes and pushes my hair back off my face. "How's my queen doing?"

I smile. "Are you really going to call me that now?"

He kisses my neck. "Do you like it?"

"Princess is cuter."

"Princess, it is. But just know, you rule me."

My heart flutters in my chest. "Is that so?" I whisper.

"It is." Running his hand down my hip, he scrunches the hem of my silky sleep shorts in his hand. "I'm desperate for you."

I laugh quietly and kiss him on the end of the nose. "How many times have you, you know, in the shower?"

"None."

I pull back and stifle a yawn. "Really?"

"Waiting for you."

"Ugh, that must be killing you," I mock.

"Yes and no. Yes, because the only place I belong is inside you, trying to give you more of my babies." He smirks, but I can tell he's half serious. "But also no, because I'm used to it."

"Used to..."

"Waiting for you. It's what I do best."

"JJ, you don't need to wait for me anymore. I'm here." I push a hand through his hair.

"I know. I have it written in ink."

Lying on his side facing me, he pushes back the duvet until the side of his rib cage is exposed.

I look down at the writing again, something I've seen a thousand times but never Googled. I wanted him to tell me. Besides, I have a history of jumping to conclusions when it comes to Jensen Jones.

"Donec shes parati. What does it mean?" I ask.

He bites down on his lip and smiles. "This might be your last surprise about me. 'Donec shes parati' means 'until she's ready,' and tomorrow, I plan on adding the date next to it. Even though I probably shouldn't since I'm in the hockey season, but I can't wait any longer."

My heart leaps into my throat. "When exactly did you get this?"

He smiles. "Right after you told me you were expecting my babies." His eyes shine in the soft light creeping under the door. "I told you, Princess. You ruined me that night in Riley's Bar. From the moment you kissed me, I felt something I never had for anyone else, and the more time I spent around you, the more infatuated I became. But the more time that passed with you thinking I was the biggest asshole alive, the more I worried you'd reject me. The more I could see how way out of my league you were. Then you got with Tom and...yeah." He kisses me. "I tried to move on, but eventually, you invaded every part of my mind. I couldn't see past your face. You were everywhere. So when you told me you were pregnant, I knew we were soulmates. I just needed you to see it, too." He points to the tattoo. "I left a space for the date when it all changed, but I didn't want to add it until you finally fell into my world as mine."

If every nerve in my body was a bulb, I'd light up like the fourth of July. "You're going to tattoo JJ and Will's birthday next to it?"

He shakes his. "No, I'm going to tattoo the day you came to this apartment and told me you were pregnant with my babies. July sixteenth."

I don't know what to say. What can you say about a declaration like that? To love so deep it engraves itself on your soul. "I want you inside me."

He shakes his head. "No, Kate, I'll hurt you. I'll also likely get you pregnant again with the way I'd take you so deep."

"Oh, well, you'd love that, wouldn't you."

He rolls on top of me and pushes down my sleep shorts, and we both stop dead as JJ stirs in her bassinet.

"I would love to breed you every day of the goddamn week. But we have to wait."

"Fuck my throat then."

He looks at me. "Don't play with me, Princess."

"I'm not." I slide down until I'm under the duvet, and his boxers are level with my eyeline. He quietly rises to his knees and pushes them down, lust filling his features.

His huge, thick cock hovers above me as I rise onto my elbows in front of him. "Fuck my throat."

"Princess."

"Just be quiet, and don't wake them."

Reaching out, I take his dick into my hand and pump him silently before leaning forward until he's all the way down my throat.

He throws his head back and groans quietly, his ripped torso on full display, making my mouth water around him.

"I'm gonna blow straight into your dirty little mouth."

Pulling back, I look him dead in the eyes. "Then be a good boy for me and do it. Fucking mean it. I want all of you."

He wraps his hand around my throat and wastes no time as he pumps in and out of me. His taste, his feel, and his darkened, feral eyes overtake my senses as my husband takes from me what I'm only all too willing to give.

I love him with every last fiber of my being, with every part of my soul. As he watches me swallow down his release, I know he's marking me for an eternity.

ONE THING that has blown my mind about being a mom is my body's ability to wake me up in the dead of night to check on my babies.

This night is no different. But the bed is empty, and so are the bassinets.

"JJ?" I whisper-shout into the darkness. Nothing.

Peeling myself out of the bed, I check the time. Ugh, five a.m.

While quietly padding through to the living area, where I expect to find them, I'm distracted by a crack of light coming from under the nursery door and then a soft but deep voice.

Pressing my ear against the door, I realize he's singing to them, and my heart explodes in my chest.

He's singing the lyrics to "You Are My Sunshine" by Christina Perri.

My body aches, and my head pounds from lack of sleep, but I could stand here and absorb this moment for an eternity.

A few more lines into the song, he stops when June makes a whimpering noise I've already become familiar with.

She's hungry.

Ready to push through the door and help out, I once again stop myself when I hear the cap on a bottle pop and the whimpers die down.

"Shhh...we don't want to wake Mommy, do we? You're both going to be good when Daddy has to go away next week, yeah? Aunty Felicity and Aunty Luna will be here to help Mommy, but I know she's got this. You both want to grow up to be like Mommy, and you both want to find someone who feels the same way for you as Daddy feels for Mommy. I know you both will."

I consider leaving them in peace and heading back to bed. But I'm too desperate to see what I can only picture right now.

As I quietly open the bedroom door, I see it—my husband in his gray athletic shorts, sitting in the rocking chair, June and Will tucked under each arm, feeding from a bottle of my expressed milk.

This sight alone is enough to make me want to lay down and ask him to give me all of his babies from now until the end of time. But truly, it's the look of awe in his eyes as he watches them both fall into a milk coma that has my legs almost giving out underneath me.

"Hey," I whisper.

He looks up, startled to see me watching them.

"Hey, Princess." He smiles sweetly, but I can tell he's as exhausted as I am.

"You could've woken me. I don't have work tomorrow, and you have early an morning skate in, like...baby, in like an hour."

"I also didn't give birth a couple of days ago, Princess. Go back to bed. I'll bring June and Will back in when they're settled. I think you might be able to get a couple more hours of sleep."

I shake my head. "No. Can I get you anything? You need something to eat or a coffee, at least."

"I'm good."

"Jensen," I scold.

He raises a brow. "JJ. I can look after it myself."

Propping a hand on my hip, I offer him the same look. "You do know I'm just as stubborn as you and equally refuse to ask for help even when I need it, right?"

"Perfectly aware."

"Right. So what coffee do you want?"

He laughs silently. "You're going to be the death of me, you know that?"

"Oh, I know."

Turning to head to the kitchen, he stops me before I leave. "Kate?"

I'm always surprised when he calls me by my name. "Yeah?"

He pinches his lips together and looks around the sage green nursery, at the light wooden furniture, and at Will and June's names above their bassinets, something Jessie stopped by to gift us earlier today. He then looks back at me, a glossy sheen to his beautiful brown eyes.

"We have our whole lives ahead of us, everything to share and look forward to together and with our family. But I just want you to know, this moment right here, you standing in the doorway of our nursery, me holding our babies as they sleep. If I died tomorrow, I'd have lived a life filled with happiness many can only dream of. Thank you for letting me prove you wrong."

EPILOGUE

JUNE

"What's that look for?" I turn to Jensen, who's unloading the trunk.

Days out with two four-month-olds are not for the faint of heart. I swear we packed more into this SUV than we did when I finally sold and packed up my apartment.

"Just thinking about you in a bikini and me rubbing sunscreen on you."

I smirk in response and begin unclipping June from her car seat when she pulls my sunglasses from my eyes with her tiny hand. "That's right, baby girl. Glasses," I giggle. "Daddy insisted on high-end ones because he's a great big snob."

"Heard that."

"I meant for you to," I call from the back seat.

Will brings his chew ring to his mouth and starts chomping down. June immediately follows but on my glasses. "Oh, no, baby. Not the glasses," I say, replacing it with her purple ring. "There we go."

It's a gorgeous day at Alki Beach. We load up the strollers and make our way down onto the soft sand, finding a place to set up for the day.

"I'm going to set up the canopy." Jensen starts unloading it from the bag and setting out the pieces.

The salty air whizzes past my face as I roll out June and Will's blankets and set them down for some tummy time. Both can already push up onto their elbows and are becoming increasingly inquisitive. Even though they aren't identical twins, they are so similar with their mass of black hair and deep brown eyes, just like their daddy. At this point, I'm the odd one out in this family.

"Do you think they will stay dark forever, or do you think their hair color will get any lighter?" I say to Jensen as he starts putting up the canopy to provide us with some shade.

He looks down at me through his sunglasses, clearly checking me out in my black plunging one-piece swimsuit. "I don't know. They'll probably get lighter, I guess. They got lucky and got their daddy's genes." He pulls off his glasses and winks.

Brat.

"It looks like you could use a hand there." Jon and Felicity approach from behind, and Jon immediately starts helping Jensen with the canopy.

In her huge "out of the office" straw sunhat, Felicity comes to sit next to me and kisses me briefly on the cheek. "Hi, babe."

"That's it?" I say as she glides past me and straight to June and Will, picking them both up in her arms.

"Yep." She pops her p. "You and Luna will always be my girls, but now I have aunt responsibilities. Don't I?" Felicity says as she looks between them.

"Is that so?" I reply in a mock tone.

"Look, don't get offended." Felicity sets June and Will down and then passes June a bucket and shovel to explore. "Even my own husband has taken a backseat to Aster, June, and Will."

"I'm sorry, what was that?" Jon says from behind me.

I turn around to face him and throw my hands in the air. "Join the club, Morgan."

"Well, if you can't beat them, join them." Jon fixes one of the poles into place and then walks across to his wife, picking Will up and throwing him in the air.

"Shall your favorite aunty and uncle take you for a walk along the beach?"

I watch as Felicity observes how he is with Will, her eyes full of hearts.

Quietly, I nudge her in the side. "Never too late, you know?"

She scoffs. "You have *got* to be kidding me. Anyway, he's one to talk; I barely see him. He's dropped me for Jack."

"Still as intense?"

She nods. "I'm so damn proud of them both. Jon sees he has what it takes, and Jack is working so hard to follow his dreams."

"You think he'll make it? To the NHL, I mean."

She takes a deep breath. "Yeah, I do. He has Jon and all the guys in his corner. He has all the ingredients to make it happen if that's what he truly wants."

"He'll make it." A deep voice joins us, followed by a cheeky three-month-old giggle.

I jump to my feet. "Aster!"

I take him from Zach and plant a huge kiss on his mass of red hair. "Why is it that you got all your mommy's genes, but mine got their daddy's, huh?"

Zach sets down all the bags as Luna catches up with the stroller. "And why is it that the beach is the most beautiful but inconvenient place to visit when you have a baby?" She crouches down to say hello to June.

"Tell me about it. I have sand in places where it should never be," Jessie adds.

"When did you get here?" I ask, taking a sip of water from the bottle Jensen just handed me.

"Around five minutes ago. I was just on the phone with my agent." He eyes Jensen.

"All okay?" he responds.

Jessie scratches the back of his neck. "Hope so." He looks anything but sure about the call with his agent.

With Will still in his arms, Jon crouches down and kisses the side of Felicity's forehead. "Let's take these little guys and girl for a walk. Give their mommy and daddy a breather."

Felicity lights up in response and looks over at me and Luna. "We'll be back in three to five business days."

Luna snorts a laugh. "You're going to need a lot more than just one diaper, in that case."

We watch as Jon and Felicity walk toward the ocean, the two boys with Jon and Felicity swooning over June.

With the canopy all set up, Zach walks over and takes Luna's hand, pulling her to her feet. He wraps his arms around her pink tie-dye beach dress, and I can tell he's already thinking about adding to Aster. "Come take a swim with me, Miss Johnson."

She kisses him lightly on the lips and then rips her beach dress over her head, tying her long auburn hair into a messy bun. "Race you!"

She flies down the beach as Zach races after her.

"Pair of teenagers," Jessie calls after them, but his smile is interrupted by his phone ringing. As soon as he sees the name flash on his screen, he stalks off in the opposite direction.

"And then there were two." Jensen comes to sit next to me on the now empty blankets.

"Are we still heading off to Zach and Luna's new place for a barbeque after this?"

He nods. "Yeah, I have to swing by and pick up the sliders."

"I won't lie. I'm relieved I can eat meat again, or at least not want to throw up on sight."

Jensen stays quiet and kicks the sand in front of him. He looks troubled, which makes my heart drop. "What's wrong?" I ask, twisting his baseball cap backward.

"I, uh, I think Jessie might be getting traded."

"What?!" I shout and then quickly look around to check no one heard my outburst.

"Other than Coach, no one knows, not even Zach. It's..." He grips at the back of his neck. "It's really complicated and not my business to tell, but he has a lot going on, which is why he played like shit in the playoffs. He also thinks that's why we lost out to Dallas."

"When did you find out?"

He shrugs. "About ten minutes ago when he showed me the email from his agent on his phone. Nothing is confirmed yet, but he doesn't want to go."

"Can you do anything to help?"

He shakes his head. "No, because I don't even know the full details of what's going on, but Coach Burrows wants to keep him. I want to keep him. He isn't just my best friend. He's one of the greatest forwards our sport has ever seen."

"How can I help?" I ask, feeling all kinds of useless.

Jensen looks over at me and takes my chin between his thumb and forefinger, our lips almost touching. "I told you, Princess. All I need you to do is breathe and be mine."

Butterflies swarm my stomach. "I can definitely do that."

He kisses me softly. "When is East coming over again?"

More warmth fills my chest, knowing I'll see my brother for the first time since he came to visit after the birth. "He should arrive tomorrow morning. Violet and Henry want him to stay at their place, but he refuses. He's staying at a hotel."

"They got what was coming to them, you know?" Jensen's jaw ticks. "Tax evasion and cooking their books." He shakes his head. "Karma always finds bad people, sooner or later."

I wish I felt some sort of sadness for my parents. But I can't. They made their bed. They'll likely lose their business, and the Feds are looking into their personal finances. Perhaps they did Mark and David Preston a favor after all when they disassociated their business.

Lying back on the blanket, I decide now is the perfect time. "Hey, come lie with me."

On our sides and almost nose to nose, I pull off his sunglasses and take in his deep brown eyes. "I want to show you something. Can you cover me with a towel?"

He looks confused but grabs one anyway, holding it behind me for privacy.

Unhooking the swimsuit strap from over my shoulder, I peel it down until the left side of my ribcage is showing, along with the plastic wrap covering it.

Jensen's eyes bug out at the sight.

"Peel it off," I say.

"When did you get this?"

"Two days ago. I've been trying to hide it from you, but I can't wait any longer."

As he removes the medical tape, it slowly reveals coordinates and then a date—December fourth.

"What's this?" he says, shock in his voice.

"An important date for my calendar. And those are coordinates."

"For where?"

"To Riley's Bar. That was the date I wore your jersey and sat on your knee." I lean forward and kiss my husband. "The hour that changed both our lives, even if I was a way behind you."

He goes to open his mouth, but I press my finger against his lips. "Thank you for showing me the definition of unconditional love. Because I love you so fucking much, JJ."

THE END.

Jessie's story is coming in January 2025. Pre-Order his book now!

ACKNOWLEDGMENTS

My Husband: Forever my heart, my cheerleader, and the man who cheers with me and wipes away my tears in the dead of night. Thank you.

My Dad: Another book, another journey with you holding my hand and guiding me through life. Forever blessed to call you my dad.

My little boy: Every book I write is for you, my LB. Your sunshine and resilience power me through long days and late nights. I love you.

Sam: Your girl is here. Thank you for your friendship, it means the world to me.

Tina: Thank you for all your help and guidance, but mostly, thank you for being such a wonderful and supportive friend. I'm so honored to be working with you.

Nay: This journey has given me great friends and none greater than you. I'll admit your cupcakes are a huge part of it but mostly, your kind heart. Thank you for always offering me honesty and love in the perfect balance.

Shann: My lovely Shann from across the other side of the world. One day we'll meet, and I'll be able to squeeze you so tight. Thank you for being one of the first pairs of eyes on JJ, and thank you for loving him so hard. I love you.

Maggie: Thank you for everything. I feel so fortunate to work with you and call you a friend.

To all at Wordsmith Publicity: Autumn and the whole team at Wordsmith, thank you. I've learned so much and cannot wait to continue working with you as we release the rest of the series. You go above and beyond, and I am forever grateful.

To the Bookstagram community: Thank you for loving my characters and stories as much as I do. I can't wait to bring you the rest of the Seattle Scorpions family.

To all my readers: Most importantly, to everyone who has picked up and read Boarded Hearts, Frozen Over, and now Dead Rinker, THANK YOU. It continues to be an absolute honor to share my stories and characters with you. Never did I think someone would love my words as much as you have shown.

ABOUT THE AUTHOR

Ruth Stilling is an avid romance reader turned writer. Having spent many years reading about and dreaming of her ideal book boyfriend, she finally decided to create her own and to share them with the rest of the world.

Living in a small town in Derbyshire, England, Ruth is an introvert by nature and spends much of her time talking with her equally book-crazy friends from across the globe.

When she isn't writing your next book boyfriend, Ruth enjoys watching all kinds of sports and is an Aston Villa and Derby County fan. The outdoors is a real favorite, and if the British weather were kinder, she would spend all her time writing outside.

Ruth is a wife to her best friend and number one cheerleader, whom she married in 2015, and a mom to her beautiful son, who has shown her a new perspective on life—enjoy and celebrate who you are as a person and cherish those who are there for you through rain and shine.

Ruth is incredibly excited to share the rest of the Seattle Scorpions Series with you!

You can follow Ruth and keep up to date via Instagram and TikTok by searching @authorruthstilling

Made in the USA
Middletown, DE
13 September 2024